Gladys the Vampire

by Heather Hein

A Kiki's Castle Independent Press, LLC publication

Kiki's Castle Independent Press, LLC

625 Riverbend Dr

Fort Collins, CO 80524

For information or permission requests, contact Kiki's Castle Independent Press, LLC 625 Riverbend Dr, Fort Collins, CO 8052

First Edition-2024
Cover and art design by Leia Sage
E-Book ISBN—978-1-964683-02-7
Paperback ISBN—978-1-964683-01-0
Paperback ISBN—978-1-964683-03-4
Hardback ISBN—979-8-9886527-9-3

Dedication:

To Darren, my love, my muse, to my kids who still remember who I am when I emerge from my office, and to CoCo, who enjoyed putting her cold feet on me and shoving me into the crevice between the bed and the wall when we were kids.

Table of Contents

1. THE SUPPORT GROUP

A slate sandwich board stood outside the VFW hall with *XP Support Group-Tuesday Nite 8 pm–10 pm* written in scraggly white chalk. Gladys frowned at the spelling of the word *nite* as she clambered up the steps. That word...*nite*...set her teeth on edge. Just like the word *Shoppe* on a vitamin store. As far as she knew, they never sold things like bull testosterone supplements or Essence of Jennifer Aniston's Collagen in a medieval apothecary.

Just spell it like it is.

She pushed the heavy metal door open and walked into the large meeting room. Three chairs were arranged in what would have been a circle had there been two or three more members of the group. Her right knee throbbed like seven bells of Hell.

Karen perched on the edge of her chair, a legal pad at her feet, wearing a baby blue twinset. The click-clack of knitting needles echoed in the empty space as she attacked a pink ball of baby-soft yarn. Not a single hair on her head was out of place and her makeup was flawless, in spite of the thick foundation.

Gladys hated that she used so much of it, but Karen was self-conscious about her pale skin. The least she could have done, Gladys had always thought, would be to blend it gradually into the rest of her skin. As it was, it looked like a high-end Halloween mask.

Karen sat ramrod straight—the kind of posture they'd taught girls to have back in the 1950s by making you walk around with a book on your head. Some things you just can't unlearn.

She looked up as Gladys sat down with a groan, knees popping like dry twigs. "Glad!" She set her knitting aside and got up to hug the older woman. "How you been, hun?"

Gladys gave her a strained smile. "Okay. You know, same old thing." She rubbed her right knee. The overhead lights reflected off the pink of her scalp through her thin cap of white permed curls.

Karen nodded. "I know. This humidity must—"

A sharp crack reverberated through the room as the door smacked against the wall. A small, balding man entered; head scrunched down between his shoulders. His face held an expression of one who expects to be eternally dissatisfied. His bushy grey eyebrows tangled together in the center of his forehead, falling into a crevasse. The emotion wasn't necessarily genuine. Hans always seemed to have that look of disapproval on his face.

He looked behind him, almost as startled by the thunderclap of the door as Gladys was as he made his way across the room. "Sorry," he said in a thick German accent. "It seems I still do not know my own strength." He sighed. "How are lady-friends this evening?"

"Good!" Karen chirped with sunny, good cheer.

"I'm good, Hans," Gladys said and stretched out her right leg. "Of course, the knees—"

"Yes, we all know. Knees hurt all the time. Is a pity." His frown of disinterest was as if Gladys' pain was a simple annoyance, nothing more than a pestering fly which returned again and again to land on someone's birthday cupcakes.

Gladys stood, ready to get the ball rolling already. "Welcome to the XP Support Group. My name is Gladys."

"Hello, Gladys," the other two chorused. It was a pointless response. They'd known each other for years, but procedure was procedure.

"I'm a vampire. It has been twenty-six days since I took blood from a living person." She sat down and the other two clapped softly.

Once everyone had stood, introduced themselves, and confessed their most recent transgressions, the meeting fell into a light, conversational chat among old friends. Tonight, the conversation turned to food. A little depressing, but then, so was their very existence.

"I'd kill for a taste of good, broiled salmon," Karen said and then blushed—at least as much as a vampire who hadn't fed recently *could* blush. She shook the foot crossed over her right knee. "Sorry, poor choice of words. What I mean to say is, I miss it so much. I miss it so much that I actually bought a beautiful fillet from the Hy-Vee on Tuesday. I did a nice lemon and honey glaze."

Hans rolled his eyes and crossed his arms, a gesture they'd all seen before.

"Then I stuck it under the broiler. Just so I could smell it, you know?"

"You didn't eat it, though?" Gladys said this more like a statement than a question.

Karen looked at the floor.

"Karen! You didn't!"

"I couldn't help it." Anger flashed across her face and her eyes glowed like hot red coals for the briefest moment before returning to their soft blue color. "I wanted to *taste* something for once! Something that doesn't taste like dirty pennies! And if you want to feel smug about it, you should know that I vomited two minutes later, okay? Satisfied?"

Gladys drew back. Karen rarely lashed out at anyone, let alone her friends and confidantes. "I'm sorry, sweetie. I didn't mean to sound judgey."

Karen shrugged and frowned. "Well, I didn't get to savor it if that makes you feel better. I gave it to Simon. At least someone can enjoy my cooking."

Gladys' face softened with sympathy. The change had been hard on Karen. The only other friend she had to talk to was her Siamese cat. After her "incident," she had no choice but to quit her job. She had been sitting at home living off savings ever since.

Hans put his hand out to comfort Karen and faltered. It fluttered like a piece of paper in the wind. Affection never came easy for him. He settled for patting her lightly on the bicep before returning his gnarled hand to his lap, where he studied the fingernails on his left hand.

Karen, who knew how stoic he was, looked at him thankfully. "Maybe if they had essential oils that were like filet mignon and loaded baked potatoes, this would be easier."

Gladys chuckled.

"I would wish for Polish sausage," Hans offered without further elaboration.

He had a strange gift for creating awkward silences instead of filling them, but the two women had become so used to his faltering lack of social skills it no longer bothered them. He was like the foundation of a house. Necessary, appreciated, but hardly noticed unless he missed a weekly meeting.

"What about you, Glad?" Karen asked.

"What about me, what?"

"What would you eat if you could have anything in the world?"

She gave the question the serious thought it did not deserve. There were so many things she'd loved to cook in her former life, and none of them had been healthy by today's standards. A picture of her old dining room formed in her mind. She and her husband—never blessed with children of their own—gathered together with Donald's parents, aunts, uncles, and their children for a grand holiday meal. Roasted turkey, mashed potatoes slathered in butter and gravy...starch and meat, starch and meat. The backbone of any midwestern meal.

Then it came to her. "Pie."

"Pie? Just pie?"

"Isn't pie enough?" She chortled. "No, I would have a great pie buffet. Pumpkin, cherry, apple with lots of cinnamon and sugar on top, lemon meringue. And then, to top it all off, vanilla ice cream and homemade whipped cream. Not that cruddy Cool Whip stuff. The real deal." She wiped at her mouth, which was on the brink of drooling. These thoughts did her no good. No point in pining away for things they couldn't have.

"Ice cream and whip cream?" Hans asked.

"Why? Is there some limit on the toppings one is allowed to put on one's pie?" The question was rhetorical and evoked no response. She changed the subject. "How's work been, Hans?"

"Is good as can be expected. I sometimes wish for more, but what is point?" His expression was one of longing and dissatisfaction, although you really had to know him well to read any of his emotions.

Gladys knew it hadn't been easy for him to step down as the manager of the produce section at Hy-Vee Food Stores. He'd been forced to stoop to being a nighttime stocker due to his rather unfortunate sun allergy.

"I am also feeling frustrated with other employees. They spend all the time talking and looking at the YouTubes. Young people are lazy."

Gladys laughed out loud. It felt good to laugh. "Hans, there isn't a soul alive or undead who could satisfy your idea of work ethic. You're the most German, German man I've ever encountered."

"I will take compliment." A shadow of a smile crossed over his face.

"Okay," Karen said, changing the subject to one which impacted all of them. "Have you sensed anyone who's been, you know, changed?"

They had to be ever vigilant in their search for others like them -vampires turned against their will and then abandoned. Having a rogue running wild through the city threatened them all. Their little group was perfect for keeping them safe and out of the hands of other vamps, who would seduce a frightened, newly made monster to the dark side. Or worse, convince them to join Estelle and her legion of drones.

Hans and Gladys shook their heads and Gladys pondered her first meeting with her best friend. She was lucky to have run into Karen at Dr. Trish's vampire dentistry clinic late one night after she'd broken a third set of dentures.

"Finding own kind is difficult," Hans offered in a rare moment of contribution.

And he was right. It was difficult, as most like them had the sense to stay hidden as much as possible. But without the right support and a lot of personal restraint, a vampire was apt to attack anyone. And it wouldn't do to have lone vampires out there running amok accosting innocent people without a group to hold them accountable and keep them safe. There were more civilized ways to get what was needed. An undisciplined bloodsucker could expose them all. The Salem Witch Hunt wasn't all that long ago in the grand scheme of things.

"I haven't seen anyone," Karen said with a forlorn, far-off look that spoke to the loneliness they all felt. Then she brightened. "Wouldn't it be great to find a boyfriend someday? One who didn't mind sleeping all day and staying out all night? It's funny, but that's what Johnathan used to do that drove me so nuts. That's the reason I divorced him in the first place." She looked to the side, betraying the lie.

Gladys knew the real reason for Karen's divorce, as did Hans, but they kept silent and played along by mutual unspoken agreement. She personally had no desire to welcome anyone at all into her dull, repetitive life and had a hard time understanding why Karen would want to make things more complicated. She flapped her hand. "Who needs a man when we have each other?"

"Perhaps young lady is not as past prime as you."

"Hans!" Karen slapped him lightly on the arm. "That's not nice."

"But is true."

The meeting lasted another thirty minutes and then they stood, took each other's hands, and chanted their closing mantra.

The blood and the heart are for beating, not eating…

After fifty rounds or more of their ruminative chorus, they walked out into the humid night, which felt close and suffocating. They walked together toward Gladys' aged Camry, cancerous with rust spots that would eventually devour the whole thing. Hans carried their sign in one hand,

Gladys popped the trunk. "Hold on, let me make room." She hefted out a canvas tote that bulged at the sides and set it gingerly on the ground.

"One for you." She handed Karen a plastic grocery bag tied at the top.

"And one for you." She handed another to Hans.

"Should we have one?" Karen asked. She licked her lips twice with a flick of her tongue, the tips of her canines barely visible in the moonlight.

"Is no better time than present." Hans pulled out a one-ounce bottle that had long ago contained Jim Beam whiskey. Now it was filled with pure, tested, and, most importantly, *fresh* blood. This week's flavor was O-positive.

"Bottoms up!"

2. GOLDEN PEAKS

Gladys arrived at work at ten-thirty and stowed her belongings in her work locker. Light jacket, gloves, floppy sun hat, headscarf, dark glasses, and a giant tube of SPF 80. It would never do to be caught out in the early morning light without protection if her shift went tits-up. It was a precaution she'd employed ever since the day that Old Mr. Strabala had inconveniently passed away at four in the morning. The paperwork had taken hours, and the sun would have turned her to fricassee had she gone out. As soon as she could get away, she'd made a beeline toward the nearest basement corner and holed up, doing her best to become a part of the jumble of discarded, forgotten equipment and abandoned belongings.

Her white shoes squeaked on the polished floor as she made her way to the nurses' station with her motorboat-like gait. The familiar smells of antiseptic, urine, and floor wax should have been unpleasant, but after two decades of service to the aging and infirm, it was just part of the scenery. A big wipe-off board hung over the coffeepot that was half-full of lukewarm sludge. Gladys didn't care. It wasn't like she could drink it. She could still savor the smell, though, which partially explained the cup that she kept with her at all times. The other reason was the need to blend in whenever possible. All healthcare workers drank coffee and half of them smoked. It was a universally accepted way of life, especially on the night shift.

The overnight nursing assignments were scrawled in red marker on the board. Twelve patient names were listed in scarlet beneath her own. She groaned. Three nurses should have been on duty, but one had been crossed out and their patients had been added to the lists of the two remaining Angels of Mercy. Angry, frustrated slashes of blue marker scratched through Kayla's name. She had called off. Again. Gladys and Corrine were the oldest nurses on staff, and, with a few exceptions, it seemed like the younger millennials had no qualms about their frequent call-offs. What was it Hans said? Young people are lazy? He wasn't always wrong.

She logged onto the computer, which was science fiction back when she had accepted her nursing certificate in her white cap and dress, but those times were long gone, and she'd figured out long ago that she'd better get hip or she'd get left behind. She reviewed the care plans and updates for her charges.

"Evenin', Gladys," the other night nurse said as she zipped past, heading toward the locker room. Corrine. Ten minutes late, as usual.

"Hey, Corrine," Gladys responded, but the other woman was already out of hearing range. Her cheerful feelings evaporated. It wasn't that they were friends, but this was one place that gave her some sense of camaraderie. And people to talk to. Corrine was small, birdlike, and always seemed to have a frantic quality about her movements. Gladys wouldn't want to have her as her own nurse. She didn't trust Corrine's shaky caffeinated hands or constant frantic haste.

The three evening shift nurses approached the station as their workday ended. Shift change was a joke. In another place and time, nurses would convene around a table for a half-hour to share updates and discuss any issues that had come up during their shift. And snippets of juicy gossip. The computer had changed that, too. Gladys stood with effort to exchange polite pleasantries as they approached, but they walked right by, hardly looking in her direction.

"Have a good night!" she called after them.

One looked over her shoulder and gave a brief flick of the hand, but the other two didn't acknowledge her at all.

How lovely.

Shift nurses always seemed to stick together, and the night shift was treated like second-class citizens. Or perhaps third. It was like dealing with high school cliques. Gladys frowned. She would never have been so rude.

Gladys had been working at Golden Peaks for fifteen years, and she considered this to be a step up from her previous post. She'd worked at a real shithole before this, Pleasant Hill Long Term Care, a job she'd only taken out of desperation. She hadn't seen decent benefits since her nurse manager days at Dr. Snodderly's office back in '96. Forced early retirement from his practice meant giving up her pension. A bitter memory she'd never forgotten.

Gladys sighed and turned her attention back to the computer. As far as long-term care went, Golden Peaks wasn't so bad. At least they seemed to care about their residents. This care trickled down to the staff, and the night shift came with a shift differential of $4.50 an hour. As a bonus, she didn't have to worry about being fried to a crisp like a slice of bacon in the sun.

Corrine breezed up to the desk and fell into a chair beside Gladys.

"Everything okay?" Gladys asked, rubbing one knee, which was already beginning to stiffen.

"Oh, sure. Just always hectic trying to get out of the house, you know."

Gladys didn't but nodded anyway. "It's just the two of us tonight."

Corrine face-palmed in frustration. "Again?" Her voice croaked like a palsied old woman's.

"Easy now. We'll be okay. If we need help, we can always call up to another floor."

There were five floors at Golden Peaks, each floor housing thirty-two patients. That was a lot of old people. Gladys hated how it felt like a storage facility for the old and unwanted. At least she knew she'd never end up in a place like this.

Corrine groaned. "You okay with your assignments? Need to swap any?"

Gladys shook her head. "I think I'll manage."

Corrine turned her attention to her own computer as Gladys jotted her notes on the pad of paper she kept in her scrub top pocket and began her rounds.

Gladys peeked into four rooms, jotted notes, and then stopped suddenly outside of Mrs. Mortensen's. The hairs on the back of her neck prickled. Ethan, the new night custodian, had his dirty mop propped against the wall. He'd arrived here from the day shift. Gladys assumed he was another one of Hans' "lazy young people," looking for an easier shift.

She walked to the doorway as quietly as her knees would allow and looked inside, the tingling sensation along her skin cranking up. Mrs. Mortensen stared up at the ceiling with unfocused eyes. Gladys thought for a moment that she was dead, but that wouldn't have explained what the nineteen-year-old clean-up guy was doing with his mouth clamped on the elderly woman's neck. A spring/winter romance? Necrophilia? She shuddered.

Then she saw it as well as felt it. A dark shadow, barely visible to her and certainly not to the regular people walking around, surrounded Ethan in a swirling nimbus. She hadn't seen it before, but then again, she'd barely noticed him. It was always much easier to pick out ensanguined nightwalkers when they were feeding. Now her alarm bells were clanging away. "Ethan!"

The young man jerked at the sound of his name and backed away from the patient with a stumble, bumping his shoulder against the wall with a little yip. The room smelled dank and was lit only by the gloom of the hallway light.

Gladys stood with her hands on her hips, looking from Ethan to Mrs. Mortensen and back again. She tapped her orthopedic shoe, awaiting an explanation. She knew what was going on, but this would be Ethan's first test. Quick thinking and explanations were something all vampires needed to master. She wondered what kind of excuse he'd come up with. Two tiny rivulets of blood made their way down Mrs. Mortensen's neck with glacial slowness.

Ethan coughed into his hand and wiped at his mouth, looked at his hand, and shoved it in his pocket. Gladys noticed the blood, despite his efforts, and shook her head. This was going to take a lot of patience.

"Well?" she said.

Ethan glanced from side to side, looking like a first-grader who'd just farted in class. It seemed he was hoping an emergency exit would appear and he could escape into the night. He walked toward the door, attempting to reach past her to grab his dirty mop. "I'll just get back to—"

"Oh no you don't." She put her hand across the door to confirm that he wasn't about to go anywhere. "What's going on in here?"

"Um. I was just checking. I mean, I thought I heard, and so I was just making sure..." He stammered, petered out, then shifted on his feet as if he had to use the bathroom urgently.

Gladys gestured to the woman, still looking up at the ceiling. "What were you doing with my patient, exactly?"

Ethan bit his lip and looked at her helplessly. His hands were large fluttering moths looking for a landing spot. He opened and closed his mouth like a fish, but no sound escaped his lips except for the squeak of the world's smallest balloon leaking air.

"Come up with something, Ethan. Anything." She bit back the little smile that tried to invade her lips.

"Um, I thought she was choking? So...I wanted to make sure she could breathe." His eyes shifted toward the figure in the bed. Guilt was written across his features, and Gladys' heart went out to him.

"Come with me." She reached out toward his arm.

He flinched away from her.

She rolled her eyes and clamped her meaty palm on his forearm, pulling him out of the room and down the hallway toward the janitorial closet.

Ethan squealed but allowed himself to be dragged along in her wake.

"Shut *up!*" She spat in a harsh whisper and doubled her grip, being mindful not to pulverize the kid's bones in her irritation.

After a quick glance up and down the hall, Gladys confirmed that they were alone and unseen. She opened the door, shoved Ethan inside, and then stepped in, closing the door behind her with a soft snick. It was pitch black, but Ethan's eyes were dim red embers. She flipped on the light switch and squinted against the glare of the buzzing fluorescents.

"Look, Mrs. Knight, I'm sorry. About what you saw back there, really. I—"

"Can it. I already know."

"What do you know?" Ethan twisted the class ring on his right hand around and around, his eyes wide with fear.

Gladys sighed. "I want you to tell me. Tell me the truth. You've got ten seconds." She waited for Ethan to acknowledge his existence. It was part of taking control of this...this disease or whatever it was.

"I...I don't know what you mean."

"Yes, you do. You've got seven seconds to come up with an explanation someone would buy before I call security."

"I'm a vampire!" he shouted.

Gladys clamped a hand over his mouth, pushing herself into his personal space. She grimaced. He had a yeasty, onion smell about him and terrible acne. "My God, will you *please* stop shouting?" She hissed. "How stupid can you be?"

He grunted and snorted behind her hand, clawing ineffectually to escape her iron grip.

"Can you try to play it cool for five minutes? Or do you want to get yourself killed?"

Ethan nodded. Then he shook his head and mumbled.

Gladys removed her hand and pressed it gently into his right shoulder. She didn't want to terrify him, but she needed him to take the situation gravely. As it was. "I'm not going to hurt you. You're not alone, Ethan. There are others like you. Like us."

Understanding brightened his face, and tears of relief plopped onto his grey uniform shirt in dark splotches. "Like us? Like you?"

Gladys nodded. "Like us. Now, if you listen to me and follow my lead, you're going to be okay. But if you keep going the way you are," she gestured in the vague direction of his most recent victim. "You're going to get caught and you're going to die. Do you want to die?"

He shook his head, hair flopping around.

"Fine. Neither do I. Now, very quietly, why don't you tell me what happened."

Ethan opened his mouth and took a deep breath, as if he were about to rattle off rapid gunfire.

"Slowly," Gladys said.

3. COFFEE TALK

Gladys had called Hans and Karen the moment she'd gotten home from work and spilled the tea about Ethan. It was exciting to have fresh blood, so to speak, but also nerve-wracking. He was young—only nineteen. A post-pubescent, newly turned vampire, with no direction and no mentor. As for the vampire who made him? If Gladys' suspicions were correct, he certainly wouldn't be getting any help from that quarter. This wasn't a gift; it was a punishment and a curse.

She'd convinced Ethan to promise not to take blood from anyone until they could meet, and she'd sacrificed three of her precious shooters to tide him over.

"Don't drink it all at once," she'd told him. "Only take what you need and save the rest." She waggled a finger at him. "This is going to have to last you three days." She grimaced, knowing she'd have to ration her own meager supply to make up for what she'd given the little pipsqueak.

He had agreed sullenly; Gladys gripped his chin between two very strong fingers and forced him to look up at her. Her eyes burned like red-hot coals. Ethan agreed to hole up out of sight until they could devise a plan for his survival.

"And for God's sake, don't draw any more attention to yourself. There are worse things to upset than law enforcement. Best to put your head down and keep making the mustard."

"Huh?"

She rolled her eyes. "Making the mustard. Doing the job. Everything's normal. That mustard."

That Friday, after Ethan had called in to Golden Peaks with stomachache three days in a row, he was due to meet with the support group at the Village Inn on College Avenue at ten PM, well after the sun had sunken below the horizon.

By ten-fifteen, Gladys was worried that he was going to stand them up. By ten-thirty, she had visions of a skinny kid galloping across town on all fours on a blood binge. At 10:33, Ethan stumbled into the smoky restaurant looking dazed and pale, clothes rumpled. At least he'd shown up.

"You're late." Gladys' mouth twisted in a slant of disapproval.

Ethan pulled his head into his jacket like a turtle. "Sorry." He waved his hand in front of his face and wrinkled up his nose. "It's smoky in here."

Karen slid over and patted the cracked vinyl bench. "I know. Sorry about that."

He squeezed in beside her.

"This place is one of the few remaining holdouts where customers are allowed to smoke, being technically outside the city limits and all." She put a comforting arm around his shoulders and pulled him against her. "We can't get cancer, Ethan."

His body went rigid from Karen's touch, but she'd always had a hard time reading people's discomfort and didn't get the hint. Plenty of kindness, little respect for personal space.

"Besides," Gladys added. "Half of these people are practically vampires themselves." She gestured toward the hunched-over habitues of the second-rate coffee and pancake shop, thick with the smell of fake maple syrup and singed coffee. Some sat dazed, with filthy hands and dirty clothes. Some had obviously come from drinking at a bar and talked too loud. "This place is perfect cover."

"Welcome to our little group," Karen said. She picked up her coffee cup, sipped it, then spit it into a water bottle that sat beside her.

Ethan watched, fascinated.

"We can't really drink it," Karen said in a low voice. "But we can't afford to look conspicuous." She slid him the remaining empty cup from the middle of the table and filled it from the coffee-stained carafe.

"Yes," Hans said. "Conspicuous is bad thing."

"That's why you need to tone things down—quite a bit," Gladys hissed. "We can't afford to have you expose our world. That's why you're here."

Ethan looked confused. "Why am I here?"

"To leeeaarn." Hans drew the word, demonstrating with his hands as if to a child.

Ethan stared blankly.

"Young people are lazy." Hans shook his head in sorrow at the thought of such misspent youth.

Gladys looked into her coffee cup, searching for patience. Ethan was the youngest vampire she'd ever met. It was a shame he hadn't had a chance to enjoy his life before it had been completely altered. Although he'd been turned in the prime of his manhood, he must have been a late bloomer. Acne spread across his nose and forehead, bright red blossoms in contrast to his pale skin. His tan hadn't even faded yet. His voice still cracked as though puberty had almost left him in the dust, then circled back out of sheer spite. Estelle had arrested his development, and he'd be stuck in post-pubescent awkwardness for all eternity.

She reminded herself to give him a break. "There's too much to explain here in public, but this needs to be said again: Don't draw so much attention to yourself. And for God's sake, leave the living alone. We have a reliable supplier for what we need. Not as good as fresh from the cow, but it'll do. You don't want to end up a mosquito who gets swatted. Got it?"

Ethan nodded, but still seemed a little befuddled. "The cow?"

Karen covered his hand with hers and he jumped like someone had goosed his keester. She patted his hand. "You'll get used to things. It's not so bad, really. I always was more of a night owl, anyway." She looked out the window with a sad, wistful expression, as if to prove this was not the case, but she was trying to make herself believe it. "Just stay out of the sun. In fact, just stay home for now." She slipped him a business card.

"You carry cards?" He looked incredulous.

"Read card," helpful Hans said.

"XP Support Group Meetings. Tuesdays, Iowa City VFW. 1022 S. Center Street. 8 pm." He looked up at Karen, squinting in an effort to solve this new conundrum. "What's XP?"

"It's a genetic disease, xeroderma pigmentosum," Karen said. "It's a condition where you can't go out in the sunlight. We don't really have XP." She looked up at the ceiling, thinking it over. "I mean, I guess we kinda do have XP. A form of it, anyway. People who have it can't repair sun damage on the skin. Like us. Only their skin doesn't burst into flames like ours. They just put themselves at an astronomical risk for cancer."

"Is why we have support group name." Hans sipped his coffee, made a face, and spit it into his own water bottle.

Ethan made a gulping sound that seemed very loud in the restaurant. "So, I can't go outside ever? In the sunlight?"

Gladys spoke up before the other two could supply him with caveats and options like SPF 80 and UV-protectant clothing. She cut to the chase. "No. You can't go out in the sunshine. Meet us there next week." She tapped the card Hans had left on the table.

Ethan looked at it distrustfully.

"You'll get all the information you need to know about your new condition."

"But what's XP got to do with it? And why can't you just tell me now?"

Hans clenched and unclenched his hands on the table, beside himself with impatience. "Is cover story. Nothing to do with genetic disorder." He threw his hands up in exasperation and shook his head.

"Ohh, I get it." Ethan's face broke into a grin, like the sun sailing out from behind storm clouds. It improved his looks and made him seem marginally intelligent.

"Yeah," said Gladys. "Didn't you work on the day shift before?"

"Well, when I went outside after...you know. I burned my arm as soon as the light hit it. I couldn't figure out what the problem was, because why would that happen, you know? So, I kept trying to go outside, and I kept getting burned. Even being too close to the curtains made my skin smoke. I decided I better stay out of the light until whatever was happening to me went away." His face fell glum again. "I guess it's not going away."

"No, it's not," Karen said and reached toward him again, but he sank against the cheap vinyl booth, pulled his hands off the table, and stuck them into his pockets.

"But do you see?" Hans asked. "You beat head on wall, but then you understand. Not all stupid."

Gladys squeezed Hans' forearm, cutting his words off before he could say something even more insulting. "What he means is, even though you had to burn yourself a few times before you got it, you made a change to keep yourself safe. You must have some semblance of self-preservation. Just use that the next time you think about doing something that might get you seen." She pointed at him. "See you at the meeting." It wasn't a question.

Gladys had almost reached her car when Ethan trotted after her. "Hey, Gladys! Gladys? Wait up!"

Patience.

"Yes?"

"Do you have any more of those things? Those bottles?"

Her lips thinned into a fine line. "Follow me." She opened the passenger door and rummaged under the seat until she found what she was looking for.

Ethan looked at the vintage Spider-Man lunch box and grinned. "What's that?"

She released the clasp and opened the box. Inside were three shooters and an ice pack. "Emergency supply. For me, mind you. But here." She handed them over and he held one up to the light from the streetlamp. "Jesus!" She pushed his hand down.

"Stick that in your pocket! You're not even old enough to drink alcohol. What if someone sees you?"

"Sorry." He shrugged, and the bottles disappeared up his jacket sleeve along with his hand.

"This is what we mean. You need to be smart about things." She looked around the parking lot. No one was in sight. "Make sure you come to the meeting." With that, she got in the car and drove away from him as quickly as she could without breaking traffic laws.

4. GROUP SUPPORT

Gladys sashayed in her awkward gait into the VFW hall at ten to seven. A fourth chair had been added to the room, changing what used to be a triangle into a square.

Karen waited with an excited gleam in her eyes, her cheeks rosy under the heavy makeup.

She must have fed before she came.

Gladys hoped it was from the bottles they received weekly from their supplier and not some outside source. She'd slipped before. All of them had at one time or another.

Karen held a small yellow notepad on her knee, pen at the ready. She took notes at every meeting. She would hand out a type-written piece of paper with "*Meeting Minutes*" in italics at the top of the page to everyone in attendance at the next meeting. Gladys had told her multiple times that meeting notes and attendance forms (and half their procedural nonsense) were a waste of time since they knew each other, not to mention they left a paper trail that could lead to questions. This time, though, it might be useful. At least it would help Ethan.

Hans arrived just as the church bell down the street clanged eight times. He ducked his head, looking guilty as he entered the metal double doors. He'd been a devout Catholic until he was turned and was still bitter about not being allowed back into the house of God. He'd said on numerous occasions that he thought there ought to be a caveat or addendum to the rule about the undead not being denied entry if they hadn't *chosen* to be undead. His private appeals to God had yet to bear fruit, but that didn't stop him from asking. The unsightly burns from his first attempt at entry had left holy scars on his hand that spread up his arm to the elbow. Sun damage and the wrath of God, it seemed, were two things vampires couldn't heal from.

"Ethan will probably be late," Gladys said. "So, we have some time to talk before he gets here."

"Young people are lazy," Hans began.

Gladys shot him a look. Her eyes flashed red for a moment, telling him to *die klappe*, then went back to their muddy brown color, floating in her slightly yellowing sclera.

Hans shut up as directed.

"You're gonna have to get over that," Gladys said.

"Over what?"

"That thing you do. About young people. You're going to need to knock that off as long as Ethan's around. It's not fair to make him a whipping boy for your grudge against anyone under thirty."

Hans shrugged, looking sullen. "Is true."

Gladys continued. "Whether it is or not, you don't need to keep on hammering away at the point. If I said, 'German men are as exciting as white bread,' over and over, wouldn't you get sick of it?"

Hans mulled her question over much longer than was required. "Well, sometimes it is truth."

"That's not the poin—"

Karen intervened before Hans and Gladys could get into full swing. "Alright, you two. That's enough banter."

Gladys rolled her eyes and huffed. She knew they were both acting like sulky grade-school kids, but sometimes it was hard not to engage.

They sat in gestating silence for nearly five minutes.

Gladys kept looking over her shoulder at the doors, hoping to see Ethan's lanky frame. Finally, she couldn't stand it anymore and broke the standoff, if that's what it was. "I'm worried about our young friend. It seems like he's going to need a sponsor."

"Like in AA?" Karen asked.

"Exactly like in AA." She shot her friend with double finger guns. "Someone he can call when he's on the verge of getting himself burned up or killed. Or thrown in jail and *then* killed."

"Doused by holy water," Hans offered.

"Eats a garlic pizza?" Karen continued, a half-smile forming on her lips.

Gladys ignored their foolishness. "Someone who can talk him down, tell him he's being a dumbass." She looked from Hans to Karen.

Hans had turned his attention to his hands and was concentrating on removing invisible dirt from under his thumbnail.

Karen stared back at Gladys with an eager half-smile, waiting for Gladys to acquiesce.

"Ugh," Gladys huffed. "Okay, fine. I guess I'm Ethan's sponsor."

"It seems only right." Karen nodded with enthusiasm and jotted a note on the page.

"Why is right?" Hans asked.

"Why bother to ask?" Gladys snapped. "You don't want to do it, anyway. And besides, Karen's right. I tagged and bagged him. The Chinese say that when you save someone's life, you're responsible for it. Lucky me."

"We're going to have to work together to keep him out of trouble," Karen said. "You're really going to have to keep an eye on him."

As if she didn't know it already.

"What is concern?" Hans murmured.

Gladys rolled her eyes again. "Everything! He was taking an involuntary blood donation from one of our patients the other night. Like I said, that's how I caught him. If I can keep him from draining the elderly, that'll go a long way toward keeping him safe. And everyone else, too."

Hans hadn't looked up from his manicure project. "But you also drank from patients, yes?"

Gladys clamped her jaw shut and glared. Her face flushed with anger. "It was only in an emergency. Back before I found you all."

Karen averted her eyes, embarrassed on her friend's behalf.

"But also recently," Hans pressed.

"We were out! It had been four days since my last feed, and I needed something. And they were right there. Sleeping. They never felt a thing."

"It is mortal sin."

Her eyes went red again. "It's a mortal sin in *your* book, Hans. I don't believe in any book, so I'm not going to trouble myself with worry about the nature and classification of sins."

"Then why not drink from elderly at all times?" Hans was goading her.

Gladys was losing the ability to control her anger.

"Hey," Karen said. "I don't think we need to—"

Gladys rose to her feet, ignoring the cracking of her knees. "I don't need a book to help guide my conscience, *Hans*. So quit thinking you have some moral high ground. You're no better than me. *I* never drained anyone dry."

The door squeaked open, ending their discussion.

Gladys retook her seat and concentrated on looking normal. The door thudded closed as the tall, awkward kid who pushed a broom for a living at Golden Peaks walked in looking around like a tourist. Ethan wore dark glasses, the kind the cops wore on that show from the 1970s—CHiPs or whatever it was. He spotted them sitting together and made his way across the large room, one halting step at a time.

"Well?" Gladys stirred the air, beckoning. "Come on. And take off those ridiculous glasses."

"It's my disguise," Ethan said with a conspiratorial smile.

She grinned. "Well, you don't need them in here and you look like a holdover from 1976."

This kid was ridiculous, but that gave him a childish charm that made it impossible to remain irritated with him for long. The distraction from her argument with Hans eased the tension in the room. She knew he wouldn't be able to keep himself from insulting the boy. Good. That would end the uncomfortable conversation about her indiscretions.

Karen started the meeting with her usual preamble and then explained the rules of the group—anonymity, confidentiality, that whole "what happens in Vegas stays in Vegas" mantra. "This isn't a recovery group like AA or Overeaters Anonymous. There *is* no recovery." Her face clouded over. "We're here to get support, learn to live with our disease, and share resources. It's something we all need, especially at the beginning."

"Technically," Ethan said as he crossed his arms. "There's no cure for alcoholism either."

Hans groaned and covered his eyes. "Why must young people always argue?"

Ethan either didn't hear or chose to ignore this. "Wait. Is there an Overeaters Anonymous?"

Karen patted Ethan's hand.

His leg kicked out at her touch like he'd been struck by a doctor's reflex hammer.

"That's not really important."

With a grunt, Gladys cut them short, stood, and recited their opening oath. "Our curse is our own to bear."

The other veterans joined in. "We do not benefit others or ourselves by feeding off the living or taking human life."

Ethan chewed his thumbnail.

Gladys pointed an accusatory finger at him. "That means no sucking blood from the elderly. Now, who wants to start us off?" She sat, grimacing as her knee popped.

"And no others, also." Hans glared at Ethan.

Ethan shrugged and slid his hands into his pockets.

They took turns standing, introducing themselves, confessing, again, unnecessary but a part of their process none of them had been able to abandon. Doing the whole AA thing, in other words.

Ethan went last. He kicked his legs out in front of him and crossed his ankles, as well as his arms. "Hey. My name's Ethan."

"Stand, please." Karen motioned with her hand for him to get to his feet. "It's more formal if you stand." She jotted a note on the yellow pad of paper.

Maybe that's his first demerit. Gladys nearly laughed out loud.

Ethan got to his feet, accidentally tripped over the chair leg, then righted himself. He cleared his throat. "Hi, I'm Ethan," he said, more loudly this time.

"Hi, Ethan," they replied in unison.

His voice echoed through the vast and mostly empty space. "Umm...I'm a vampire?" His voice cracked on the last syllable, as if he was still uncertain that was the truth. "It has been, umm..."

"Seven days," Gladys offered.

Ethan's glance cut to her briefly, and he shifted uncomfortably on his feet, looking guilty. "It has been four days since I last fed on a human being." He cleared his throat again and sat down.

"Ethan!" Gladys shouted. "What did I tell you?"

He shrugged. "Couldn't help it. And it wasn't at work, so it wasn't a patient. I haven't been back to work since that day. The day you found me. Anyway, there was this guy under the bridge, see? Down on the bike path. And he...well, he was sleeping. Or maybe he was unconscious. I don't know—it made me feel all spinny. But I was so hungry!" He looked at each of them indignantly, as if this excused his behavior. "I already tried eating everything else. I even got a package of raw hamburger from the store. But it made me sick. Even the juices."

"Holy hooters. How could you be so dumb?" Gladys' nostrils flared.

"Now, now," Karen said. She waggled her finger at Gladys for effect. "This is a place where we don't judge. Remember?"

Hans huffed. "Perhaps it should not be a place without judgment. I think judgment is sometimes necessary. Especially for—"

"Young people. Yes, I've got it, Hans," Karen said through clenched teeth. "We all need to remember that none of us here are without sin. We all need a little guidance, and we're all bound to make some mistakes along the way." Karen rubbed her temple.

"So long as no one died," Gladys said.

Ethan was silent.

"Right, Ethan? No one died, did they?"

Her heart did a little flip-flop in her chest. If he had accidentally murdered someone, it was going to take a long time before he could forgive himself. Maybe he never would.

He clenched his fists at his sides and shuffled his feet. He looked down at his battered Converse sneakers as if he'd never seen them before and gave no answer.

"Ethan?" Karen soothed. "It's alright. You can tell us. This is a safe place, *free of judgment*. Isn't it?" She looked at the two other aged vampires for confirmation.

Gladys gave a slight nod of affirmation.

Hans remained stony.

Ethan shook his head but didn't look up. "I don't think so. I called 911. From the emergency box."

"You what?" Hans was on his feet, jabbing a finger in Ethan's direction. "We can't have you calling police! It will bring destruction down on all of us!" He took a step forward, seemingly unaware he had done so. "This is most important rule of all! No authorities, no police snooping around. Do you want to die? If so, I can do this now. Say word and I will be ending this for all our sakes."

"Hans!" Karen shouted.

This got his attention. She never shouted. Well, almost never.

"Is it taken care of?" Gladys leaned forward and held her hand out in front of Hans as if that would stop him from having a go at the boy. "All I want to know is that it's taken care of, and we aren't going to hear any more about it." She looked at Hans with daggers in her eyes. "And you ought to know better than anyone how hard it is at first."

Hans rose and headed toward the bathrooms at the other end of the meeting hall. They didn't have to use bathrooms, of course. Vampires didn't excrete. But the habit of commodial escapism was difficult to overcome.

"Yeah. It's taken care of. I was just, you know. Afraid the guy would die. And I watched from down on the riverbank. You know, made sure he got help and everything. I think he might have been overdosing when I bit him, cause that feeling I had was like being super drunk. End of story. They injected him with something—I don't know what it was. Then they took him away."

"Narcan," Gladys said, more to herself than the group. "What did you do then?"

"Passed out." He flashed the goofy version of his smile. It was the one that charmed you into forgiveness.

"See?" Karen beamed. "It's fine. He cleared things up. Now let's move on."

Gladys had one more thing to say on the subject before letting it drop. Ethan's safety and well-being were the whole reason she had insisted he come to the meeting in the first place. "You have to be careful, Ethan. Whatever's in your victim's blood can affect you, too."

"What do you mean?"

"I mean, if someone's high on drugs, it'll make you high, too."

"Really?" His face lit up.

"That's not an option," Karen said. She pulled him back to his chair by his sleeve, pinching it between her fingers. She finally seemed to have grasped the fact that Ethan was skittish about touch. "We can't have vampires running around high on drugs. You see what could happen. Right?"

Ethan nodded.

Hans returned and thumped into his chair, looking as though a hapless puppy had just peed on his favorite rug.

"Gladys, would you like to testify?" Karen said in a desperate attempt to change the subject from anything unpleasant or confrontational.

"Fine, okay. Here goes." Gladys stood up, though she would have been much happier to remain seated. Her knees were bad tonight and there wasn't anything that could be done about it. Ice was little comfort. Though she'd thought about snagging someone coming out of a methadone clinic and absorbing a little pain relief for herself, she'd not been able to bring herself to do it.

5. GLADYS TELLS ALL

"Okay, Ethan. Since you're new here, it only makes sense that you get to hear everyone's story." She put a finger to her lips, thinking. "Probably can't get through all of them in one night. There's too much. We'd turn to dust before Karen stopped talking." She shot Karen a friendly look.

Karen nodded back. No offense taken. Good.

"This all started fifteen years ago" Gladys held her hands in front of her like goalposts as if checking for just the right camera angle to look into the past. "So, there I am, sitting at the nursing station, working the night shift. This is at Pleasant Hill Long Term Care. It's your basic shithole, but I'm the lead nurse supervisor, so not too shabby for a workin' gal. It had been a hell of a day. Call lights going off like it's Christmas in New York City, one code blue, and an impressive shit in Room 1202 that covered the bed sheets and part of one wall. The gal in charge of that one walks off shift with feces in her hair halfway through and I know she isn't coming back. This isn't a job for sissies."

Ethan snickered.

Gladys raised her eyebrow. "Something funny?"

Ethan laughed out loud and actually slapped his knee. "The impressive shit thing. That's hilarious!"

Karen elbowed him to shut up and gestured for Gladys to continue.

"I'm enjoying a cup of coffee now that the dust of the day has settled. Not that the coffee is good. It's an evil shade of sludgy black. It's gone cold, too, but at this point in the day it's caffeine and that's enough. I've got two ice packs strapped around my knees because they're aching like rotten teeth. The ice isn't a cure, but it feels heavenly. I've been on my feet all day and haven't even had my lunch yet.

"The knees are getting worse, and I've been waiting for my ortho doc to approve a knee replacement, but he keeps telling me I need to exercise and lose some weight before he'll do surgery. Isn't that what they always say? He doesn't seem to understand that in order to exercise, I need new knees. You know, the kind that actually bend. I can't get new knees until I lose weight. I can't lose weight without new knees. Around and around we go and there's never any progress. I'm enjoying the cool, quiet moment and thinking of a way to get Dr. Peterson to agree that I'm strong enough to rehab. If he'd just follow me around for a day, he'd see that I have plenty of get up and go.

"My mind is a million miles away when a severe, *severe* looking woman comes up to the desk. She's so...severe—that's the best way I can describe her—that she seems sharp enough to cut someone and draw blood. I plaster on the face I save for difficult conversations."

A grunting sound interrupted Gladys' story. Ethan shifted in his seat, looking ready to bolt from his chair. He was nearly hovering in his excitement with his hand up. "I know that lady—"

"Hush yourself," Hans said, cutting him off. "Settle movements of buttocks and listen. You will have turn later." He crossed his arms. "Young people are—"

"Lazy," Gladys finished for him.

"Twitchy," Hans corrected.

Ethan settled, but she could tell it was taking a monumental effort for him to sit still and shut up.

Gladys continued. "The woman stands on the other side of the counter glowering like someone just pissed in her Cheerios. I'm staring at her hair. It's cut painfully straight, and doesn't seem to move at all, like she's a cartoon character or something. This was the first time I've seen her so I couldn't even connect her with one of our residents. I thought maybe she was a medical equipment rep or something. The weirdest thing is she's wearing all white from head to toe. White pantsuit, white gloves—*what is this, 1960?*—floppy white hat that looks like it would be right at home on the beach. Her skin is so pale that her face seems to blend in with the white of her fancy suit. Clearly, it's been a while since she last visited the beach.

"Fancy-Suit Lady slaps her gloved hand on the counter as if I can't see her standing there. *'Hello!?'*

"I say, 'Hello,' with a smile, but all signs are pointing to the fact that this is going to be a nightmare. Sometimes the patients' families are more work than the patients themselves. In fact, that's often the case.

"She asks me, 'What are you doing, exactly?'

"Her accent is just as sharp as her looks, and it's not quite British, but almost... I'm trying to puzzle out the origin when she makes that exaggerating throat-clearing sound people do to not-so-politely show how damn impatient they are.

"I realize I'm just kind of staring off into space and I look down as if I'm not sure what I'm doing. The capering animals on my scrubs seem to be laughing at me. I have my ice packs on, swollen ankles being squeezed to death by my support hose, feet propped up on a chair, and I think, *yeah, this could look like laziness to the outsider.*

"I realize this woman isn't going to be placated with words, so I sigh and put my feet on the floor. The ice packs slide down and slap the polished floor like dead fish. I'm too tired to argue or play games. This is my fourth ten-hour shift in a row, and I have two more to go before the weekend. Why couldn't this have happened thirty minutes from now after shift change? I'd have been heading home toward a well-deserved evening beer, singing to classic rock on KUVO radio. There's no one else in sight. I have no choice but to deal with it, so I ask, 'Is there something I can help you with?'

"The woman's lips thin to a bloodless slit, practically disappearing altogether. 'My mother needs assistance!'

"I glance at the bank of call lights, almost wishing they were blinking like morse code so I could claim that duty calls elsewhere. For a wonder, none of them are currently flashing red. Any other time, I'd have been running my butt off. I ask, 'And who is your mother?'

"'What do you mean, who is she?' She's so riled up I can see spit coming out of her mouth. 'What kind of stupid question is that?'

"I thought it was an honest question at the time," Gladys told the group with a shrug.

"Then Snow White says, 'She is in Room 1408. She hasn't even had her supper yet.'

"1408. Our newest resident just arrived this afternoon. No wonder I don't recognize her. I look up at the clock over her shoulder. It's only four-thirty in the afternoon. These may be older people, but four-thirty is too early for dinner even when you're over seventy. 'Dinner isn't ready until five-thirty,' I say, knowing full well this won't placate her. I've been in the nursing game long enough to identify an overbearing relative lurking about, waiting to make the lives of the staff as miserable as possible.

"The woman presses her hands into the counter—seems to press them through the counter—and leans over, appearing to grow taller as she does. A weird stretching lengthens her neck and her arms. Her already long fingers creep toward me, and I back away. I'm kicking myself for succumbing to the whim-whams. It must be my imagination. What I'm seeing is just not physically possible."

"Often, we see what is not possible. Mind cannot match reality, so we disbelieve," Hans said.

Everyone stared at him.

"Is true. Young man must learn this lesson. Believe what you see. Or you have a downfall." Hans shot a piercing look at Ethan, who, for once, hadn't butted into her tale.

"Fantastic advice," Gladys said, not minding the sidestep into helpful hints for the newest member of their group. "That would have been really helpful a long time ago. If I had known then, I wouldn't be—"

"Go on," Karen said. Her eyes sparkled with excitement, even though she'd heard the story countless times already. "I want to hear what happens next." She licked her lips, the points of her teeth poking out just a little.

"Okay, okay. Yes. Believe what you see." She nodded at this little nugget of wisdom. "Moving on.

"Fancy Suit Lady snaps at me, 'I don't care! She's been here all day with hardly anything to eat! She's hungry. Do you people make it a standard practice of starving your patients?'

"I can't imagine it'd be possible for her to be any angrier, but she's a pro. Probably she's been at this a long time. 'Okay,' I say. I kick the ice packs aside and my knees hurt so bad I actually wobble as I get to my feet. It defeats my efforts to make me seem like an authority figure of any kind. When I catch my balance I say, 'Let me see what I can find for your mother to tide her over until dinner. Which,' I emphasize, 'is at five-thirty.' I try to meet her eyes for a moment, so she knows I'm in charge. But when I do, they flash red for a moment and my courage runs out of the soles of my stupid orthopedic shoes, right into the floor."

Gladys flapped her hand to ward off any comments, but none came. The three others nodded in understanding, as if an undercurrent of intuition had settled over their little circle.

"I look away from her freaky eyes because they're so disturbing and start for the commissary. 'What's your mother's name again?' I ask. 'I didn't catch it the first time.' I have this strange compulsion to yammer away and fill the silence because I'm afraid I might be going crazy—or I might start screaming because I'm not crazy.

"'That's because I didn't tell you. Her name is Rose Getty. Room 1408. Rose. Getty.'

"Something, I don't know what, makes me turn around to look at her. She's smiling, but it's not a nice, friendly smile. It makes my skin crawl, and I can feel rivulets of sweat coursing down my face.

"'Now go,' she says, making a shooing gesture with her hand that might be hilarious if I wasn't hot, tired, and in pain. And afraid. 'I'll be waiting in her room.'

"My knees pop as I shuffle to the small kitchen where we keep snacks like Jell-O, applesauce, and pudding. It's like my feet are stuck in blocks of cement and they're too heavy to lift. I open the cupboards and know something right away. None of these offerings will satisfy that woman. I realize that I forgot to ask Fancy Suit Lady what *her* name was. Maybe it won't matter. Maybe I'll never have to deal with her again. Probably wishful thinking on my part. A good number of our residents don't tend to spend very long with us before they 'graduate' and move on to a higher realm."

Gladys replayed her last words and felt embarrassment wash over her.

"I'd never wish for someone's death, you understand, but I'm starting to feel absurdly panicked because all I can find are saltine crackers, 7-Up, orange popsicles, and Jell-O cups. Sweat pops out in my underarms. Even though I remembered my deodorant, I smell the astringent stink of B.O.

"Finally, in the second to last cupboard, I hit the goldmine. Bagels. And fruit cups. I slice a bagel in half, almost cutting across my palm for my trouble. I flinch as if I can see the blood welling up in an invisible cut. But there's no blood, so I pop the bagel into the toaster, hoping we have one of those weird triangular single-serving packets of cafeteria cream cheese in the fridge. Thankfully, we do. I slather the bagel, pull the plastic cover off the peaches, not failing to splash that sticky syrup they call juice all over myself, and put all the stuff on a tray. My goal is to get this over with as quickly as possible. In my mind's eye, I see myself getting in the car and locking the doors.

"One of my knees completely locks up on my way to 1408 and I nearly dump the whole thing onto the floor. You have to understand, there's only ten percent of the cartilage remaining in my left knee and fifteen on the right. Lose weight. Ha."

"Is hard to do," Hans said.

"I knock on the door frame, holding the tray like a waitress at a fine dining establishment.

"'*There* you are,' Fancy Suit says. 'I thought you'd decided to let her starve.'

"I flash my best, cooperative, understanding smile in her direction and set the tray on her bedside table. An ancient woman—presumably Rose—sits in the plastic recliner, staring into space. I wheel the tray over and adjust it so the lady can reach. She seems so normal compared to her daughter, who reminds me of Cruella de Vil, minus the two-toned hair. Rose makes no move to eat anything, and I can't tell if she really is hungry or if her daughter just needs something to do to fill her time. The old woman seems positively vacant.

"I say, 'If that's everything, I'll leave you to it,' and then I can't remember her name. I can't remember if I asked her or not. The last fifteen minutes seem kind of blurry at this point. 'Mrs....'

"'Estelle,' she says. 'Estelle Getty.'

"I know it's unprofessional to laugh, but it's a struggle. *Estelle Getty? Rose? Who are these two, the twisted* Golden Girls?"

Ethan looked confused.

Karen chuckled, turning toward him. "It's an old TV show, honey. An old sit-com."

He looked at Karen, still baffled.

"Never mind," she patted his hand, "it doesn't matter."

"I'm able to swallow the laughter, but it feels like she can read my mind! I watch her face and I'm almost certain she knows that I've had that thought and that inside, I'm laughing at her expense. I reason that I'm just exhausted and everything will seem normal when I'm home and changed into a comfy gown watching *Wheel of Fortune*.

"'No relation to the actress,' Estelle says in her clipped accent."

"Did she hear you? Do you think?" Ethan asked.

"I still wonder about that," Gladys responded, looking thoughtful. "It seemed like it at the time, but who knows. I never had a chance to ask." Gladys returned to her story.

"'Alrighty then.' My voice sounds croaky, breathy. I don't want to talk to this woman anymore. I look at my actual patient. 'Goodnight, Rose. We'll see you tomorrow.'

"The woman doesn't respond at all. Not a word. Not a flinch when I squeeze her hand in comfort. I actually have to check to make sure she's still breathing. She is, of course. I leave her and head to the desk, but I can't get Snow White Pants Suit Lady out of my head, you know?"

6. GLADYS DESERVES A DRINK

A look of understanding spread slowly across Ethan's face as he listened with rapt attention. It was as if some great epiphany had just occurred to him. The others had experienced this same emotion before, and Gladys recognized it for what it was. She shook her head. He raised his hand to double down, shifting his weight from one butt cheek to the other like a third grader with the right answer.

"No, Ethan," Gladys said. "You're going to have to wait until I finish. We don't interrupt with cross talk."

Incredulity faded to confusion. "Cross talk?"

"She means," Karen said, leaning toward him, "we don't share our thoughts on someone's experience until they're all done talking. It's an AA term. We use lots of those." She patted Ethan's shoulder.

His body went rigid, but he didn't jerk away. He was learning to master his new reflexes.

Karen wrote something on her notepad and then looked up. "Go ahead, Glad. Finish telling."

"Enough cross talk has been happening already," Hans grumbled. "We should be here all night with this." He crossed his arms.

"Thanks," Gladys said, marveling at how all three of them had interrupted and how two of them had done it to get the first one to stop. Her lips quirked up in a little smile, and then she focused her concentration, trying to pick up the loose threads of her story. She cleared her throat. "Okay, so it's a few days later."

"The day, not to mention the week, seems like it's gone on for a year, and I wish the weekend would just come already. I'm completely wiped out, but I have a couple of hours yet to go before quitting time. The halls are quiet, so I pour myself a cup of coffee and sit down for a little breather.

"Rose, the patient in Room 1408, is settling in, but she hardly talks and when she does, I'm not always certain it's me she's talking to. It's strange—Estelle hasn't been by to see her mother since she moved in. Most patients are so clingy their families practically have to get their groping fingers surgically removed so they can go home. But this hasn't been the case here, and I can't figure out why. It leaves me feeling unsettled.

"I'm ruminating on all of this when an elderly gent zooms up to the desk in his wheelchair and opens his robe, exposing all his shriveled man parts. I close my eyes, wanting to shut out the vision of Mr. Flanders's fuzzy white pubes. I'm hoping to find a nursing assistant, a nurse—hell, even an administrator—to drag the old pervert back to his room, but they're either hiding or helping someone else. There are a ton of reports I need to finish before I can go home, but the duty still falls on me. I set the coffee cup down and hope it doesn't get dumped out before I can make it back. It was the last cup of mud in the pot. 'Come on, Clyde. Let's get you back to your room. You can put some pants on, so you don't scare the staff.'

"At this point, I don't care if he strips down naked and flash dances all afternoon as long as his door's shut. The CNA is still nowhere to be found. Probably outside smoking. I take hold of the joystick—the one on the wheelchair, not the one on his person—and guide him back to his room. As we pass 1408, there's a small squeaking sound. The room is dark. 'Go on now, beautiful. And don't come out flashing us again,' I tell him.

"Clyde giggles like a kid and pilots his chair into 1406 as if this was the funniest prank he'd ever come up with.

"It will happen again. Guys like Clyde, whether they're the epitome of robust health or decrepitly limping along in God's waiting room, always seem to be able to get a rise out of people. With him, it happens at least once a week. I want to see him safely tucked away, but I don't like the sound from 1408. Or the darkness.

"I hold my breath and tap on the metal door frame of Rose's room, not wanting to startle her if she's just sleeping. 'Hello? Rose?'

"Even with the light streaming in from the hallway, I don't see her silhouette in the bed. The curtains have been drawn, and that's strange since we open everyone's curtains in the morning to let in some natural light. The recliner is empty as well. Maybe she's not here. Maybe she's visiting...but no. I hear it again. A squeaky, reedy sound, but there's a word in there all right.

"'Help.'

"The voice is breathless. I flip the switch and light floods the room like a camera flash. *Oh shit.* My stomach does a little dive roll when I see poor Rose sprawled out on the tile, reaching for me like Mrs. Fletcher in the Life Alert commercials. This couldn't have happened at a worse time. Or for a worse resident. Part of me—a cowardly part—wants to shut off the light, put on my jacket, and head home an hour early as if I hadn't seen Estelle's mother on the floor. But I'm a sucker, right? So, I stay and do my duty.

"'What happened?' I push the call light and get down on the floor. Not a pretty sight, and I'm afraid of what it's going to take to get me back up again. My right knee pops with a sound like a gunshot. 'Rose? Are you alright? How did you get on the floor?' I glance around the room, checking for any hazards.

"'I was trying to go out to the garage.' Rose's voice is pitifully weak and confused. 'I'm late for bridge.' Her eyes flood with tears as she looks up at me. 'How did I get down here?'

"'I'm not sure, but let's check you over before we get you up, okay?'

"Julie, the AWOL CNA, finally sticks her head in the door. 'You got it?' She asks me as if she can't tell that I don't.

"I try not to snap at her, but I'm kinda at the end of my rope by this time. 'No, I don't *got it*. That's why I called. Rose fell.'

"The twenty-something nitwit slouches against the door jamb and smacks her gum. 'And?'

"I can't stand that sound. It's like a herd of vaginas stomping through the mud, you know?"

Karen snickered with a look of distaste. Ethan gaped at her, no doubt believing that his elderly mentor would never say such a thing. Hans just looked embarrassed.

"Anyway, I ask her, 'What's our protocol for a fall?' And she just looks at me like I've posed the question in Mandarin. 'You know there's a protocol, right?'

"She smacks her gum again before answering, 'Yeah, but nobody ever follows it.' She says this right out loud, without the slightest hint of shame. Technically, I'm her boss! I just don't get it."

"Young people are lazy," Hans said with a self-satisfied smile.

Gladys ignored this with a roll of her eyes.

"The snarky look on Julie's face makes me want to punch her, but obviously I can't do that. I say, 'Yes. We do. And we will follow it. Now come over here.'

"With a groan, Julie comes over to where I'm crouched on the floor, down on one knee and trying to stay up with the other. I know that the longer I'm down here, the harder it's going to be to get vertical again, and the last thing I want to do is try to get up with Gidget in the room. Not a very dignified process.

"We check Rose over from head to toe; things seem in order. Somehow, I'm able to get back up but a tiny fart sneaks out, and I can see this chick's face buckling under the pressure of trying not to laugh. Finally, we get Rose back on her feet, help her to the bathroom, and then get her settled in the recliner with *Jeopardy!* and a cup of applesauce. If I didn't know better, I'd have said Rose doesn't remember that anything happened at all. She's happy as a clam. But I'm not. I know what comes next, and I'm the one who has to do it."

"What? Do what?"

"Shh," Gladys said, quieting Ethan. "I'm about to tell you. Believe me, this is the last thing you *ever* want to do when you're a nurse. Other than to tell someone that their loved one has expired."

"Expired?" Ethan's eyebrows knit so closely together in confusion, they could almost shake hands.

"She means dead," Karen explained.

"Oh."

7. GLADYS TAKES A DRINK

"Once the incident reports are written, the FALL RISK sign is taped over Rose's door, and the administrator is notified, I know I can't put this unpleasant task off any longer. I dial Rose's emergency contact. The phone rings. Once...twice...three times... four...Just as I think I'm in the clear, and I'm going to get her voicemail, a woman's voice on the other end says, 'Hello? Yes?'

"For a minute, the words are caught in my throat, and I almost hang up. But this is my job, so I better do it. 'Hello, I'm calling for Estelle Getty?'

'Yes, you've reached Estelle.'

'This is Gladys from Pleasant Hill. Rest assured, everything is fine, but Rose took a little tumble today. Again, she is totally fine, but our policy is to notify our patient's emergency contact or guardian anytime there's a fall or an incident, so—'

"'She what!?' The feedback from Estelle's screech penetrates my eardrums. 'What are you people doing there? How could you let this happen?'

"*You People.* I squeeze my eyes shut and hold the handset away, but I can still hear the vitriol coming out of the phone, which seems like it's dripping with venom. I wouldn't have been surprised if it puddled onto the counter and started to eat a hole through the fading Formica. That's how awful it was. You know what I mean?"

They all nodded. They knew what she meant.

All of a sudden, Gladys felt overwhelmed with gratitude for this oddly cobbled together group of misfits.

"Thanks. That actually means a lot. Anyway, when the sounds on the other end dwindle, I put the phone back to my ear. 'I'm sorry,' I break in. It's rude, but there's no other way to get this call over with before the end of time arrives. 'I don't know how she fell. She was alone in her room and when I walked by, she was on the floor, as simple as that. I think she may have been a little confused. She said she was trying to get to the garage and was late for a bridge game.'

"And then she said the magic words, 'Well, of course she's confused! She has Alzheimer's disease, you stupid cow!'"

Ethan gasped. "She said that to you?" Hero-worship was painted on his face,

Gladys was both touched and tired. She never wanted to be anyone's savior, dammit. Now here was this kid.

"Yeah. She said it. But of course, that's not the worst thing she'd ever done. And I don't think I need to tell you that Rose *wasn't* her mother."

"She wasn't?"

"Nope. Great-great-granddaughter, actually. I don't know when the woman was turned, but it had to have been several hundred years ago. Otherwise, she wouldn't be so powerful."

Karen and Hans nodded sagely.

Ethan looked perplexed.

"That diagnosis wasn't included in Rose's intake paperwork. I had read the whole thing, of course. That's my job. 'We don't have that diagnosis in her chart, Ms. Getty. Patients with Alzheimer's disease require care on a different floor with heightened supervision. Did you alert our admissions office of her diagnosis?'

"The lengthy pause says she hasn't done any such thing. I have her right where I want her. She can't hold us responsible if she lied on the admissions forms to get her mother on this floor instead of Memory Care. Intense supervision means a bigger monetary investment. Talk about being a cheapskate. The satisfaction I'd felt just seconds ago quickly gives way to anger, which I have to stifle. 'Ms. Getty?'

"'I'm here.' Estelle is otherwise silent.

"'Does your mother have Alzheimer's disease?'

"Another long pause. 'Well, yes, but it's not advanced. She's perfectly fine.' She sounds positively indignant.

"At that point, I can tell you I was only slightly surprised. People do this all the time—long-term care is expensive, you see. But this lady seemed loaded, and I thought, If this crazy lady cares so much about her mother, why stick her in a place where she's not going to be safe, you know?"

Everyone nodded except for Ethan, who once again raised his hand.

Gladys felt as if she had the mother of all migraines coming on, and her knees were orbs of fire and ice. The kid was too curious, and that was dangerous for a beginning vampire. There were things they could do...and Gladys knew exactly what they said about curiosity and cats.

"Did you have a question, or are you going to let me finish?" Gladys asked. "I don't want to be here until sunrise. I'm not Scheherazade."

Deflated, he lowered his hand, made a zipping motion across his lips, and stared down at his lap.

"I flat-out told her, 'Your mother's needs can't be met on this floor of our facility.' I tried to sound polite, authoritative, but also sensitive. You have no idea how hard that is."

No one chimed in, so Gladys kept on, wanting to get to the end of it all and go home to put her feet up.

'Thankfully, she didn't break anything this time, but because of her diagnosis, she needs a higher level of care than we provide here on this unit.' *Keep cool,* I remind myself. 'Can you come in so we can sort all this out? Maybe this afternoon?'

'What do you mean, she didn't break anything? Is that what you're worried about? Your precious *unit*? Your precious *furniture*? I think you ought to be more focused on MY GRA—' For a second, I think the phone line is dead, but I hear her breathing deep gulps of air and I'm worried that maybe she's having her own medical emergency. Then she clears her throat, which is relieving. Mostly.

"I grip the phone. 'I'm sorry, you misunderstood me. I mean, nothing on Rose is broken. She *is* the most important thing in this whole scenario, and I'm sure we can get this all worked out. So, if you could come in—'

"'I can't be there until after sunset.'

"Sunset is two whole hours after my shift ends. There's nothing I want more than to pass the buck, but I check the whiteboard to see who's coming in as my relief. I'm not relieved to see that Patty Stonewall and Jess Norman are the nurses scheduled. Neither one will be able to handle this monster.

"'Ms. Getty, I'm afraid it will have to be before five o'clock. My shift ends at—'

"''You'll just have to wait until I get there.'

"In my mind's eye, I can see the woman's saliva splattering the phone.

"'I can't get there any earlier than seven-thirty. I will deal with you then.'

"The phone goes dead in my ear. 'Well, fuck you very much,' I say. Thankfully, no one is around to hear. *I'll deal with you then. Jesus, what does that even mean*? I don't have a clue, but something about the statement feels ominous. Especially the way she said it.

"It's nearly eight when Estelle breezes into Golden Peaks, this time dressed in a flowy art frock that billows behind her like white stratus clouds in her wake. 'Where is she?' Her movements are jerky, and her face flushed and hectic.

"I struggle out of the chair I've been sitting in, reading a paperback romance. 'She's still in room 1408.'

"Estelle's eyes dance in their sockets, flickering everywhere. Her irises darken to a color that pulls me into them like teeny black holes. It's a struggle to stay focused and that eerie feeling I've been ignoring comes back. 'Not my mother, you imbecile! The one who called! And where were you when my mother needed you? Huh? Sitting out here with your feet up?' She snatches the book right out of my hands. 'Reading smut?'

"I have to remind myself to have patience, at least for now. 'I *am* the one who called you. And when your mother fell, I was helping another patient. Rose isn't the only one under my care.' It's a barb, I know, but I smile gently. It's the one I use to disarm my sometimes fractious charges."

Gladys showed off the smile as if that would help further the plot.

"Estelle chucks my book against the wall with more force than I would have thought she possessed. Luckily it was a paperback, or the facility might have sustained some damage.

"'I will have you fired before the sun rises, call your manager,' Estelle snarls

"*Facts and regulations will work best with this one*, I think to myself. I've seen it before. Facts are irrefutable and this lady needs to understand the facts. 'I feel the need to remind you that the patients on this unit don't require one-on-one care. They aren't monitored and are free to move around at their leisure. If your mother needs a higher level of care, she needs to be re-evaluated and moved to another unit where that kind of staffing is possible.'

"I'm amazed at how steady and measured my tone has been so far, but I'm not sure how long that will last in the face of abuse from this snippy bitch. What I'd really like to do is punt-kick her scrawny ass down the hall and out the door, but my knees are long past the football career stage.

"Estelle shakes a long, thin finger in my face. No gloves today. The nail is painted scarlet and filed homicidally sharp. She could do a lot of damage with those nails. 'Someone should have told me. Someone should have been there with her.'

"My legs touch the chair as I retreat a step back from this tempest of a woman. I pull myself together. 'Our policy is clearly stated in the paperwork you were given at the time of admission.' That sounds lame and I know it, so I call for reinforcements in the form of our policy manual and admissions paperwork. This is where the indisputable facts that will end this conversation live.

Both are in a file stacker on the desk, so I fish out a copy of each and slide them across the tall counter. I'm thankful for the barrier between us.

"'I don't have time to read all that drivel.' She shoves the papers away and they float in the air like some strange magic trick.

"I'm goggling at them because they seem to defy gravity.

"Then she breaks the spell, the papers fall, and I'm back on Earth.

"'I'm going to see to my gra...mother.' She shakes her head and I wonder why she keeps tripping over that word. Speech impediment maybe? 'I'll be calling your manager, you know.' She whirls, frock flying, and heads off in the direction of room 1408, and certain stereotypical name flashes through my mind."

Karen cleared her throat harshly, and Gladys flashed her a look of apology.

"I know, but really, *call your manager* is such a stereotypically entitled move by someone like her."

Karen clenched her jaw.

"You know I won't say it, now, and I didn't know you then."

Ethan burst into laughter, finally understanding.

"Shut up!" Karen snaps.

Ethan's childish giggling was cut off like a light switch.

Karen looked back at Gladys and gave her a winding-up gesture. It was getting late.

"Again, sorry Karen. If everyone can just be quiet for a few more minutes, I'll be done. No more interruptions." The other three vampires nodded, so Gladys continued.

"So I'm thinking. *Oh great. Call the manager. She'll tell you exactly what I just told you and you'll be lucky if your mother isn't kicked out of here altogether because you lied on the admission form*, but I don't say that. 'I'll get my supervisor's card and leave it for you on the counter here,' I call after her. 'Tomorrow, Rose is going to have to move upstairs to one of our secured units. It's policy.'

"Policy usually has the effect of shifting anger from a single person to a larger entity. Not this time. Rose's daughter turns and approaches me without seeming to move at all. 'You don't know who you're dealing with.' Her voice is low. She pokes her finger in my chest. It feels like a bee sting. I hadn't even realized I'd moved out from behind the safety of the desk! Her eyes swirl, shifting from that deep, bottomless black to red, and back.

"Out of nowhere, an overwhelming urge to embrace this strange, bird-like woman like a lover washes over me. A distant

part of my brain is yelling at this slack-jawed version of myself—
screaming, in fact—that the woman is dangerous. But the part of
my brain where Freud's fabled id impulses lay uncensored by the
ego wants to be held in the light of her regard. To be loved by this
woman—no matter the cost.

"When I get my wits about me, I see that ten minutes have
gone by. I've been standing in the hallway with my mouth slack,
like a catatonic patient. I wipe my hand across my mouth and find
that a runner of drool has formed at the corner. There are little
splats of saliva on the floor. I am completely alone.

"I walk as quietly as I possibly can to the door of Rose's
room to see if Estelle is still inside. She is. The two women are
speaking in low voices. It's time to go home before she wants to
talk to me some more. I'll just call the boss from the road and fill
her in on the details. I have this bad—and I mean bad—feeling
about the whole afternoon, and I just want to get home. I think it's
important to mention here that I am not exactly afraid of Estelle,
but I am afraid of something. It feels like a storm cloud inside my
skull.

"The parking lot is mostly deserted and the dark cloud I'd
felt is lifting now that I'm outside. Shift change was three hours
ago, and no one comes calling on their elderly loved ones at this
time of day, hence the deserted parking lot. The confused ones are
likely to be sun-downing and the rest are engrossed in Fox News
or Wheel of Fortune. Maybe it was the long day, being inside,
being tired, or maybe even just stress that made everything feel
weird.

"I'm juggling my keys and my bags, and I've got all this
shit in my hands that I'm trying to balance and of course, you
know I'm not the physically gifted type. My purse slides off my
shoulder to my elbow and bangs against my right knee which feels
like fireworks have just gone off in hell. I have a paper bag of
romance novels in my other hand. The nurses trade them around
like cigarettes in prison. One of the handles starts to rip. I'm—"

"Bags not to be being supported by handles, you know,"
Hans interjected. "On bags, it says clearly do not use handles on
heavy bags. You should have read."

"Thank you oh so much for that nugget of wisdom,"
Gladys said with her hand pressed to her chest. She didn't have a
shred of patience left. The story always stirred up a toxic
concoction of emotional upset. "Can I *please* just get through?"
Tears threatened to fall and Gladys preferred almost any emotion
to sadness. There had been enough of that over the years.

"Sorry," Hans said.

Gladys took a moment to get back to her place, then cleared her throat.

"I just touch the key to the lock when I feel it. It's not a sound, not something I can see, either. It's a feeling. A hot breeze that brings the sickeningly sweet scent of lilies. It's a nice spring day but not nearly nice enough for a hot breeze. Suddenly, there's someone behind me. I turn around, thinking I'm about to be mugged and my lunchbox just sort of drops from my hand. It bursts open. I'm actually watching an apple roll underneath the car as if it's the eighth wonder of the world as Estelle advances on me. I can't do anything but watch. My mouth is smiling even though I'm trying to scream. It's like my lips are attached to marionette strings. I can't scream. I can't make any move to get away. I can't even breathe. I try to fight back, attack her, you know? But my arms are dumb things that are no longer under my control. I'm powerless.

"Estelle slices a gash in one of her wrists with a pointed nail. A splash of scarlet spills across my scrub top—today's version is dinosaurs—and hot blood lands on the side of my face. I'm having that out-of-body feeling again and I want to run, but I remain still. Estelle presses the thin flesh of her wrist to my lips and..."

Gladys drew in a giant, trembling breath and released it with a sob of such heartsickness that Karen winced.

Hans wiped at his eyes.

Ethan looked sorrowful, no longer antsy to add commentary or ask questions.

Gladys sniffed back the snot that was threatening to drip from her nose and finished. "I drink. I can't help myself. It is horrible and wonderful, tasting of life and of death. A combination of those intoxicating lilies and dirty copper. Filthy rotting leaves and sweet citrus."

8. TAKING IN THE STRAY

Gladys gripped the back of the metal chair until her knuckles turned white and looked down at the floor for a moment. No matter how many times she told her story, it was never easy. She felt weak and pale—more than usual—like her soul, if she still had one, was exposed in the bright overhead lights.

A crackle of applause shot through the silence and Karen let out a little chirp of surprise.

Hans kicked out one leg and looked ready to jump out of his seat.

Not Ethan. He leaped from his chair, giving Gladys a great big standing "O" as if he was at Carnegie Hall.

"Good God! You would give coronary if the heart of mine was beating. What is problem with you? Do you have the brain damages? The woman pours out heart and you applaud like at Mottled Crew concert." Hans swore under his breath in German for nearly ten seconds straight, then crossed his arms and sat back.

"Hans," Karen said softly. "He didn't mean anything by it. And it's Motley Crue, not Mottled Crew." She giggled behind her hand.

Hans frowned.

"Don't worry about it," Gladys said, but shot a disapproving look at Ethan. "Not appropriate, but don't worry about it. Just try to be more sensitive next time."

"Sorry, but Jesus! That Karen-chick Estelle really fucked you up!" He snickered. "Maybe you should have let her talk to the manager."

Gladys' mouth fell open; Hans stood, glowering. But Karen—Karen's entire body vibrated with anger and fury. A light wind stirred and tousled her hair. Lamps of fire lit her eyes.

Ethan looked from one to the other, completely oblivious of his gaffe. "What? What did I do now?"

Gladys had a feeling that was a question he'd asked often in his former life. The one he'd lived without a bizarre thirst for sanguine sangria. "Geez, Ethan. Can you guess? If you just took a minute to think?"

Realization bloomed on his face like a flower. "Oh, I'm sorry. It's just that—you know. It's a normal thing to say."

Karen's voice cracked. "Yes, I know what it's just like. I can't stand it! I hate that every time I hear my name, it's got this negative attachment." She looked on the verge of tears.

"I'm sorry, okay? Like, it's just a thing, but I get how it sounds." He looked at Karen, imploring her for forgiveness.

She sniffed back tears and the light breeze that had begun to blow petered out. She dabbed at her fading eyes with a hanky she produced from her shirt sleeve. "It's okay. I guess. Just try to be more aware." She looked at her wristwatch. "We should adjourn for the night, don't you think?"

Where do you even get a handkerchief these days? Gladys wondered. That was Karen in a nutshell. Neat, polite, and proper. And always kind. Well, almost always. "Let's wrap this up, shall we?"

They stood and linked hands. Ethan hesitantly grasped Hans' calloused palm.

The three seasoned members recited in unison: "We are vampires. Alone we could not manage our illness. No human power can relieve our burden. No higher power can save us. We must look to each other and summon our own strength to remain on the righteous path."

"And remember," Ethan added with a goofy smile on his face, making him look sweet and childish. "People are friends, not food!" No one laughed. "You know, like that one kid movie about the fish who got lost? Whatever his name was?"

Gladys just shook her head, squeezed the hands of her fellow members, and waddled out into the fragrant night, relieved to be out of the VFW hall whose temperature seemed to have risen thirty degrees by the time the meeting was finally over. Her tale was told, and now she could shove it back in the dusty filing cabinet in her subconscious, where it belonged. The night had brought with it the sweetness of hyacinth and the blue chicory that lined every ditch in Johnson County. Curse or not, being a vampire had heightened her senses.

"Hey Glad!" Karen trotted after her. "Wait up."

Gladys turned and Karen took her hand. "I know he's annoying." She looked back toward the building where Ethan stood with his hands jammed deep into the pockets of his cargo shorts, looking at his scuffed shoes for a cosmic answer unlikely to be found on his Converse sneakers. "It takes a special talent to insult almost everyone in a room in a single night, but please. Give him a break. Go to him. Make sure he knows you're a safe person he can turn to if he gets in trouble. He's like a child out there. A dangerous, confused child."

"Yeah." Gladys shook her head as she watched the kid skipping down the stairs and heading toward parts unknown. "I hate this, you know?"

Karen nodded. "I know." She patted Gladys' arm.

"My life is quiet and contained and predictable, just the way I like it." Gladys' eyebrows came together, forming a little groove in between them.

"Did you think you could survive eternity that way?" Karen asked. "It's good to take risks and do new things." She shook her finger. "You can't shut people out forever."

Gladys squinted with skepticism. The riskiest thing Karen had done recently was give up on finishing *Pride and Prejudice* half-way through.

"I know, I know." Karen waved her hand as if to contradict anything Gladys might say. "I should follow my own advice. But you *have* to do this. If not for Ethan, do it for us. It's not safe with him wandering loose. You're the one he'll listen to."

"Why me?" She didn't say it out of self-pity, but out of genuine curiosity.

"Because he's afraid of Hans..."

He ought to be afraid of you. Even more so.

"And he doesn't take me seriously."

"Oh, he will, I'm afraid. Not sure I want to be around when that happens." Gladys rubbed the back of her neck looking uncharacteristically angry, but it might have been the story she'd just told. She simply said "Okay," and walked as fast as her worthless knees would carry her toward the darkness the scrawny kid disappeared into.

She found him beneath a big oak tree on the north side of the granite monstrosity the Veterans of Foreign Wars had commandeered from the Masons decades ago. Ethan had his nose pointed toward the sky, like a dog scenting the air for a bitch in heat. Karen was right. The kid needed guidance.

"How are you getting home, Ethan?" There were no other cars in the parking lot beside hers, Hans' Beamer (efficient German engineering), and Karen's little Kia.

He turned back slowly, and she saw hunger in his face. His eyes were Halloween orange. "I'm walking. I don't have a license." His voice was dreamy and far away-sounding.

Go figure. A picture of a post-teenage vampire assaulting innocent citizens as he moved across the city flittered through her mind and she groaned. "Want a ride? I'll drive you home."

"Umm, okay. I guess." He looked back toward the way he'd been headed with something close to sorrow.

"Great. Let's go. Besides, I have something for you." She pointed to her aging Honda and walked to the last row of parking spaces. Ethan followed, opened the passenger door, and dropped into the seat.

"Isn't that kind of redundant?" He pointed.

"What?" she asked, as she pulled the seatbelt across herself and buckled it.

"The seatbelt. I mean, we can't die, so what's the point?"

"*Blending in* is the point." She reversed and turned onto 6th Avenue.

"No one's looking in the car, though. And if someone did see you without a seatbelt, they wouldn't be like, 'Oh she's not wearing a seatbelt. She must be a vampire'. It's not the first thing that comes to mind."

"It's more than just what you look like. As a vampire, safety means always thinking two or three steps ahead. Let's pretend you get into an accident. And you do a big ol' dive through the windshield. Something like that. You follow?"

Ethan nodded.

"Now imagine there are innocent bystanders who witnessed you flying through the windshield. You can't just somersault, land on your feet, and do a dismount like Mary Lou Retton."

"Who?"

She sighed. "An Olympic gymnast, but that doesn't matter. You get what I'm saying?"

"Yeah, I guess so."

"Then the paramedics come. The police come. They might want to know how you survived. They might see your wounds magically healing. That might draw a little bit of attention, don't you think? You're going to have to be smart about this. As difficult as that may be for you."

"What's that supposed to mean?" He frowned and fiddled with the window button until Gladys hit the child safety lock. Ethan squished himself down in the passenger seat, sulking.

Gladys thumped the steering wheel. "You're just a kid! You're not used to thinking things through a whole lot before you act. That's not your fault, really. That's just how people your age are."

"Hans doesn't like me."

"Hans doesn't really like anyone. The fact that you're part of the group means he's decided not to murder you. So, for Hans, that's affection." She looked up at the intersection signs. "Where am I taking you, anyway?"

"Home," Ethan said.

The pulse of irritation throbbed in her forehead. "Yeah, I got that, but since vampires aren't psychic, you're going to have to tell me where that is." This was only a partial truth, but she wasn't about to give the kid ideas.

He chewed his lip. "Gilbert Street and Kirkwood Boulevard."

Gladys made a right turn, heading to the west side of town. "Wait, there's nothing out there, Ethan. Just the train tracks and some university office buildings."

He ducked his head. "I don't live at home anymore. I was afraid I'd, you know, eat my roommates or something."

"You're telling me you don't have a place to stay? A safe place to be out of the sun?"

"Well, it's pretty dark way under that bridge."

Gladys had to make a decision, and she knew she wouldn't like it, no matter which way she went. Did she leave him out in the cold? At risk of combustion or attacking an unsuspecting jogger or two? Or should she invite him to move in temporarily and subject herself to his incompetence twenty-four-seven? Resigning herself, she decided.

"You'll move in with me."

His face brightened up like it was Christmas morning. "I will?"

"Just for a while. Until you find a better solution." It was important to clarify that she wasn't looking for a long-term roommate. She liked her peaceful, drama-free life and knew that Ethan would muck that up. It would be hard to have him there, but she saw no other viable choice.

"Oh, thanks Glad! I mean, Gladys. Mrs. Knight?" His eyebrows drew together again in confusion. "I don't know what I should call you outside the group."

"Gladys is fine. And don't thank me too much. I'm not putting you up in the penthouse or anything. I need to stress this again—this is not a permanent arrangement."

His idiot grin was full of teeth, four of which were unnaturally sharp. He was going to have to learn how to control that. Gladys smiled in spite of herself. She made a legal U-turn and headed back toward her little house.

"This is so cool!"

"Sure it is. Now, open the glove box."

After fiddling with the latch, Ethan got it open, and a little bottle fell out—a whiskey shooter like one you could get at the liquor store for ninety-nine cents. He held it up to the light. As they passed under streetlights, the color of its contents shifted to red, then back to black once the light faded behind them.

"Is this what I think it is?"

"Yeah. Now bottoms up." She made a shot drinking gesture.

He twisted off the cap and chugged. "Thanks, my dude—I mean, Gladys—I needed that."

"I'm sure you did. Now shut up and let me drive." She was giving him bottles from her own supply. Hans and Karen had helped with the blood donations, but her supply was scant. She could be strong, though. Holding out wouldn't be as much of a struggle for her. She'd had plenty of practice.

Ethan turned on the radio to a classic rock station, which was fine with her, but at an ear-splitting volume that would get them noticed with the windows open. She gave him a disapproving look, of which he was oblivious and then returned her concentration toward piloting the car through the nearly empty city streets deciding to deal with the not-so-dulcet vocal signature of Steven Tyler at full volume as he waxed poetic about love and elevators.

9. HOME SWEET HOME

The Honda's headlights flashed across the low roofline of a little ranch-style house. White shutters stood out in stark contrast to the dark brown siding. Gladys shifted into park and killed the engine.

"This is where you live?" Ethan asked.

"This is it." She removed the keys and gathered up her massive handbag, grunting as she struggled out of the car. Seeing Ethan hadn't opened his door, she braced her hand on the frame as she leaned inside. "Well? Are you coming or not? I'd rather not have you sleeping out here in the car if it's all the same to you. The sun can be unpleasant for people like us."

Ethan frowned, confused, but got out of the car and stood beside it, one hand clasping the other wrist in front of himself like a good little choir boy. "You live here?"

She sighed. Why couldn't this kid make anything easy? "What were you expecting? What part of this isn't measuring up to your standards?"

The gravel grated under his shoes as he shuffled his weight from one foot to the other. "It's fine, I just thought..."

"Thought what?"

He cleared his throat. It was loud in the stillness of the sleeping neighborhood. "I guess I thought it'd be, you know, cooler or something. Like the Bat Cave."

She groaned inwardly. "You got to quit thinking this is a movie, Ethan. This is real life. There's no bat cave, no Transylvanian tower, just a nice, safe, sunlight-free suburban abode. Now get in the house before the neighbors spot you." She came around the car and bumped her bag against his butt to get him moving.

He stumbled up the concrete steps, then she bumped him aside so she could unlock the door. Once it was shut behind them, she engaged all three locks and flipped on the light switch.

Ethan stood on a small square of wood flooring in front of the door, looking around the living room of Gladys' small, neat house. The incongruity of expectations versus reality was painted on his face. "This looks like my grandma's house!"

"Well, we'd probably be about the same age, Ethan. Actually, I might be older than your grandma by now. If I hadn't stopped aging at sixty-five, I'd be older than dirt. Sorry it doesn't have all the newest technical gadgets and updates. Alexa doesn't live here."

"No, it's fine. It's just not...not what I expected."

The overhead light cast shadows into the corners. Ethan stared at the couch as if it was a strange specimen of insect. Maybe, to him, it was. It was straight out of the seventies, with brown velour scenery print and heavy wooden arms on stubby feet. A recliner sat next to a small end table with a hand-stitched sampler draped over the headrest. It said *God Bless this Home* in neat little crisscross stitches. Ethan laughed out loud and pointed.

"That's funny," he explained when he noticed Gladys wasn't smiling.

"What's funny?"

"The thing. The stitched thing on your chair."

She'd never considered the irony of that piece. It was something she'd made almost three decades ago. There had once been two, in a time when two recliners sat side-by-side to display them on. She shrugged.

"Come on. I'll show you your room and give you a tour."

Ethan giggled as she led him down a short hallway.

On the right was a bathroom. She flipped on the light switch. "Bathroom."

He gaped at the pink toilet, tub, and sink—just as she knew he would. He looked suddenly embarrassed.

"What?" When there was no reply, she repeated, "What? What's the problem now?"

"It's just that I...I haven't...I mean, that is..." He cleared his throat. "I haven't taken a shit since all this happened. Or peed." He gazed at the toilet as if it was a holy relic.

"Well, congratulations, kid. You'll never have to use it or worry about constipation ever again. We don't do those things. No need anymore." She shut the light off, not wanting to talk about things they couldn't do anymore. Not tonight. The next door on the right opened onto a small bedroom. Gladys turned on a standing lamp next to the bed and moved aside, ushering him in to have a seat on the pink and green quilt covering the bed.

"This is your room. The windows are covered, obviously, but I don't want you sleeping in here. I use the basement to sleep. You will, too. Don't want to take any chances with hurricane-force winds, rock throwers, footballs, frisbees, or baseballs."

"Huh?"

"I'll explain later. My room's over there." She pointed to the room across the hall. "Off limits."

"Why do you have a bedroom if you don't even sleep in it?"

She pondered for nearly a full minute. "I guess it's because there's still some part of me that wants things to be normal. Or as normal as possible. My clothes are in there, my memories are there...but, I don't trust the safety of a room above ground for sleeping. Nope, don't relish the idea of being disfigured until the end of time."

"You can keep your stuff in your room while you stay, though, and you'll have privacy." She realized he didn't actually have anything with him. She raised an eyebrow. "Where is your stuff, anyway?"

"Some of it's down by the bridge. But most is still back at my old apartment."

"How much? If we went to get it, how much space would you need to store it?"

"I don't really have any furniture. I made my bed out of pallets and milk crates." He snickered. "Stole the pallets from Menards and the crates from Hy-Vee!" He bounced on the bed and flopped backwards with his arms open wide, with a little kid smile. "This feels so good!" He made snow angel movements on top of the quilt.

"Don't let Hans know where you got your milk crates, and don't get too comfy on that bed. Like I said, I don't really want you sleeping in here. I'd rather not have to clean up the mess if you get incinerated."

Ethan rose up, disappointed, onto his elbows. "Okay."

"Do you want to go collect your belongings? Because we can. It's no trouble."

Ethan shook his head. "I don't think I'd be welcome there again."

She guessed why but didn't press him for an explanation. "Come on, I'll show you the rest of the house."

He climbed off the little twin bed in the room with light green walls and a ruffled bedside lamp and followed her back down the hall.

"Dining room," she said, pointing to a small space with an oblong oak table and chairs tucked in on both sides. They had cushions on them that tied to the rungs. Behind the table was a matching hutch with delicate plates and glassware inside. One whole shelf was filled with small china shoes.

Ethan walked over to the hutch and traced his finger along the glass, peering into the cabinet. "I like this one with the little birds on it." He reached for the cut glass knob and Gladys stopped him.

"Nope. No touchie."

Ethan withdrew his hand as if he'd been burned. The look he gave her with his puppy dog eyes was sorrowful.

"Sweet Christ, Ethan, I didn't slap you. Just don't touch the breakables, okay?"

Ethan nodded, clasped his hands together, and followed.

"This is the kitchen."

Ethan immediately opened the refrigerator but was surprised when the light didn't turn on. He looked accusingly at her.

"I'm not going to waste electricity keeping a big old box cool if there isn't going to be anything in it."

He looked confused.

"We don't eat, remember?"

A cloud passed over Ethan's face. No doubt he was remembering the first days after his turning.

Gladys remembered those dark days all too well, how hungry she'd been. Everything she'd eaten made her violently ill, but she kept trying. By the third night, the desperation was so unbearable that she'd attacked Smithers, the neighbor's cat who'd made the mistake of jumping off the privacy fence into her yard. She'd run after the animal with lightning speed, her knees sounding off like playing cards in the spokes of a child's dirt bike, scooped up Smithers, and rushed back inside with him, mewling and scratching. She'd buried her face in his soft underbelly before she even knew what she was doing and drained him of his fluids right over the kitchen sink. It had taken a week of scrubbing to remove the blood and entrails from the ceiling. She had no animosity toward her neighbor at the time, or her cat, but after three days without eating, the furry critter was just too tempting.

She left that little detail out of her story, not to save Ethan's delicate feelings, but because she still felt terrible about it. Afterward, Gladys had driven through the snow to the nearest pet store and sat in the car, wanting to do the right thing and find a quick replacement. Finally, summoning her courage, she approached the Pet Depot doors, but the thought of driving back home with a living, breathing entity with life-sustaining blood coursing through its veins had sent her right back to the car.

Things were easier now, thanks to Dr. Cooke.

"Mrs. Knight?" Ethan looked into her face with concern.

She grasped the counter, flooded with painful memories. "I'm fine." She shook her head to clear away the haunting thoughts. "This is the kitchen." Gladys spun a finger in the air without looking around.

"Yeah, you said that already."

"As you might have guessed, not a whole lot happens in here anymore. It's funny how much time people spend shopping for food, cooking meals, eating, cleaning up. I have a hell of a lot more free time since I don't have to cook every night."

Once, long ago, there *had* been someone to cook for. And she missed him every damn day.

The door just off the kitchen gaping open like an evil maw led to the dank basement lurking in the dark below. She pulled the chain of the dangling overhead lightbulb and descended into the depths with agonizing slowness, strangling the railing as she tilted one way, then the other.

Ethan trailed behind; his tennis shoes whispering on the stairs. When they reached the bottom, she pulled the chain on another light.

The floor was basic concrete, and the walls were painted cinderblock. In the corner, a huge sleeping bag and a small end table sat on a rectangular scrap of carpet. A neatly folded tarp and a small pillow were nestled on top.

"That's where you sleep?" Ethan looked horrified to see that his new mentor slept in such squalor. He wandered over to investigate her humble bed chamber.

"Yep, that's it." The embarrassment she felt was unexpected, and she resented the little pipsqueak for making her feel that way.

Ethan picked up a cloudy glass from the table and swept his finger around the rim. He made a face and set it back down next to a packet of tablets.

Gladys put her hands on her hips. "I suppose you need something better? Honestly, Ethan, it's just not necessary. Who would notice anyway?"

"Where do I sleep?"

"The windows down here are blocked out, and that's a mummy bag." She pointed to the dark blue lump in the corner. "I just slide in and wrap up in a tarp. No risk of incineration. I'll have to get you something like that tomorrow. I wasn't expecting company." She raised an eyebrow at him, giving him the once-over. "Until then, you can sleep in here." She ushered Ethan over to a long, skinny closet and opened the narrow door.

"You want me to sleep in a closet, Mrs. Knight?"

"Gladys," she reminded him.

"No offense, *Gladys*, but it's pretty creepy to pick up a nineteen-year-old kid and suggest that he sleep in your closet."

The corner of her mouth twisted into a little frown. "I don't think—"

He waved his hands, grinning. "I'm kidding. I'm not complaining. Really. I'm grateful. But maybe we can, you know, make something nice?" He rocked back and forth on his feet, scanning his new home. "I thought you'd have a cool coffin room or something. All draped in red velvet and black paint and stuff." He smiled a little as his brain played out his great vampire bed chamber scenario.

She gave him a minute to come back to the conversation. "Yes, I suppose there's always room for improvement, but will this do for now, your highness?"

He glanced around the cavernous, unfinished basement again.

Hulking appliances crouched along the far wall: washer, dryer, water heater, furnace.

"Yeah. It'll do. It's better than being the troll under the bridge."

The space was dark and depressing. She knew it wasn't very inviting; it had just never occurred to her to care. After all, she was the only one who'd been down here since her run-in with Estelle. Now that Ethan was here... she shook her head, reminding herself that he would *not* be staying. This was a short-term situation. Temporary.

10. A HEART TO HEART

Gladys was thrilled to get Karen's invitation for an evening coffee before picking up their shooters. It was nice to get out of the house for a couple of hours, especially since it wasn't for work. Gladys' knees had been aching like mad bastards and there wasn't a thing she could do about it. Other than the ice. She longed for the healing effects of ibuprofen. Hell, even the blood of a stoned teenager or two would do, but that was a terrible idea, and went against the whole "don't attack people" idea, not to mention that intoxicated vampires were apt to do all kinds of things that could get them into trouble.

She squeezed the life out of the Honda's door handle in her attempts to free herself from the entanglements of the steering wheel and seat belt, nearly hitting the pavement. A normal person would have dislocated their shoulder, but Gladys' normal human decay processes had been halted back in 1996; about the time when Lady Di and that putz, Prince Charles, called it quits.

Later, she and Karen would be paying a visit to a certain county coroner who'd been successfully flying under the radar for longer than Gladys had been taking her nutrition from people instead of plants. For now, she and Karen were happily squirreled away in the back corner of the Java House, coffee cups sitting in front of them. Touched often, for show, but never ingested. She missed coffee the same way she missed arthritis medication.

Karen sat in the chair opposite her. Tonight, she wore a light yellow twin-set instead of that hideous Pepto-Bismol color she liked so much. Gladys thought pink was too girly a color for a woman of Karen's age to be wearing, but kept that opinion to herself. They had so little enjoyment; she didn't want to rain on her friend's pink parade.

"How's it working out with Ethan?"

Gladys grimaced. "He's an okay boy, but he's already thinking he should change things around the house. 'Décor is old-fashioned,' he said. 'Doesn't like the sleeping arrangements,' he said. Blah, blah, blah. I don't think he gets it. This is just until he can find a place of his own. I know apartment living isn't ideal, but I want to get him out as soon as possible. Whatever it takes."

"Oh? Is he somehow unsatisfied with his living situation?" She still hadn't quite forgiven him for the "Karen" comment at last week's meeting.

"More like his nighttime quarters. He doesn't approve of sleeping in the basement closet."

"Neither did you." She pointed at Gladys and winked.

"Yeah, I know, but I got him a nice, new sleeping bag. It's not like I rolled him up in a tarp like a cigar."

"I suppose." She didn't look convinced. "Speaking of tarps," Karen said as she took a deep whiff of her coffee, "you could treat yourself better too. There's nothing glamorous about sleeping on the concrete floor."

"At least he has a door! What's the point, anyway? Why would I care what I'm sleeping on if I'm dead to the world? You think it'll make these any better?" She stuck out her leg and flexed her knee. It crackled.

"Sometimes it's okay to pamper yourself. It's alright to treat yourself to something nice. Once in a while."

Karen's "den" as she called it, was in the furthest corner of her basement behind some folding screens. A plain wooden box she'd managed to cobble together herself, stuffed with fluffy bedding (pink) and 3000 thread-count Egyptian cotton sheets (also pink) provided cover for her during her daytime slumber. She refused to call it a coffin, but that's what it was. A medieval pauper's coffin. Gladys had mentioned this only once, and Karen had been so offended, she hadn't spoken to her at the next support group meeting, asking *Hans* to tell *Gladys* that she expected an *apology*. Which she'd already given.

Laughter crept out of her mouth. "Ethan said just about the same thing. But again, what does it matter?"

Karen nodded. "It's the principle of the thing. Would it be so bad to let Ethan do a little remodeling while he's there?"

Gladys considered for a minute and took a fake sip of her latte, inhaling the glorious fragrance. "I hadn't planned on him staying long enough to do anything that extensive. There's the logistics, the planning, the cost, and—I feel I need to state this very clearly one more time—Ethan. Is. Not. Staying. For. Long."

Karen nodded, as if she knew better.

Gladys wondered in her own heart if it would be possible to rid herself of the child and knew the chances were fifty-fifty at best. A shudder ran through her as she contemplated the idea of him becoming a permanent installation in her home.

"What was that?"

"Oh, just envisioning spending eternity with fortune's fool, that's all."

Karen's cold hand grasped her forearm. "Things will get better. He'll learn, Glad. You just have to be patient. More than anything, he needs your guidance and wisdom. Just like I did." Her face clouded over as she thought about all the times she'd tried to end her own life after being turned and then abandoned by the same monster who'd gotten Gladys and the rest of them.

Gladys patted her clammy hand. It felt dead, like a fish pulled from the river. Karen hadn't fed for two days, and her face was pale as porcelain.

Which reminded her—they had an appointment. "It's time to pay a visit to the blood man." She grinned. White tips peeked out of her smile and disappeared. "Let's go."

Once they'd tossed their full cups into the trash (Gladys made the sign of the cross as they thunked to the bottom of the bin) they climbed into Gladys' car and headed for temporary salvation.

11. A WITHDRAWAL

The back loading dock of the hospital was usually deserted by two in the morning—the perfect place and time to have "a meeting with a man". They'd only had to abort their mission once when a group of kids on skateboards showed up. Karen's had been poised to get out of the car and tell them it was 'against the rules, can't you see the signs?' when Gladys laid a hand on her shoulder.

"Don't," she had said in a whisper. "We can come back later."

Karen had licked her lips, hungry and weak, but had agreed. Better to avoid confrontation and to stay under the radar. Someone could have gotten hurt. Someone could have ended up bleeding.

Tonight no one was malingering near the dock. They watched as a small man in a white coat stepped out of the unmarked door and looked around furtively. It reminded Gladys of a noir film where a bad guy in a trench coat made an illegal transfer of guns or drugs, or maybe the Maltese Falcon. He wedged something in the door to prevent it from closing all the way and emerged from the shadows into the otherworldly orange cast of the streetlamps. Moths fluttered under the lights like junkies with a platter of cocaine. The car vibrated with energy as both women felt their hunger stirring.

Gladys nodded.

Karen took a deep breath and exited the vehicle. She approached the man with his iridescent bald head.

His glasses flashed in Gladys' direction and she shut off the headlights, leaving only the dim glow of the orange foggers.

The man in the white doctor's coat handed Karen a heavy canvas tote bag, and she handed him a lighter one containing a paltry eighty dollars and a bunch of empty one-ounce bottles in exchange. The real payment for this service was their silence. They'd had to negotiate a new rate once Ethan had arrived on the scene. It hadn't taken much to convince Dr. Cooke that it was in his best interest to up the quantity if he wanted his secret to remain a secret, but he hadn't been happy about the early pick-up.

Karen scurried back to the car, moving across the parking lot more quickly than she should have, but Gladys couldn't chide her for it. She knew how her friend felt.

Karen got in, breathless with her hands shaking. Once the door was closed and Cooke had retreated into the massive hospital, she tossed a small bottle to Gladys and struggled with the cap of another.

After tossing back her shooter, Gladys took the other bottle gently from Karen, whose fangs were out in full display.

Karen lunged, but Gladys held her off with a well-aimed elbow and unscrewed the cap.

Karen snatched it and gulped with greedy enthusiasm, then leaned back against the seat with her eyes closed. Light steam escaped from her exposed skin. "That's so much better."

"You got a little gloop on your chin there, chum." Gladys wiped a red splotch from her friend's face and stuck her finger in her mouth.

Karen tilted her face toward Gladys, still pale in the orange light. "Sorry about that. I should have better control." She pressed the palms of her hands together and put them between her skinny knees, looking chastened.

"It's fine, I get it." She did, too. Karen had donated two of her weekly bottles to Ethan out of pity—they all had. The donated shooters had kept him satiated enough until the day before yesterday. He'd nabbed a rabbit from under the porch in the wee small hours as dawn drew near. He'd taken it into his closet and nursed from it like a baby. The mess had been awful.

Gladys hefted the bag into the back seat. Instead of seven, it contained nine one-ounce booze bottles for each of them, filled with the refrigerated blood of some unfortunate sap who'd died in the last week. Two extra, so they could get back to their regular schedule next week.

Dr. Cooke (Chip was his first name, but cookie jokes had not gone over well in the past) had worked out a deal with Gladys after she'd spied him taking liberties with a dead resident one night at Golden Peaks. She'd seen the telltale dark, nebulous aura surrounding him and realized he wasn't kissing the poor old woman's wrist. When their eyes met, she allowed hers to flash red. He flashed his back, and just like that, they were known to each other.

It was poor form, she thought, to take blood from a resident at work. Not only did it seem somehow wrong to take blood from someone she had once cared for and genuinely liked, the danger of being caught was just too great. Hence, blackmail. She promised not to expose him as a vampire doctor if he promised to give her enough blood for her and her friends to survive. In return, *he* promised not to expose *her* as a vampire in exchange for twenty bucks from each of them every week. It was mutual blackmail but seemed to work out. The money wasn't something he needed. Gladys assumed it was the principle of the thing and had wondered if there were others in the city who had similar arrangements. She couldn't be the only one.

An ounce of blood a day was never enough to feel satiated, but it was enough to curb the urge to run around at night, attacking unwitting joggers. Safer, too.

Dr. Cooke did a complete drug panel on each of his unfortunate, deceased admissions before taking their involuntary blood donation. Once, before he started testing, they'd gotten a batch from a methamphetamine user. Sleeplessness had been the least of their problems during that incident. Hans had nearly been arrested for running around in his boxer shorts, howling, and shaking his fists at the moon. His defense was that boxers were just the same as shorts, and howling wasn't against the law. Luckily, the police had let him go after sticking him in the back of the car for a half-hour while Karen and Gladys promised to take him home and get him back on his medication.

They drove across the river to Hans' modest cottage up on the bluff to find him pacing in front of his door, hands gesticulating wildly. When the car pulled into the drive, he ran toward it, bent over like a great ape. It was hard not to laugh. Strange behavior was not unexpected when their hunger was at its apogee, and they'd all gone without their typical rations.

A gruesome image smashed itself against Gladys' window; Hans with his nose flattened and eyes wild. His lips smeared foamy saliva on the glass.

Karen reached behind her seat, snatched a shooter from the bag, cracked the window open, and tossed it into the lush Kentucky Blue Grass lining the side of the pebble drive. "Over here!" She shouted and rolled up the window.

He lifted his head in a quick, jerky movement and followed Karen's gaze. In an impossible motion, he leapt at the hood of the car, slid like a seventies action star, and came down on his knees as if he was in the starting blocks at a track meet. His hands fumbled in the grass until they found the bottle. His Adam's apple bobbed as he swallowed this elixir of their not-exactly-life and then he lay down on the ground in a fetal position.

Both women got out of the car now that it was safe. Gladys opened the back door and pulled a plastic grocery bag from the little pouch on the back of the driver's seat. She counted out Hans' share of the bottles and tied the bag shut.

Looking down at him with pity, Gladys nudged his khaki-clad hip with her Birkenstock. Her yellowed toenails looked especially gruesome in the small circle of light cast by the sconces that lined the driveway. She held out the bag. "Here."

Without opening his eyes, Hans snatched the bag with a snarl and pulled it to himself like a teddy bear. He'd recover in a minute or two and be back to his frozen-chosen self. With his eyes squeezed shut the way they were, he could have been a sleeping child, rather than a grown, stoic German man who worked as a night manager in a grocery store.

Two minutes passed. His tense muscles became buttery, and he sank more deeply into the grass as he relaxed.

Karen reached out with her hand, ready to withdraw it if Hans showed any sign of rabid blood lust. He blinked twice and took her hand so she could help him to his feet.

"Is better now. Thank you." His lips twisted into a frown. "I am not in the future giving my blood to lazy young man." He sulked like a pouty child, but perhaps that was just an after-image inspired by his previous position in the grass.

"We all gave him some, Hans. And guess what? It worked. He didn't attack a single patient. You're a hero." Gladys leaned a hip against the car.

"Thank you, but I am not hero." He patted Gladys' shoulder.. "You are hero. You bring to me, and I thank you." He gave her a little bow.

"Sure thing," Gladys replied. "You can stop the bowing, though. It's not necessary."

"Thanks given to saviors is always necessary."

"Whatever," Karen broke in. "Look, we have to get going. Ethan's alone and hungry. Glad made him promise to wait until we got back, but I worry. I don't want him getting out and...doing something." Her face took on a wistful expression. Karen missed her own children terribly. They'd been quite young when she last saw them. Now here was Captain Clueless, a nineteen-year-old man-child she could smother with mothering.

Gladys frowned.

Why don't you have him live with you, then?

Then she felt the same urge to get back to her new roommate. There was a tickle in the back of her mind...not a psychic thing, but an inkling that he was getting himself into trouble. Intuition. Gladys feared for the general public.

"Fine, go." Hans flapped one hand, the other still clutching at the plastic Hy-Vee bag full of bottles to his chest. The bag looked like a cradled child. "Will see later, yes? At coffee?"

"Yep," Gladys said. "You got it." She crooked a finger at Karen and got back into the car. It sagged on the driver's side in protest.

"Well, that was quite a show, wouldn't you say?" Karen folded her hands in her lap.

"I expected him to start baying at the moon. Again."

Karen snickered, which made Gladys snicker. By the time they pulled up to the curb in front of Karen's neat little house, both women were wiping away tears of laughter.

Karen collected her bottles and gave Gladys a peck on the cheek. "See you at coffee."

Gladys saluted her friend, shoved the gear shift into drive, and zipped away as fast as she could without bringing attention to herself. It was time to get home to Ethan.

12. NO SNACKS BEFORE DINNER

Arlyss Maitland had her ass sticking out of the hedge between her driveway and Gladys' when Gladys pulled up to the house and killed the headlights. The beam of a flashlight swept across the bushes and front lawn like a lighthouse beacon. Gladys wanted to put the car into reverse and drive somewhere else. Anywhere else. Bermuda, maybe. Something was up and whatever it was, she had a bad feeling that Ethan was involved. She shut off the engine but remained in the car, wishing the woman would go back inside, saving her from a long conversation.

Finally, she sighed, hauled herself out of the car, and closed the door. The canvas bag containing the blood-filled bottles remained in the backseat. And there it would stay until the coast was clear, no matter how desperately Ethan must need a shot by now.

Arlyss poked her curlered head around the hedge and waved. She wore one of those old lady house dresses Gladys had never completely succumbed to, and ratty slippers over socks which had lost most of their elasticity and clung to her veiny calves for dear life.

"Glad! How nice to see you out." Her voice was syrupy sweet. And false.

"Hi, Arlyss. Yeah, I'm out. For a wonder."

Jesus, woman. What do you want?

"I see that." She frowned as her all-too-sharp eyes scanned Gladys, searching for God knew what.

Gladys frowned. It wasn't a secret that she worked nights at the nursing home and slept days. A sign posted on the door reading, *Day Sleeper—Please Do NOT Knock or Ring Bell!* made it clear to anyone who ventured up the concrete steps. It ensured that neighbors like Arlyss wouldn't come be-bopping over for a cup of sugar or midday gossip session. Which is how Gladys preferred it. That never seemed to satisfy her interloping neighbor, however.

"What brings you out so late?" Gladys asked. For Arlyss, it really *was* late.

"I was hoping to catch you. It's the darndest thing. I let Cleo out earlier to go potty, but he hasn't come back. Have you seen him around?" She wrung her hands.

What Mrs. Maitland *should* have said was that she'd let the cat out so he could come over and take a nice shit in her flower beds and then scratch around, digging them up. Cleo, one of those smashed faced cats with stupid eyes and long orange fur that needed a hundred-dollar grooming job every other week, loved the tulips best. Gladys' mouth went dry and sweat popped out on her forehead.

Crap. Ethan.

"No, I just got home from work."

"Oh? Where's your uniform?"

Think quick, Gladys!

"Got stuff on it at work. One of our patients had this massive diarrhea—"

"Never mind. I guess I don't want to know." Mrs. Maitland frowned as if she'd stepped in it instead of just hearing about it. "But that reminds me. Did you get a dog or something?"

"Nope. No dogs here." She shook her head and offered a tired smile, wanting to get this exchange to be over as soon as possible so she could investigate.

"Well, what about the young man?"

"Young man?"

She gave Gladys a knowing look. Sly, side-eyed, like she thought she knew what Gladys had been up to.

"Oh!" Gladys slapped her forehead for dramatic effect. "You mean Ethan! He's my nephew. He's staying with me for a while."

"Kinda young to be your nephew, isn't he?" She winked, clearly mining for some nugget of juicy gossip.

Mind your own business, why don't you.

"Change of life baby. He's considering school at the university in the fall and wanted to spend some time getting the lay of the land." It was amazing how easily cover stories came to her now that she'd been in hiding for so long.

"Oh." Arlyss seemed disappointed. "Well...does Ethan have a dog?"

"No, I assure you, Ethan doesn't have a dog either."

"I just wondered because I thought for sure I heard some growling in the backyard earlier."

The urge to bolt and run was an overwhelming, almost physical need. What was the kid up to in there?

"Nope. No dogs."

Christ woman, just release me from this purgatorial conversation and take no for an answer.

"Well, keep an eye out for my Cleo, and let me know if you see him anywhere. Poor thing must be scared to death out there. And after losing Smithers, I try to keep a good eye on him." She shone the flashlight into Gladys' face.

Gladys raised an arm to ward off the bright light, her pupils shrinking to pinpoints. The last thing she wanted was for Arlyss Maitland to see a suspicious red glow in her eyes. The world came into sharp focus. She needed to get out of here. Self-control could only go so far.

"Will do," Gladys said brusquely, and turned to go. Then she remembered the canvas bag in the car.

She went back to retrieve it. The nosy neighbor couldn't possibly know what was in it.

Could she?

"Just let me know!" Arlyss shouted into the darkness.

Gladys turned back to see her still watching. She waved at the busybody, then hustled up the sidewalk.

The door was locked, which was good. It meant Ethan had at had the sense to follow at least half of Rule #1: Keep yourself in and others out. She pawed through her gigantic purse, nearly dropped the canvas tote, and finally had her keys in her hand. She inserted one, braced herself for what she'd find, and opened the door.

The feel of the house was all wrong. It was too quiet, for one thing. Not actually silent—there were muffled noises coming from somewhere—but as if a vacuum had pulled the sound out of the world. The only light was what seeped through the blinds from the streetlights outside. A humid mist, almost like perspiration, lay in the air and coated her skin. It smelled like a wild animal den—and sweet copper. Her nostrils flared and a feral hunger kindled in her stomach. Her heart sped into a full gallop. She scanned the dark living room, taking in all the scents at once—a heady mix of blood, panic, and meat. Unbidden, her canines elongated, pressing into her lower lip. Something clattered to the floor.

Another muffled sound came from the kitchen. The darkness was cave-like, but she didn't need the light to see. All her vampire senses were awake and hypervigilant. She had a pretty good idea of what had happened while she was out with Karen. Her olfactory senses led her to the source of the smell. She twitched the curtain aside and scanned the yard outside for movement, but Mrs. Maitland must have given up her search.

Ethan was probably in a state much worse than what she and Karen had found Hans in earlier. The hunger was the same, but the paltry experience Ethan had nothing compared to the years of self-restraint Hans had accumulated.

The door closed behind her with a little snick that made her jump. "Ethan? You here?" She left her bag and purse by the door, not neglecting the lock.

The house wasn't just silent, she thought. It was holding its breath, waiting to see what would happen. What could she do if Ethan went savage and attacked her? Not much. She could throw him across the room, sure. She was bigger than him, and had been a vamp a lot longer, not to mention she was freakishly strong, even for a vampire, but if he knocked her on her ass, she'd be helpless. She pictured herself as a turtle on its back, unable to get up thanks to her God-rotted knees.

Gladys grabbed the fireplace poker. "Ethan? I'm back!" Still no answer.

She could sense him close by; could feel his vibration. She rounded the corner slowly, poker held out in front of her like a medieval sword, and there he was. Blood splattered the cupboard behind where he sat on the kitchen floor. It covered the tile and even the upper cabinet doors. The refrigerator looked like a Jackson Pollock painting done in scarlet.

Ethan looked up when she walked through the doorway, an aching expression of misery on his post-adolescent face. In his arms he held scraps of muddy-looking fur. The fur was orange.

Well, Mrs. Maitland, I believe I found Cleo.

Clear streaks ran down his face from tears of guilt and sorrow. Poor kid. His eyes filled with helpless pleading—as if silently asking for her to reverse time. His mouth opened and closed like a goldfish. Pearly white fangs glinted in the moonlight.

She walked slowly toward him, hands down, trying to be as unthreatening as possible. The poker was still in her hand. At this point, she wouldn't need it. She set it on the counter and got down on the floor with great effort, knees cracking loudly in the quiet house.

Ethan was trying to pet the matted horror that was once Cleo.

Gladys soothed the boy with quiet words he didn't seem to hear, but her tone of voice managed to get his hands unclenched.

His shoulders dropped down away from his ears.

She stroked his hair, sticky with blood, and curbed the urge to lick it off her own fingers. "It's okay, Ethan. It's okay."

He looked into her face with a haunted expression. "I...I don't know how this happened."

"I know, honey. You can put him down now," she said and helped Ethan lower his arms. She set the mess of the former cat aside. "You didn't mean it." She scooted closer to him with a grunt and did a half-assed job of putting her arms around him.

He leaned his head on her shoulder and sobbed. Great, hitching wails perforated by tearing breaths nearly broke her heart. She knew how he felt. Unfortunately.

"I'm sorry I left you here alone. I should have brought you along. I'm so sorry." She cradled his head to her bosom, petting him like a wounded animal. She hummed softly and rocked him until his sobs began to peter out. He looked up, and she smoothed his hair back from his face. "I think we owe Mrs. Maitland a new cat, though."

He laughed once, hiccupped, and lay his head back on her chest.

13. WHAT EVERY YOUNG MAN NEEDS TO KNOW

"Hans, you've got to do something," Gladys said, cupping the phone. Ethan was developing excellent hearing in addition to his other new gifts, and she didn't want him to know she was calling in reinforcements.

She heard a sigh from the other end of the line. "I do not know why you are asking me for this help. Karen seems like more reasonable—"

"Karen's still pissed. She's got some maternal protective thing for him, but I don't think it'd be enough right now. You know how she holds a grudge. I don't think she'd be the best one to guide him right now. Besides. You're a guy. He needs a father figure. Be that guy."

"Young people are lazy. I should not waste time."

Gladys paced the length of the basement, as far as the coiled cord would allow. "Time? All you have is time." With the hand not holding the phone, she made emphatic gestures that were wasted with telephonic communication. "I think I've done more than my fair share and after last night's escapade with the cat, someone needs to step in. You're the one this time. Besides, he's not a bad kid, he just needs...you know. A different perspective."

Silence, but no refusal. "If I do this—that is big if—when is good time?"

Now. Yesterday. Last week.

Gladys calculated. "Ethan's got a shift tonight at Golden Peaks. But I'll be there, so I can watch him and make sure there's no trouble. He had more than enough to hold him over for tonight, with...the cat. But you have to talk to him tomorrow. Before anything else happens." She pictured Ethan sitting in the kitchen, clutching not the cat, but Mrs. Maitland herself, and shuddered. "Think of it as the "Guy Talk.""

"I had no children for good reason. I am not authority on growing up! My own youth is far away."

Gladys' patience was on the verge of breaking. "You have to do it, anyway," she hissed. "It's not about youth, it's about his new condition, and I think I'm doing more than my part here. If I can handle him living here and messing the place up—I was cleaning cat guts off the kitchen ceiling yesterday, for Christ's sake. You need to handle this one, single chat with him. Capiche?"

"I do not understand this capiche."

Hans was playing the dumb card, but Gladys wasn't letting him off the hook.

"Yes, you do! It means, 'yes Gladys, I get it, yes Gladys I understand, yes Gladys, I'll do it, it's important', yadda yadda yadda. You can pick him up tomorrow just after sunset."

"And where is it I am taking him?"

The headache was returning. Shouldn't vampires be superhuman enough not to get headaches? There was so much about this other life that didn't seem fair. The knees, for one thing. The dentures for another.

"Take him for a ride. Take him to your house. Take him to the Goddamn county fair. I don't care, just take him." Gladys rubbed at her temple. This was like trying to find a babysitter for an awful child so the parents could go to the yearly Christmas party.

"I will take him, but not with happiness."

"Gee, Hans. What a gentleman you are." She didn't care whether he was happy or not. No one had asked if *she* was satisfied with her new living arrangement. No one asked her what it was like to have a nineteen-year-old, awkward, weirdo kid living in her basement closet. Let Hans have a turn. What else did he have to offer the group, anyway? Surly, grumpy commentary? It was time for him to step up and do his part.

"I will want to make note of dissatisfaction with assignment."

"Fabulous. I'll have Karen put it in the minutes as some sort of addendum. Happy?"

"No."

"See you tomorrow." Gladys hung up before Hans could make any more objections. The ancient telephone bell tolled in protest. Slamming down a real phone was much more satisfying than the little digital things everyone had nowadays.

She'd never bothered with a cell phone, let alone one of those expensive pocket computers everyone was obsessed with now. That would mean a trip to a store and what amounted to a tracking device in her hand.

Ethan had been mystified by the thing's purpose and design. He'd bemoaned the loss of his own cellular device. Gladys had chosen to hold off teaching him the ways of the rotary dial. He might decide to call up an old buddy and go have himself a little evening drink. Of both kinds.

At the sound of her approaching footsteps, the basement door swung open.

Ethan stood, silhouetted by the kitchen fluorescents at the top of the stairs.

Gladys flinched involuntarily.

"Ready to go?" Ethan asked.

"Yep. Ready." She gestured to her scrubs—little panda bears in primary colors. "Did you drink?"

Ethan nodded. "It's not enough, though. Isn't there some way we can get more?" His voice had taken on that teenage whine that all kids got when they were denied something vital, like the latest pair of jeans or an outlandish haircut.

Gladys didn't like the way he looked out the big picture window at the houses that lined the street. "I hear you, Ethan, but it's the best we've got."

"For now."

Her eyes narrowed in suspicion. "Yes, for now."

Whatever you're planning, Ethan, don't even think about it. I'm not in the mood to clean up another mess.

Disposing of Cleo's remains had been a nasty business, a task to be done under cover of darkness after nosy old Arlyss's lights were turned off for the night. Now there were two unmarked graves in the backyard instead of one. Three, if you counted the rabbit.

Ethan had offered to help, but after one look at his pale face and shaking hands, she dismissed him so she could do it herself.

After the incident with the cat, Gladys made it her business to keep him surveilled at all times. He'd complained that he didn't like her tagging along after him at work, though. The other nurses had started whispering to one another, going silent when she or Ethen came within sight.

"I'm not a child. This is like having your mom follow you around at work." He leaned against the door to the janitorial closet.

As if she was having the time of her life, keeping up with her daily rounds, and most of Kayla's, while also keeping up with a skinny janitor making his rounds.

"Until you learn to control your urges, you *are* a child. A dangerous one. I'm going to be right behind you every step of the way, every minute." Gladys sighed. "It will get better, you know."

"How will it?"

"I don't know. It's a mystery. But it will, I promise."

Work your magic, Hans. Please get this kid straightened out. Before...

But she didn't want to finish that thought.

Gladys was exhausted by the time she was able to roll up in her vamp-tarp and go to sleep, but she didn't cover her head until Ethan was securely tucked into his closet. Nothing should be left to chance when it came to this one. When the door closed behind him, Gladys ducked inside her big blue burrito.

The next day, Gladys was up as soon as the sun slipped below the horizon. She unlocked the basement mini-fridge and knocked on Ethan's closet door.

"Rise and shine, buttercup. Hans will be here to get you soon."

"I'm not coming out."

"What? What do you mean, not coming out?"

"I *mean*, I'm not coming out."

"You need to—"

"Not if I have to get in a car with *Haaaans*."

"Ethan..."

"No."

"Don't make me come in there." She tried the doorknob and pushed, but it was locked from the inside.

That was new. When had he installed a lock? Maybe he was craftier that she gave him credit for. She banged on the door and little flecks of dust drifted down from the door jamb, dancing in the light from the overhead bulb.

"You can't come in unless I invite you in. So, ha ha."

Gladys rolled her eyes. He had much yet to learn. She rapped with one knuckle.

"Still not coming."

She choked down her frustration. "Yes you *are.*" She grabbed two bottles from the refrigerator and, with as much noise and commentary as possible, downed hers in two gulps, followed by a big 'aahhhh' and theatrical belch. She thumped her fist against her chest. "Delicious!" She tapped the other bottle on the door, just a light little knock. "Come on out and get it!" She waited.

"No. I...no. Not coming."

But she sensed his hesitation. "Get out of there and come get your breakfast. Now!"

She tapped her foot and banged on the door again.

The door creaked open, and light spilled into the crack. He'd constructed a nest of old blankets and quilts from around the house that Gladys hadn't even realized were missing.

What else is he hiding?

The boy emerged from the swaddling mass; a hedgehog coming out of hibernation in the spring thaw, blinking in the light. His eyes burned like candles.

That red stare frightened her a little. Although he could gain no nourishment from her—she hadn't eaten enough herself—the boy was looking pretty desperate. She held out the old whiskey shooter to him and shook it. "Just like my mother used to make." She smiled, but it felt like a mask on her face.

A skinny white hand jutted through the crack and snatched it.

She stumbled backward and nearly tripped.

His underdeveloped Adam's apple bobbed as he drank down the contents. He wiped his mouth with the back of his hand.

"Better?"

He nodded. The burning hunger and anger had left his eyes.

"Okay then. Up and at 'em." She pushed the door inward, but it stopped halfway, its movement halted by bushels of Gladys' bed linens.

"But I don't *want* to go with Hans. He's about as much fun as a...a root canal." That five-year-old whine was back, nasally sliding up and down the musical scale.

"Have you ever even had a root canal?" Gladys was genuinely curious. She reached for his hand, caught it, and pulled him out of his cotton womb.

"No, but I don't like the dentist, so it can't be much fun. I don't suppose that's a problem now. It's not like I can get cavities."

Gladys snapped her fingers twice. "Chop, chop. Hans will be here soon." She went to the stairs, grasped the railing for dear life, and made her way slowly upward, one grunt at a time.

She still went to the dentist, as a matter of fact. Iowa City had its very own vampire dentist who specialized in unique dental applications and serious plaque removal, not to mention advice. She was one of the oldest vamps in town, by her own account, of course. Decades and centuries of existence could result in a heck of a lot of tartar build-up, so there was a definite need. After yesterday's fiasco, she needed to go again to get her dentures fixed. That tumble onto the hard floor had cracked one side, and she was wearing her spares.

Ethan opened the door the rest of the way and shuffled out.

"It'll be fine. You'll see," she said over her shoulder. "Hans is actually a decent guy once you get past that frozen German exterior."

He clumped up the stairs behind her. "Doubt it."

She reached the top stair and was startled when a knock on the front door announced that Hans had kept his appointment and was here to explain the facts of life to this juvenile blood junkie.

Thank God. Now I can have a moment to myself to breathe.

Ethan begged with his eyes, looking frantically from the locked front door to Gladys, all but clasping his hands in prayer.

She shook her head. "Nope. You gotta go."

Hans stood in the doorway framed by an overcast, moonless sky. Streetlights cast yellowing shadows into the deep corners of the night. The air was still. Mrs. Maitland must have given up searching the bushes for her missing cat, but posters were tacked up on the lamp posts. She could see them fluttering in the breeze.

Hans' fists were hard stones shoved into the pockets of his standard issue Eddie Bauer khakis. Today's polo shirt was dark green with an alligator embroidered over the left breast. He looked like he was ready to meet up with a herd of middle management assholes for a round or two of golf. All he needed was a pair of shoes with fringey little tassels.

"Ahh. Hans. So glad you came."

He gave her a look that would have curdled milk. "I have no choice."

She ignored him and hollered down the hallway. "Ethan, Hans is here!"

Ethan appeared from the bathroom without a sound, looking nervous and sullen.

The two of them would drive her to an early grave. If only that were possible. She gave them her sunniest, aren't-we-just-the-best-of-friends grin and shooed Ethan out the door.

She watched as they made their way to the car.

Hans slumped as he walked, like he'd finally agreed to take out the garbage after it had spilled across the floor and attracted roaches.

Gladys waved and then slammed the door. She flipped the locks and waddled to her recliner.

Alone at last. How long has it been? A week? Two?

Time moved so differently for a creature of the night. It was often hard to know just how much had passed. Gladys clicked on the TV, more than ready to spend the night watching old re-runs of Dark Shadows on AMC. All that was missing was a bowl of popcorn. She hit pause, nuked a package of microwave popcorn she'd squirreled away in the back of a dusty cupboard, and reveled in the smell despite not being able to eat it. Her mouth watered, but she lost herself in the show and ignored the old hunger that returned now and then to remind her of what she was missing.

14. THE MANAGER

When the silence in the Mercedes became too uncomfortable, Ethan cleared his throat. "Thanks for picking me up."

Hans gave no reply but seemed to talk silently to himself as he drove. He hunched forward toward the windshield and clutched the wheel, reminding Ethan of Ahab the sailor as he sought his white whale.

"Gladys said you wanted to talk."

Again, Hans didn't reply, just glowered at the dark road from beneath his bushy eyebrows while his gnarled hands piloted the steel beast with its efficient, German engineering.

"Where are we going?"

Hans shook his head. "So impatient. Sit. Wait quietly."

Ethan shifted in nervous discomfort and all at once the air inside the car was too stifling, threatening to choke him. He opened the window and stuck his head out, breathing in fresh air. A smile began to creep across his face, but then froze as he realized the window was going up and the space he occupied was shrinking fast. He yanked himself back in before he was trapped.

"You are vampire, not dog."

"Mmm nt thewun..." Ethan attempted to swallow his words.

"What was that?" Hans cut his eyes sideways to Ethan, sharp as thinly honed blades.

"Nothing."

"Yes, was something. Out with it."

He cleared his throat again, summoned all his courage, and glared at Hans with his arms crossed. "I said, *I'm* not the one growling like a dog."

Hans' frown carved more deeply into his face. "We cannot pull in attention to ourselfs. We must be quiet like cats. Invisible like vapor, forgotten like wisp of smoke."

"Poetic." Ethan shrugged and fiddled with the knob on the glove compartment.

Hans smacked his hand away.

Ethan put his finger in his mouth and whimpered.

Hans rolled his eyes in exaggerated exasperation and made an abrupt turn onto a gravel road, mumbling under his breath.

Ethan clutched the Oh Shit handle on his side of the car as the back end of the Mercedes slid sideways before gaining traction. "Where are you taking me?" The certainty that he was about to be murdered by a short, angry, German vampire filled his head with white panic.

"We will chat. Then you ask questions."

"But—"

Hans held up a finger and reached across the seat, pressing it to Ethan's lips, then returned his attention to driving.

Ethan leaned back into his seat, his eyes as wide as ping-pong balls and his body plastered against the door, trying to create as much space between them as possible. Maybe Hans was crazy. After all, he seemed to be talking to himself. Wasn't that what crazy people did?

After fifteen minutes of left and right turns, Hans pulled the car to a stop and backed into a small lane between two cornfields.

Now that the chance for escape was upon him, Ethan pulled the door handle and jumped from the car, kicking up dust from his heels as he sprinted away from this crazy old coot of a vampire. Except that was only in his mind. The child-safe locks were engaged and all he managed to do was flip the door handle and whimper. When it was clear that his escape was thwarted, he crossed his index fingers and held them out toward Hans, warding him off.

"Back away! You just back away from me! I know what you are."

Hans frowned, but the expression was half amusement. "Put those down." He swept Ethan's hands apart. "We are same, and you know nothing. You are *kinder* in *winder*. Shush the mind." He poked Ethan in the forehead with a stubby finger. "Listen." He clapped Ethan's right ear and set his head ringing.

"Ow! That hurt!"

"You will live." Hans twisted his mouth in a sour grimace. "Or at least not die. Now listen and I will tell all." Hans gazed out over the waving corn. "I will tell story one time. So young man will listen and shut up while I say it. Is it deal?"

Ethan nodded, afraid of Hans but excited to hear this story. He'd been wondering how a guy like Hans got turned.

"I am at Hy-Vee, stocking vegetables. Is third run-in with The Lady. She's swaddled from head to toe in white, wearing ridiculous floppy hat. Looks like misplaced celebrity, plucked from LA or New York, dropped into shit-splat Iowa City without map or credit card, looking for white sands beach party. 'Is your turn,' I say to inept store manager. 'I dealt with her twice last week. First for no arugula. Second because no orange beets. I point out red beets, but woman cannot be satisfied.'

"'You're the produce manager on duty,' Sheila says. She snaps stupid pink bubblegum. It smells of rotted watermelons. 'Whiny customers are below my pay grade. You deal with it.'

"I am angry and glowering. Manager is young and lazy. 'It will not matter the cause!' I am not wanting to shout, so I raise my hands like surrender. 'She will be unsatisfied always. I cannot placate this woman. She is not normal.'

"Of last part, I am certain. There is something *off* about her, but I am not quite putting finger on what that *off* thing is.

"'Hans.' She says in patronizing tone I now have come to hate. She blows another pink bubble. 'It's your job to placate the public. My job's to make sure you do your job. Get it? Now git out there and make a difference!' She swings arm with bent elbow like she is at square dance in Mississippi barn.

"'It will not matter what I say!' I once more am raises hands in the air. 'Can we not ask her to leave? She can find fancy-dandy vegetals elsewhere. Is not my job to make sure this Ms. Getty has everything.'

"I put hands on hips so I can be more better at making point. But I see it will not be working.

"'Hans. Buddy. If you wanna throw away twelve years of your career on this pasty twat, be my guest. But I think you got it in ya to handle the situation.' She pats my shoulder like child, and winks. I wishes to wrap her lanyard around her wattled throat. 'I believe in you.' Sheila stomps up stairs then turns around with head over her shoulder, and points at horrible woman. 'She's waiting. Don't forget, Helpful Smile in Every Aisle!' Then manager disappears to break room where she will watch minions on the security cameras.

"I clench fists in frustration and—"

Ethan's laughter disrupted the story. The kid was beside himself. He aborted the laughter when Hans reached out and slapped him upside the head. Not hard; barely a tap, really. Hans had perfected both his aim and self-control long before being turned into an unclean parasite.

"There. Now you have learned. Do not stop my story with words.

"But I—"

"Or laughing. Or whining, crying, moaning, shrieking! None of these things! You are to learn not to laugh. That is why we have come to here."

Ethan glanced around. The cornstalks were nearly waist high. It had been a good wet spring. They whispered and crackled in the breeze. Ethan felt the stirrings of anxiety beginning to hum to life.

Hans' angry face resembled a stubbly red radish. His eyes were shot through with angry lightning. Ethan could clearly see the scenario in his mind: Hans had dragged him out here and placated him with the beginning scenes of a story so interesting he'd have no choice but to listen. Then, as soon as he dropped his guard, this crazy guy would be all over him.

As if hearing the lanky kid's thoughts, Hans said, "If hurting you were goal for me, it would be already done. I am here because Gladys ask. So please? Let me to finish? Is painful enough to tell without this disrespect." Then, almost to himself, Hans said, "Young people are disrespectful."

"Okay. Sorry." Ethan sat quietly for nearly a minute.

Hans was still silent.

The boy looked over at the older man.

Hans scrutinized him as if he was a science experiment in a petri dish, making him squirm.

"I'm sorry! I'm sorry! I'll shut up! Just quit staring at me like that."

Hans nodded. "I will go on, then."

"I think in my head I should walk away. Get in the car, go home, and look at the want ads. Find new job more suited. But Sheila is right. After much time and work, I rise high up food chain here and am not wanting to start over again. In the shiny paper towel dispenser over the handwash sink, I take a moment to straightens my tie, smooths back my hair, and tame down my eyebrows."

Ethan laughed out loud, then his eyes widened. "Sorry."

Hans glowered at him. "What is this funny thing you laugh for?"

"I'm sorry. It's just that...your eyebrows..." He motioned to Hans' eyebrows which resembled more of a 1940s caricature of a vampire than anything else and snickered again trying to stifle it. Although Hans had not torn him to shreds yet, he wasn't sure that he was in the safe zone. Sure, the guy was at least a half-foot shorter than him but was much older and more experienced. By forty years? Fifty?

Hans' frown deepened, forming long grooves in his cheeks. "Yes. This is hilarious, no?" Hans shoved his face into Ethan's personal space and waggled them like Groucho Marx.

Ethan shook his head.

Hans was definitely not joking.

"I continue then, and you will not interrupt."

Ethan shook his head.

"Young people are disrespectful."

Ethan chewed on the inside of his cheek, wanting to defend all the Gen Z and Millennials of the world. He listened to his intuition, catching that he would be making a big mistake by doing so. For a kid like Ethan, it was quite a feat of self-control.

"When I am certain I look my best, I feel confident to approach horrible woman. As I come to her, she is angry. Lips looking scrunched like big butthole."

Ethan guffawed involuntarily, but was gratified to see that this time, Hans was actually cracking a joke. His response wasn't going to see him under a mound of dirt somewhere out in the endless miles of cornfields.

"'How may I help you?' I ask of her. I would like to help out the door and into her car.

"Pale white lady says 'Finally. Come over here...what's your name?'

"I go closer. 'My name is Hans.' I tap name tag because is obvious and also I have been telling my name each time she comes in to assault."

"Assault?" Ethan was confused. "You mean she came in and started attacking people?"

"Not assault." Hans thinks for a moment and then brightens. "Inn-sult. Insult. Sorry. English is nonsense."

Ethan had no idea how to respond, so he reserved his right to remain silent.

"She does not listen. She never listens.

"'Yes, *Franz*. I want you to see the deplorable state your so-called Fresh Salad Bar is in.'

"I follow, but am wishing I was anywhere else. Even colonoscopy would be better. 'That's *Hans*. Not Franz.'

"She pivots like fashion model, white jacket flares like Marilyn Monroe dress. "You know of Miss Marilyn?"'

Ethan nodded.

"Ah. She was quite a beauty. I remember...never mind this now. Later we can speak of stars of the cinema. Before movies were made to nonsense. I will continue story now.

"'Hans, Franz, it doesn't matter,' she waves her hands beneath the sneeze guard of the salad bar.

"I am thinking now how we must disinfect.

"'You see how inadequate this is,' she says, indicating the items on the salad bar.

"I do not see. 'Do I?' I say.

"This woman is waking anger inside me, and I think I will not cooperate this time. I will remember dignity.

"'If not, you are a blind fool! This is *iceberg lettuce*! Iceberg! No one uses that anymore! There's no nutritional value in *iceberg lettuce*. How am I supposed to feed my gran—myself if all you have is ICEBERG!? Would it kill you to provide some spring greens? Or romaine? Oh, and look at this.' She is pulling shirt sleeve, pointing. I am not liking her to touch me. She feels cold and I think there is something else. I surprise myself at personal restraint in face of verbal abuse. Behavior is *verwerflich*."

Ethan couldn't have defined this concept even if Hans had said it in English. Reprehensible wasn't a word in his personal repertoire, but he got the context and didn't bother to ask.

"I know if I do what is impulse and punch snippy lady in face, job would be lost. Is hard for foreign man to find work in America. Especially a not young man," Hans informed Ethan before continuing.

"Then harpy says, 'these mushrooms are dirty! Disgusting!'

"They are not. They are mushroom colored. 'I do not see—

'

"Long thin fingers tipped with sharp nails pull at sleeve again, dig into the flesh of my arm. I am nearing point of break. If soon she does not leave—

"'Look at those tomatoes!' She plucks one out from under the sneeze guard. Disgusting, and against rule to touch. It is now certain I must clean whole thing before leaving. I am now very anger and soon will explode.

"'You must use tongs for—'

"She holds cherry tomato inches from face, turning it so I can examine shape and color. 'This!'

"It is so close I can almost count seeds inside. I do not know what I should see. Tomato looks perfectly fine to me.

"'This tomato is four days away from wrinkling. Four days! Can't you put fresh food into your Fresh Salad Bar? This is ridiculous!'

"What is ridiculous, I am thinking, is standing in the middle of grocery store taking abuse from uppity woman with geometric haircut and monochromatic fashion. In Germany was respected professor of history! Appreciated by colleagues, loved and respected by students.

Ethan doubted Hans' claims of adoration but was too wrapped up in the story, though he had a pretty good idea how it ended.

"Most important, I was well paid for this knowledge. Here in America, I come to find new life. 1946 this was. Wife and I lived through war and came for promised new start. Prejudice in Americas means I cannot get job at university. I had job in restaurant, in factory, many places where they think I am dumb German. Ha! They must think I am almost Hitler myself. Now I have good job as manager, but still is underling job. Americans are so—"

"Prejudiced," Ethan supplied. "You're sure right about that, Hans bubbie."

Hans raised an eyebrow. "What is bubbie?"

"Don't tell me you never saw *Die Hard*."

Hans said nothing.

"Okay, we definitely *have* to have a movie night."

No response.

Ethan flapped his hands. "Later. Go on."

"I know woman's name from visits before. Many visits. 'Ms. Getty,' I find courage and stand as proud German man and say, 'I am not caring for your tirades in store. You want better? Get down on hands and knees and grow vegetals yourself! In dirt!'

"Estelle makes big gasp and puts fingers to her throat. 'How dare y—'

"But I march on; I am not quitting now. No retreating. I am not wanting to go on but march ahead. 'No longer will I take shit attitude from you,' I tell.

"Yes," Hans said, responding to the younger vampire's shocked expression. "I use shit word in middle of store. Customers get close to action to watch. If it was now, all young people would be recording with phones to put on the internets where I would become next internet sensation. Young people are addicted to smarts phones," Hans made a face of sour contempt. "The ticks and tocks and bookface."

"Yeah. That's probably true," Ethan said.

Hans had a good point, though it wasn't just young people. Everywhere you looked, people, regardless of age, had their heads bowed before their hand-held device gods. He realized that relationships were something he'd taken for granted before. Now that he understood their value, it was too late to make new friends. Not to mention, he would have liked to have had a steady girlfriend before he had been turned.

Ethan opened his mouth to make these points, then decided against it. He was more anxious than ever to hear about how Hans became the cranky guy he was. Perhaps Hans had pretty much always been that way.

Hans eyed Ethan, seeming to dare him to speak.

Ethan remained silent.

Hans nodded with satisfaction.

"I am thinking this is last shift at Hy-Vee with Helpful Smiles in All Aisles, but I am no longer caring. I am no longer taking abuse from uppity woman—will not be cowed by flowy white ghost in store. I admit, I am frightened. Just this case, more angry than frightened. I tell you angry is better. 'You go now, out to car.' I am getting as big as possible, so I am now intimation. *Imitationed*. You know what I am meaning."

"Intimidating," Ethan said.

Hans ignored him.

"I say, 'go cross town. Find Co-op or Whole Foods or other fancy places. We no longer want business from woman who looks like pig and screams like banshee!' This is almost enough swears, but I cannot help to add, 'Harpy! Backpfeifengesicht!'"

"Sorry," Ethan interjected. "But what was that?"

"Backpfeifengesicht."

"Back-a-whatica?"

Hans frowned. "Back-fife-fen-guysicht."

"What the heck does that mean?" Ethan's face was the very picture of rapt attention. He got to hear Hans' great and terrible story and learn German swear words at the same time. Could this day get any better?

Hans put a finger to his pursed lips for a moment and tapped. "It is not having translation. Is no exact word in English for this. It means 'face which deserves being punched.'"

"Oh yeah," Ethan said, and actually rubbed his hands together fiendishly. "I'm gonna use that one from now on. Bagfiffennugatshit. Got it."

Hans didn't bother to correct his pronunciation. That could come later. "You understand? Is not nice thing."

Ethan nodded and made a little twirling motion with his finger. "Go on, please."

"I poke her in side to make point, and she yelps, jumps away. She is shocked from touch, but I am also shocked. She feels like low electric. Like small zap of the wires. She slaps back my hand and advances with stuttering steps."

Hans' face took on a cloudy bitterness that made Ethan uncomfortable.

"A mysterious growling rumbles up from deep in lady's throat. Two bright red spots like roses bloom on her pallid face. I think I have never seen this kind of angry, not even in Germany, and I wonder where Lady comes from. I am beginning in back of mind to wonder if she is human being. She seems to grow taller, and now I am feeling more afraid than anger. Maybe is my imagination. Maybe is real thing. No matter, courage begins to disappear, and I want to shrink down and get away. She is…" Hans paused, looking for the exact word, probably in German, and then translated his thought. "Woman is not a natural person. Supernatural is what is called.

"She says to me, 'you will regret speaking to me this way! You…you uncouth monster! Where is your manager?'

"This she is not yelling, but is whisper yelling. Only inside head is loud like gonging bells.

"I am now regretting my way of speaking. Would maybe have been better idea to walk away. My hands are gripping edge of salad bar, and I am afraid of falling over. Still, I am holding ground.

"Ms. Getty's eyes are red and black and red again.

"I am all manager needed here,' I say. 'Now go.' I make shooing motion with hands. They tremble.

"A screech that could not come from human throat escapes her lips and now I am terrified and cannot stop from showing this. I throw arms up, squeeze eyes closed, and wait for attack. I fear there might be release of bladder, and then, nothing. I open eyes and see people dispersing. Excitement is over and they are returning to their shopping.

"Ms. Getty is nowhere in sight. I wait for Sheila to descend stairs angry for unprofessional way I handled crazy white lady, but she does not leave ivory tower.

"I am clocking out late at seven-thirty for I am having to replace all things in salad bar after lady concomb…contcamp…contampunated…whatever is word. Spread germs. So happy I am to be outside where air is sharp and cold and stings nostrils. November winds rustle trees like skeletons. Leaves are making chitter noises in the gutter. I am reaching for car keys when warm breezes are on neck, too hot for cold night. I smell rotten meat smell, and all my mind is filled, and I feel like as if I am spinning around.

"I turn around slowly, hoping for mugger but an unholy presence lurks. Here is the white harpy but not with same face. Face is no longer human.

"All air in lungs goes away in whoosh and I am not able to scream. Only whistling noise leaves mouth as I am trying to pull air into lungs. I am become human teapot.

"Thing asks me, 'How about a drink after work?'

"I shake head no, leaning on door of car. There is no running away now. But then, in next moment, I do not want to run. I am wanting to go to her—wanting to spend rest of my life with her, marvel at her horrid beauty. In this moment, I would be happy doing anything she asks.

"You must understand, young Ethan, a power is in woman that never have I felt before. She is strongest evil ever I have seen in life. More evil even than war and Nazi camp. I hate and love her in this moment and cannot choose which is more."

Ethan nods. He knew exactly what Hans was feeling.

"Estelle pulls up sleeve and slices thin skin over veins with fingernail like dagger. Red splatters on ground, on car. A violent color spattered on the long white coat she wears. Dumb brain thinks there's no way to get those stains out. When she presses her wrist to my mouth, I grab her forearm and drink like have been Moses in desert for forty years. I am greedy now and she shrieking with laughter."

Hans wiped his eyes furtively, but not before Ethan noticed the tears pooling on his lashes, then falling down his cheeks.

Ethan was quiet for once. Sitting in the car with his hands between his knees, he felt like a helpless child.

"You have nothing to say?" Hans' hands were intertwined, the knuckles white.

"I..."

"Let us go for walk."

"What?" Ethan looked around nervously at the wavering corn. "Out here?"

"Why not? World is oyster. Let us get fresh air. I think head out window was not terrible idea." He clapped Ethan on the leg twice, favored him with a rare grin, and opened the driver's side door.

Ethan sat for a moment, undecided, then with no other option, he opened the door and stepped out onto the soft earth. If Hans wanted to kill him, there was likely nothing he'd be able to do to stop him. "What are we doing out here?" His post-pubescent voice cracked. He rubbed his hands along arms dappled in goosebumps. He couldn't feel the cold anymore, but it seemed to seep into his marrow, nonetheless.

"Taking walk. To clear the head."

"Is that it?"

"Is what it?"

"Like, is that the whole story?" In a rare moment of intuition, Ethan had assumed there was more that Hans wasn't telling him. That Hans didn't *want* to tell him.

"What would you like? Happily ever after?" Hans sneered at him, then continued walking down the dirt track between the fields with his head down.

"No, but you just left it at 'you were at the car'. What happened next? Did you fight back? How did you get blood? How did you find Gladys to help you?"

"That is many questions. Which is most important? Pick one. Dawn is not far off."

Ethan thought it over. "What did you do? After you were turned. Right away, I mean. How did you get blood?" Ethan licked his lips as if tasting a memory.

Hans sighed, looking like someone had just run over his dog. "I am Catholic. When first I was bitten, I ran to church. Of course, handle of door burned me with electric fire. God's church was closed to me." Hans' voice cracked as if he'd been the one whose pubescent growth had been arrested right before its departure. "Nowhere to go. I went home. I thought I knew what would happen next, but also knew it was only fairy tales and books where vampires lived. To bed I went. For sleep. But dreams were not good."

He looked up at the crescent moon, as if the answer would be there. "I could not go out next morning. Sunshine hurt my eyes, burned skin. I roamed empty house for days and was sick. So sick."

Hans paused, and Ethan's heart went out to him. He remembered all too well what the first day was like. He reached out to comfort his new friend, but hesitated and dropped his hand to his side.

"I made chicken soup, best thing for bad stomach, is it not? But all things in stomach came up, and still I felt bad. On third night, with courage, I went out into night. Drove to west side of city where hobos sleep under bridge. I not knowing why it was that I was there, but I sat with hobos and feel sharp teeth in mouth, coming from top but not hurting. Then hungry feelings overcome, like something outside is driving me like a car. Then I know nothing for a while.

"When daylight approaches and I woke, I see man beside me not moving and no throat. I am covered in blood. I drank from him until nothing was left." Tears formed in his eyes as he recounted his shame, but this time they did not fall.

Although it'd be a coincidence, Ethan bets it was the same place he spent countless days after fleeing from his roommates.

Hans' eyebrows knitted together until the bushy threads seemed to tangle. His face was filled with sudden anger as he remembered how he got the shaft so many years ago. A wind began to stir and leaves from the growing corn lashed at Ethan's face. He took a step backward. Hans appeared to be vibrating and—a weird shadow radiated off his body.

"But what happened to the guy you killed?"

Hans flinched as Ethan spoke the word out loud. The small German man looked stooped and weak, even though Ethan knew better. He thought perhaps it was shame that made the old man hunch over.

"How did you get home? Covered in blood like that. You must have looked like Carrie."

"I do not know this Carrie. Is a vampire you know?"

"It's from a movie, but never mind. What happened after that?"

"I wrap myself in dead man's clothes. Push him into river. No time to get home, I move under bridge where sun does not shine and sleep like dead." The man allowed his tears to fall in tiny rivulets that rolled in tributaries down his wrinkled cheeks.

"Finally, I am feeling better for first time. I am feeling powerful now. I call work and ask for night shifts. I say there is family situation. They were happy to put me in night shift. No one wants to be working the nights. Pay less, sleep less." Hans smirked at Ethan. "Everyone assumed it was because of customer who wanted to speak with manager. They weren't wrong. They were right for the wrong reasons."

Suddenly Ethan felt sorry for making Hans recount this story. It's worse than his own.

Ethan extended a shaky hand toward Hans' shoulder making contact this time, and Hans jumped at his touch. "You did what you had to. How could you know? And since Gladys hadn't found you yet…"

A bark of harsh laughter rang out across the fields. "You think it was Gladys who found me? I find *her*. Together we help each other. We did our best not to hurt people but had no luck in finding blood supply until much later. Even then, sometimes urge is too strong."

"Well, what do you do? Like, when the urge gets too strong? Don't vampires get a familiar or something?"

Hans scowled at him. "Too many movies. You must think you can also turn into bat." He shook his head. "Is witch who has familiar, anyway." He waved his hand. "We do the best we can."

Hans turned around without another word and walked back to the car.

"That's not really an answer," Ethan called after him. He jogged to catch up.

"Is best to end story for now. Let us get in car. Would not do to be out when sunlight comes."

Ethan looked to the east and saw the horizon was turning into that strange green color that happens just before dawn.

They drove in silence all the way back to Gladys' house. When Hans put the car in park, Ethan paused for a moment before opening the passenger side door.

"Thanks for telling me all that. I'm not sure I understand everything even now, but thanks for telling me. I guess I'll learn more as I go, right?"

"Only do not make same mistakes. You are in good position to learn from others and not all have such bad luck so early. Important not to do foolish things. We have good arrangements now and is best not to upset apple cart."

"I don't know what that apple cart thing means, but yeah. I promise not to kill anybody or do anything dumb." With that he got out, closed the door behind him, and watched Hans reverse down the driveway before stepping inside.

He was surprised to see Gladys in her recliner with a bowl of popcorn next to her on the end table. She had a strange expression on her face—one he'd never seen before. He shut the door quietly. She looked dead. But then, she was dead. She was undead. The floorboard squeaked, and he released a tiny fart. Gladys blinked once. Twice. Then seemed to reanimate.

"You're home. Already. What time is it?" Her words were slurred. She rubbed her eyes.

Ethan pointed to the clock above the fireplace. "It's four-thirty. Almost dawn."

"Wow," Gladys said and worked to get herself out of the chair. She stumbled, grabbed the back of the recliner, and almost went down as it spun in a lazy circle.

"What's wrong with you?"

"Nothing. It'sh fine, I'm just a little out of shorts." She giggled and pressed her hand to the wall, inching her way toward the kitchen with plodding steps, away from her troublesome roommate.

"Out of shorts?"

Her heavy shoulder thudded against the doorframe. "I feeehl fine." She slapped a hand across her mouth and stifled another giggle.

"Woah. Are you, like, drunk?"

Gladys burst into gales of laughter, nodding. "Shhh," she said and pressed her finger to her lips. "It's our little secret. Yerz and mine."

"But how can that be?" His eyebrows knitted together in concentration. "How can you be drunk? We can't drink, right?"

"No," Gladys' voice had lowered into a harsh, conspiratorial whisper. "But other people can!" She broke into fresh laughter. "This one tasted like Tequila." Then she burst into song. "My favorite wi-i-ine, is tequilaaaaa..." She grinned, all teeth.

Ethan stepped away, for the first time not fully trusting her with those pointed canines.

"There 'uz a Tres Margaritas commercial on. It sounded so good, I just wanted to shmell it. *Smell it.* So, I went there and stood outside." Her face became stormy. "And then thish creep came outta nowhere and bumped into me." She hiccupped like a cartoon drunkard. "He uz so rude, shmelled so much like a margrida. I just had to have a taste." She licked her lips.

Ethan felt ill. And angry for the first time since he encountered Gladys and crew.

"You go downstairs right now and roll yourself up in your damn tarp. Go to bed!" He pointed his finger at her like a disappointed parent.

Gladys cackled but allowed him to guide carefully down the stairs. She stumbled at the bottom, and went to her knees. It should have hurt, but she just laughed.

Ethan helped her up with a grunt of effort and wondered if vampires could get hernias. Once he got her to her corner, he unzipped the sleeping bag. She struggled to get down on the floor and slid partway. He pulled it up around her, zipped it up and watched as she rolled herself up into the biggest joint in the world. A pink-and-white object flew from the whole thing. He caught it without thinking Then another, which he also plucked from the air. He frowned down at the misshapen blue lump that was his mentor and landlady and then at the wet things in his hands. Dentures.

"Ack!" Ethan held them out away from himself and tipped one and then the other into the clouded glass on the table next to the mound of Gladys. He wrinkled up his nose. "Gross."

After securing all the doors and windows, Ethan nestled himself into his closet and locked the door. He fell asleep wondering how he could change himself into a bat. He hadn't used his best listening ears when Hans had discussed bats and familiars. The idea was most appealing.

15. HANGOVER

Ethan and Gladys were due at Golden Peaks in forty-five minutes, and Gladys still hadn't worked her way out of her bedroll. Ethan dressed in his janitor's uniform and combed his hair back from his forehead like Fred Astaire, although he wasn't so light on his feet. He waited on the sofa for fifteen minutes, glancing up compulsively at the clock. If Gladys didn't get up soon, they'd be late for work. Finally, when he felt like he couldn't wait anymore, he considered taking her car. But that wouldn't do. Her job could be at stake if she failed to show up and so could his. He stomped down the stairs in his heavy black work shoes and kicked at the edge of the bundle that was Gladys, the very hungover vampire.

"Unnfh." She turned over and issued a grand snore.

"You got to get up. We're gonna be late!"

"Uhhhhhgh." After a good deal of rustling and wiggling, Gladys worked her torso out of the mummy bag and tarp. She looked up at Ethan with bleary contempt. "What? What do you want?"

"A ride. To work. Where we need to be in like, twenty minutes. You gonna get up?"

Gladys stroked her tongue with a finger. "Blech. I feel like crap."

"Well, you went on a bender or something last night. You should have seen yourself. I don't even know how you managed to get home without being pulled over."

"Is that all?" She started to snuggle back into the sleeping bag.

"Oh no you don't." He nudged her with his foot.

With her eyebrow raised, she looked up at him in irritation. "Can't you just bugger off and leave me alone?" Her tight, white curls were mashed to her head on one side.

"No." He held out a one-ounce whiskey shooter to her. "Bottoms up. Let's get going."

She took the bottle, spun off the cap, and gulped. "Ahhh. Better already." Color washed into her face.

"Well go get better in the shower." He paused and sniffed. "You smell." He turned and stomped up the stairs.

Fifteen minutes later, Gladys was more or less put together, and they went out into the night.

"We're definitely gonna be late."

"You drive." She shoved the keys into his hand. "I'm still wobbly."

"Can you actually work like this?"

"No problem. Just drive."

Nervous, Ethan adjusted the mirrors and backed slowly out of the driveway, hitting the brakes and causing the car to lurch every few feet.

"Haven't you ever driven?"

"Well yeah, sort of. But I never had a car, so never had a chance to really do any driving." He looked over his shoulder each time the car stopped.

"You're gonna give us whiplash." She belched from down low in her belly and put her hand to her mouth. The tequila fumes were still gurgling up from her nether regions. "You'll be fine. Maybe you could earn your keep as my personal valet. My chauffeur."

He grunted and finally got the car moving down the street in the right direction. "What happened to you last night?"

"That bothers you, doesn't it?"

He nodded.

"Well, shit happens. Sometimes when you least expect it. The feeling just comes over you."

"And you vamp out? Yeah, Hans told me that last night."

She raised an eyebrow. "Did he, now? What else did he tell you? Did he mention the hobo?"

"Yeah." Ethan flipped on his turn signal at the corner of First Avenue. "But you shouldn't say hobo. That's not really politically correct anymore. It's not 1933."

"What's not 1933?"

Ethan pulled hesitantly into traffic and then slammed on the brakes, bringing them to a jerking stop when he got a loud honk from a black Chevy pickup with "Dirty Deeds" painted across the back.

It swerved around them, and a hand stuck out the window and gave him the finger.

Ethan wiped his sweaty palms on his pants.

Gladys gripped the dashboard in terror. "Jesus! If you're gonna go, then go. Otherwise, we're going to get creamed."

"I told you I hadn't driven in a long time." He got going again. "Anyway, as I was saying, 1933 was the end of the Great Depression. Lots of people lost everything. Calling people hobos back then might have been okay, maybe, but nowadays they're called *homeless people,* or better yet, people experiencing homelessness." He glanced her way with a pedagogic little grin. "They're people first, homeless second."

Gladys reached over and nudged the steering wheel as he drifted toward the curb. A light pole loomed ahead. Ethan corrected course.

"Sorry," Gladys crossed her arms. "I didn't know I was living with the PC police. I'll try to do better."

"Are you going to be okay? I mean, you're not gonna try to attack people to get rid of the hangover, are you?" He frowned, again attempting a parental look of disapproval.

Irritated, she said, "You walk a year or two with my knees and tell me how it is before you preach."

For a few minutes, the only sound was the whisper of wheels on the rainy street.

Ethan, feeling guilty about razzing her, cleared his throat and changed the subject. It was better than discussing this heavy topic. "So, what cool things can you do?"

"What are you talking about?"

"I mean, what cool shit can you do? Hans said something about turning into a bat."

She looked utterly gob smacked. "He told you *what*? That he can turn into a bat?"

"Well, no, not in so many words. But he mentioned turning into a bat, so I just thought maybe that was something we could work on. You know, together." His face took on a wistful look. "That'd be so friggin' cool."

"What?" Gladys stared straight ahead. "Are you serious?"

"Well, it *would* be cool, you know? To fly around like a bat. Think how much faster we'd be? And we wouldn't be contributing to carbon emissions and global warning, so why not?"

"Why not? Because that's ridiculous! And dangerous! Hans, I promise you, cannot turn into a bat or anything else." She turned sideways in her seat, not wanting to miss anything in case his face might give something away. "Now, what exactly did he say? Verbatim."

"Verbatim?"

"Word-for-word."

"He said witches have a familiar and vampires can turn into bats. I heard it loud and clear." He turned into the Golden Peaks parking lot, double parked, and killed the motor.

Gladys put one hand over his, completely eclipsing it, and turned his face toward hers with the other, forcing him to pay attention. "Listen to me carefully, Ethan. Are you listening?"

He nodded and tried to remove his chin from her vise grip.

"Vampires can't turn into bats or birds or anything else. You got that?"

Ethan nodded. "Okay, okay. I got it." He sat silently with the keys clutched in his hand. "But can you do anything else that's cool?"

Gladys sighed, looked down at her lap, and yearned for the time when she was lonely in her home, but things were simpler. "Yes. And no. It takes a while for you to come into all your powers, and you never know how strong they'll be."

"That's not a real answer, though. What are your powers? Oh! How 'bout Karen? I bet she can do some cool stuff. So what about you?" He was practically begging. "Come on! What can you do?"

"I can go in that door," she pointed, "and keep twenty-four old people alive. Let's go."

Ethan was unconvinced that she was telling him the entire truth. It seemed more likely that she just wanted to control him. As if she was in control of herself. Obviously not, based on what happened last night.

16. WHO'S WATCHING WHO?

During her break, Gladys called Hans.

"What did you tell him?" She hissed through the receiver in the break room once she verified that she was alone.

"What did I tell him? I tell him truth. This is what you asked for. So, I take him out to country, and tell him about my fall from grace. What is there to tell more of?" Clearly irritated, Hans huffed into the phone.

"What's this thing about witches and bats and stuff?"

"I do not know what it is—"

"Ethan is going off about vampires turning into bats and witches' familiars. Whatever you said, he's totally confused." She twisted her lanyard around in her hand. "Now he thinks we can do weird things. So, what did you say?"

"I told him none of these things. He asked if we have familiars to drink from, but I say no. That is for witches."

She pressed her fingertips to her forehead and closed her eyes. She wanted to keep a lot of information from Ethan at the beginning. This was not a time for him to try anything that might get him killed or noticed. Sure, there were familiars and there were human servants, but if she told him about this now, he'd go out in search of one as soon as he woke up tomorrow and he'd get himself obliterated. He'd gotten some of his wires crossed and now everything he thought about powers was mixed together with half-truths. Maybe they should have told him everything all at once. It was hard to tell what the best course of action was. They'd never tried to help someone as young as him before. The young ones often went in search of someone to serve. Like a twenty-year-old kid seeking out an older woman to teach him the mysteries of sex. She was going to have to do some damage control.

"I wonder what kind of books he read growing up."

"Was probably movies," Hans replied.

"Are you coming for coffee tomorrow night?" Gladys asked.. "Because we need to nip this in the bud before he gets other crazy ideas.

"Some myths are true, and some are false. Is easy to be confused. Yes, I am coming to coffee. Will be good to put out young one's fire with hose." Hans paused for a moment. In an unnaturally small, almost childing voice he asked, "I wonder can you get early withdrawal from blood bank?"

Her and Karen's weekly visits to Dr. Cooke at the hospital morgue for freshly squeezed blood kept them honest (most of the time) and kept things quiet. It wouldn't do them any good for people to report that they'd been attacked in the night by senior citizens and had their life fluids drained. It had been successful so far, though it never felt like enough.

Cooke was a fellow vamp who'd been in the game a long time but wanted nothing to do with their way of life. He was a loner, a medical examiner on the night shift. Whenever a fresh cadaver came in, he bottled up the blood supply. So far it had kept their merry band alive in exchange for their silence, but Cooke was a stickler for their strict schedule. Gladys had a feeling they weren't Cooke's only customers and had often wondered if he and Estelle were linked in some way.

"Why do you need an early delivery? You should be fine until next week."

"I have given some to Mr. Ethan."

Shock that he would be generous toward the kid reverberated through her, then outrage. "Hans, we can't get an early delivery. Dr. Cooke is very, very clear about his boundaries. I don't want to shake things up by asking for more. He could cut us off completely, and that would be very bad. You realize this, right?"

"Yes, but he seemed to need some extra. Is growing boy."

"You can't do that, Hans." She was nearly pleading. "Ethan needs to learn how to get by just like the rest of us and—"

Gladys covered the receiver with her hand. The other nurse on duty had poked her head in the door to ask a question. She held up a finger and removed her hand from the receiver.

"Hans, I've got to go, but I'll see you tomorrow, yes?"

"Alright. I will see you then. And if you have any extra bottles, please bring some. I may be getting...desperate."

Gladys hung up and looked at the phone for a moment before getting up. This was getting complicated.

She kept a keen eye on the night janitor during their shift, making sure he did nothing that would get them into trouble. She checked each of her patients for puncture wounds to the neck or wrist, but nothing seemed out of the ordinary.

Ethan seemed to be watching her just as closely. A look she didn't care for came into his eyes each time they passed. What was it? Hunger? Irritation? She thought it was more like disappointment and it burned her that this kid—this clueless, bumbling idiot—had the gall to pass judgement on her.

During break, they sat across the table from each other in the room which was really reserved for the nursing staff. Custodial had their own breakroom.

"Are you watching me?" Ethan asked.

"Of course I am. You're new to this and—"

"And what? You think I'm gonna bleed a patient?"

"Didn't you do that before?"

His eyebrows drew together as if concentrating on a difficult math problem. "Well, yeah. But I didn't know any better then. *You* do and *you* know what happened last night. Maybe *I* should be watching *you*."

He wasn't wrong, but she still felt pissy about his holier-than-thou attitude. Or maybe it was an *un*-holier than thou attitude. Sometimes the undead thing was confusing, even after all the years.

"Like I said, I didn't go out in search of a victim. I went out because I wanted to smell that tasty Mexican food. Sometimes the urge is just too strong."

Ethan shrugged and studied his hands.

Gladys had finally had enough. "I'm going to get back to work. I suggest you do the same. And stay out of the patient rooms."

"I will if you will," he muttered under his breath.

She paused at the door and looked over her shoulder. "Watch yourself." She consciously allowed her eyes to flash one time as a warning and then went back to her doddering charges.

17. ETHAN SNITCHES

Ethan was almost at the door of the Village Inn while Gladys was still struggling to free herself from the car.

"Ethan, wait up," she puffed.

He stopped with his hand on the door frame and looked back.

She grunted as she finally righted herself and took those two baby steps she seemed to need in order to get her knees working again.

Ethan raised his lip in disgust. He still hadn't gotten over Gladys' drunken escapade the other night. Although her victim wouldn't know anything had happened and would experience no lasting harm, she could tell he was still mad about it. As if he hadn't disemboweled Cleo the cat on the kitchen floor just last week.

"Will you hold on a second?" She plodded over to him in her waddling walk, rocking back and forth on her stiff legs like a tipsy rowboat. She reached for his shoulder.

He pulled away, not wanting to be touched.

"Come over here." She grabbed him anyway and guided him away from the door, off to the side. "I know what you think. All of us have these little stumbles along the way. Think of an alcoholic. Sometimes they trip, but then they get back up and dust themselves off. They go back to the meeting and get their priorities straight. It's the same with us. That's why we have our group."

Ethan didn't look convinced. "It's not the same. When you have a beer, no one gets hurt."

Gladys gave him a little side smile. "Young man, I can tell you from experience that when an alcoholic takes a drink, it *does* hurt other people. Mostly the ones they love. I can promise you that the young man in question was mostly unaware of my presence, and afterward, his only thought was that he must have spaced out for a few minutes. It takes resolve and restraint. And even though I was on the way to tipsy, I've gotten to the point where I'm able to stop myself from—"

"If you can stop yourself from killing someone, you can stop yourself from taking their blood! Sounds like you're justif...justly...whatever the word is. You're making excuses."

"You mean justify." Gladys thought about it and repeated her own words in her head, then nodded. "You might have a point, but that doesn't mean you're right. It doesn't change the fact that we all fall every now and then. Again, that's why we have a support group."

"Hans doesn't."

"He does. And it nearly breaks him each time. And by the way," she shook her finger at him, "you wouldn't feel so smug about Hans if you'd seen him the other night."

Ethan's eyes grew wide. "Did he—" He couldn't finish the thought.

Cripes. He always leaps to the end conclusion, doesn't he?

"I'm not saying he did what I did or that he attacked anyone, but he was nearly feral by the time I got to him with his bottles. Blood thirst makes us do strange things. Things we can't always control, like hunting house cats."

Ethan nodded but still didn't seem completely convinced despite the faint flush of shame that filled his cheeks. "Can we go in now?" He was back to sulky teenager mode.

"Sure."

Hans and Karen were seated at their regular corner booth. The fellow patrons were night people and looked almost as vampiric as they did. Maybe more so. Dark circles under half-wild eyes, clearly here at the twenty-four-hour Village Inn because they had nowhere else to go. They guarded plates of greasy eggs and held onto coffee cups for dear life.

Karen waved with a perky smile, and they slid into their places.

A waitress with the half-dead look of most of the patrons smiled sardonically. "Let me guess, coffee as usual?" Her name tag read *Felicia*.

Gladys nodded.

"Great. Always love serving people like you. Big tippers." She stomped off toward the kitchen for cups.

"She seems...chipper." Gladys said. "It's not like we're demanding. And we do leave a decent tip."

"We do not take away table from busy restaurant," Hans flapped his hand around. The place had at least ten empty tables.

Felicia returned, plunked down the cups, and left without a word. Gladys poured from the fresh carafe.

"Bye, Felicia," Ethan said.

Karen laughed, but Gladys had no idea what the joke was. It didn't matter.

Gladys inhaled the intoxicating scent of crap coffee. "So how is everyo—"

"Gladys attacked a guy at a Mexican restaurant last night and got drunk." Ethan announced to the table.

"Shh!" Karen said with her finger pressed to her lips. "You don't know who may be listening!"

The half-asleep regulars continued to look dully into their food. She returned her attention to the table and shot a piercing look at Gladys with her mouth twitched down in disapproval.

"What is this?" Hans asked, looking from Gladys to Ethan for an explanation.

Ethan scrunched down in his seat and sullenly stirred the coffee he couldn't drink. The silence spun out.

She threw up her hands, surrendering. "Yes, it's true. I did it. It wasn't planned, but there was just this commercial on TV, see? And Mexican food sounded so good. And then there was a guy in the parking lot. I wouldn't have bothered him at all, but he bumped into me on purpose! Shoved me into the wall at Tres Margaritas. I could tell he'd had a few. I could smell it on him. I thought about how long it had been since I had a good margarita and I just..." She held out her hands as if to say, *what can you do?*

"Oh, honey." Karen stroked her forearm. "I'm so sorry."

Ethan looked stricken. "You're *sorry?* What about the guy?" He looked at Hans. "Didn't you call it," he concentrated, looking for the right word. "A moral sin?"

"Mortal sin," Hans said.

Gladys felt the corners of her mouth lift and stifled the smile that wanted to form. *Oh, you summer child, you.* He didn't understand the full impact of what he was yet. The hunger that was ever-present, waiting to be satisfied by more than a stupid little whiskey shooter of the good stuff.

Karen saw his expression and raised an eyebrow. "You have no idea what you really are," she said, echoing Gladys' thoughts.

"What's that?" Ethan stuck out his lower lip, looking almost comically like an infant. An infant with acne and an Adam's apple that had a habit of bobbing up and down when he talked.

Hans' blue eyes shifted into a dull red glow.

Ethan sat back against the back of the red vinyl booth, trying to disappear.

"You. Like a child. You learned nothing!" A light breeze fluttered the napkins on the table. "You see world in black and white but is not black and white. You know nothing about hunger! Thirst. Guilt. Anger. You will learn. You will fall. But bigger question is can you get up? That is where real courage is. How do you think it is with me? Cannot even go to confess sins." The fluttering increased and a paper placemat blew onto the floor.

"Hans…" Karen said with a warning. She covered his hand with hers.

Hans turned those red, glowing eyes toward her. When they locked with hers, they began to fade. The breeze died down. He took a deep breath and grimaced at Ethan. "Fine. But he must learn."

"Okay, okay," Ethan said. "I get it. We're all monsters doomed to hell."

"This is Hell," Karen said quietly and fake-sipped from the coffee cup.

An awkward silence fell over them, each with their own thoughts of guilt and frustration at their unfortunate circumstances. A life that none of them had chosen for themselves.

Finally, unable to bear the quiet anymore, Ethan cleared his throat and swallowed. His golf-ball Adam's apple bobbed. "So, how many of you can fly?"

18. MYTHS AND MISCONCEPTIONS

"What do you mean, you can't fly?" Ethan asked. "Can't all vampires fly once they, you know, get the hang of it?"

"Cartoons," Hans lied. There were some who could, but most of them were ancient and it wasn't the same as flying like a bird. It was more like floating on a wave of energy, but one could not sustain that level for long. "Nothing but cartoons for this one." He shook his head in disgust.

"Honey, we can't do anything like that," Karen said, shifting her eyes toward Gladys who nodded imperceptibly.

"What about mesmerizing people? Can you do that?"

Gladys shifted in her seat. Although it was possible to visually sedate a human being and make them experience amnesia, it just wasn't something they did. Usually. The only real reason for that was to drink from someone, and since they spent a good portion of their time ignoring this drive, it wasn't something she wanted to encourage. "There's no reason for it unless you plan to attack someone."

Ethan's eyes lit up like he'd just been handed a Christmas candy cane. "So we *can?*"

"We can, but we don't. And it takes practice." Gladys shook her finger at him for the second time that night. "I don't want you going around trying it." She knew, given the chance, he'd start trying out this skill on her residents at Golden Peaks and wanted to shut that idea down as soon as possible. "Besides," she lied. "Sometimes it backfires."

"Okay, I won't." He bit his lip and didn't look convincing.

Thus, Gladys wasn't convinced. He was going to require continued watching over the next few weeks.

"But now we're getting somewhere." He rubbed his hands together fiendishly. "So, Karen," he turned toward the younger of the two women with her short, brown hair, cut into a bob, "read my mind." He put his index fingers to his temples and squeezed his eyes shut. "I'll try to block you out." He held his breath and sat that way for nearly a full minute before cracking one eye open.

"You are ridiculous," Hans said.

"Well? Can you?" Ethan asked Karen.

"Of course not," Gladys snapped. "Where did you get all these crazy ideas from anyway?"

Head vampires could sometimes reach the minds of those who they had turned if they maintained those lines of communication immediately. That ability faded over time and although vamps could intuit feelings, a few words, things like that, very few were true telepaths. It was easier to touch the minds of mortals—fewer barriers—but true hypnosis of mortals was a skill that took years to cultivate. Ethan would figure this out when he was ready. Like how kids start to explore the idea of sex gradually.

"You know. Movies. Interview with a Vampire, Dark Shadows, Blade, that stuff."

"Well unless you want to end up a Blade victim, I suggest you get these crazy ideas out of your head. Keep your head down and keep making the mustard," Karen said.

He gave Karen a questioning look, much like the village idiot, with his mouth slightly open and a glazed, dull look in his eyes.

She groaned, looking up at the ceiling as if a trap door might appear with a ladder conveniently attached so she could make a speedy exit. "It means keep quiet, keep unnoticed, and try to behave like a normal person. Or you're going to get us all killed."

"Killed?"

Hans banged the table with his fist. "*Dummer jung*! How can you be so stupid? Have you not heard of 'grab torches and pitchforks'? Why do you think there are so few of us? Only vampires alive are keeping their quiet. Imagine authorities discovering secret blood lust! We would be jailed or worse."

"I never thought of it that way," he said. "Wait, were there other ones? In this group of yours, I mean?"

The three of them exchanged glances using the very kind of power they'd just insisted to Ethan didn't exist. It wasn't telepathy. More like sharing strong intuition. But the same level of sharing could be found among close siblings. Or husbands and wives who'd been married a long time.

Karen gave a little nod. "Not our group exactly," Karen said. "There was someone I knew. Before I met these two. I...I'd rather not go into details now." She looked around the room at the half awake, half dead patrons. "Suffice it to say, human beings are incredibly creative when it comes to barbarism," she said in a low whisper.

Ethan's pale face went a shade lighter. It was nearly translucent under the dusty light over the table.

"You see? You don't want to let on to the general public that you have certain...hmm...desires. So you'd *better* start thinking that way," Gladys said. She was fed up with this line of questioning, but it did get the subject off of her little indiscretion.

The truth was, there were a few tricks of the vampire trade. It just wasn't time to share them with him just yet. He wouldn't be able to keep himself from trying them and knowing Ethan the way she did, he'd do something that would make people question his motives. No one would believe that there were actual vampires living in a small midwestern city, but everyone was more than happy to believe in mass murderers, psychopaths, and dangerous criminals. Probably due to all the true crime shows that were on nowadays. Maybe it would be better for him to get caught. They'd be rid of his dangerous behavior, and she'd have her house back to herself.

Gladys shook her head to banish her unkind thoughts. She didn't wish any ill will toward him. He would learn eventually, and until he did, he needed them to guide him. "You need to be careful. One wrong move and you're toast. Literally. Remember what happens when the sun comes up? You don't want to be caught anywhere like, say, a jail cell when daylight arrives, now do you?"

Ethan thought about the burn he'd gotten shortly after his run-in with Estelle—the run-in he still hadn't had a chance to talk about. He shook his head.

"Great. That's settled," Karen said.

"So, who turned you?" Ethan asked her.

She raised an eyebrow, coffee cup halfway to her mouth. She breathed in the aroma as though it were intoxicating. "Gee, Ethan. Who turned *you*?" Her voice was sad.

He shrugged. He hadn't gotten a chance to tell his story yet, but it seemed like they already had an idea. "Some Karen bitch who got mad at me for skateboarding on the sidewalk."

"What?" It was Karen's turn to bang her fist on the table. The silverware rattled and coffee splashed out of the cup onto the paper placemat.

Several customers swiveled their heads to take in the scene. It was probably the most interesting thing that had happened for them all night.

Her pale cheeks flushed with color. Her eyes flashed, but she closed them and took a deep breath. When she opened them, tears glistened in the light of the globe overhead. "You think that's funny? Do you have any idea how much I hate—I mean HATE that term? How would you like it if every time someone did something stupid, they said 'Way to go Ethan'? Does that sound like a lot of fun to you?" Droplets of saliva landed on the table between them. Foamy.

"I'm sorry, it's just something we say. Like 'okay, Boomer.'"

"Well, you should quit that too," Karen growled. "Think before you speak, Ethan. And don't ever say that again or I don't know if I'll be able to restrain myself."

"But you're totally not like that. You're like, nice, you know? It's just a joke."

"Well, it's an old joke, and it's not very funny." She gathered up her leather handbag and slid out of the booth. "Gladys, Hans, good night. Ethan, grow the fuck up." With that, she left the restaurant. All three stared after her with open-mouthed wonder. It was not a word she used often.

"You shouldn't have said that," Gladys said as they drove home, tires whispering on the pavement.

"I know, I get it. You don't have to scold me like I'm a kid."

"But you are a kid, Ethan. And you have a lot of growing up to do. I just hope you live long enough to do it."

"What's that supposed to mean?"

She glanced at him. "Don't worry. I won't be the source of your demise, but you probably want to hear Karen's story before you accidentally piss her off again. She may seem like someone who'll bake you cookies and mix the chocolate milk just the way you like it, but she has a dark side, too. You'd best remember that."

They pulled into the driveway and Gladys scanned the area for nosy Arlyss. She was nowhere to be seen.

"Wait up!" Ethan tagged behind her up the walk to the front door like a terrier. "How can you move so fast sometimes?"

"Just come on. Let's get inside before someone sees you."

Ethan stopped. "Why? Why can't anyone see me?"

Gladys paused with her key in the lock and turned back toward him. "Because Arlyss over there has already noticed that I have a young man staying in my house. I told her you were my nephew, but I'm not sure she bought that. I can't have the neighborhood thinking I'm shacking up with a kid young enough to be—" She stopped there. If she had continued aging the way she should have, Ethan would be about the age of a great-grandchild. "Just trust me, okay?"

Gladys flipped on the light and closed the door behind her, securing the locks and breathing a sigh of relief.

"I almost forgot!" Ethan broke into a sunny grin, the night's admonishments forgotten for the time being. "I want to show you something,"

Her innards coiled. What could he possibly want to show her? She wasn't sure she wanted to know. "What?"

"Hold on," he said, grinning wide enough to show his teeth.

Gladys noted they were normal at the moment.

He jogged back to the bedroom, which served as storage for his few belongings and a place for him to be alone when he wanted privacy. It was a room he didn't dare sleep in. Gladys had warned him that there could be a catastrophic blinds mishap while he was asleep, and she'd wake to find nothing but a pile of ash.

When he returned, he had a piece of folded graph paper. He opened it and spread it out on the counter. It was the size of a desk blotter. She examined the lines and shapes while Ethan chewed on his thumbnail.

Finally, the silence got the better of him. "Well, what do you think?"

Gladys wasn't sure what to think. Ethan had reconstructed a vampire crypt which could be found in any cheesy vampire movie from the seventies or eighties. After more careful consideration, she realized it was more blueprint than drawing and included measurements and materials.

"Well?" He bounced on his feet like he had to pee.

"What do I think? Are you actually proposing the idea of building this in my house? Is that your plan?"

"Of course! I'm not a complete idiot, you know. I was in construction management classes at Freakwood when this happened to me." He gestured at himself.

"Freakwood?"

"Sorry, that's just what we call it. I hate that name. Teakwood Community College."

Gladys nodded and went back to studying the blueprints.

"So? can I?" He asked.

Gladys had to admit this was a lot nicer than a sleeping bag and a tarp. She had never considered that her current sleeping arrangement was sadly plebeian before Ethan brought it to her attention. It wasn't like she'd had overnight company since all this had happened. Now that he had, she realized that there were people in the world without homes, who weren't vampires, that slept in more luxurious accommodations. The kid looked so hopeful, she couldn't resist his little boy enthusiasm.

"Sure. Go right ahead. Only how are you going to get materials and lumber?"

"You forget about the power of the internet."

"I don't have internet," she said and frowned.

"No, but the library does. And they're open until ten. I can go as soon as the sun goes down, order my stuff for delivery, and be back here in time to go to work at eleven. What do you say?"

"That's a very public place. Do you think you can control yourself?"

"Maybe you should come with me. Keep an eye on me so I don't attack the librarians." He laughed.

Gladys wasn't laughing. He had articulated one of her worst fears, but he'd done at least as well as her lately. "Just take a shooter before you go. And call an Uber. Your driving is atrocious. I'm off to bed now, Ethan. I suggest you do the same."

"Back to my closet under the stairs where all the unloved children live," he said with dramatic forlorn misery, but grinned at her.

19. FACE OFF

Karen quivered like an over-tightened bowstring when Gladys and Ethan arrived at the weekly VFW meeting. Her yellow pad was balanced on one crossed knee, and she clenched a pen in her fist without mercy.

Uh oh. This doesn't look good.

Surprisingly, Ethan picked up on Karen's energy. He stopped in the doorway as Gladys shambled into the hall. An icy breeze lifted her thin, tightly permed hair, like ruffling wild clover. Static electricity played across her arms. She shivered involuntarily and looked back at Ethan.

Ethan stood in the doorway with his arms wrapped around himself, looking nauseated.

Karen's short hair blew in wisps around her head, and she seemed to be hovering an inch above her chair.

Uh oh is right.

Gladys hesitated, then turned back to Ethan, who remained rooted in place, eyes wide. A whimper escaped his lips as she tugged the sleeve of his T-shirt to get him moving. Heat waves danced before the hovering woman, and the air had a coppery tang to it.

"Karen," Gladys nodded to her in greeting. "How's it going?"

"Fine," she said. But her teeth were clenched together, and her incisors were looking decidedly long.

"Uh huh. You don't look fine." Gladys gripped the back of the chair and sat down with a groan. She rubbed at her right knee and frowned.

"*I'm* not the one with the problem." Karen turned her attention to the pad on her lap and resumed her furious scratching. She could have been carving the words out of a chunk of maple.

"Okay. You want to talk about it?"

"Let's wait for Hans to arrive, shall we?" she said, without looking up.

Ethan squirmed on the metal folding chair, looking like he would have been happy to be anywhere but in the VFW. Maybe Gladys should teach him a little bit about shielding at least. Surely no harm could come from that. Karen's anger was a tangible thing, hot and metallic. Ethan must have been awfully uncomfortable.

Gladys was glad it wasn't directed at her, but she closed her eyes and shielded herself anyway. She visualized a shroud surrounding her body; like a jelly-filled bag where some things could enter through osmosis, but some couldn't. Each vampire used a different strategy, their own helpful imagery, but the result was the same.

The wheeze of the old air conditioner was the only sound in the room until Hans came through the door. As usual, it swung harder than he intended and smacked into the wall.

Ethan ducked and covered his head. Once he realized he wasn't dead, he lowered his arm and looked pleadingly at Hans to…what? Protect him? Gladys seriously doubted Hans would pull him into an embrace, pat his head, and tell the world not to be so hard on the boy.

"Why are we quiet? Who has died?" Hans flashed a rare German grin at them, lopsided and without much enthusiasm.

"No one *died*, Hans," Karen said through her teeth. Her jaw line became chiseled iron, and Gladys could see muscles twitching under her skin. "But that could change."

Hans shifted his gaze from Karen to Gladys, then to Ethan. Understanding filled his face. "Ah. I see we are still angry with the boy, yes?"

"You could say that."

Gladys stood, staggered, and then regained her footing. "Look, I know you're pissed at Ethan, so let's talk about it and get it all over with. Then we can get on with things."

Karen pointed her pen at Gladys, who'd moved a little, so she was between the small angry woman and the clueless teenager. Tiny, invisible ants bit at her skin.

"You want things to be better? You uncomfortable with the anger around here? Is that it?" Karen asked.

"Actually, yes," Gladys replied carefully. "That's part of it."

"Until that…thing over there," she threw a red-hot glare at Ethan. Her irises filled with what looked like arterial blood. "Can learn to have a little bit of respect for his elders, I reserve the right to hold on to just as much anger as I want."

Suddenly, Gladys pictured herself as a mediator in a hotly contested divorce. One of those celebrity breakups where everything is televised, and you find out way more about people's personal lives than you ever wanted to know.

Ethan looked everywhere except at Karen, who seethed like a viper. Gladys felt sorry for him.

"Ethan?" Gladys said. Her voice was low and calming.

"What?" He looked up at her and seemed on the verge of tears.

"Do you have something to say to Karen?"

"Is time for apology. Contrition," Hans chimed in.

Gladys bit the side of her cheek to keep from smiling. Hans would have dragged Ethan to the confessional at Saint Mary's by now, had he not been barred from church entry under threat of spontaneous combustion.

"Do it. You'll feel better. So will our friend." He gestured to the tempest that now hovered a full six inches above her chair. Every muscle was flexed until her whole body seemed like a fist.

"I'm sorry, geez," Ethan said as he raked his fingers through his greasy hair. "I don't even know what I'm sorry for, but I'm sorry, okay?"

"Not. Good. Enough." Karen said.

The draft in the hall picked up, and a breeze blew loose papers off the podium at the front of the room. Dust kitties ran for cover and the pages of Karen's note pad flipped by themselves.

"Ethan, think about it," Gladys said as gently as she could. She was getting freaked out by this display of aggression. It was true that Karen was kind, soft-spoken, and sweet. But she'd also killed a whole family inside their camping tent one night shortly after her life reversal. Gladys hadn't seen it, of course. Karen had been turned long before either she or Hans had had their own misfortunate encounters, but she remembered very well the look on Karen's face when she'd told the story.

"Are you still hung up on that stupid Karen thing?" He actually laughed.

Gladys could have shaken him. He had no idea what he was dealing with, even now. Couldn't he feel it?

It was time for him to be educated. Gladys stepped away and allowed the full force of Karen's energy to hit Ethan.

His short hair—not slicked back a-la-Astaire style tonight—blew back from his face. His lips flapped and his eyes flickered open and closed like he was standing in front of a jet engine. Fear filled his face, and his mouth dropped open. Fangs descended from his upper gums. Fear was too small a word, Gladys decided. Terror was a coat that Ethan wore now, and it was time for her to keep herself out of it and let things play out. She might end up short a tenant or a best friend before the sun rose, but that was up to fate, not her.

Karen's arms extended away from the sides of her body. She rose on the updraft of her fury.

Ethan leaned back, trying to distance himself, until his chair fell over with a crash and a clatter. He went sprawling onto his back and bumped his head on the chipped linoleum.

She hovered five feet like a cover model for a superhero comic, except she wore a pink and white flowered shirt and dark pink capris pants instead of spandex.

Ethan's hands rose to cover his face, and Gladys saw that his nails had grown and sharpened into talons.

Hans jumped to his feet, but Gladys grabbed his arm to hold him back. He whirled to face her, and she only shook her head. Hans turned to watch the whole Show Case Show Down.

If one of them didn't win, they'd find a truce. She hoped.

An ungodly shriek filled the room as Karen's lower jaw unhinged itself. Corded muscles and tendons stood out in her neck as she drew nearer to the dumb kid on the floor. Her face was horror unmasked. Crazed eyes filled with burning hate, hollowed cheeks, eyes sunken. A snarling monster.

Ethan took his hands away from his face and Gladys was dismayed to see small flames flickering inside his eyes. that could easily burst into a forest fire. He got slowly to his feet, never looking away, and then stood tall before Karen. His hands were clenched, and blood flowed from his palms.

"OK. I. AM. SORRY! SORRY I CALLED YOU THAT!" He advanced on her, and although his anger was sufficient, his experience wasn't. He rose a half foot into the air and then whatever puppet strings controlled his body broke and he fell to the floor.

Karen descended to land softly on her toes in front of him. The wind died down. Her face slowly returned to its former shape. The energy in the room dissipated. She reached down for Ethan's hand.

With his face full of wonder, he took the offered hand and allowed mild-mannered Karen, former manager of the Iowa City DMV, to help him back to his feet. She dusted off the seat of his pants as if he was a toddler who'd fallen in the dirt and righted his chair.

"I think we understand one another now, don't we?" She sounded as sweet as sugar.

Ethan swallowed. "Yes, ma'am. I believe we do. And I'm so sorry, okay? I'm really sorry I insulted you. I never meant to." He held up his hand to ward off the opposition Karen hadn't offered. "But just because I didn't know doesn't mean it didn't bug you. So, I'm sorry. I won't do it again. Promise."

Karen pulled Ethan in for a hug, cradling his head against her small chest even though he was easily four inches taller than her. "I know you won't." She looked up at Gladys and winked, but Gladys could still see the fire behind her eyes. She knew Ethan wasn't all the way out of the woods, and if he wanted to live to see his twentieth birthday, he needed to make sure never to slip up again.

20. QUEEN OF THE DMV

After the dust settled from Ethan and Karen's little tête-à-tête and Gladys righted the chairs, they resumed the weekly meeting as if nothing had happened. As if there hadn't just been an otherworldly battle of wills that could have left Karen or Ethan dead. Or all of them, if Gladys or Hans couldn't have kept themselves from stepping in.

Everyone in the group came to a consensus; it was time for Karen to tell her tale. Ethan's could wait. He needed to know the truth. Gladys had already heard it. Ethan was about to understand that they all had one very unfortunate thing in common, aside from needing a swig of blood every day and having a serious sensitivity to the sunlight. Estelle.

After roll call and confessions (Hans confessed to staring at a customer's collarbone for too long and had needed to go out to his car for a nip from a spare bottle he kept in the glove box. His Catholic guilt dripped from every stilted, German word. Gladys mentioned the incident that—thanks to Ethan's big mouth—everyone knew about already.) Karen stood, still vibrating a little, offered the group a tight smile, and began.

"In my other life, I worked at the Johnson County DMV. I loved my job, although the building was a bit run down. The Iowa river had overflowed its banks, drowned half the town, and flooded out the rest in 1990. After the water receded, Emergency Management declared that the office had been "cleaned and sanitized." It reopened in the spring of '91. The dank, musty odor remained, as did my suspicion that little mold spores had been deposited and were growing inside the walls and behind the baseboards.

"'Hey, girls!' I say when I walk in through the employee entrance. If I had realized what was in store for me that day, I'd have gotten right back in the car and gone home.

"The three lovely women I work with reply with a cheerful 'Morning!' like a rehearsed chorus. I smile as I breeze through to the break room, but wrinkle my nose when I stow my lunch in the communal fridge. It's funky in here too and it desperately needs to be cleaned. Mysterious Tupperware containers have been shoved into the back and are now growing like junior high science experiments. They weren't left there by any of my girls. More likely it was Ed the security guy or the night auditor. I can't think of his name...Sidney? Sheldon?"

"Simon." Gladys replied dully.

Karen frowned. "Do you want to tell it?"

Gladys could detect an edge to her voice, her frustration lingering after the argument with the kid.

"Sorry, sorry. No. That's fine. Tell it your way, that's always the best. Didn't mean to interrupt."

Karen nodded.

"I decide to delegate this unpleasant chore to one of the girls. Their enthusiasm is genuine, even when they're assigned something as distasteful as cleaning out the fridge. They've told me enough that even though I'm the boss, they all adore what they think of as my 'sweet smile and pleasant attitude'. Which, according to them, makes our DMV the only DMV in the US that people don't mind having to go to. Good morale goes a long way toward dealing with the frustrated public day in and day out. I'm lucky to have them on my team.

"I'm wearing a brand-new outfit that was pretty pricy for me despite the discount, so I make a show of twirling into my desk chair and giving it a little spin so my pink skirt flares as I sit down. It's one of the things I liked about it so much. My makeup and hair are perfect, too, and I feel like a million bucks. Plus, it's springtime. The sun melting all the snow away for the year always puts me in a good mood. I wish I could play hooky and spend the day soaking in the sunshine at the park, but duty calls.

"I pull the cover off my computer, something we were privileged to have back in the day.

"'Love that skirt, Karen!' Melissa says with a genuine smile. 'It's so cute!'

"I twirl one more time for effect. 'Isn't it just? I got it last week at Maurice's. On sale.'

"This is something I said with traditional midwestern pride."

She looked directly at Ethan as she said this.

"Anything of quality purchased at a bargain price is a true accomplishment; worthy of a brag or two in this neck of the woods. It isn't how much you spend; it's how much you *don't spend* that makes people envious. Thriftiness and cleanliness are next to Godliness in the Tall Corn State."

Ethan was entranced by the story and this little side-step takes a moment for him to wrap his head around. "Uh-huh."

Karen frowned, clearly wanting more acknowledgment from him, but she continued her tale.

"'Well,' Melissa says, 'it looks so good on you!'

"I tuck a loose strand of hair behind my ear, not wanting a single hair out of place."

Gladys thought Karen's hair was a magnificent architectural wonder. It always looked exactly the same, and never fell out of shape. She'd been captivated by its obduracy when she first met Karen, but hardly noticed it anymore. It was as much a part of Karen, as her passion for pink.

"'How was bowling last night, Cindy?' I ask as I power on the IBM. Cindy is in her mid-fifties, divorced, and childless, and has only one love in her life—a ten-pound burgundy bowling ball she calls Rosie.

"Cindy huffs and blows her big bangs off her forehead. They barely move, thanks to copious amounts of Aqua Net. 'I was totally off my game. Never broke one-fifty.' She sticks out her tongue, her face twisted in disgust.

"'Aww, that's too bad,' I say. Nothing bums Cindy out more than a crappy bowling score. 'I bet you'll get your groove back next week, though.'

"'Always the cheerleader,' Melissa says. The perky little blonde has primary counter duty today and doesn't look thrilled about it, but she'll keep her customer service face on despite any crankiness that walks in the door.

"'Well, of course!' I say. 'I'm happy to celebrate my friends' major accomplishments.'

"'And if you had outside interests, I'd be sure to cheer you on as well.' Melissa winks.

"Although I'm the only one who's currently married, it never really seems to enhance my happiness. I feel like I spend most of the day complaining about Carl, but they never discourage me from blowing off a little steam. This is just about the only place I can, which just confirms my theory that marriage doesn't necessarily make you happier. I've even thought of asking him for a divorce, but there's the kids to consider—

"Melissa's chipper voice interrupts my downward spiral 'Is it time?' Melissa asks.

"I look at my Timex—a cheap anniversary gift from Mister Wonderful—and compare it to the clock on the wall. 'Two minutes. Places everyone! Places! The show is about to begin.'

"We all laugh. It's an old standby joke around here. Cindy unlocks the glass double doors and turns the sign around to say "OPEN".

"'Here we go,' I say and settle into my work day.

"It's fifteen minutes before our first customer arrives, dressed head to toe in white: white sweater, white linen slacks, wrapped up in a gauzy white shawl. A pair of gloves and a wide-brimmed hat, also white, complete the outfit.

"If it hadn't been 1991, I might have seen her as a character in a tampon commercial, or drug ad for some menopausal remedy. As it was, advertising medications on TV weren't a thing until 1997, and the only tampon ads featured girls barely into their teens gallivanting on a pristine beach with jaunty music in the background."

Ethan's face reddened—as much as the face of a bloodless walking dead person could anyhow.

"Melissa addressed the woman, 'Hello, may I help you?'

"The woman's reply is sharp, clipped, and irritated. 'Yes'.

"Her accent is not one I've ever heard before. I wonder where it comes from. I wonder how much trouble this one will be."

"Most people who come into the DMV aren't there because they want to be," Gladys pointed out.

Karen ignored her. She was deep into the memories and the enjoyment storytelling brought. Even if the story being told was awful. One need only look at how many people make a living off scary movies to know there is pleasure in horrible stories.

"So, the lady says, 'I need to get my driver's license renewed.'

"'Well, you're in the right place!'

"Melissa is being overly perky, trying to get on the lady's good side. She taps the keys and opens the database she needs. 'Do you have your current license with you?'

"'It expired, and I need a new one. That's why I'm here.'

"Melissa bends down and rolls her eyes toward Cindy as she pulls a clipboard from under the counter. She notices me watching and ducks her head a little bit like she's embarrassed, then slips a triplicate form under the clip and slides it across the counter. 'Okay, there's a few things we'll need in order to get you a new license if you don't have the old one. Would you perhaps have it at home? It would simplify things for you.'

"The woman in white glares at Melissa, 'I told you, no.'

"Melissa is no rookie, though, and pulls out the right forms, setting them on the counter in front of her. 'In that case, I'll need a photo ID, a social security card, and a birth certificate,' she uses a red pen to draw three red circles on the form and pushes it across the counter, 'which will get the process started.' Melissa smiles tentatively. 'Unless...you wouldn't happen to have those things with you today, would you?'

"The customer's lips thin into a line so fine it could be a scar. 'No,' she says. 'I don't have those things with me. Why would I? Who carries those around with them?'

"*People who don't have their previous license*, I think to myself. I'm trying to look busy, but really, I'm listening in, waiting for the moment I'll be summoned to smooth things over. We get at least one of these customers a day and they're never satisfied.

"The door opens with a little jingle of the bell and a man walks in with what can only be his teenage daughter. She looks nervous. They usually do.

"'I need to get my license,' the woman repeats. 'Today. It's crucial.' She leans forward and stares intensely at Melissa.

"'Yeah, I hear ya,' Melissa's words become slurry, 'but we need some documentation. Surely you can understand that. Is it possible for you to get these items? That's the only way...'

"Her voice seems distant even though she's just a few feet away.

"She drops her hands to her sides. 'Maybe you could...' Melissa swallows and sways on her feet. She grabs the counter for support. 'A passport. A passport would...you have a passport, right?' Her words taper off completely and she just stands there at the counter saying nothing at all.

"Something isn't right here in this scenario. I can feel it. And it isn't just the way Melissa seems like she's in a daze. It's the woman. She seems scary somehow. Unnatural, but that's ridiculous.

"The people in line look embarrassed, but also curious. I collect myself, getting ready for the moment I need to offer assistance, and smooth back my hair. That one little lock seems to be misbehaving today. And what's with that get-up, I wonder. No one around here dresses like that. Maybe California or Long Island or Martha's Vineyard...

"Hectic red splotches appear on the woman's neck and crawl upward toward her pale cheeks.

"I'm still watching, even though I don't want to get involved. I know I'll probably need to, though. I can see the signs.

"Melissa shrinks away from the woman on the other side of the counter. This is a big deal, because Melissa, although she's as nice as can be, is also surly, seldom intimidated, and direct to a fault. But not now. She walks backward until her butt bumps against my desk, nearly knocking my coffee cup to the floor. She turns to me, looking meek and powerless. Her hands look like they're wringing out a dishrag and her eyes are wide with fear. She opens her mouth and closes it when no sounds come out, pleading with me to take over.

"The woman shakes a finger at Melissa. 'I want to talk to your manager.'

"There they are. The magic words that mean it's finally time for me to do the manager thing.

"I whisper in Melissa's ear to go back to the break room and rest for a moment. She looks ready to faint. I gesture toward Cindy to help her in case she really does faint. And I want her to get away from the argument that's sure to follow.

"I approach with all the confidence I can muster. 'Hello. How can I help you?' I ask. I'm cordial but professional. I don't want her to think she can push me around.

"'I said I want to talk to a manager, not a secretary.'"

Hans rolled his eyes and crossed his arms.

Gladys could almost hear another one of his famous "young people are" or "Americans are" fill-in-the-blank statements. But he keeps it to himself.

"Now, this was the early nineties, mind you. It was a long time before gender equality, sexual harassment, and mansplaining were really a thing. Even so, I hated the attitude back then, and I hate it now. I'm angry and offended, but I still need to be professional. 'I am the manager, ma'am. Now how can I help you today?'

"She narrows her eyes and looks me up and down, assessing.

"'A woman manager?'

"My patience is starting to wear a little thin, but I keep it together.

"'Yes. Wonders never cease, do they? Now, if you'll allow me to—'

"'That girl,' the lady in white points at the door marked "private" that Cindy and Melissa disappeared through, 'told me I can't get my license renewed. Just what kind of place are you all running here? You're supposed to serve the public, are you not?' The lady's eyes aren't right. Her pupils seem to be growing larger and then smaller. Back and forth.

"I look away and, just to have something to do with my hands, I fiddle with some of the paperwork in the little file sorter on the desk. Then I see the Rules and Regulations form. I think this should do the trick. If she sees that it's not my rules, that it's just policy—"

"Ha!" Gladys barks and snorts. "I know how much good that does."

Karen flashes her a sympathetic smile.

"I turn the form around so the lady can see. 'If you look here, it shows each of the documents required.' I smile over the woman's shoulder at the father and daughter duo waiting on the plastic chairs lined up against the wall, at the two older ladies who came in just a second ago and are still milling around trying to figure out what they're here for, at the clock on the wall—anything to avoid making eye contact. I don't like those fluctuating eyes. 'Surely you have some of these documents. In a safe, somewhere? In a filing cabinet?' I feel my courage slipping.

"'I do NOT have those things sitting back at my home. I DON'T have a photo ID because my license is EX-PI-RED,' she enunciates.

"I feel my attention being pulled to the woman's face, but I can resist this. The feeling of that tugging is awful, but I concentrate on the form instead and soldier on. 'I'm sorry, ma'am,' I say. 'Do you happen to have your old license with you today?' My voice is so small it seems to come from miles away. In another century. My ears are so fuzzy, they feel like they're full of cotton.

"'I don't. as I told that other one.' She gestures toward the break room door. 'And don't call me ma'am. Have some respect.'"

"Respect? I thought I was being respectful. I take a deep breath. 'Alright, Mrs....'

"'It's MIZZ. Ms. Getty,' she says. She sweeps her hand, as if she was clearing the counter of invisible cracker crumbs. 'Ms. Estelle Getty. You won't forget it, believe me.'

"'I won't forget it,' I hear myself say. What's wrong with me? I shake my head to clear away the cobwebs that seem to have formed in my mind and I'm able to get control of myself. 'Ms. Getty, do you happen to have any form of identification at all?' Surely no one walks around without an ID of some kind. No adult would—

"''Here!' Estelle shouts.

"For a second, I think she's going to attack. I put my hands up as if the weird lady's going to punch me in the face right here in front of these people. Instead, she opens her white leather handbag and extracts a matching pocketbook. The material looks soft enough to be made of kittens. For a second, everything seems so out of sync that I actually think maybe her bag *is* made of kittens."

"Ooh! Was it?" Ethan asked.

Gladys smacked him lightly on the arm. The truth is, she was surprised that he'd been able to keep this quiet. Usually he'd be shouting questions, raising his hand, heck even his breathing was loud. He must be really invested. Or morbidly curious. Probably the latter.

"I don't know," Karen snapped. "I never really got the chance to investigate the question with the seriousness it deserved."

For a moment, Ethan seemed to ponder her response and then sighed with understanding. "Yeah, okay, I get it. Shut up, Ethan. No crosstalk." He looked glum.

Gladys had another one of those flashes of sympathy for the kid. It wasn't his fault he'd been the last one to leave the house with all the lights on and the doors unlocked.

Karen cleared her throat. "Ms. Getty pulls something out of a plastic sleeve. Tattered paper, yellowed with age and curling up at the corners. 'Here.' She thrusts it across the counter at me.

"As I examine the folded card, I understand the situation less instead of more. I can feel a line forming between my eyebrows that feels like a face cramp. The card's twice the size of a regular license and unlaminated. I open it, but I have to be careful because it's so ancient the edges are actually crumbling and the fold lines look like ancient denim, a moment away from fraying. The ink is faded, almost to unreadability, with a blurry black-and-white photo in one corner. It's the woman standing in front of me. I'm sure of it, but how could that be? She looks exactly the same, outfit and all. I'm trying to read the expiration date, but I have to squint, and it makes my head hurt. 'This expired in 1976,' I say.

"I'm completely bewildered by this ancient relic from a past long gone. I know what I'm looking at, of course, but I can't believe this woman thinks I'd honor this document. I look from the photo to the woman in front of me, and back again. The similarity is unmistakable.

"'Yes. So?' Estelle taps her foot impatiently. It echoes in the suddenly silent room.

"The few people in the lobby seem to be holding their breath. Someone thought to shut off the Muzak.

"'I've been...away. For a while. I was pulled over the other day and if I don't get my current license, I'm to be detained. Detained! Have you ever heard of such drivel?' Another hand flutter.

"My heart feels like it's gone to the races. I can feel her—*actually* feel her demanding that I look up into those blazing eyes. The urge is so strong that I squeeze my own shut tight just to keep them from defying me. I can feel it in my bones that looking at that alabaster face would be a terrible mistake.

"And then, just like that, the spell is broken. Behind me, Cindy, who must have returned to catch the finale of this spectacle, chuckles loud enough for me to hear. I'm thankful for the distraction, but now I'm afraid for her as well. I shoot her a look which must not have been a very "me" look because her eyes go wide, and her hand moves to her chest. I turn my head over my shoulder. 'Shut up and get out,' I say, and that's not a very friendly way to talk to a co-worker."

Ethan mumbled something.

Karen's eyes flicked to his. "What was that?"

"Nothing."

"No, not nothing. Spit it out. You wanted the floor? It's all yours."

He shook his head, refusing to make eye contact.

"Oh, no. You said something, now out with it." She crossed her arms over her chest.

Ethan shook his head again and mimicked locking his mouth shut and throwing away a key.

"He says that these women are not co-workers," Hans reported. "He said *employees*."

"What difference does it make?" Gladys asked. The night was wearing on and she was ready to be home with her feet up. "Get on with it." As soon as it was out of her mouth, she felt bad about being short-tempered. "Didn't mean for it to come out that way. I think I'm just tired."

Karen nodded once, then resumed.

"'I'm sorry for your difficulties, Ms. Getty,' I say. 'Truly I am.' At this moment, it is the truth. Like all truths, it hides in an unspoken desire, however. The desire to believe that none of this was really happening. *Am I about to give in?* It seems like it. Giving in is not an option. I need to stay in charge. Calm, but firm. That's the best way to handle situations like this. 'I don't want to be the one to tell you this, but I can't give you a new license based on just this document.' I push it back to her, making sure our fingers don't touch. I don't want her skin to come in contact with mine.

"Estelle taps the photo of herself on the open card. 'This is clearly me, so there shouldn't be a problem.' She looks at me with piercing dark eyes. It seems to me that even the whites have turned to black. *She's trying to pull me in again*!

"There's a throat-clearing sound behind me I recognize as Cindy's—when you've been smoking for twenty years, you develop your own, distinct hacking cough. I'm grateful for it right now because it might be the only thing that's keeping me from falling under whatever spell this is.

"The door jingles as the two older women decamp for parts unknown. Maybe they'll come back later. Maybe they won't. At this point, I don't care. I just want Estelle out of my DMV.

"Estelle sniffs, as if the air offends her. Maybe it does. The ancient smells of river and mildew offend all of us day in and day out, but I don't think that's what she's scenting. The woman tries a new, more patronizing tactic. 'Perhaps there is a different manager I could speak with? Someone who's above you? Someone who knows what he's doing?'

"He, again. As if women are incapable.

"'I am the manager. First last and foremost.' My courage is like tattered flags fluttering in the wind, but I will not let this woman intimidate me. She's scary for reasons I can't articulate. I'm not afraid of being yelled at, of being disrespected—that happens all the time. But this one, she's just...scary. There's no other word that fits.

"I feel my eyes being pulled back in as Estelle's oscillate from dark brown to a black that's almost red.

"*It's just an illusion. Isn't it?*

"Estelle snatches the ancient license and plastic envelope off the counter and turns in a military-style about face. 'You'll hear from me!' She nearly collides with the dad-and-daughter team who've come in for a learner's permit or her first license.

"The girl yelps as her elbow is clipped in the wake of the white gale whirling past.

"I hold tight to the counter for a moment while I catch my breath.

"The dad is staring at me in disbelief.

"I shrug as if this happens every day. 'Excuse me for a moment, please. We'll be right with you.'

"'Take your time,' he says and ushers his daughter to a chair as far away from the door as possible, as if the lady would come back and finish what she started.

"I turn toward the employee lounge and Melissa steps aside so I can enter, then shuts the door quietly behind us. 'Well, that was a heck of a thing.'

"She laughs shakily. 'You alright?'

"I take a few deep breaths. 'Melissa, go out and help the two out in the lobby, would you? Cindy, you could go as well. I just need a minute, but in the meantime, let's get back to work. I'm sure Ms. Getty will come back when she gets all her ducks in a row.'

"Melissa pats my shoulder as she makes her way back to her desk. 'You handled it like a pro.'

"I still feel unsteady, but already the fear that I felt seems out of proportion to what just happened. I was jumping at shadows but it's over now.

"I take a moment in the bathroom to touch up my makeup and fix that one darn lock of hair, then I go back to the desk like nothing at all has happened. The rest of the day is fairly uneventful—only two unsatisfied customers, one sketchy dude in a Def Leppard T-shirt who I dub Heavy Metal Larry, (he proceeds to ask Melissa out on a date), and a not-guide-dog who accompanies his owner and defecates on the floor when they were asked to leave. Typical, in other words.

"As soon as the little hand points at four and the big one at twelve, I flip the sign around and lock the door. After I shut down the computers and finish the day's reconciliation, I close up, feeling mentally exhausted.

"The girls left a half hour ago, and now that queasy-uneasy feeling is coming back, though I can't say why. I walk across the parking lot with my keys fanned out between my fingers, a trick I learned in a self-defense class after a series of muggings on this side of town. I don't notice the shadow of someone walking behind me, even though I'm watching everywhere. I don't notice because, unbeknownst to me at the time, Estelle Getty is incapable of casting a shadow.

"The first hint I get that I should have paid more attention to my heebie-jeebies is a whisper in my ear. Tiny hairs on my earlobe flutter with the breath of the unseen whisperer. I whip around, brandishing my keys as a weapon to stab the Def Leppard T-shirt guy who I'm sure is responsible, but there is no one. Just my imagination, after all. It's been that kind of a day.

"The DMV building blocks out the last few minutes of the sunset. Spring is knocking on the door despite the snow, and I'm mentally planning summer activities with the kids and with Carl, if I can convince him to take a few moments away from work or the TV, that is.

"That's when I see a flicker of movement out of the corner of my eye. I turn toward it. It's over in the bushes somewhere and I bounce on the balls of my feet, ready to fight off the person who's about to come bounding out of them wielding an axe or a machete, or sprint back to the safety of the office. But again, there's nothing there.

"The streetlights flicker on, coming to life automatically in the twilight. My breath looks like the steam from an old locomotive."

A sharp whistle pierced the silence in the hall. Everyone jumped, and Karen let out a tiny squeak. Ethan, whistling in awe at the circumstances, had just scared the shit out of everyone present. If they could shit, that was.

"Jesus Christ on a Crutch, Ethan!" Gladys shouted. "Can you please just can it until she's done? Then you're welcome to whoop and holler all you want."

"It's okay, Glad," Karen said. "It's quite an unusual story. At least, it would be for people who weren't here getting support for their sun allergy." She smiled, but it was wistful and sad and very far away. "I'm almost done, anyway." She took a deep breath, closed her eyes for a moment, and then opened them again. The sadness in them is almost unbearable.

"The car is just a hundred yards away, and that thought eases my nerves a little. Just three hundred feet and I'm safe and sound. When I reach the door and turn the key in the lock, a tap on my shoulder makes me let loose a shriek. I spin around, ready to use my keys to scratch the face off of whoever is going to rape, rob and murder me, but they're still stuck in the lock. I grab them with both hands and try to get them free, but my hands are shaking.

"I'm still scanning the area for whoever touched me, but it's no good. Isn't this what always happens in the movies? The door won't unlock, or the car won't start? No one stands behind me with a rag doused in chloroform. I relax my grip on the keyring and extract them easily. Amazing what adrenaline can do to mess up your thinking. A little laugh escapes me, and I can hear my heartbeat like thunder in my temples. I break out in an instant sweat, even though the evening temperature has dropped to the forties. I reach up to wipe off the little dots of perspiration on my forehead and that's when my purse falls and hits the ground. Everything scatters from Hell to breakfast.

"*Dammit!* Now I'm more irritated than afraid, which feels a whole lot better. I crouch down to scoop everything back in, arranging my skirt so my knees are covered and no one's going to get a free show. I feel under the car and find my lip gloss, wallet, and everything except the kitchen sink, and then I hear the can of hairspray rolling away. That's when my hand brushes against something cold and hard. There's a sharp point at the end of that something.

"I look up and there is the towering visage of Estelle Getty, who seems to have gained two feet of height. The pointy object is a white patent leather pump. I can't scream. I can't breathe. The taut face of the first visitor of the day to the DMV is now a terrible rictus. Lips drawn back from pointed teeth that glint in the overhead lights are the last thing I see before the pain starts. And after the pain is a languid, almost sexual acquiescence that overwhelms me, more than Carl ever did. Something is placed against my lips that smells like spring lilacs. I suck it in and drink, swallowing the sweet elixir on offer. But then I detect a tang beneath that taste, and as I look up, a creature in a white dress suit is cackling madly. I lose consciousness and awaken hours later in the driver's seat of my car.

"My pink sweater is stained scarlet."

21. HOME IMPROVEMENT

"I knew you could fly," Ethan said from the passenger seat as he and Gladys headed home.

"What you think and what's true are two very different things," Gladys said. The windshield wipers screeched each time they wiped right. The rain wasn't hard enough to warrant their use, but too hard to drive safely without them.

"Looked like it to me," He mumbled. He scrunched down further into the seat and crossed his legs with his calves on the dashboard, fingers steepled beneath his chin.

Gladys glanced over and then back at the road. She bent over the steering wheel like an ogre looking for a fresh, tasty princess to devour. All she wanted to do was get home. The evening had been emotionally draining. "Look, don't go getting any ideas, okay? The kind of anger and energy it takes to levitate like that takes years and years to develop."

"Well, then I better get started now."

"You're impossible! Do you have any idea how close you came to being torn apart?"

"Karen wouldn't have done tha—

Gladys slapped a meaty hand on her thigh. "You don't know shit one about Karen and what she's capable of. You really should count your blessings."

"Oh, yeah. Like, I'm totally blessed. Look at me. I have pizza face acne and it's not gonna get better no matter how many Stridex pads I use. Which, by the way, I'm out of and we need to get some more next time we go to the store."

"Dammit, Ethan, you're not listening."

"I'm listening." He closed his eyes.

"You're listening but you're not *hearing*," she reached over, lightning quick, and whapped the back of his head with her open palm. Not hard. Just for emphasis. "This is the time to clear your mind of that constant carnival that goes on back there and focus. Can you please focus?"

"Yeah," he said, sulking.

"You don't know it, but there was a big part of the story Karen didn't get to tonight. Can you guess what that might have been?"

A little smile crossed his face. "Yeah. I wish I knew what happened after."

Gladys pulled over to the side of the road and threw it in park. "What happened after? You want to know?" She turned toward the kid in the seat beside her. "The day after she was turned, she kinda went nuts. She went really nuts. She had a husband and two kids. Did you catch that?"

Ethan shook his head.

"Well you should learn to listen better. What she didn't say was that she went home that night, after she came to in the car. She went to bed and in the morning, she stayed in bed; said she was sick. Which was true, of course. She slept until that evening and when she woke up, the hunger was on her. She chased the kids, chased her husband, though what I know of him he was no prize. They fled to the car and locked themselves in."

Gladys looked away for a moment, remembering the look on Karen's face as she told her story. "She attacked the car, scratched at the windshield, tried to get at the kids through the back windows. She never saw them again. They took off and never went back. Carl changed their names. You've seen her now—when her face changes?"

He nodded and swallowed the lump in his throat. He'd gotten considerably paler. Ethan nodded.

"Imagine what that might have been like to a six-year-old." She let that sink in for a moment before continuing. "She stayed inside the house that night and the next day, sick with shame. But there was a greater sickness brewing. That evening…" Her lips pressed into a line so thin they seemed to have disappeared.

Ethan waited. Just as he feared Gladys wouldn't continue, she resumed.

"That night—the second one after she was attacked—she drove around the countryside just south of here, looking for answers and no doubt hating herself. Eventually she ended up out by Hills Access. Just wanted to contemplate the river, but there's a little campground there, too. You know the place?"

"Yeah," he croaked. He cleared his throat. "I've been there. My dad used to take me fishing."

"Well, you should feel fortunate that you weren't there that day. She went on a rampage. Tore through six tents and fifteen people. All of them shredded—the tents and the people. They said it was a bobcat. Or a cougar. Everyone knew a bobcat couldn't have done that much damage. What else could they say, though? I'm sure the police just wanted to keep everything quiet because they didn't have a single clue. One of the victims was only four years old."

Ethan looked like she'd slapped him across the face. "Are you serious?"

"Yes, of course I'm serious. If you value your life, you'll never say one word about this. There's a reason she didn't talk about it. I'm sure you can imagine."

He nodded, but Gladys grabbed his hand in a crushing grasp. "Not. One. Word." In the glow from the dashboard, he looked green. Gladys could tell there was a serious reevaluation going on underneath his pimply surface. It was a hard truth at the beginning, having to constantly realign what you thought you knew, changing from your old reality to your new one.

She released his hand and turned back toward the windshield. She wiped her eyes and then put the car back into drive and continued toward home.

The silence in the car drew out and finally Gladys said "So, how's the remodeling plan coming along?"

Ethan perked up and sat upright in his seat. "Oh, I have big plans."

"Like the ones you showed me?"

"Better."

Gladys woke the next evening and headed straight for the shower. Ethan lounged in her favorite chair while she puttered about, getting ready for work. He'd taken vacation time so he could work on his building project. She'd be leaving him to his own devices for the week, a nerve-wracking thought. There came a point at which you had to give kids a little leeway. This would be his first real trial of alone time.

Once dressed—tonight's tent-size uniform had giddy green frogs galivanting across her boobs—she prepared for her shift. Her white nurse's shoes squeaked as she went back and forth from the kitchen to the bathroom, to her own room. She watched Ethan carefully, trying to glean his level of hunger as she readied herself. He was hard at work with a pencil and pad of paper, one foot slung over the recliner's arm. The look of deep concentration was almost comical.

"Comfy?"

"Huh?" He looked up, barely focused on anything other than his makeshift blueprints and then turned his attention back to his work. His tongue stuck out the side of his mouth. He could have been her own son, working on his social studies homework after school so long ago.

She tipped her whiskey shooter into her mouth and swallowed. "Whatcha got there?"

"Want to see?" He looked like a five-year-old with a crayon drawing; eager and full of desire to please.

She shuffled over and leaned in to see his work. A pop and thunk in her right knee made her grimace. She swore under her breath.

"You alright?"

"These knees are going to be the death of me."

"Why don't you just get them fixed?"

Clearly, he had not thought the problem out to its inevitable end. Sure, the doctors could replace her knees, but what would they say when her bones reverted back to their current condition? When, the next day in recovery, her fancy new knees got pushed out by her bone regeneration and sent a team of nurses and medical assistants screaming into the parking lot, only to return with torches and burn the place down with her inside. "Can't do that, Ethan. Think about it."

He did, giving the question due diligence. "Oh. Oh yeah. Sorry."

She waved it away. "Tell me what you've got here."

"Okay, so this is your half of the basement, and this is my half." He pointed with the pencil.

She didn't correct him by reminding him that both halves of the basement were actually hers.

"I know you said you didn't want a bunch of fancy stuff, so here's what I put together for you." The drawing in front of him was actually very good. A wooden box (she refused to call it a coffin) stood on a pedestal, flanked by electric chandeliers on either side. Heavy drapes lined the concrete block wall, obscuring its white brick. The hardwood floor had a dark red, Turkish rug in the center.

The box itself had a whole side that lowered and steps that folded out automatically. "This is so you can get up into bed easier."

She saw the ingenious design and realized he had made it so that she could be spared any embarrassment or indignity when it came to getting herself in and out of the thing.

"The whole inside is gonna be velvet." Ethan tapped the eraser end of his pencil with a faraway grin. "A nice soft pillow for your head, and it's padded all the way around. So it's a lot more comfy. More comfy than that tarp."

She didn't burst his bubble by reminding him that she wouldn't know if she was comfortable or not, as the undead have no feelings during their solar slumber.

"The outside I'll finish with oak and stain a nice medium-dark color. I didn't think you'd want something that looked heavy like mahogany or maple."

"It's beautiful, Ethan." She smiled. He blushed a little bit—as much as he could. There was only so much blushing a vampire could pull off without a full feeding. The shooters just took the edge off. They were always hungry, deep down. "Really, I mean it. This is just so...so nice."

"Well, it's the least I could do for letting me stay here."

"What about you?"

He grinned, showing his teeth. "Wait'll you see." He got up and padded toward the dining room table. His cotton pajama bottoms were a little too loose around the hips for her taste. He unfolded a giant piece of paper that took up most of the space.

"How long have you been working on thi—," she stopped and stared. "Ethan...really?"

What he had put together looked like a combination sex den and castle, straight out of Bram Stoker's Dracula. Crushed red velvet everywhere, a huge coffin-shaped coffin (*you could fit two in there*. She shuddered, not wanting to form a mental picture of any kind). Any exposed wall was to be covered in faux limestone blocks. Arched doorways added to the castle effect.

"Yeah. Really. I always wanted to be cool, so now I'm gonna be. Even if no one will ever see it, I'm the Vamp Vamp Vamp of Iowa City and the Seducer of All Its Virgins."

"Oh?" Gladys asked.

"Yeah," Ethan said. His enthusiasm was not to be deterred.

"Okay, well I have to get to work. You're going to be a good boy? No funny stuff? Stay in the house?"

"Yeah. Except I'm gonna have to go to the library. I have to order all this stuff."

"Well, call someone to pick you up. Hans or Karen, I don't care which. You can't drive worth a dang." She didn't add that there was no way she would trust him around people unaccompanied. He wasn't ready for that. She looked over at his supply list. It was very, VERY long. "How are you planning to pay for all that?"

"Yeah. About that. Can I have your credit card?"

22. THE BAT BOY OF MILLER PARK

Halfway through her shift, Gladys felt that little tingle; more than instinct, more than a hunch, but it wasn't alarm. At least, not yet. She brushed it aside when Elmer Brenneman hollered for her to come get him off the pot and wipe his arse. It was the fourth time he'd taken a dump since she arrived on shift, but it only amounted to a couple of poop-berries each time he went. She got him cleaned up and back in his chair, and she'd almost escaped fully when he called after her.

"Nurse Ratched, ya a got anything for piles?"

"Sure." She sighed, hating the dreaded nickname he couldn't seem to stop using, no matter how many times she told him to stop. Eventually, she stopped bothering and just accepted it. What he really needed was some Miralax and a stool softener, but the old coot refused to take them. She wished she could tell him he was full of shit.

That itchy, twitchy feeling washed over her again. Anxiety shot through her veins, making her tremble and her upper lip sprouted little dots of perspiration.

Ethan!

There could be no other explanation. She felt that tingle like a psychic tuning fork vibrating at his frequency. In the med room she opened the topicals cabinet and found the packets of Preparation H for Elmer's broken butthole. A jolt of hot electricity shot up from her feet to her hands and she dropped the bum butter on the floor with a gasp.

"Glad? What's wrong honey?" Sheila stuck her head in the med room, looking concerned. "You went all funny there for a minute."

Gladys put her hand out on the counter to steady herself. "It's fine. Everything's fine." But it wasn't fine. Nausea crept up her throat and her hands felt like microscopic earthquakes. "I'll just sit for a bit and get some charting done. Have a little something. Maybe it's blood sugar. Could you take those to Elmer?" She bit the inside of her cheek to keep from cracking a smile at her unintentional blood sugar joke and pointed to the scattered packets of ointment on the floor.

"Well, okay. If you're sure." Sheila gave her a worried look. "Is there anything I can do?"

"Just help Elmer with his ointment."

Sheila bent to collect the hemorrhoid cream.

"Thanks. I'm sure he'll be most appreciative."

"It's no problem." Sheila said, and went off to help her patient.

Gladys sat down at the nurse's station. As much as she wanted to shrug this off, she was pretty sure something was about to hit the fan, and it wasn't going to be Elmer Brenneman's great bowel breakthrough. It could be paranoia, like a mom who'd left the kids at home alone on the first day of summer vacation.

I'll just call. If he's at the house, he's fully capable of answering the phone.

Sheila and the other night nurse they'd dragged in from another floor were nowhere in sight. She punched in the numbers that would surely put Ethan's quavery voice in her ear. The phone rang five times before her ancient answering machine picked up. She didn't leave a message.

Shit! Where are you?

Ethan had said he needed to go to the library to use the computer, but Gladys had made him promise to go with Hans or Karen. She doubted that he would have called Karen after hearing the rest of her story. He wasn't ready to go solo, and she wasn't sure it was safe for Karen to be his wing man. Or woman. Whatever. She wasn't sure Karen was completely over the fiasco at the VFW and the anger inside her was a vicious monster barely kept in check. Most of the time. If Ethan slipped and said something stupid again, that just might be the end for him.

Gladys tapped her pen on the counter, fighting the compulsion to run out the door, get in her car and drive around the city hollering his name out the car window.

And how, exactly, did you get yourself into this situation, anyway? Whose fault is this? You got nobody to blame but yourself, lady.

She picked the phone up again and called Hans. No answer there, either. Was he working tonight? She couldn't remember, but it was worth a try. She dug the dusty old phone book out of a bottom drawer and looked up the number for Hy-Vee on Governor Street. A jaunty robot voice took the time to remind her that the Fourth of July was fast approaching, that the deli would be more than happy to take her order for party trays and pre-made salads. After this shameless advertising spiel, the disembodied voice reaffirmed that there was, indeed, a helpful smile in every aisle, before it switched back to Muzak.

Finally, a real person answered. They sounded bored. "Hy-Vee, North Governor Street."

"Hello, I'm sorry to bother you, but I'm calling for Hans Klauffman?"

"Who?"

"Hans. Hans Klauffman. In produce?" The fight-or-flight response was quaking through her, and she gripped the phone tighter in her hand.

"Oh, sure. Hang on." The Muzak resumed, followed by the same goading encouragement to really do up the next Fourth of July party. It circled all the way through a rather somber version of *Night Fever* and then she was graced with Cyndi Lauper's, *Time After Time*, arranged for the Beige-Clad White Boys. She wished she could reach through the phone and shake the customer service agent who put her in the land of eternal hold. *Was* Hans working? She didn't think he was—hoped he wasn't. If Hans was at Hy-Vee, where was Ethan? She'd given him strict instructions to stay home unless he had a chaperone.

She drummed her fingers maniacally and checked her watch. Six minutes now. Ray Charles was next in her ear. He'd have turned over in his grave if he'd heard what they'd done to massacre his masterpiece that was *I Got a Woman*.

Where is everyone?

If she couldn't get Hans in the next couple of minutes, she'd call Karen. It was ten-thirty. The library had closed two-and-a-half hours ago. Perspiration trickled down her sides, reminding her of a slow-drip IV bag.

Elmer's call light went on. He was probably ready to recommence whatever miniature loaf pinching activity he'd been working on all night. She flipped it off and ignored it.

Hurry up, hurry up!

"Hello. Thank you for calling Hy-Vee stores. This is produce manager, Hans. How may I help?"

Shit!

"Hans, it's Gladys," she said, speaking quickly and formulating a plan to get out of work and go find her juvenile roommate. "Have you heard from Ethan?"

"Ethan calls to say he needs help going to library. I pick him up, I drive him to library, I drop him off."

"Well did you give him a ride back home?"

Hans sounded irritated at being interrogated. "No, I have work, as you know. He said he would get ride home on bus."

"Well, he's not home!" She looked around the nurse's station. No one was present, but that didn't mean she could sit and yell into the phone. She lowered her voice. "We need to go find him. I think..." What *did* she think? She thought that her young friend was about to get himself into a serious pickle. Something dangerous for him or for the public, she didn't know. But now she was certain. That little tickle was now a bass drum from a marching band booming within the confines of her skull. Panic rose like stomach acid after a spicy burrito, and she took a deep breath to keep herself under control.

"I cannot leave now," Hans said.

Of course he couldn't. His perfect German work ethic didn't allow him to sign out of a shift even a minute early. So predictable.

"Fine. Okay, I'll go myself."

"Call Karen. Perhaps she will be search for party with you."

"That's a search party."

"Whatever is you said. You and Karen will find boy and bring home. For now, I have orange beets to arrange. You understand? *Orange* beets. Who is liking those?"

"Look, I can't deal with this right now. I've gotta go." She hung up and started to get up, but then realized she had one more call she could make. Maybe Ethan had called Karen for a ride home.

Elmer's call light beckoned again.

Sheila emerged from Mrs. Foster's room and looked at the blinking call light beacon with a question in her eyes.

Gladys asked if she wouldn't mind getting it. "I feel pretty cruddy, actually. Maybe I'm coming down with something."

Sheila approached the station, and Gladys hoped she couldn't smell the feral coating of sweat she'd accumulated in the last twenty minutes.

"You go home. We can take care of the zoo for tonight. Go, get some rest." She patted Gladys' shoulder and went in search of the very constipated Mr. Brenneman.

Gladys picked up the phone as soon as Sheila disappeared and dialed Karen, praying she would be home. Or praying that she *wasn't* home and was out with Ethan at the Home Depot buying hardware. She answered on the first ring.

"Gladys?"

"Yeah, how did you know?"

"Had a feeling."

"You too?"

"Uh-huh. You want to pick me up, or do you need me to come get you?"

"Meet me at my house in twenty minutes. I need to get some things. I have a bad feeling about this."

"Me too."

Gladys hung up and collected her stuff. She stuck her head into the room where Sheila was currently assisting a very cranky patient back to his bed. She smiled in spite of her frantic need to get the heck out. "Success?"

Sheila nodded and dropped a wink. "Go on." She shooed Gladys out.

Gladys was more than happy to be gone.

Karen's headlights flashed across the front of Gladys' small ranch-style house. When she'd gotten home, she'd done a quick search inside and out, not neglecting to check over the fences on either side of the property. His remodeling plans were neatly stacked in little scrolls on the table, but his supply list was gone.

Had he made it to the library then? Hans had said so, but did he know *for sure?* Had he watched the kid enter the library? Or was it more of a drive by, telling him to tuck and roll as he slowed down to thirty and shoved the door open? The credit card she'd left on the table was gone. There was no sign of the boy.

Shit!

A number of possibilities ticker-taped through her head as she changed clothes. He could be at a stripper bar. He could be at the county fair. He could be...

Anywhere.

Headlights flashed across the living room window and for a second, she felt a wave of relief. He was back. But no. It was Karen. Ethan didn't have a car. Before she could knock, Gladys yanked the front door open. "He's not here."

"You're sure?"

"I looked everywhere. Let's go to the library. First, I mean. I know it's closed, but he could be lurking around in the park or something. Maybe someone saw him."

Library Park was loaded with unfortunate people who had nowhere else to go this time of the night, most of whom were just looking for a place to sleep. Many of whom utilized substances to help them obtain that sleep.

"Oh no. You don't think..."

"After the cat incident, I'm not about to rule anything out. Ethan could be..." Gladys shook her head.

Don't think about it.

She pulled on Karen's sleeve. "Come on! Let's get going!" She yanked Karen toward the car, still idling in the driveway.

At the library, Karen whipped into the closest parking spot, and they went to search Miller Park for a lanky vampire with a case of arrested development.

After a quick search, they concluded that Ethan wasn't there. The individuals lying in the grass adjacent to the library confirmed that he had, indeed, been there earlier. Gladys groaned inwardly. This couldn't be good. These people remembered him.

"Kid was raving by the time I got here," an older man said. His voice was a conspiratorial whisper. Spittle flew from between his few teeth as he enunciated. "He was kissing everybody. Like some weird sex fiend. Those ladies over there got a kiss." He cackled, gesturing with a grubby finger toward three women; two passed out on bedrolls and the other lying on a flattened cardboard box looking up at the sky with slack-mouthed wonder.

Gladys exchanged a look with Karen and raised her eyebrows in a question. Karen gave a tiny nod.

No bueno.

"Thanks for your time, sir," Karen said.

"Sir?" He shouted to his friends near the bushes. "She called me *sir*. Didja hear that?" He cackled maniacally, then turned back to Gladys and Karen. "You wouldn't have a cigarette on you, would ya? A little information's worth at least that, ain't it?"

"Sorry, I don't," Karen said, backing away with her palms out as if the man was going to get up in attack mode and maul her.

He was swaddled in a heavy jacket and had a bottle in a paper bag. He wasn't going anywhere. Besides, Karen had probably killed more people than this poor schmuck.

Gladys twitched the sleeve of Karen's lavender sweater. "Come on, let's get going." She rambled across the grass at a speed that was uncanny. She *could* be fast if it was required. She moved around the active sprinklers quickly, but with little grace. An onlooker might have thought she was enrolled in a deranged Arthur Murray dance course. The dewy grass kept an imprint of her progress.

"Don't you think we should talk to them? The women, I mean?" Karen looked back over her shoulder at the people who lived at the park when the sun went down. Were they really that much different from her group?

"There's no point. And the less I do to cement Ethan in their memory, the better. Christ! Where is that kid?" They'd reached the car and she stood against it with the fingers of one hand massaging her temple.

A police car drove by but didn't look like it was on its way to an emergency. It gave her a chill. What if they thought she was a drug dealer? And Karen was an addict?

"Should we just get in the car and drive around looking?" Karen was wringing her hands together like a damsel in a fifties drama.

"I mean, yeah. We could, but do you really think we'd just spot him? Maybe I should go back to the house, and you should stay and search."

Karen's eyes widened in alarm. "Oh no you don't! You can't leave me out here to find him on my own."

"Why? Are you afraid of him all of a sudden?" Gladys' voice was thick with irritation and impatience.

"No," Karen said in a small voice. "I'm afraid of *them*." She pointed over Gladys' shoulder.

Gladys turned to look in that direction and saw a group of five or six people heading their way. They weren't loud and raucous like people out on the town having a good time. They were quiet. Nearly silent. She could almost see the elongated incisors in some of their mouths. One was wearing an acid-washed jean jacket loaded with patches. Her well-tuned eyes could see a button on the lapel—*will work for food*. Seeing others like themselves was rare, and this was a whole gang. They weren't exactly sending out positive vibes. Her skin prickled as if it was electrified. Whatever they wanted wouldn't be good for any of them. "Get in the car," she said.

Karen clicked the unlock button, but Gladys insisted on driving.

Karen reluctantly handed the keys over, and Gladys cranked the ignition and gunned it a little.

"Easy!" Karen said and strapped on her seatbelt with a look of fear.

Gladys reversed, and the back end of the car slewed slightly as she peeled out of the parking spot.

"Slow down," Karen said, grabbing the oh-shit handle and looking over her shoulder. "It's not like they can catch us. They were on foot."

"Sorry." She let up on the gas a little bit. "I just want to get out of this place as quick as possible. Not to mention, we need to find Ethan. God knows what he's up to."

"What were they?" Karen asked.

Not who, but what. Good fucking question.

"I have an idea. I don't think they were like the others. The bush-dwellers, I mean. They..."

"They felt different." Karen nodded. "I felt it too. Vampish. Let's go! We have to find Ethan, Glad. He must be freaking out by now."

Like I'm not.

The little car sputtered as they sped toward the square. She turned the corner where the pedestrian mall squatted in the middle of town and slowed to a crawl, eyes looking everywhere at once.

Karen grabbed the wheel when they became dangerously close to a collision with a parked Lincoln Continental.

Gladys corrected, nearly rear-ended another car, then came to a screeching halt. She gaped up through the windshield and felt her pulse quicken. There was a parking ramp up ahead. Below it, a crowd had gathered, their collective attention turned upward toward the top where a figure stood.

"What do you see up there?" She pointed but had to keep her eyes on the street in front of her. "You see someone freaking out? Or maybe someone doing something unforgivably stupid?"

Karen clapped her hands over her mouth. "Oh my God."

"Something unforgivably stupid, then. Got it." Gladys whipped into a handicapped parking space and groaned as she struggled with the door and the seatbelt. The last thing she wanted to do was walk all the way over there. She'd been one medical form away from her handicap permit before her run-in with Estelle. She leaned in and slapped the top of her car with an open palm. "Come on, come on!"

Karen's face was paler than usual—if that was possible. Her huge eyes looked like a frightened animal's. She shook her head and clutched at the seat belt.

Gladys leaned down to look Karen directly in eyes. "We *have* to! Do you think I want to go intervene in this madness? No! I want to go back home and put my feet up. But we need to do it before a cop comes. Now come on!"

Karen released her grip on the seatbelt with maddening slowness and finally exited the car. She nearly stumbled when Gladys grabbed her by the arm and yanked.

The excruciating pain in Gladys' knees impeded her first halting, running steps, morphing into more of a lurching Quasi Modo shuffle as she headed into the crowd. "You go up, and I'll stay down," she puffed.

Karen shook her head. "No, you go up."

"What? Why? We don't have time to argue."

"Because he trusts you, Glad." She put her hand on Gladys' shoulder. "It has to be you."

Gladys threw her hands up. She was right. "Fine." She gritted her teeth and handed the keys over in case Karen needed to make a quick getaway; in case things turned out badly. She turned to go, then turned back. "I mean, you can see how it is." She gestured to her misshapen and mostly useless legs, then turned away again and made her way over to the parking garage door as quickly as she could, hoping the elevator would be working and she wouldn't have to climb up ten flights of stairs. Ethan would be nothing but a puddle on the ground below by the time she got there, and she'd be a pile of flab and bones in the stairway.

"Ethan!" Karen had her hands cupped around her mouth and was looking up at the spectacle. "Get down!"

Ethan didn't look desperate or sad or depressed. Just the opposite; he looked euphoric, smiling like a lunatic and waving his arms around. And what was he wearing? Karen squinted, trying to make it out, but she couldn't. The darkness and the lights behind him made him nothing more than a silhouette.

The elevator *was* working, but Gladys cursed the thing for its snail-like pace. When she reached the top floor, the elevator doors creaked open as she pushed through. She smashed the crash bar on the door and burst out onto the top of the ramp. "Ethan!" She waved her hands furiously. "Get down off of there before you fall." She came toward him like a logging truck in low gear.

Ethan turned toward the sound of her voice and raised his arms, beaming a sunny smile.

Good God. He's high as a kite.

He was wearing a cape, though she couldn't have guessed where he'd found it.

"Ethan," she said through gritted teeth. "Get down off that damn ledge. They're gonna call the cops and they're gonna slam you into the mental ward at the hospital. Do I need to explain why this would be very bad for you?"

He giggled with his hands over his mouth like a toddler who'd just discovered the joy of mud puddles. "But I can fly! Look!" He raised the corners of the cape, a ridiculous caricature of a vampire in an old black-and-white movie.

Gladys held her hands out, palms facing her young friend like a traffic cop.

Ethan skittered on the edge and the noise of the people below intensified into a shocked and slightly anticipatory scream.

Vultures.

He wheeled his arms and finally caught his balance again. The gathered throng let out a chorus of disappointment.

Gladys ignored them. Her focus was pared down to just one thing: talking him off the ledge. "Get. Down. Now." She pointed to the flat tarmac of the parking level with one hand on her hip.

His smile melted, and he lowered his arms. He took a step off the wall toward her with his arms open for an embrace, looking forlorn and chastened, and fell flat on his face in between a Saab and a light post.

"Well, that's that," she said out loud to no one. She leaned over the wall of the parking garage and gave Karen the thumbs up. The crowd erupted into applause.

Fickle assholes.

She made a hand motion that suggested driving and was satisfied when she saw Karen heading back to the car. She helped Ethan roll over onto his back. His eyes were glazed over, and he had that idiotic smile plastered across his face again. Blood trickled from his nose. Her dentures began slipping, and she took a deep breath to calm herself. The smell of blood and the closeness of the encroaching crowd were awakening her primal hunger. There was enough attention on them as it was, without putting rumors of a vampire in the mix.

A few minutes later, she and Ethan reached the ground floor. The headlights of Karen's car doused them in a harsh light. Gladys supported him with his arm across her shoulders, hoping the dissipating crowd would think him a drunkard. She waved her hand in a come-on gesture.

Karen parked illegally and got out to help Gladys throw Ethan's useless, seemingly inebriated body in the back seat. "Let's go, Glad. Get us out of here before some curious so-and-so comes up to investigate." Karen ran around to the passenger side.

Gladys dropped into the seat with a groan and drove toward home and safety. The skyline was just beginning to turn the color that said dawn was not far off. She wondered what the junkie he'd fed off of had been using tonight.

23. IT'S ECSTACY WHEN YOU'RE NEXT TO ME

Ethan snickered to himself in the back seat all the way home, occasionally bursting into gales of baffling laughter. Karen let Gladys out in her driveway without further discussion of this nearly catastrophic escapade; the sun was coming soon and there was no time to get into it.

With great stumbling effort, Gladys helped Ethan into the house and shoved him into his closet.

Thank the gods that Arlyss isn't an early riser.

She had just enough time to get herself wrapped up in her cocoon before the sun breached the horizon and she became still for the day.

The next evening, Gladys rose and thudded up the stairs to the kitchen. Ethan hadn't stirred from his little warren, and she was glad she'd have time for a shower before the Come to Jesus Meeting. She needed reinforcements. Karen would arrive shortly, but she still needed to call Hans. Hopefully, he could make it before he had to head to Hy-Vee.

"Hans, I need you to come. Part of this is your fault, you know. You can spare me a half hour, can't you?" She spoke quietly, one ear listening for the sounds of creaking doors and shuffling of feet on the stairs.

"What is my fault? I have done nothing."

"That is *precisely* the problem. Now can you come over here or what?"

"I will make time for meeting, but there is no reason."

Gladys clenched her teeth and ignored the last part. "Fine, see you in thirty minutes." She hung up without waiting for further confirmation and headed to the bathroom.

She tossed the suction-cup non-slip mat down in the tub before stepping into the shower. A fall wouldn't do any lasting damage. Anything she could do to hurt herself would almost instantly revert to its previous form. It was the indignity of floundering naked in the bathtub, hollering for help that she didn't want to endure. Life was full of injustices. No need to add to it.

She stepped out into the steaming bathroom and swept her hand across the mirror out of habit. No reflection looked back.

She wondered, not for the first time, how Karen managed to look so perfect all the time. *Maybe she sleeps in formaldehyde.*

Wrapped in a furry green bathrobe, Gladys chuckled on the way into her upstairs bedroom and donned her scrubs. Today's pattern of enforced gaiety would be clowns. She sighed. It was past time to do some laundry.

She heard the TV from the living room and finished dressing, ran a comb through her baby-fine hair, and found Ethan sitting in the recliner looking dazedly at the news without seeing it.

"There you are," she said.

He turned the chair around with little tap-dancing movements of his feet. The look on his face came as a relief. The expression he wore was one of equal parts shame, illness, and contrition. Good. No arrogance or defiance. She put her hands on her hips, and they regarded each other in silence for nearly a full minute.

"Well?" she asked.

"Well, what?" He was putting up a good act, but she knew he felt guilty. Here was a great learning opportunity.

"You have any enlightening meditations on your actions last night?" She tapped one foot, clad in its Velcro-strapped orthopedic shoe.

"Man, I can barely remember what happened last night. I remember going to the library, having a couple of shooters, and then the rest of the night is a blur. What happened, anyway?"

"Hold that thought for a minute, won't you?" His statement gave her a little tickle in her mind, and she needed to go check something.

With the sound of popping ligaments echoing off the stairwell, Gladys got herself down the stairs and opened the mini fridge that she had only recently started to leave unlocked. There were two batches of Dr. Chip Cooke's bottles of blood in there. A few from the week before and a bag of fresh ones. She frowned. Ethan had untied the plastic grocery bag.

He must have gotten one of the new ones.

She frowned, took one bottle from each stash, then grabbed two more from the current week's supply, and hobbled back up the stairs.

"Have you had yours yet this morning?"

He shook his head, his feet pushed into the carpet, rocking the chair in tiny, compulsive movements.

She tossed him one of the older bottles and he snatched it out of the air. Even hung over as he was, his reaction time was getting quicker.

"Did you get last night's out of the door of the fridge, or out of the bag?"

"I got it out of the bag. That other stuff was starting to taste stale."

Gladys rolled her eyes. "Don't take anything else from the bag, got it? Last night might not have been completely your fault."

A small smile began to spread across his face.

"Not so fast," she said.

Ethan's smile froze before it could blossom into a grin.

"You're not off the hook yet." She left Ethan to drink and stew on his misdeeds and went to phone the hospital morgue.

"Chip speaking," a gruff voice said on the other end.

"Doctor Cooke. This is Gladys."

"I told you not to call me here," he snarled.

"Well, I don't have a phone number for you so how else am I supposed to get a hold of you?"

"You aren't."

"Anyway, just listen. I think there might have been something in the blood you gave us for this week."

"Something?"

"Yeah. Did you test it? Like for drugs or knockout drops or something? Or more specifically, Ecstasy?"

Dr. Cooke was silent on the other end.

She could hear the sound of turning pages.

"That autopsy was not handled by me. Why do you ask?"

"Because young Ethan had a pretty serious reaction to something last night, and if my theory is correct, the entire shipment could be contaminated. I need to know if the rest of this is safe. He got amorous with some homeless people yesterday, which makes me think Ecstasy. So, was it tested?"

"Hold, please."

A dreary, instrumental version of *My Funny Valentine* erupted in her ear at full volume. She held the handset away.

Several minutes later, Dr. Cooke was back on the line. "No, that batch didn't get checked. The new intern missed my notes."

"Are you serious?" Gladys paced, fuming and angry. "How could you be so careless? Ethan nearly did a swan dive from the top level of the downtown parking garage last night! He could have been taken away. And what do you think would have happened if someone had done a rudimentary little physical on the boy and found out he had no heartbeat? Or that his body temperature was below eighty? Or, God forbid, kept him overnight? We can't afford to blow our cover."

"Look. It was a mistake. I'll make it up to you. Just bring me the full bottles and I'll get you new ones."

"Why full?" Suspicion filled her mind. Dr. Chip was corrupt, greedy, and impossible to work with. She had an inkling that if Cooke had more...unorthodox clients than herself, he might be tempted to sell this tainted blood as a drug and make a butt load of cash on the side. A danger to both the drugged vampires and any humans in the vicinity. He was without scruples.

Cooke gave no answer.

"Hey, I'm talking to you. Why do you want them full?"

"Because I don't trust that you aren't just trying to swindle me into getting a double batch of bottles. For all I know, you just want to live high on the hog for a week or two."

"First of all, even if we had double rations, that would hardly be living high on the hog. We barely get along with what we have. Second, I don't trust you not to give this stuff to someone else. I know you must have other clients."

Dr. Cooke sighed, resigned. "Fine, empty them out first. I don't care. Let me run a test to make sure it's contaminated before you go dumping it all down the drain, okay? I'll call you back in an hour." A click in her ear told her he'd hung up the phone to prevent any more discussion.

She glared at the receiver, seething, until a heavy knock on the front door made her jump. It sounded like a fist. The phone clattered to the floor. She reached down, grunted, and picked up the phone, returning it to the cradle. "Sit right there, Ethan." She stomped toward the door. "I'll get it."

24. THE EVENING OF THE AGE OF AQUARIUS

Ethan's eyes were wide with worry as Gladys opened the front door.

"Who is it? Is it the cops?"

Hans entered, wearing his fussy white shirt and red tie—standard uniform for all grocery store employees, male or female or otherwise. Gladys stepped aside to let him in. Ethan saw who the visitor was and tried to disappear into his chair.

"So? Why am I summoned?"

"Wait until Karen gets here," Gladys said. "I don't like repeating myself." She was still holding the shopping bag filled with the suspect shooters.

Hans' attention was pulled toward the bag, and he turned stone still. His eyes darkened and swallowed his sclerae.

This blood supply needed to get back under lock and key until they decided what to do with it.

He raised a hairy fist to swipe at his mouth.

"Don't even think about it," Gladys said in a low voice, tucking the bag under her arm.

Hans snapped his head toward her and licked his lips. Two tiny dots of white poked out under his upper lip, lifted in a snarl.

"Get a hold of yourself. We can't have any of this until Dr. Chip calls back." She turned and made a beeline toward the basement, not wanting to hold the temptation in her hand. She kept an ear out for the sound of creaking stairs, but there were none. If he had been stalking her, she probably wouldn't have heard him anyway. She'd just end up pasted to the concrete floor below. She'd seen Hans do some pretty interesting things in the name of bloodlust.

Once the bag was stowed in the mini-fridge, she locked it and spun the dial of the padlock to the right. If one of them really insisted on getting in there, it wouldn't take much to pop the lock. This was only a deterrent.

The stairs creaked and groaned under her as she climbed back up the stairs, huffing and puffing. By the time she reached the top, Karen had arrived and was perched on the edge of the sofa, glaring at Ethan.

Ethan looked like he was actively trying to become invisible with his hands stuffed between his knees and his head turtled into his shoulders.

Gladys leaned against the wall by the kitchen, panting, and was about to begin the lecture when the phone rang, unnaturally loud in the quiet house.

"Hello?" Gladys said into the phone. Her visitors seemed to be hanging on her every word.

"Uh-huh."

A pause.

"You did?" She leaned her forehead against the wall with her eyes shut. "Okay and what?"

Another pause, longer this time.

Her guests leaned forward, waiting for a verdict.

"You're sure?" She jerked upright. "So, it was drugged?" Gladys' face went through a series of emotional expressions before it reached the point of aghast. "You're *serious?* Sweet Christ, Chip!"

Gladys listened, becoming angry.

"Of course we're going to need more! No, I'm dumping it all."

She listened her mouth screwed up into an angry grimace.

"Just fix it! Tomorrow, doctor. Not next week." She hung up the phone and walked back to the living room where all eyes were large and round and focused on her.

"Ecstasy. Like I thought." She looked at the floor and shook her head in disbelief. "The blood came from someone high on ecstasy."

Karen raised her hand to her mouth, eyes wide. "Ecstasy?"

"Yeah. And psilocybin."

The furrow between Hans' eyebrows deepened into a chasm. "What do you mean, they are drugged? And what is this silly silo bin?"

"Exactly what I said, Hans." Gladys sat at the dining table with her elbows propped on the placemat, fingertips kneading her forehead. "The bottles we got from Dr. Cooke are all laced with ecstasy and magic mushrooms."

"Mushrooms? We sell all the time, mushrooms. They do not—"

"*Magic* mushrooms, Hans," Gladys reiterated. "He gave us blood tainted with ecstasy and *magic* mushrooms."

Ethan's face lightened. "So that means it wasn't my fault! Everything that happened. It wasn't my fault at all!"

Gladys pointed at him. "If you'd gotten the blood out of the *door* of the fridge instead of the *bag,* then this never would have happened. And if you'd stick to just one a night, we wouldn't have to sacrifice our own supply for you."

His face clouded over again, chagrined.

"But Glad," Karen said in her soothing voice, pawing at Gladys' forearm. "If Ethan hadn't found out, we could have all been in the same shape. It could have happened to you while you were at work. I think we should count ourselves lucky this time."

Gladys shook her off. "Hans? What do you have to say about all this?"

"I think it is unwise to act rashly." He caught Karen's eye and winked.

"Maybe we need to take a moment," Karen said.

Gladys' eyebrows knitted together, and she squinted one eye, looking at Hans and then Karen. "What are you talking about?" She looked from him to Ethan who was grinning like the village idiot, and then to Karen, who merely looked thoughtful.

"We should be cautious. We have opportunity now. So little we are enjoying life. Maybe this is time to remember fun?" Hans asked.

"You know, Gladys," Karen said as she studied her hands, "we really don't get many opportunities to cut loose and enjoy life a little. What if we…"

"No. No. Terrible idea." Gladys was shocked at the both of them. She never would have suspected her two compatriots— Hans the "frozen chosen" and Karen the goody goody—would have any interest in getting high at this juncture.

All three were looking at her with that look Oliver got in the musical when he asked if he could please have some more.

"*All* of you? You're serious? You really want to do this knowing what could happen?"

Three heads nodded in choreographed synchronicity.

Ethan raised his hand. "I mean, I'll just watch this time, but yeah."

What could possibly go wrong?

She threw her hands up in the air and went back to the kitchen and called off her shift. Stomach flu. It was easy for them to believe her—she had left the night before looking positively ill. She gave her friends a look that said she couldn't believe they were actually going to do this and then stomped down the hall and shut her bedroom door, leaving the others in her living room to wonder.

Fifteen minutes later, she returned wearing socks, earth shoes, and a billowy caftan with a middle eastern print. She wore a little wreath of flowers and ribbons on her head. "If we're going to do this, then let's do it right. Hans, lock the door. Call in to work. We're going to have a little psychedelic experience."

Karen looked at her unbelievingly. "Really?"

"Really."

Ethan shook his head. "Like I said, none for me, thank you, Mrs. Knight. But I would love to watch a bunch of old people stumble around tripping balls." He grinned with all his teeth on display.

"Well good." Gladys said, "because you're the designated Trip Sitter."

"Trip sitter? What's that mean?" Ethan asked.

"You're the co-pilot. That means it's your job to keep us all out of trouble while we lose our minds. Now, how many did you have last night?"

"Eight."

"*Eight?* What in the hell! That's supposed to last a whole week!"

"I guess it was just so good I couldn't stop. When Hans got here, I was pretty fucked up, so I didn't say anything. When I got to the library I was, like totally whack-a-doo. By the time I was done ordering the stuff on my list, I felt invincible. Like I was flying high. Don't be surprised if there's some stuff that got ordered that wasn't on the original list."

"Don't forget to give me my credit card back, you little vagrant." Gladys pinched his cheek.

She turned to the other two. "It'll be fine. We have a guide! We used to make sure we had a trip sitter back in the sixties when some really good acid landed in our laps. Less trouble that way."

"You?" Ethan asked. His jaw dropped open so far it had nearly landed on his chest.

"Yeah. Me. You think I was born this way?"

"It's not like we've never been on drugs, Ethan." Karen looked at Hans.

This admission surprised Gladys—she'd expected a long-winded speech would be needed to get Karen to join the fun.

Karen shrugged. "Before the kids came along. Carl wasn't always such a stick." A grimace crossed her face and then it was gone.

"Yes. Has been a long time. Maybe too long," Hans said.

Ethan stared at Hans with his mouth open.

"What? I have been to Amsterdam. Was not far from Germany, as one might know." His brow furrowed, and he crossed his arms. Hans, too, it seemed, had a history he'd never talked about.

"Great!" Gladys clapped her hands together. "Then let's get this party started." She gave them a very un-Gladys grin and did the peg-leg stomp back down to the basement, returning with the big plastic bag of one-ounce bottles chugging like an engine with a glass pack muffler.

"All those?" Karen asked.

"All these. I told Cooke we'd only return these babies empty. I don't want that sleazebag selling this shit to God-knows-who. Or trip-trapping alone all over the countryside attacking stray dogs and stray people. So, let's empty them. There's twenty here. Ethan doesn't want any, so that leaves..."

"Six for each," Hans said. "Remainder two."

For once, Hans seemed to be excited about doing something spontaneous and mildly scandalous. Gladys wondered, not for the first time, just what kind of life Hans had lived before joining their little band. He'd always been tight-lipped on the subject. Not one to cast his mind back to the past. It must be painful.

Karen rubbed her hands together. "Do you know how long it's been since I cut loose?"

Gladys would have thought never was about right, but not all pre-conceived notions were accurate. "When was the last time?" She opened the bag on the dining table and set about splitting up the bottles.

"College," Karen said and helped her divide them into three piles. Remainder two. "You know what would make this really special? If we poured it into glasses. Like they were Bloody Marys. Pun intended."

They all agreed. Gladys took three glasses out of the cupboard, dusted them off, and meted out the supply.

She waggled one at Ethan. "You sure?"

"Yeah, dude. I had waaay too much yesterday. But I'm glad that I, like, didn't attack those people in the park. I mean, I guess I kissed them and stuff, but at least I didn't attack anybody to hurt them or anything."

Gladys frowned, sourly. "It wasn't an offer. I meant, are you sure you'll watch over us? You'll be in charge." She cringed. Was she really about to put *this kid* in charge of their safety?

"Well, yeah! Are you kidding? I wish I still had my cell phone. This'd go viral on YouTube."

"Oh no," Karen said. "No photos."

"Okay." He looked disappointed. "You guys have fun. I'll protect you." He puffed out his chest and raised his arms like a body builder. A very thin body builder with low muscle tone.

"Yes. Is the least you could do." Hans lifted his glass and peered into the thick, red liquid. "Now let us lift up our bottoms."

Karen stifled a giggle. "It's *bottom's up*, Hans."

He flashed a rare smile. "Very well. Bottoms up." They clanked glasses, drank, and ventured out into the cool, moonlit backyard to wait for...whatever happened next.

Ethan eased himself out of the sliding patio door and made a comfy spot for himself with a couple of pillows and a blanket on the top step of the deck, resigned to his fate of watching a bunch of old people wander a suburban backyard high on psychedelic drugs for the evening. A bunch of old people *vampires*. At least it would be interesting.

25. MIDNIGHT IN THE GARDEN OF GOOD AND EVIL

The crescent moon looked down on the melee, casting its light upon three gallivanting, drug addled people. Three vampires, all over fifty, capered in Gladys' yard, listening to Jefferson Airplane, who posed the question of if you wouldn't, indeed, as a matter of fact, perhaps, just maybe...want somebody to love. In the distant part of Gladys' brain where rational thought still lurked, she worried that Mrs. Maitland would happen to step out her back patio door and see them cavorting, but the part of her mind that was currently occupied with visual distortion and tangential thought didn't care one bit.

It *had* been a long time since the 1960s and Hans was right—there was so little fun in their lives now that they'd been forced into hiding. She planned to enjoy it to the fullest extent possible. Without getting the cops called, of course. Ethan had reminded them that tonight was the Summer Solstice, and was there really any better way to celebrate than by staring up at the moon and enjoying a really good psychedelic experience?

Gladys and the others danced barefoot on the lawn for a time that was impossible to calculate. Ethan could have told them he played the Surrealistic Pillow album on her ancient boom box three times, and each time Gladys informed him it was Airplane's *second* studio album, and the first one to feature Grace Slick. He switched to taking requests from Hans and Karen, when he could find the tape, while Gladys sat on the backyard swing grinning at her companions. Grinning like an idiot, in fact. Her sharp teeth were prominently displayed.

Feeling like she was swaddled in soft, warm wool, she watched Karen and Hans grooving out to the vibes. Karen hugged herself and smiled sweetly, swaying back and forth, still wearing her conservative peach colored sweater twin set. Her face was heartbreakingly beautiful, Gladys thought, and tears streamed from her eyes as she continued to smile. How lucky was she to have found a friend like her? Especially after years of being alone. It wasn't that she liked being a vampire, but if it hadn't happened, they never would have met, and Gladys would have been a poorer person for it.

Hans was...what? His movements were erratic. He jumped and turned all over the place, making jerky motions with his hands like he was a poorly animated zombie—as if a necromancer had done a crappy job and split the scene before it was finished.

Ethan approached him cautiously and handed him a glass canning jar with a screw-top lid. Hans opened it, slapped his hand over the top, and closed it again quickly. Ignoring Ethan, he tucked it under his arm like a football player and ran out toward the taller grass at the back of Gladys' property line. He continued his spasmodic gyrations, pausing every few minutes to open the jar. And then she got it. A tiny arrow seared her heart. He was chasing lightning bugs. The look of childish glee on his usually pensive face was unmistakable. The jar contained eight little blinking lights.

In the waist high verge, she could see them swooping and looping in their little J-shaped flight trajectories with drug induced trails behind them. She rose from her place and joined him, caftan billowing out behind her, shoes long since cast away. Hans had even ditched the bow tie and unbuttoned the top button. They giggled like children in the night, on the longest day of the year, reclaiming the lost shreds of their young adult lives when everything was simpler. Not to mention, a good deal less bloody.

Ethan curled up on the back stairs with his head on the quiet boom box, still watching his mentor and her friends when Gladys tapped him on the shoulder and told him it was time to go inside. The four of them trooped in together. Ethan had the presence of mind to tell them all it was too risky to go home and that they should all plan to spend the day in the basement.

"Unless you want to risk the death rays of the morning sun. I'm sure we have plenty of blankets and stuff around."

It didn't take much convincing. He dug through the closets and found enough bedding for all of them to safely roll up in. Gladys directed him to the garage where there were more tarps, and he dutifully retrieved them. He reminded her of a kindergarten teacher laying out mats for nap time.

Before he went into his own closet, he laughed. "Y'all look like three little cocoons lined up together. You look like insects wrapped up by a spider to be saved for dinner."

Gladys laughed, bitterly.

But we're the spiders.

He closed the door before the sun birthed itself over the horizon and they were all dead to the world.

The next day, Gladys was the first to struggle out of slumber. She worked to escape the layers of fabric which separated her from the world beyond. She sat up and looked around, bewildered and adrift as to time and place. This was her basement, alright, but there were two extra bundles. Then she remembered: the psychedelic blood, the dancing, the lightning bugs. She smiled, but the memory stung. Today it was back to real "life" and living beneath the radar of normal folk.

As she was fighting to free herself (Ethan had really wrapped them up tightly—no light was going to breach that armor) the closet creaked open like the door to Dante's Inferno and Ethan stepped into the dim light cast by the Mickey Mouse night light Gladys had purchased at his request. He laughed out loud and then slapped a hand across his mouth to stifle it.

"What?" She sounded groggy and her mouth felt like it was lined with cotton batting. She smacked her lips and patted her tongue with one arthritic finger.

Ethan got control of himself. "Nothing, it's just, you look..."

"How do I look?" She raised an eyebrow at him and resumed her efforts to escape her tightly wound wad of blankets.

"You look like you were up all night partying. Which, you know, you were." He crossed the room and offered his hand.

Frowning, Gladys grasped it and he yanked, heaving her off the floor with little effort. He was, after all, a vampire. Something fell out of the mass and clattered on the floor.

Ethan bent down to pick it up, looked at it with fascination, then dropped it like it was a burning ember.

"Gross!"

Gladys looked down. Her dentures. Cracked again, dammit. She scowled, picked them up, and went into the small bathroom to wash them off.

Ethan followed and watched over her shoulder as she pulled out a packet of Efferdent and dropped it into a glass of water. It fizzled, and she released the dentures into it. They sank slowly to the bottom. Time to schedule another appointment with Dr. Trish.

She turned around, glass in hand, and met Ethan's eye.

"Yes? You have something you want to say?"

"No. I mean, are those your *teeth?*

She pushed past him and set the glass on the old wooden table by her bedroll. "No, they're my dentures."

He shook his head, trying to solve this mystery. "But, you have, you know. Fangs and stuff." He looked utterly flummoxed and tried to peer into her now toothless mouth.

"You really are clueless. I had dentures before I got turned into a vampire. Didn't you ever wonder why they were so pearly white and straight?"

"Yeah, but how..."

"How does it work?"

Ethan nodded.

The others were beginning to hatch.

"When the pointy ones come out, the dentures fall out. Good enough?"

He shook his head and looked down into the mussed rumple of her blankets. "Where did they come from, exactly?"

She sighed. "Maybe they fell out, and I stuck them in my pocket. How should I know?"

"You lost your teeth? How does someone lose their teeth?"

She rolled her eyes and went to the fridge. Everyone would be wanting breakfast. "Dentures. If yours popped out when you were in the midst of blood lust or under the influence, you might lose yours too." She unlocked the padlock. "At least I didn't lose my mind."

"Oh. Well, I guess I'll keep an eye out for them the next time you go all savage. But where do you get them fixed? Is it a mail order thing?"

She laughed. "No, not a mail order thing. That would be Dr. Trish. She's a dentist. Moved here way back in the 1800s, I can't remember exactly when. She came from New Orleans. A vampire turned her husband, and things were going fine for a while, but then he made the mistake of trying to get revenge on a very powerful vampire who hit on his wife. They arrested him. Can you guess what might have happened next?"

Ethan shook his head, looking green.

"He was arrested and thrown in the town jail. Which was fine until the sun came up. Get my meaning?"

Ethan nodded.

"That's good." She put a hand gently on his shoulder and gave him a peck on the cheek. "Thanks for looking out for us last night. You're a good kid, Ethan."

His face broke into a sunny smile of gratitude.

She shook a finger at him. "Don't let it go to your head. You still have a lot to learn."

"Should we help them up?" Ethan motioned to the two lumps on the floor, squirming around like woodlice on steroids.

"Nah. They'll get up when they're ready." She stretched and yawned. "I have a feeling we might all need a night off to recover." A look of embarrassment crossed her face. "Listen. About last night. If we did anything weird—"

"Nope," Ethan said and held up his hand. "No need to explain. No need to apologize. Don't worry about a thing. It was kinda fun, you know?"

Gladys nodded and shuffled to the stairway, strangling the railing in her fist, and made her way up.

Ethan followed.

She opened the sliding patio door and looked out into the yard with her hands on her hips, still wearing the caftan, though it was horribly rumpled. The flower garland was gone, lost somewhere in the night. The yard seemed smaller tonight, now that she was on the other side of things. She lumbered down the stairs and crossed to the swing.

Ethan followed and sat down beside her. She pushed off, setting the swing in motion, and felt a sudden melancholy wave wash over herself.

"What's wrong? I'd think you'd be pretty happy about last night."

She looked up at the moon, a little fatter than the night before, and wiped a tear from her eye. "I am, it's just something Hans said last night that stuck with me."

"What's that?"

"He said, 'So little we enjoy life,' and he's right." She sighed and sat back in the swing, moving it with her feet. "I'm tired of just existing. It's been a long time since I *lived*. Sometimes I wonder if it's worth it."

Ethan's eyebrows knitted together. "If what's worth it?"

"This!" She gestured around the yard. "All of this. All the hiding, the constant restraint. Is it really worth it? There are times I think about walking out my front door to watch my last sunrise before I turn into a pile of ash."

They sat in uncomfortable silence until Ethan couldn't take it anymore. "You don't really mean that, do you?"

She sighed. "Well, not exactly, no. But I am beginning to wonder just what the point of all this is."

"If you could go back, you know, to the way things were, would you do it?"

Gladys thought about it. Her old life was gone, and she had her new friends. She had a job, and she had some pretty extraordinary gifts. But she also had a bit of a sun allergy, terrible arthritis, and a little problem with wanting to feed off the living.

"I'd reverse it in a heartbeat."

"Is there any way to do it? To reverse this? Because as cool as all this is, I really want my friends back. And my family."

"Well, it wouldn't be too late for you, but for the rest of us, this is all we've known for so long. My husband is long dead. Karen's family is gone, who knows where. Hans..." She realized she didn't know much about Hans except for his life in Iowa City, even though he'd lived and loved elsewhere. "Besides, the only way things could go back to normal would be to kill Estelle Getty."

Ethan sat bolt upright. "Say what?"

Shit! Shit, shit, shit!

"Oh, no." She shook her head and turned his chin so she could look into his eyes. "Don't even think about it." But Gladys could tell Ethan was going to think about it. Really hard.

26. THE MORNING AFTER

Ethan and Gladys were sitting in the kitchen taking tiny sips from their shooter bottles when Hans straggled up the stairs looking more like a wet, distempered rodent than an irritable German.

"What is the time?" He sounded cranky, even for Hans.

"It's eight-thirty," helpful Ethan offered.

"I will be late!" Hans paced from the kitchen out to the living room and back, rubbing his hand over his head. "I must drive to home. I must change, yah? Out of party clothes. Shower," he counted things off on his fingers. "There is no time! No time! I will be late for—"

"Hans," Gladys said gently and struggled out of her chair. She put a hand on his arm with gentle reassurance. "It's alright for you to call in. If you could look in the mirror, you'd agree that you have no business going to work tonight."

"What is wrong with way I look?" His chin jutted out with wounded pride.

"Nothing, exactly, you just look like—"

"You look like you've been up all night trippin' balls is what you look like," Ethan offered with his customary tact and snickered. "You go in and they're just gonna send you right home thinkin' you're still sick."

Hans gave Ethan a considering look with a bushy eyebrow raised.

"Trust me on this one, buddy...sir. You don't wanna go in tonight. Just play it cool, tell them you need another day, and chill out for the evening. Can you? Like, are you able to just chill out?"

"Did I not get chilly last night?"

Ethan chuckled. "No, you weren't *chilled out* last night. Last night you were on another total plane of existence, my dude. You should have seen yourself chasing after lightning bugs and stuff! It was hilarious."

Hans' frown deepened.

"I don't mean any disrespect or anything, I just mean, it seemed like you busted loose for the first time in forever. It was probably really good for you to, you know, branch out and stuff. And they say shrooms are great for depression." Ethan offered a helpful smile.

"I am not depressed. I am German."

Gladys cackled.

Karen stumbled into the room, rubbing her eyes and looking disoriented. "God, what happened? I feel like I've been pulled through a knothole." She looked at Ethan sitting relaxed at the kitchen table while Hans and Gladys were engaged in what looked like a stand-off. She gave Ethan a questioning look.

"It's cool," he said with a shrug. "We're trying to get Hans to take the night off, chill out with us, hang out before he goes home to shower off the paisleys and rainbows from last night." He dashed into the living room and came back brandishing a DVD. It had a library sticker on it. "Look what I got!"

It was *Twilight*.

Gladys grinned.

Karen rubbed her forehead. "What time is it, anyway?"

"Almost nine," Gladys said. "Would you two like a little breakfast? Such as it is? We need to go find Dr. Cooke later and get a new batch of bottles. There's just enough left for the two of you."

Karen nodded and Hans sat down in the recliner, his silence meaning consent. At least, to the breakfast part.

Gladys retrieved the last two bottles and handed them to her friends. "Drink up."

"So, I need to go to the library again," Ethan announced as Karen and Hans wiped their mouths. He looked at the others and cleared his throat. "I promise to keep myself under control and I'll keep it on the DL."

"The DL?" Gladys asked.

"The down low. Like, I'll keep my head down and keep quiet and not be noticed," he grinned. "You know, keep making the mustard. Can I borrow your car?"

Gladys shook her head at once. "No way, Ethan. You still need some minding. At the very least, a driver."

"Well, will you take me?" He looked doubtfully at Gladys who, to his eyes, barely seemed capable of taking herself to the shower right now, let alone driving across town.

Gladys opened her mouth to say no, but Karen spoke up to volunteer.

"I'll take you, okay? But just in and out and that's it."

"Yeah, cool. I need to finish my supply order. I can't wait for you to see how kick ass this is gonna look." He grinned. "Like, we'll be totally vibin' down there." He saw the blank look on Karen's face and realized he had left her behind with his slang.

"Never mind." He shook his head, blond bangs flopping all over the place. "You'll take me? Tomorrow?"

"Yes, I'll take you. Tomorrow night. It will have to be early-ish though, okay? I have a big date with Outlander." She waggled her eyebrows in a mockery of salaciousness, and Ethan looked away uncomfortably.

"If we are to watch movie, then let us get on," Hans said.

Ethan opened up the DVD case and turned on the machine Gladys barely used.

"How did you manage to keep hold of that last night?" Gladys asked.

"Slid it into the back of my pants as soon as things started feeling weird. I wanted to watch the jet trails my hands were making."

"Very resourceful," Karen said, snickering. "Just don't ask me to carry it to the return slot."

Karen and Gladys shared the couch since Hans had already commandeered the recliner. Ethan sat on the floor between them and leaned against the couch.

The movie struck everyone but Ethan as utterly hilarious. Hans snorted with laughter when Edward went outside and started to sparkle. Gladys pointed out that Bella had a constant expression of dull surprise on her face, and Karen thought the idea of werewolves, especially those who could change at will, was ridiculous.

When it was over, Ethan got up without a word and removed the disc from the player.

"What's wrong, honey?" Karen asked.

"Nothing." He snapped the case closed and looked at his mentors.

"Ethan?" Gladys said. "If you have something to say—"

"It's just that. This movie...you know..." He stomped his foot and looked at them with reproach.

"What is wrong with movie?" Hans asked.

"This was something important to me. From my old life, you know? I took my first girlfriend to a Twilight marathon at the Englert. You know that theater by the square? They had a night—Halloween it was—they played all the movies one after the other. Everybody dressed up."

He could have been performing a monologue to an empty theater. No one knew what to say to this. Ethan soldiered on. "I just wanted to share something that was important to me, you know? You all have this great big history I'm not a part of. And I know I haven't even been around the block once, while all of you..." Ethan stopped. "Not trying to be disrespectful to you, but you're like—"

"Old," Hans said, nodding. "Is true we are not chickens in spring. Is okay to say what is true."

This seemed to give Ethan the courage he needed to continue.

Three sets of eyes looked at him as he took a deep breath.

"I just want to belong. All I've ever done is want to belong. That girl? The one I took to see this?" He held up the DVD case and flashed it at them. "She only went out with me that one time. Decided I wasn't worth going out with again, even though I bought the tickets, the popcorn, and the drinks." He frowned. "I've never fit in. Not with anyone."

Karen reached out and grasped EtHans' hand and dabbed at tears in her eyes with a hankie she'd produced from Gods knew where.

"So...I wanted to...I don't know." He was almost out of steam.

Gladys stood up with effort. "We're sorry, kid. Didn't mean to be disrespectful. We're glad you wanted to share something with us." She looked at the couch where Karen wept silently.

Hans stared at the shag carpet from his seat in the recliner.

Gladys nudged him not too gently with her foot. "*Aren't we, Hans?*"

He nodded. "Yes, is true also, that we are glad to have you in group."

For Hans, that was quite a statement, and Ethan seemed to know it. His face began to brighten up again.

"I'm glad," Karen said softly and then blew her nose. She looked up at him with her lovely eyes, wet with tears. "I, for one, am very glad you're here. I, um..." She stopped for a moment, looking off into the distance. Then she cleared her throat. "I lost my own children. And now I have you." She smiled, stood, and pulled him in for a hug. He was nearly a foot taller, and his chin rested on her shoulder.

"Alright then. It's settled." Gladys smiled. "Who wants to play Scrabble?"

"Oh, no thanks," Karen said. "I've learned my lesson about playing you in scrabble."

"I also will not scrabble you," Hans said.

Ethan shook his head. "Not me. I suck at spelling."

"Is because of the spell checking. Young people are—"

"Adept at using technology?" Ethan asked with a grin.

"Precisely as young man says. I would play a game not needing spelling," Hans said.

"Monopoly?" Gladys suggested.

"That game lasts forever!" Ethan said. "I'll just hang out if that's okay."

"Karen?" Gladys gestured toward the kitchen table.

Karen favored Ethan with a motherly expression.

Ethan looked down at his sneakers.

"I think the young one and I will just hang out. Maybe see what's on TV."

"Suit self," Hans said. "You only are nervous about bankrupting."

Ethan flashed a Hans smile that evaporated instantly.

Gladys set up the board and she and Hans set about dominating the world financially.

"I just need to get myself tidied up a bit," Karen said. "Mind if I use your bathroom?"

Gladys nodded, but noted that Karen didn't need a lot of cleaning up. Her twin set remained unwrinkled from the night before and, inexplicably, her pants still seemed freshly pressed. As usual, Karen's hair was in perfect order. Gladys wondered if she had looked this put together before her change.

"Ethan, why don't you find us some true crime? The bloodier the better!" Karen said as she resumed her place on the couch. "Oh yes!" The *dung-dung* sound that marked the beginning of a *Law and Order* episode played through the speakers.

"This is okay, then?"

"Perfect. Here, have a seat." Karen patted the empty space beside her.

Ethan sat, trying to keep a polite distance. "You guys all okay?"

"The movie wasn't really scary, Ethan."

Ethan shook his head. "I mean from last night."

Karen looked at him sideways as Jerry Orbach began setting up the scene. "Ethan, I think it's a common misconception by people your age that older people had no life before hemorrhoids and arthritis claimed them. Gladys was part of the Rainbow Gathering. Did you know that? She used to travel the country with a band of hippies. Kind of like a caravan commune."

Ethan concentrated. "What's a *Rainbow Gathering*?"

"Really?" Karen laughed. "Have you ever heard of the Grateful Dead?"

"Oh, was that who we listened to last night?"

"Well, that was mostly Jefferson Airplane, but same era. You really don't know what a Rainbow Gathering is?"

He shook his head.

Karen sighed. "It's too much to explain. My point is just this: we all had lives long before age and Estelle changed things. Trust me, they'll be fine. Hans grew up in some crazy culty place in Sweden for a while."

"I thought he was German."

"Well, yeah, but he lived in Sweden for a while. Let me tell you, Swedish people are weird."

"Weird like the people in Midsomer and that movie about the hiker dudes who wandered into the camp of these elk worshipper people?"

"I have no earthly idea what you're talking about."

"It's just these movies, they're made by A-24 and they're all like whacked out and stuff and these Swedish people—you know in the summer it's daylight all the time there—anyway, they live in this place where, like, it's all happiness and flowers and shit and before anyone knew what was happening this dude ended up paralyzed wearing some kind of bear suit."

Karen watched the flickering screen silently with her mouth open a little, trying to digest the meaning of what Ethan had said and then gave up. "Umm, no. At least, I don't think so. Let's just agree that there's something up with the Swedes. And I can say that because my grandma was half Swedish."

"Yeah, like how black people can say stuff white people aren't allowed to say." He nodded at his own 'wisdom'.

"Shit!" Gladys said, slapping her hand on the table. Karen and Ethan jumped.

"What's the matter?" Ethan asked. "You lose Park Place already?"

"No! We were supposed to meet up with Cooke tonight!" She pushed her chair back and was about to rise.

"Don't worry about it, Glad," Karen said. "We'll go." She turned to Ethan. "Won't we?" She got up without waiting for his agreement.

Gladys raised an eyebrow. "You sure?"

"Of course! Don't worry, I'll protect him." She gestured with her thumb over her shoulder at the boy, already collecting her purse.

Gladys settled back into her chair. "Wonderful. I didn't want to go, anyway."

Karen and Ethan got in her car and drove in silence while Ethan opened the window and hand-surfed in the cool night breeze.

Karen was the one who finally broke the silence. "I wanted to thank you for sharing your movie with us. It really was special."

"Sure! Thanks for taking me to meet Dr. Cooke." Ethan looked eager. "I can't wait to meet him! What's he like? I bet he's pretty cool. Plus, he gets to like, do autopsies and shit. That must be really cool."

"No, you don't get to meet him," she said. "And no, he's not cool. He's a selfish, blackmailing prick."

Her comment was so unlike her that Ethan's smile fell. She looked at her gold Timex, gritted her teeth, and increased her speed to five miles over.

"You okay?"

Karen looked at the dashboard clock and swore under her breath. "We can't be late. He won't wait around. And you're going to sit in the car like a quiet little mousie and not bring any attention to yourself. He's not going to like that you're with me in the first place."

"I'm so sick of feeling invisible," he grumbled as he got in the car and fastened his seat belt. "I mean, if I actually *was* invisible, that would be something." His face became animated. "*Can* we be invisible?"

Karen backed out of the parking spot and zipped toward the river and the hospital. "No, Ethan, we can't be invisible." She thought for a moment, knowing the others wouldn't appreciate her giving him more information about powers. They were all devoted dental patients of Dr. Trish, but they had, by unspoken agreement, decided to keep some of this to themselves until Ethan had more time to adapt to his condition. "Dim, maybe. Still enough so that others take no notice of you, but it takes a lot of practice being still."

Ethan, who had been fidgeting, settled in his seat and concentrated on the dashboard in front of him with his face screwed into a rictus. "I can be still."

She laughed. "Keep working on that part for now." He really was adorable. At least he was being quiet.

They pulled into the loading dock behind the hospital and Karen looked at Ethan, still concentrating on the dash. "That's right. Just keep working on that." She tapped the steering wheel, impatient for the blood Dr. Cooke would be bringing, even though she tried not to show it. She struggled to maintain a look of poise and self-control at all times. It's what had kept her safe for so long.

Finally, the door opened and a man in a white lab coat stepped out with a bulging grocery bag. "That's him. Stay put."

Ethan started to speak, and she shushed him. "Keep trying to be dim. I'll be right back."

Dr. Cooke didn't glance at the car parked out of the circle of light from the streetlamp.

She handed him the empties. "Are these tested this time?"

He sneered. "Yes, they're tested. They're fine. Now take the bag and go." He shoved it into her hands, making her stumble back a step from his unexpected strength.

"Thanks, Doc."

He gave her a sardonic smile. "You forgetting something?"

"I don't think so," she said.

"Payment?"

"Oh no. We paid you for the others and they turned out to be contaminated. You'll have to consider these returns."

Dr. Cooke pressed his lips together in anger, but seemed to understand that she was right. "See you next week." He disappeared behind the door, which closed with a metallic ring.

Karen walked back to the car, a little lighter on her feet, a feeling of hunger mixed with greed rising. She tamped it down, stowed the goods in the trunk, and took off back toward Gladys' house.

27. ETHAN'S BIG OFFENSE

"Hi, I'm Ethan."

"Hello, Ethan," the others chorused, well-rehearsed and completely unnecessary. After all this time, Karen still insisted on standards and protocols. Probably a leftover habit from taking crap from the public at the DMV.

"It has been two days since I last took blood from a living person." He cleared his throat. "It wasn't exactly my fault, though." He held up his hand as Karen opened her mouth to say something. "I'm taking full responsibility, even though I didn't exactly drug myself, you know?" He looked hopefully at the group.

Gladys crossed her arms over her impressive ta-tas and frowned at him.

"Of course, if I hadn't pigged out and guzzled all those shooters, it never would have happened. But it's better than eating Mrs. Maitland's new cat, Mr. Fuzzles." He shrugged, a crafty little grin blooming on his face.

Gladys grimaced.

Karen looked from Gladys to Ethan. "New cat? What happened to Cleo?"

"You don't want to know," Gladys said. "Go on, Ethan. It's time."

"Yeah. I guess it's my turn to tell my story. Probably past time, but I don't really like thinking about it. Anyway, I guess it's what we do at the "ol' XP" Support Group.'" He indicated air quotes around the words with the first two fingers on each hand.

The XP Support group thing was, of course, just a cover story for anyone who might be curious. Gladys had come up with the idea long ago, after reading one of Dean Koontz's books about a guy with XP who went around at night solving crimes, thinking it the perfect excuse for a bunch of people who couldn't go out in the sunlight. And since XP was incredibly rare, the likelihood of someone coming to them who actually had it was low. They'd never talked about what might happen to any poor schmuck who *did* show up unexpectedly for a meeting.

"Tell your story, Ethan," Karen said. "You'll feel better."

"It all started because of my stupid skateboard. I'm leaving Teakwood Community College on the afternoon of April 28th, which is a lot warmer than usual, especially after all the rain. It's been raining for eight days straight, and I've been stuck taking the bus to my classes 'cause it's too gross out for skating or riding my bike. But this day is like, awesome. When I wake up on this morning, the clouds are gone. The sun is shining like it's the first day ever. You know, after God did the thing and said, 'Let there be light.'"

Hans coughed into his hand and looked at Ethan with disapproval.

"Oh, sorry. Didn't mean to take the Lord's name in vain or anything."

"It's fine, go on." Karen gave him an encouraging smile.

"The birds are singing and everybody's walking around like they're on happy pills. There are people biking around and even my roommates got up early, which they never, ever do. So instead of heading straight home from class, I head downtown where all the action is. I want a foot-long sub from Clark Brothers and a smoothie from the Juice Stop. I think I'll go to the ped mall. I'll sit and enjoy this early dinner, and then maybe head to the skate park. It is, after all, a glorious day in the hood. I always stick to the side streets as much as I can. You know how Iowa City drivers are."

"These drivers are not being known for patience and attentiveness when driving, especially on sunny days," Hans offered. "So many crashes with cyclists in summer."

"Yeah, right? And I have no interest in getting a pavement facial. I may be clueless about a lot of things, but I've always had a keen interest in self-preservation, so I'm not about to let anyone smear me into the concrete. I have too many goals to end up living out my days moving an electric wheelchair by breathing through a straw.

"Once I turn off Teakwood Boulevard, it's just residential streets until I get to the University, where I'm planning to finish my construction management degree when I'm done with pre-reqs at Teakwood. I hate it when some of the other kids joke about it by calling it "Freakwood." One of my roommates is already at the U and he LOVES to give me a bunch of crap about going to—"

"Fast forward," Gladys said.

"Yeah, yeah. It's just, Teakwood is great for kids who don't want to be in debt forever or don't get sports scholarships. That's all I wanted to say.

"Anyway, I'm kick-kick-gliding toward the pedestrian mall, and I'm thinking all about Amber DeLotta. She sits in the front row of my algebra class. She hasn't noticed me, not yet anyway, but I've noticed her plenty. She likes short cutoffs—even when it's cold out, and she wears these soft, loose, low-neck sweaters.

"Since we're supposed to be honest, I guess I have to say that I spent a lot of my class time checking her out. Unnoticed, I hope." He rubbed the back of his neck, donning the look of one who is reliving one of their best memories. "She had great hair. It had these blonde streaks in it. And her eyelashes were super long and so were her legs. Truly great legs. I was just trying to get rid of my acne, so there was no way she was ever going to talk to me first."

Karen squeezed his hand. "I know it's hard, honey. I know."

"I'm so busy thinking about Amber's sweaters and her boobs that I forget to think about what I'm doing. Before I know what's happening, I'm bouncing off the hood of a big white Beamer and scraping across the pavement on the opposite side. Which sucks 'cause that's the whole reason I take the back streets in the first place. I just lay there, trying to figure out if I'm broken anywhere and if I am, how bad it is. Mostly, I'm just happy I'm still able to think at all. Like I said, I don't want to end up a veg.

"I hear this whistling, keening sound and at first, I think it's a weird noise from the car, and then I realize it's me. I can't breathe because the car knocked the wind out of me. So, I think I'm okay. Nothing is injured but my pride, right? My breath is returning and I'm inhaling and exhaling like one of those yogis from India, and then I hear the car door open. I expect them to come around and make sure I'm okay and see if I need an ambulance or something.

"I turn my head, and I see white high heels and the bottom of a pair of white pants step out of the car. Those heels make tapping sounds so loud as the person walks toward me. But then they go right by me. This asshole is looking over their car! Trying to see if there was damage instead of asking me if I'm okay!

"'You've got to be kidding me!' a voice as sharp as a knife says.

"I wince as I try to sit up. Although I'm pretty sure my arms and legs are still attached, my head throbs each time my heart beats. I reach up to touch my head because it hurts like a son of a bitch. My hand comes away slick with blood and suddenly I think I'm gonna faint."

"I can't stand the sight of blood," Ethan said. "Well, at least, I couldn't just then. After that…" He raised his hands as if to say 'well, that's it. You know the rest.'"

The members of the support group looked at Ethan expectantly, as if they didn't know all of it, so he continued.

"I lay back down, hoping the grey that's clouding my vision doesn't turn into full blackness. I don't want to pass out on the street, but I close my eyes anyway. The pain in my head is too much, and it feels much better when I'm not looking up at the sun.

"'How could you be so careless?' A shrill voice, like a mom who just found you stealing money out of her purse, makes me murmur something. I don't know what.

"I just want to be left alone here to get my bearings back, and that's when the greatest pain ever flashes through my left side. My eyes fly open and all thoughts of fainting fly away. The owner of those white shoes has just kicked me in the ribs! I can't believe it! She's towering over me, and I have to shield my eyes to look at her. Part of me wishes I hadn't. She's...scary. And not because she just assaulted me. 'W-what?' Things aren't connecting in my mind just right. Is she trying to say that *I* was the one being careless? Because if she is, I have a whole lot of time to argue. And, thanks to my debate class, I'm pretty good at it."

"Oh, I'd agree with that one. Case in point, my new room," Gladys said, softening the words with a smile of compassion. There are tears of understanding in her eyes. She can't imagine how awful it was for him to go through that. She knows part of the story—he spilled some of it back in the janitor's closet when she busted him with Mrs. Foster. It seems like years ago now. But she wanted to hear him tell it all. He'd left out all the details during their tet-a-tet. She thought about all the years he had ahead of him. Being turned at nineteen is almost as bad as being turned as a child. The more she thought about it, the more her tears turned from those of sadness to those of rage.

"Fixing up your room was the least I could do after you saved me from living under the bridge," he said.

"We wouldn't have let you live on the street anyway," Karen said kindly. She elbowed Hans. "Would we?"

Hans grumbled. "Is true. Young man would be cared for in either way."

"Thanks, guys. Really. Thank you for saving me." He clears his skinny throat. "Ok. Here we go."

"She screams at me, 'You heard me!' Her face is shaded by a huge, wide-brimmed white hat, and she has little white gloves on, like my ancient great-grandma wore to church. She's wearing an old-fashioned looking white suit. Reminds me of a gangster movie like Scarface or Goodfellas or something. Underneath that, she has a white turtleneck pulled up to her chin. It's weird how I can notice all these details even though she practically stabbed me with her shoes.

"I wonder why she's wearing all that on a nice day like today. It's like 75 degrees out! She's not even sweaty, but her face looks like it has white goop on it.

"'I *said*, how could you be so careless?'

"I'm still kinda staring at this lady because she's sorta fascinating and my head is kinda messing up. She has crisp, angular features. Even her hair seems crisp, like it's screeching on her head."

Ethan stopped speaking. "I was just thinking. How could she even be outside in the sun? I mean, if she was a vampire like us, how's that possible? He turned his arm over to expose a faint scar from the first time he burned himself and looked at it with detached interest.

Gladys pondered the question, wondering how it could have taken him this long to question her presence on such a sunny day, and she wondered just how much information she should give him. The last thing she wanted to do was plant ideas in his head about magic abilities. But he deserved to know the truth, she supposed. "There are a lot of things that *some* vampires can do, especially as they get older—I'm talking decades, centuries older even. Plus, she's a head vampire, see? And the only way you get to be a head vampire is to grow your powers and start recruiting others to join the cause. She gets more power from them, kinda like how if you add more engines to a train—"

"You mean we could go outside? In the sun?" Ethan's face was so young and vulnerable, she hated to dash his hopes.

"There are some who can, but remember how covered up she was?"

He nodded.

"That was to keep her from being hit with direct sunlight. She's incredibly powerful, but she still has to take extreme precautions."

"But what about if it's cloudy? Can we go all sparkly like Bella and Edward?"

"I wouldn't recommend trying," Gladys said, frowning. This is exactly what she had feared by telling him about Estelle's powers. "Unless you want the rest of you to look like that arm of yours."

Ethan hid his hand behind his back reflexively. "No, not really."

"You must listen well now," Hans said. His craggy face went grey, and his frown lines deepened. "Young people are impatient, but young vampire must not be. Sun will scorch you to nothing but cinder marks on sidewalk. It is not mattering what you wear in sun. You would be dead. You think you have power because once when in argument feet left floor for a minute?" He laughed so harshly it was almost a cough. "You must *learn*. You must wait for time before any powers come." Hans had been leaning forward, and now he sat back against the chair. He rubbed his temples. "Young people are so impatient," he muttered.

"Go on, Ethan," Karen said. "We can talk about powers and sunlight and beach hats later, okay?"

Ethan nodded. "Alright. I can wait. Okay, so she says to me, 'There's a huge scratch on the fender, and a dent in the hood!' She points toward the huge car that had nearly been the machine of my death. 'I don't suppose *you're* going to pay for the damages?' She sniffs and taps my tennis shoe with her crazy high heel. Like I've never seen shoes that pointy.

"'Wh-what?' I'm totally flabbered...flayboard..."

"Flabbergasted?" Karen offers.

"I'm *flab-ber-gasted* that this lady would hit me with her car and then get mad at me for denting it. Like, what the fuck, lady? I'm the one on the ground and you're worried about your car? How sick is that?

"'You heard me. I want your insurance papers.' She taps her foot and looms over me, and she seems like ten feet tall.

"I gaze up at this cray-cray assaulter who's blocking out the sunshine like a lunar eclipse or whatever. Suddenly it's super cold in the shade she just made, and now I think she might actually be dangerous. She gives me a bad feeling, and in this light her eyes look red. I figure that can't be right. But then, I see her eyes almost match her red lipstick. It's so red it looks like," Ethan coughed and his voice stuck for a moment. "It looks like blood.

"Her face is super pale, like it has zinc oxide all over—you know that stuff surfers put on their noses and stuff, but like it's been rubbed in real good. Now that I'm scared, I'm watching her real close. She might try to kick me again and really break something. But I'm mad too. So I say, 'Are you for real, lady?' My voice is too quiet, like it's coming from far away, and I'm still trying to get all my breath back. My side hurts when I try to take a deep breath, so maybe there really is something cracked in there.

"'What did you say?'

"I can't repeat it. I just groan and roll onto my right side." Ethan paused, looking thoughtful. "I think that might be what the recovery position is from CPR. I had to take CPR in Boy Scouts. It was part of the "Helping Others" badges I collected."

None of the others replied.

"Right, so, I ask her, 'Are you gonna help me up here?'

"The woman is practically snarling. Her lip curls up like a dog, and I think for a minute her teeth are like a dog's teeth, but then I realize they aren't and she's just giving me one of those nasty sneers. Seems like rich ladies are the ones who do that best. 'You're right where you deserve to be. You came out of nowhere and now I have all this repair to do on my car. How could you be so stupid and oblivious?'

"And now I'm real mad. '*I'm* careless?' I sit up and then I gag on something in the back of my throat. I hack it up and spit out a big nasty glob onto the ground beside me. It looks like snot and lung cookies. There's blood in there, I think. Maybe just from my bloody lip, but maybe not. Now I can't help it. I start yelling too. I'm just...too mad to be nice anymore. 'You're the one who hit me! Stupid bitch! I'm the one down here on the ground and you fucking kicked me! Like, what the fuck? Did you even think about calling an ambulance? Or saying something like 'Hey are you alright'? I'm calling the cops, lady.'

"She crouches down to where I'm sitting. My head is still spinning, and I feel like puking. She smells bad, like roses and baby powder, but that doesn't cover up the smell underneath it all. I don't know what it is, but it's making me feel more like throwing up than ever. And her eyes...they aren't that weird red color anymore. Now they look completely black, but I think to myself that it's probably because she's still blocking out the sun and everything. I try to get away from her. I don't want her to know how scared I am, but I push myself away, digging my heels into the street. Her anger radiates in waves off her shoulders.

"Now I'm sorry for yelling like that, and I think that was a big mistake.

"She is right in my face. 'You are the guilty one here, young man. And I swear to you, you're going to regret ever crossing paths with me.' Her eyes flash red.

"I hold up my hand. I think I make a little tiny squeak because I'm so afraid of her now. Like what does she mean 'I'll regret it'? It sounds like something someone would say in a movie. I almost expect her to holler 'You fool!' like the cartoon villains do in those Pixar movies."

"Love of God!" Hans said, not quite yelling. "Is all you think of from the movies? Movie, movie, movie. '*This reminds me of this movie, that reminds me of that movie!*' I don't know these movies! Enough." He spoke in a high, mocking voice that shocked them all into silence for a moment. ,

"Hans!" Karen snapped, so furious with him that her hair began to rise, freeing itself from her perfectly coiffed do. "That is *not* necessary, and it's not fair! He can't help the generation he comes from! It's not the same as when you were growing up. Back before there was even a TV in most people's houses! Stop. Making. Fun of him." Her chair quivered and her hair blew in a breeze that wasn't there a moment ago.

Hans looked down at the floor, stricken and shamed.

"You have to give the kid a break," Gladys said to Hans, while shooting Karen a warning look.

Karen took a deep breath, and the breeze faded. Her chair became still, and her hair reverted back to its flawless style. "Apologies, Ethan. I didn't mean to get so angry." Her eyes flicked to Hans, who looked up at her and back to the floor in a quick glance.

Hans cleared his throat as if the words were stuck far back in his mouth. "I am apologizing for outburst. I do not understand, is true. Young man should tell story his way. I will say nothing more unless I am asked for opinions."

"S'okay," Ethan said. "I get it. But you'll have to tell me more about this growing up without TV thing."

"Anyhow, I'm obviously totally petrified now, and I'm trying to scuttle backward on my hands and feet. I feel like a crab who's about to get snatched up by a pelican or something. My ribs are screaming, my head is pounding, and the blood on the street makes me feel panicky. I kick out at her. Maybe I am aiming for her ankle or maybe I'm just wanting to get farther away from her. The crazy bitch catches my ankle. She squeezes it. I can almost feel my bones in there calling for help. How can she be so fast? And so strong? I try to scream but it's more like a yelp, and I think, *gee you sound like a wounded puppy, asshole.* I'm flailing back from her. I suppose anyone watching would think I was a drunk trying to make a snow angel.

"I'm so scared now I can't see straight, and it seems like she's getting closer and closer and her eyes flash like that nuke exploding over Hiroshima. I start to babble like I don't have control over my mouth anymore. 'I'm sorry! I'm sorry, lady! I didn't mean to get in your way, I just didn't see you and then I got in your way and it's my fault I'm sure, okay? Please don't hurt me anymore! Just leave me alone!' Then my mouth becomes a traitor and even though I know it's coming and I don't want to, I end it all with 'Jesus Christ, bitch! Take a chill-pill!'

"She drops my foot, and her eyes fill with black, murky oil. There are those weird rainbow things you see in spilled gas, or oil, or bubbles, and I can't look away from her. I'm like, frozen in place. I feel like a frog getting ready to be dissected. Her lips turn upward in an awful smile and for a second, I think of that movie Queen of the Damned…"

Ethan's eyes flickered to Hans. "Sorry, another dumb movie reference. I can't help it."

"It is okay." Hans waved the boy on. "We get point."

"I'd just watched that movie like a couple of weeks ago and I could swear it was her, except that chick was black and this lady is, like, really white. When I blink, the image is gone. I could almost laugh if this chick wasn't so damn creepy. But she's not a movie monster. She's just a short, angry woman dressed in all white with a goopy face and her spotless, massive car behind her.

"'You'll rue the day you crossed paths with Estelle Getty, you little reprobate.' She turns away from him, something which makes me feel much better, despite the fact that I'm still lying on the asphalt because she creamed me with her car.

"She gets in and drives off. I look up just in time to see the little peace sign emblem on the back of the car. Then I notice she hit the edge of my skateboard and it's rolling toward the gutter. I snag it just in time to keep it from disappearing into the steam tunnels beneath the city like a paper boat in the movie IT, never to be seen again."

"Was book first," Hans muttered.

Karen silently set her hand on his knee again.

Ethan continued, oblivious to the interruption, "I struggle to my feet and move over to the sidewalk as quickly as possible—definitely don't want to get hit again. I look around to see if anyone saw the accident or the altercation, but there's no one on the street. None of the houses have kids running around and laughing in their yards. There's no one to be a witness to the crime, no one to write down her license plate number. I'd been too dazed to think of it until she was already gone. For a brief moment, I have a dizzying sensation—like I'm not really here, that maybe I'm actually dead and still laying on the street and this is an out-of-body experience.

"Off in the distance, I hear the Gilbert Street train and the hum of traffic. At least there's someone out there somewhere. I rub the back of my head. The thudding is gone, but there's a big old goose egg, and it's sore when I touch it. My fingers come away tacky with blood and my stomach loop-dee-loops but it's not too bad. I don't think I need the emergency room or stitches or anything. So, I carry the skateboard under my arm and take out my earbuds, just in case a Mercedes comes roaring up onto the sidewalk to finish what the Beamer started.

"Fifteen minutes later, I'm at the Ped Mall. Most of my adrenaline is spent and I feel shaky all over. But it's nothing a sub sandwich and a smoothie can't cure. *Was it my fault?* I wonder. I don't think so. It doesn't matter anymore. The creepy lady is gone, and I still have a warm, sunny afternoon ahead of me. After a twelve-inch spicy Italian sub, a strawberry-mango-banana-blueberry-raspberry smoothie with an extra scoop of protein powder, and nearly two hours at the skate park (mostly watching, my head was still buzzing a little from bouncing it off the asphalt) I've just about forgotten about the argument with the crazy lady and her flashy red eyes and weird smile.

"Just another Ka—um...just another angry rich white lady making the world a worse place for mankind. I laugh as I toss my trash. Time to head back. I have homework to do and a test to study for. I wave goodbye to my skating bros and kick my board toward home. The sun's getting ready to set and it's starting to get a little chilly. I really want to get home before it's totally dark. It's gonna be sidewalks all the way this time though, and I don't even care if someone complains.

"After rounding the corner, I zoom down the uneven sidewalk toward Burlington Street. It's a busted-up path of humps and dips, from tree roots which run deep beneath the earth like Ents, and the temperature goes from cold shade to warm sun. Tree roots might tear up the streets and sidewalk, but it definitely makes for a fun ride.

"My route goes past the old Riverfront Church. The stained-glass windows above the door look like eyes tonight. The mammoth hospital looms up on the hill in the distance and casts a dark shadow. It's creepier with my earbuds out. I think I can hear something. A hiss? Maybe. More like hot breath in my ear. Goose bumps pop up on my arms and something feels totally off. I hop off the board and kick it up so I can carry it.

"I cock my head to the side, as if that would help me hear better. And I think I actually can hear something. 'Hello?' I say out loud. My voice trembles like a scared old man's. It echoes off the stone buildings and seems to answer me. After the echo dies, all I can hear is the quiet chattering of birds settling in for the night, the belch and squeal of a city bus two streets over, and the beating of my own heart.

"I look everywhere at once, searching for anything out of the ordinary—but there's nothing. *Okay then*, I think. *It's my imagination.* But I'm still kinda freaked out. There's one thing I know will help. I stick my earbuds back in and hit play. The Chili Peppers shred in my ears, and I scoot along on my way. I already feel better. I've gone more than a hundred feet when a person steps out of the shady little alleyway between the church and the condos where all the old farts live."

"Ahem." Gladys coughs into her fist and raises an eyebrow at the boy.

Ethan shrugs and goes on, his words coming out in rapid-fire succession because he's almost done and if he's almost done, he'll never have to tell it again. Which means he can start forgetting.

"I stop the board because I don't want to be responsible for breaking some old dude's hip. I nod, trying to be polite, but whoever it is just stands there in the darkness. He's so still I think maybe it's a holy statue of a saint or something, but this person has something like a dark light surrounding them. Only, that's not quite it. It's more like the opposite of light. A vacuum wormhole from outer space that sucked out the life in the world. I narrow my eyes, really straining to see what's in my way, and then I know. It's the nut job in white who tried to kill me with her car and then beat the shit out of me.

"I stop in my tracks and look around for anyone who might step in and help me. But of course, there's no one. It's like I found myself in a place where no one seems to exist. It's weird how this keeps happening. Although my balls have shriveled into walnuts and my stomach feels like a washing machine, I summon up all the courage I have and stand up straight. I'm just over six feet tall when I'm not slouching. My mom used to tell me all the time to quit slouching," Ethan struggled not to cry.

"I put up one hand, clutching my skateboard in the other like a shield, as if that would save me. I say 'Hey, lady I don't know—'

"The evil woman raises an open hand and closes it into a fist.

"I'm choking on my words, and I can't breathe. It seems like my ears are stuffed with cotton. The skateboard drops and clatters to the sidewalk. It sounds like firecrackers when you throw them in water.

"I'm panicking because I seriously can't get rid of the pressure in my throat. It's like there's a noose around my neck. The more I try to get out of it, the tighter it gets. Then this witch— I'm sure that's what she is now—starts pulling me forward like there really IS a noose around my neck, and she has the other end of the rope. The toes of my beat-up red Converse carve furrows in the leafy debris on the sidewalk, but it's like they're on another planet. She reels me in and her grin gets bigger. It's horrible, like a carved pumpkin, and I can't even scream because I don't have any air to do it with.

"'I told you,' she says, pulling me in with one arm. She's cradling me like a lost love. 'You shouldn't have messed with me.'

"My heart stops as I watch fangs pushing out through her gums, long and sharp as nails. She looks like the Great White Shark in that old movie, Jaws, as she bites into her free wrist.

"My stomach starts to squeeze, and I think I'm about to puke up my sandwich.

"She tears away her own flesh and I'm so scared I feel like I'm blind. The tendons of her wrist pop and rip. They sound like your jeans when you catch them on something and rip a hole in them. I'm trying to get away, to look away, but she's got me and I can't. Her blue veins are exposed and bright red gore splashes down her white sleeve. It splatters all over her fancy white suit and totally ruins my Zeppelin T-shirt. She raises her bloody wrist, and her face is like the most horrible Halloween mask I ever saw."

Ethan trembled like an autumn leaf that had forgotten to fall. He looked like a cholera victim—face pasty like cheese with hectic red spots of acne masquerading as plague lesions. He hadn't started crying yet, but looked like he was on the cusp.

"I try to make myself pass out because I don't want to know what happens next. I'd rather be dead than see what happens next, but it's no good. She slaps me across the face and it's a red explosion of pain and surprise. My eyes flash open against my will, and those creepy twin fires in her eye sockets bore into me like pine beetles. I'm totally paralyzed with fear. The fangs I thought I saw earlier are actually real and they're lengthening until they look like snake fangs.

"The worst part of it all is her tinny, hideous laughter. It bubbles up from somewhere deep within the woman shaped monster as the taste of copper pennies coat my teeth and tongue. I know I'm going to die, which sucks because I never made a move on Amber from Algebra. I've never even been out of the country. I try to move my face away from that horrible open wound, but her other hand clamps onto the back of my head and eventually I have no choice. I can feel the blood pumping into my mouth, and I'm totally powerless.

Ethan took in a massive, tearing breath that said everything about sorrow and loss.

Everyone in the group had tears in their eyes or rolling down their faces. The kid had turned out to be a good storyteller. It's unfortunate that the tale he had to tell was so awful.

He squeezed his eyes shut as he finished, not wanting to look at his friends. "After the first swallow, I don't want to stop. It's like a primal hunger I never knew existed that overtakes everything, even my mind. All I know how to do is suck and swallow, even though I know her blood is tainted and unholy. I feel like I've been lost for weeks, wandering the desert and have finally been given a drink of water. I don't know how long it has been because I feel like I'm floating out of time and place. I close my eyes, feeling like I'm in heaven. I want this feeling to last forever. I guess I get my wish, but not in the way I hope."

28. ETHAN'S INDECENT PROPOSAL

"Here's to us!" Karen raised her coffee cup and clinked mugs with everyone at the table, though no one drank.

Gladys wrinked her nose at the burnt, bitter odor of the coffee. For once she was glad she had a reason not to take a sip.

"Yeah," Ethan said, but looked gloomy as he swirled his spoon around in the cup. "Here's to us and the one stupid, miserable thing we all have in common."

The kid had been mopey ever since the support group meeting where he'd told the story of his harrowing run-in with the vampire who'd turned them all.

Karen's smile faded into sorrow. She placed her hand on Ethan's forearm, lending him what comfort she could. "I know this isn't the way any of us would choose to live our lives, but at least we have each other." She patted his arm.

Ethan scooted away, and the gloomy expression didn't leave his face.

He raised his head and Gladys felt pity for the pain that was so visible in his haunted eyes.

"Sorry, but that doesn't really help. That Kar—that *bitch* got to all of us," Ethan said. "Don't you wanna make her pay?"

Gladys shot a warning look across the table at Hans. *Don't encourage him*, the look said.

Hans frowned. "You think this has not crossed minds with us? Estelle is powerful, more than us. To fight would be useless and would only end in death."

"That whole "Resistance is futile" thing from the Borg, right?" Ethan said. Sarcasm dripped from his words.

"I do not understand what is this *borg*. A fortress has nothing to do with current problem."

"Huh?"

"Borg. Is like how you say—castle?"

Ethan shook his head.

"What Ethan's talking about," Gladys said, "is a super-race of cyborgs from Star Trek. The Borg. They assimilate. Resistance is futile, all that stuff." She raised her eyebrows in a question.

Hans' frown creased his jowls deeper. "I am not watching this, Star Trek. Ridiculous fantasy land. Borg in Swedish means fortress."

Ethan smacked his forehead. "Dude, you're like, so literal. Don't you ever watch TV? I mean, Star Trek has been around since the old days for, like forever! Since like, 1966. Although the Borg didn't really arrive on scene until season two of TNG," he mused a little to himself and then looked up at them, excited to share his nuggets of sci-fi wisdom. "They actually hinted at it at the end of season one. Like, there were no good bad guys because the Klingons were, you know, friendly and there weren't any Romulans around. And let's face it, the Ferengi were too dumb to be a threat. So, they brought in the Borg, 'cause they were like hella scary. 'Cause they were, like, pretty unstoppable."

The others looked at Ethan uncomprehendingly.

"What? I'm a Trekkie. So what? I also played D&D, did LARPing on the weekends, and had a collection of Pokémon cards. So, sue me."

Gladys held a faint smile on her lips. "I like Star Trek too, Ethan. How else would I have known what you were talking about?" She grinned. "And yes, they are, how did you put it? "Hella scary." I think that's the perfect analogy."

Ethan shrugged, scrunched down into the cracked vinyl booth, and turned the coffee cup around and around in his hands. "Well, I got made fun of a lot, okay? So just don't you start."

"No one's making fun of you," Karen said. "And we *do* get what you're saying. I think Estelle is exactly like this Borg you keep referring to, and maybe not unlike Hans' idea of a fortress."

The soft clattering of utensils and clinking china mingled with low conversation from half a dozen tables as the members of the group became lost in their own thoughts. It was a quiet night at the Village Inn.

Ethan finally broke the silence. "Any fortress can be taken."

Gladys looked at him in alarm, wanting to end this line of thinking before it could blossom. But Ethan was relentless in his single-minded obsessions.

"Like, it's not impossible. You just have to find the right angle. Find the weaknesses and then, you know, lay siege to the castle. When they let their guard down. No one can be on guard all the time. There has to be a way." He looked to his new friends with earnest hope.

Gladys saw with dismay that Hans actually looked to be considering this suicide mission. She felt cold all over. The last thing in the world she wanted to do was to have another show down with the ice queen who had ruined her life. And her death, if you wanted to look at it that way. She'd ruined that, too.

"Ethan, we aren't going to wage a war on a vampire who's hundreds of years old. Not with just the four of us. What would we do, anyway? Look at us!" She rubbed absently at her knee, as if to confirm that it was still a painful part of her existence. "Not really the Buffy the Vampire Slaying type." She shot a warning look at Hans again, hoping he'd keep his mouth shut and not encourage this lunacy.

"Well, I was thinking about that," Ethan said and sipped his coffee.

Karen slapped him hard on the back and it ejected from his mouth onto the paper placemat in front of him.

"What the Hell?" He used his napkin to wipe off the dribble on his chin.

"Don't drink, remember? Unless you want to be puking in the parking lot."

"Maybe I do," he said, chin jutting out in defiance, then immediately seemed to deflate. "You're right. It's just, it's so easy to forget."

Hans nodded like a benevolent sage. "It will come in time. You will learn like us. You will get used to—"

"But I don't *want* to get used to it!" His voice went up a full octave and cracked on the last word.

"Shh!" Gladys and Karen said together.

But Ethan would not be shushed. "Don't you get it? You're all, like old, and I still have a life in front of me." He thought for a moment. "*Had* a life in front of me. Now it's gone."

"It's not *all* bad," Karen said, but the look on her face made her conviction seem weak and flimsy. "We have our friends, we have our coffee, we have..." she stammered, not knowing how to make herself understood.

Gladys understood perfectly.

What do we have? I have two friends, which I'm thankful for, and a weird kid for a roommate, who isn't so bad after all. But I can't even enjoy a tuna sandwich.

"You must get over," Hans said.

It seemed as though his pondering had brought him to the same conclusion.

"No point looking behind, must look forward to future."

"What future," Ethan said in a barely audible grumble.

"Really, Ethan," Karen said. "don't you think we've thought about this before?"

He shrugged and stared at the paper placemat. He curled the end up. "I suppose, but you didn't have *me* then." A light of excitement shone in his eyes. "I could, like seduce her or something. Or pretend I was, like, on her side, and then I could get her. Move her into the light or stick her with a stake or something."

Karen laughed and then clapped a hand over her mouth.

Ethan glared.

"I'm sorry, Ethan." She snickered again. "I don't mean anything by it, but I have doubts that you're her...type. And you haven't developed your powers yet. I don't want to see anything bad happen to you."

"It already did."

"Look," Gladys said, actually shaking her finger at him. "You get these ideas out of your head. Don't go doing anything stupid that'll get you killed or make her come after us. I, for one, am just thankful she left us alone and didn't turn us into one of her...after she...after she...you know." She was thinking about the group of silent stalkers she and Karen had encountered during their search of Miller Park.

"One of what?" Ethan asked.

No one responded.

"One of what?" Ethan asked. He banged his fist on the table. "Tell me!"

"Disciples," Hans said. "Not like Christ Our Savior. No, she has many who serve. They sometimes go to her, not knowing what else to do. When bitten three times, she then has them for slaves. Slaves do bidding. Others choose to stay away. Like us. And that doctor, Chocolate Chip Cookie. He also knows to go own way. That is smart way. And why we must look for those like you."

"Like me?"

"New vampires who've only been bitten once," Karen said. "Sometimes vampires just stay hidden. Dr. Trish...you know who I'm talking about?"

Ethan nodded. "Yeah. Gladys broke her dentures the other day and had to go for an appointment."

"Right. She has a sort of tingle, you know? She was turned way back when."

"I know. I heard the story."

"Part of it, anyway," Gladys said.

Karen continued. "Dr. Trish—Patricia—was her husband's nurse or assistant or whatever you called it back then. This was over in France, I think? His name was Walt Stepford—"

Ethan broke in, smiling in that goofy way of his that made him look like a little kid. "You mean she was a Stepford Wife?" He snickered.

Gladys laughed. She couldn't help it. She was a bit of a movie buff herself and had seen both versions of the film, preferring Nicole Kidman's version over the earlier one. She grinned at the kid.

Karen frowned, not wanting to draw this whole story out. "Yeah. I guess, technically she was. Anyway, back then, barbers also did surgery and dentistry. Before they understood medicine better. Trish and her husband emigrated to the US. In, what was it she said, Glad? 1878?"

"It was 1798," Hans said.

Karen nodded. They lived in New Orleans and at some point, when she was out one evening she was propositioned by some guy. Or at least, that's what Walt thought. The truth was even more terrifying. Walt was really protective of his wife and so when Patricia told him what happened, he tracked the guy down. It took some time, but— "Yeah. Gladys told me already."

"You interrupt always, young one. Let woman tell story.." Hans shook his head with his arms crossed. "So impatient."

Karen nodded in thanks. "Let me go on. When Walt finally found the manipulating cur in some back alley near the French Quarter, he was taken aback. The man was with a child! He couldn't bring himself to hurt someone in front of their own kid. According to Trish, she was so beautiful that all he could do was stare with his mouth open. She'd enchanted him, you see. It took all his willpower to tear his eyes away. He cautioned the womanizer—I guess today you'd call him a homewrecker—to stay away from his wife. The man was handsome, he noted. Incredibly so. Velvet jacket, long flowing hair, ruffly shirt, the whole shebang. I picture a guy dressed up like Mozart. And the kid, she had acres of curly hair. The vamp sicced the little girl on him. You can probably guess what happened then."

"Wait," Ethan broke in. This sounds a lot like a movie. With Tom Cruz? I forget who else was in it. But geez, it sounds awfully familiar. Like...is it Interview with a Vampire?

"Good job. Ten points to you," Karen said bitterly. "That's a movie I actually have watched. What most people don't know is that it, and several others, are based on true stories. Most of them, anyway."

Ethan thought about that for a moment. It wasn't every day that you found out monster movies were real. His face fell. "I guess I know what happened then. He died, didn't he?" "He died, didn't he?"

Karen shook her head. "That might have been better. But no, he was just turned. That really is better revenge, wouldn't you say?"

"To be cursed is worse than to die," Hans said. "I am Godless now."

Karen waved him off. "You can go into that later. Let me finish. So, anyhow, Walt went home, and Trish was horrified to see him covered in blood. She helped him clean up, thinking he'd just been hurt, even though she couldn't find a wound of any kind. For three days he lay in bed with the shaky shivers. She used leeches in hopes that a little bloodletting would get rid of the bad humors. On the third day, he was delirious and succumbed to his own bloodlust. He bit Patricia but had the presence of mind at least not to bleed her dry. She was mad at first. Who wouldn't be?"

"Turned by her own husband," Gladys said and shook her head.

"Eventually they put the whole thing behind them, but they avoided attacking people. There were plenty of rats and cats and things, but those never really fixed the problem. As you know, only human blood really gets rid of the hunger. They continued to work together in the surgery/barbery/tooth pulling business, and as time went on, they would nip just enough from their surgery patients, when they were under ether, to slake their thirst. Of course, as you could guess, one day Walt went a little overboard and accidentally drained the guy they were supposed to be curing.

"The locals were pretty pissed off because the guy was a prominent politician whose name Trish refuses to tell 'til this day. Walt was arrested one evening and tossed into a cell. When the sun rose the next morning, he was literally toast." A shudder went through her. "Patty pulled up stakes—"

Ethan erupted in laughter and all three of them stared, unaware of the play on words Karen had just done. "Don't you get it?" He snickered. "Stakes? Vampires?" He giggled again, but his laughter petered out when the rest of them looked irritated.

"Ahem," Karen said. "Trish moved to the Midwest where she was sure no one would know what had happened. She set up a barber shop in Iowa City, where she continued to do the tooth thing as well as haircuts and beard trims. After a while, it just became too difficult. What kind of dental establishment only sees patients after sunset? As time went by, she met other vamps—her special gift is what we call "the tingle"—lots of us have it, but it isn't very developed. Some have more than others. I guess it's like athletic ability. Anyone can run, but it takes a gift to win a race at the Olympics. Dr. Trish decided it was her duty to seek others out. She set up a vamp dentistry shop in her basement, trading services for gifts of blood—no questions asked, as long as it was in a container with a lid. She's very tidy. I suppose it's a result of her being in the medical field for so long.

"So, you go to this dentist? All of you? It's not like we can get cavities."

"Sure," Gladys said. "But decades and centuries of tartar build up are pretty unsightly. Besides. She's nice to talk to. And her advice is free."

"But how do people find out about her?"

"You know that tingle I talked about?"

He nodded.

"When she gets it, she finds them and leaves a calling card, inviting them to visit her. Some do, some don't," Karen said.

"Yeah," Gladys said. "She's happy to give advice while they're in the chair, and even has a pamphlet titled, *So You've Been Turned Into a Blood Sucker*. She charges for her services, but the advice is free and she, obviously, doesn't take insurance. Talk about blood suckers!" She laughed.

"What's your point?" Ethan asked.

"Point is," Hans said, "we have been in business long time. We know what is possible and not possible. You suggest impossible things. Though," he conceded, "is nice enough dream." He sighed. "You should spend time working on remodel building project. Then you will not have mind of murdering thoughts and will get used to idea of life as quiet vampire. You will see." Hans gave him a smug "now-that-it's settled" look and reached for the steaming carafe.

"If you say so," Ethan said. "I just don't see anything wrong with putting up a little bit of a fight. Stand up for ourselves, you know."

"Hans is right," Gladys said. "What you need is a diversion to keep you distracted from these *very dangerous* ideas. We all have our little diversions. Karen knits, I read and watch movies, and Hans..." She stopped there. "What do you do, Hans? To keep your mind off it?"

"I have stamp collection. And I like puzzles."

Gladys realized she'd never actually been inside Hans' house, despite the fact that they'd known each other for years. It stabbed her heart to think about how lonely his life must be. Working at a grocery store where he was barely tolerated. His only social functions being the support group and weekly coffee. She made a mental note to ask him to go out on a social occasion. Maybe a movie.

"These are things you just shouldn't be thinking about," Karen said, and raised her hands palms out. "The best thing to do is just keep your head down. Live your life quietly." She took a fake sip. "It's really just better that way."

"Just make the mustard," Ethan said with a bitterness Gladys had never heard before. "Well, that's easy for you. And for her," he jutted his thumb at Gladys. "And him," he pointed to Hans. "None of you probably did much before this anyway." He slammed his hands on the table, causing the entire restaurant—all seven tables—to turn and stare in their direction. With that, he got up from the table and left without a look back and headed for the door.

Gladys looked at her friends, each one mirroring the stunned look that was surely on her own face. Karen started to get up, but Gladys shook her head, rolling her eyes.

"I'll go. You two "enjoy" your coffee." The enjoy part she said with air quotes. "I'll take him home." She groaned as she slid out of the booth and staggered once before securing her footing.

"Call me if you need me, okay?" Karen said and squeezed Gladys' hand.

"Will do," she said with a sigh. She collected her giant handbag and plodded toward the exit and into the night, calling Ethan's name before the door shut completely.

29. WHILE YOU WERE OUT

It was as if Ethan had completely forgotten about his outburst at Village Inn, and that had been almost a week ago. In fact, he hadn't spoken about anything related to Estelle, not reclaiming their former selves, starting a rebellion, or mounting a hostile takeover. Nothing. Gladys wasn't sure she trusted his new, serene acquiescence. It seemed too servile to be real.

She'd watched him at work while he mopped the floors, at home while he mowed the grass in the dark, and at the last support group meeting, during which he was unusually quiet. Most of the time, you couldn't shut the kid up. He'd stopped whining about his share of house chores and about there not being enough blood supply. She might have suspected him of getting a little booty on the side or having a willing lady-blood donor, but he just didn't seem to be the type. He wasn't exactly Lestat in the looks department and she doubted the kid was capable of turning on the level of charm that would net him his own personal bloodfruit.

"When do you think I'm going to get my bedroom back?"

He was dragging half a dozen sheets of plywood across the basement floor by himself, a feat he'd never have been able to achieve before his reversal of humanity.

"Oh, you'll be getting more than just that." He grinned and puffed his hair out of his eyes. A work belt full of tools threatened to slide his jeans off his narrow hips. "This is more like a concept than just a room. I can't wait until you see it."

"So, again, how long 'til then?" She'd been cocooning next to the hot water heater for the last week and, although it didn't make a lot of difference—she was dead after all—Gladys was a woman who liked her own space.

"Soon," he said and threw back the tarp flap he'd secured to keep the dust in and her prying eyes out.

Gladys gave up and struggled back up the stairs, leaving him to his work. Maybe this *was* a good idea. Ethan got to be creative. He got to work with his hands. But most importantly, Ethan wasn't thinking about waging a one-man-boy war on a powerful vampire—one powerful enough that she was able to walk in the day, albeit covered from head to toe. The sunlight could still roast the bitch, but she wasn't in danger of dying every time the sun rose like they were.

Two hours later, Gladys hollered down to Ethan that she was headed to Golden Peaks for her shift where she'd while away the hours with her elderly patients, who were just a step away from being as dead as she was. Although, they weren't likely to get back up every night after their life force faded away. "I'm heading out now. Need anything?"

Ethan's voice echoed from the basement. "Nope! I'm good!"

She drove without the radio to the care facility. Ethan always insisted on listening to music at full volume whenever she'd allow it, and it was nice that he'd taken a few days off so she could drive in silence without having to argue. Her thoughts returned to Ethan's sunny, contented attitude, but the worry that he was up to something other than home improvement refused to leave her alone.

Gladys considered Hans. Was he in on it too? Although Hans held certain stereotypical attitudes toward the failing youth of America, she also knew he was as discontented with his life as a German vampire in America as Ethan was as a teenage vampire. What would he be willing to do if it meant he could return to his homeland or be welcomed back into the church and enfolded in the love of God? Would he risk their survival on the off-chance that a dingbat nineteen-year-old kid could do something to vanquish the head vamp? Surely, he was more pragmatic, more logical than that.

She parked, scrambled at the oh-shit handle to hoist herself out of the car and went inside to begin her thankless, but somehow rewarding job tending to the increasing needs of her aging clientele in God's Waiting Room.

After eight hours of running around delivering laxatives, bed pans, and sleeping aids (specifically in that order) her knees were killing her, and she thought if she could get them replaced, she'd happily slay a dozen head vampires just to get some damn relief.

She donned her sun block, full sleeves, hat, and climbed back into the Toyota. She'd probably get home before dawn, when the sun made its early summer way up over the horizon and cast its golden light on all things living. She'd never had the nerve to do an actual trial run to see if she could survive the daylight, and it was wise to take precautions. When the sun did rise, she'd die, temporarily. If it got close, she'd pull over somewhere and bundle herself in the emergency sleeping bag and space blanket she kept in the trunk. If that wasn't enough and she *did* get caught in the rays after she fell into her immortal slumber, well, she wouldn't have anything left to worry about.

As it was, she made it home before dawn. When she unlocked the door, the smells of sawdust and paint filled her nostrils. "Hello?" She called into the still house.

There was no answer, but Ethan was most likely already tucked into his hidey-hole for the day.

She undressed quickly and clambered down the stairs, wrapped herself up in the mummy bag and plastic tarp, and quickly turned still as stone.

The sensation of being rolled over like a rotten tree stump greeted her and she sat up, bewildered, rubbing at her eyes.

Ethan stood before her like a knight errant, holding out a one-ounce shooter and looking suspiciously proud of himself. "I've got something to show you!"

Gladys raised her eyebrow and took the proffered bottle, tossed it back, and struggled out of the bundle while he watched, grinning like a quokka. The image was perplexing and heartbreakingly innocent. She didn't trust it.

"What is it?"

"Come on, you'll see!" The image of a tiny, grinning marsupial remained.

"Alright, alright, let me get up first."

He stuck his hand out and pulled her to her feet like he was lifting nothing more than a milk jug. He'd gotten stronger.

"Okay, I want you to cover your eyes." He came up from behind her and covered her eyes with his hands.

"Ethan, what—"

"Nope. Just walk forward and you'll see!" He sounded giddy.

She was groggy and bewildered, but she allowed herself to be led forward. She heard the rustling of plastic and nearly tripped as he propelled her forward.

"Ta-daa!" He crowed and removed his hands.

At first, she didn't know what she was looking at. It was like a movie set. A goofy, Bella Lugosi vampire movie set. The walls had been hung with dark wood paneling and deep, rich red velvet swags ran across the ceiling, gathered at the corners with thick, rope tasseled ties. On the far end of the room was a platform, waist high, wrapped in varnished oak with two steps leading up to it. She approached reluctantly and looked down over the edge. It wasn't a coffin, not exactly. But he'd designed it to be just like one. The interior of the box was lined with crimson silk, so red it could have come from the bottle she'd just emptied.

"It's, um, a little bit wider than your average coffin. Not that you're, you know, fat, or anything like that. I just thought you might want a little more space. And look here." He pulled the lid down over the top of the box that wasn't a coffin and opened it again. "There's little latches here, so you can lock it when you're sleeping. See?"

She nodded.

"It locks from inside so there's no danger that someone else might, you know, open it or something when the sun's still up. And feel how soft it is!"

She ran her fingertips over the satin and pressed her palm into the interior. The batting was thick, and he'd made sure it was plush and soft.

"And," he said, whirling around and flipping on a light switch, "check this out!"

The overhead light went out and electric torches on the walls came to life, spilling soft orange light across the room. The effect was like candle-lit torches in the catacombs under Paris.

Gladys turned in a slow circle and then finally settled on Ethan, who was shuffling back and forth on his feet like he had to urinate urgently.

If he could...

The silence got to him. "Well, what do you think?"

Gladys was, for once, at a loss for words. What he'd built was campy and lovely and beautiful and ridiculous. She loved it. This was a step toward embracing who she was instead of cowering in the corner and trying to escape her nature. And if you couldn't change what you were...

She opened her mouth twice, then enveloped him in a huge hug, pressing his head into her cleavage. If he was the type of being that still needed to breathe, he might have suffocated. Tears leaked from the corners of her eyes, and she squeezed him until his arms started flailing. Finally, she released him and held him out at arm's length, wiping away the rivulets as they tracked down her cheeks.

"So, it's good?"

"It's better than good. It's wonderful!" She was truly touched. How long had it been since someone had done something so thoughtful for her, with no expectations in return. She frowned a little, not wanting him to think she was ready to let him completely off the hook. "Of course, it also bears a striking resemblance to an S&M den."

A look of confusion crossed over his face. "I don't know what that is."

"Honey, if you don't know, I'm not gonna be the one to tell you. Now what about you?"

"What about me, what?"

"Where do you sleep?"

He grinned, showing all his teeth, and led her to a concealed door next to her bedchamber/coffin. "Right through here."

Ethan's sleeping quarters weren't as rich and were much more modern. Rope lights in place of torches, black satin bedding, and a similar coffin which would easily accommodate two, as if he was waiting for his undead soulmate. Or, "lack-of-a-soul mate." The walls in his room were covered in rich black pleather. Medieval weapons and whips adorned one wall, and he blushed when Gladys noticed but didn't break eye contact. In both sleeping areas, the windows were completely covered, but done in a way that erased them from existence instead of making them look like boarded-up windows in a crack house.

S and M den indeed.

With her hand pressed to her chest, she said, "Ethan, how did you know how to do all this? It's more than carpentry. It's...well, I'm speechless."

"Coulda fooled me."

She pulled him in again, but kissed his cheek with a big, wet smack.

"Jeez!" He pulled away, wiping at his cheek, but grinning. "I *told* you. I was in construction management. And I used to work with my dad building houses in the summer."

"Huh." She had forgotten that, despite his crazy ideas and lack of experience, he had been in the process of pursuing higher education. Although he often seemed idiotic, he wasn't dumb. She smiled wanly, thinking of him bent over a desk, diligently studying.

"You're not gonna be grinning like that when Karen and Hans see this. They're going to want something too."

She thought for a moment. Karen, for sure, but Hans? She had no idea what he'd want if he had the choice and made up her mind then to force the issue and create an excuse for them to gather at his place soon.

"You think so?" Ethan asked. "I already have plans for them. Want to see?" He gestured toward a makeshift workbench he'd created with sawhorses and a sheet of plywood. "Come check it out."

30. ETHAN EARNS SOME PRAISE (FINALLY)

"He really pulled it off," Gladys said, twirling the upstairs phone cord around her finger. Ethan was still banging away downstairs, though she had no idea what else could possibly be needed. Everything looked pretty complete to her.

"What's it look like?" The excitement she heard in Karen's voice made her smile. There was so little to get excited over.

Gladys thought about it. How could she best describe the gothic bedchamber he'd constructed? Then it hit her. "It looks like a vampire sex den."

"Ooooh! That sounds scandalous!"

"Well, he has plans for you, too."

"Me?"

"Not in a sexy way." She chuckled.

"Oh, I get it." She sounded deflated.

"Hans too. He's gonna die when he sees what Ethan has in store for him. If he could die."

"Can I come see?"

Gladys checked her watch and calculated how much time she needed before she had to leave for work. "If you can make it in the next hour or so, you can."

"Are you kidding? I'll leave now!"

Twenty minutes later, Karen was at the front door. Gladys opened it, ushered her inside, and saw Mrs. Maitland peeping over the hedge between their driveways. It was *supposed* to be a privacy hedge, but that didn't seem to deter her all-too-curious neighbor. Gladys gave her a half wave and Arlyss disappeared below the line of bushes. *Nosey goddamn parker.* She ducked back inside, determined not to allow the neighbor's curious meddling and gossip quest to ruin her good mood.

"So? Show me, show me!" Karen rubbed her hands together, dancing back and forth.

"You'll not believe your eyes. Step right up!" Gladys said.

They descended the stairs to her new basement dungeon.

"I'm not sure I deserve such finery." She led the way.

"Oh, come on. How long have you been sleeping like a burrito on the dusty floor?"

"I guess about thirty years? More or less." She grunted with each step and clutched the railing for dear life.

"Good grief! Has it really been that long for you?"

"More or less." It really *had* been that long. She tried to imagine infinity stretching out forever, living this life of arthritis and lack of joy. The idea made her sick to her stomach, so she banished it. No use pondering the things she couldn't change.

"It's in here."

"In the storage area?"

"Not anymore." She flipped the light switch and the mellow torch lights on either side of the (casket) bed flickered to life.

"Oh my God," Karen clapped a hand over her mouth, eyes wide. "You weren't kidding when you said sex den."

"Nope, I'm afraid not."

"This must have cost a fortune!"

"Probably. I don't want to think about the credit card bill that's going to be here at the end of the month. I'm not sure I need all this." She gestured at the room with a wave of her hand. "I guess I can't complain. Where was all that money going to go anyway?" And really, what did she have to spend it on? No kids, no husband, no vacations to distant places. No grocery bill...

"I just can't believe he did this. I mean *Ethan*?"

"I know, I know. I had my doubts too." Gladys shrugged. "The kid's got skills, even if he lacks a bit of common sense. He said he was in construction management at Teakwood before his abrupt departure, and his dad had a construction company. Poor kid spent his summers working all day in the Godawful heat." She leaned against the wall with her arms crossed and assessed her new space.

"This really is incredible. I'm blown away."

"Yeah. You know, I think he's growing on me."

"Aww..." Karen pinched her cheek.

Gladys batted her away. "Like a fungus or a bad habit."

"Of course he is, sweetie. What's not to like?"

"I can list at least a hundred things," Gladys ushered Karen forward, "but I've decided to give him a break. At least for a day or two."

"How generous you are." Karen allowed herself to be ushered. "What's back there?" She pointed to the partially hidden door behind which lay Ethan's own den of supernatural pleasures that she doubted he'd ever use for the purposes of seduction.

"That would be Ethan's room."

"Where is he, anyway?"

"Shower. And thank the Gods for that. He smelled like pizza and garlic. Go ahead and look, but you'll blush."

Karen undid the latch on the door—something that looked like it belonged in an old castle, not a ranch house in the midwestern suburbs. It swung open, and the lights came on automatically.

"Motion sensor. He said it would alert him if someone entered. Not that it would do any good if he was dead to the world."

An electric candelabra that would have been at home on Liberace's grand piano lit one corner of the space and two sconces illuminated the other. The light was dim, and she had to strain her eyes to take in all the aspects of the room.

"Here." Gladys adjusted the dimmer switch so Karen could see better.

"Well…heeello!" She looked at Gladys lurking in the doorway with a raised eyebrow. "Who does he think he's bringing back here for a midnight snack?"

"I thought the same thing. I don't think there's any special ladies in his life. Or gentlemen. At least not right now, but that does have me a little bit concerned."

Although he didn't currently have someone, he was a horny nineteen-year-old kid, and it would only be a matter of time before he thought of the idea himself. She only hoped he'd bring it up before sneaking off for a secret date. A living, breathing, bleeding human being in this space could spell real trouble. Would he be able to control himself if they made out, and he noticed an enticing pulse in her throat? An artery just asking to be tapped? Or would some poor unsuspecting sorority girl end up like Mrs. Maitland's cat?

Would I be able to resist?

Gladys quivered with anxiety.

"What is it?" Karen asked, watching the tiny earthquake roll over her friend.

"I was just thinking…"

"Yeah. You don't have to say it. Maybe you should bring it up first, though. Kinda like the birds and the bees talk?"

She grimaced. The last thing she wanted to do with her adult roommate was to explain to him that it was best if he kept it in his pants and avoided dating, at least until he learned how to manage his new lifestyle.

"Maybe Hans could?"

Karen shook her head. "No, not Hans. He doesn't have a romantic notion in his entire body. I know he was married once, but I imagine it was just *Efficient German Sex.*" She said it in a perfect imitation of Hans' thick accent.

They both giggled.

"I think this time it has to be you."

Gladys shook her head and looked up at the ceiling, hoping a black hole would appear and spare her the responsibility. "Why must I take on all the unpleasant tasks?"

Karen filled Gladys' coffee cup with some fresh brew. "By the way, I meant to ask. Is he still brooding bout the thing at coffee the other day?"

"It's funny that you ask. He hasn't even mentioned it. Or Estelle. Or anything else." Gladys stirred her coffee and brought it to her lips to inhale the steam. "Maybe he's just been so busy with this project that he hasn't had time to contemplate the future or a possible cure. But I don't believe he's forgotten. I'm pretty sure that sooner or later he's going to come up with a detailed plan that won't work and will probably lead to his untimely demise. Hopefully, he'll run it by us first."

Footsteps on the stairs ended the conversation, but Gladys knew they'd have to address that subject as well as any Casanova ideas he might be having.

Ethan walked up to the door and stood between them with his arms crossed and his signature idiot grin.

"Cool, isn't it?"

Karen tipped her head toward him. "Seems like you've been pretty busy around here. It looks great. I'm very impressed."

"Yeah. Didn't I tell you it would? It's even better than I thought it would be. Gladys says it's like, some kinda sexy torture room—"

"Sex den. Not torture," Gladys said. The idea of a torture den was just too close to what they'd just been discussing before he appeared with his moppish hair still wet from the shower.

"Yeah, whatever. But it's cool, right? I mean, wouldn't you want to sleep in here? Like, even if you weren't a blood sucker and stuff?"

"I hate that term," Karen said in disapproval.

"Sorry. How about *Lady of the Night*?"

Karen exchanged a glance with Gladys and they burst into laughter.

When she was able to catch her breath, Gladys asked, "You know what that is, right?"

Ethan shook his head, perplexed.

"That's a nice term for a prostitute, so no," Karen said with a snicker. "I don't think I prefer that one either. How about vampire? We should just call a spade a spade."

"Fine. Spade."

Gladys looked at Karen whose turn it was to do the eye roll. "Ha ha."

Ethan elbowed Gladys and flapped his hand as if it made no difference to him. They stood in silence, admiring his handiwork.

"You want to see the plans I have for you?" His excitement was infectious.

"Of course!" Karen nodded.

Ethan had made the dining room table his architectural drafting office and large rolls of graph paper sat like scrolls on one end, pencils, protractors, and a calculator sat on the other. "It's over here." He selected a scroll and spread it out for her to see, holding the corners down with four of Gladys' old canning jars filled with gravel from the driveway.

For the next fifteen minutes, a very different Ethan took over; one more confident and capable. His knowledge of the whole construction process really was impressive. Once he'd explained the design strategy, he picked a smaller scroll and unrolled it. This was a surprisingly skilled sketch of what the finished project would look like when it was completed. Full color with lots of detail.

Karen gazed at the rendering. Pink satin, ruffles everywhere. But instead of making it look little-girly, he'd created a vision of soft-spoken sophistication that would suit her perfectly. Not as gaudy as Gladys' space.

Gladys felt her heart grow. Karen's upstairs bedroom was exactly the same as it had been when Carl and the kids had decamped. Gladys didn't think Karen had done anything but reach for the doorknob and pull her hand back since then. Her lonely box in the basement made it seem as if she was punishing herself by removing any semblance of joy. It was far better than Gladys' own sleeping arrangement had been before Ethan completed his handiwork, but it was still a sad excuse for a bedroom.

"Okay, now look at this one." He rolled up the plans, handed them to Karen to hold, and pulled out another small scroll. These drawings were much more understated. Functional. No flair or flash, and so completely *German*.

After a moment of silence, Karen said, "Ethan, I think these are perfect."

"Do you think Hans will let me do it?"

"Well, sure," Gladys said, and she thought that Hans really *would* let Ethan build him something like this. "But you better make sure you use *his* credit card this time." She looked at her watch. "I've got to get going. Ethan, you working today?"

"Nope. It's my last night off."

"Well, be good."

He smirked. "Of course I will."

Gladys raised an eyebrow and grabbed her bag on the way out the door. She and Karen walked to their cars together while the boys continued to pour over Ethan's plans.

"He's going to be fine!" Karen reassured her friend. "These projects are good for him." She kissed Gladys' cheek and walked pertly to her car with her perfect posture and sensible shoes.

As Gladys pulled out of the driveway, she wasn't thrilled to see that busybody Mrs. Maitland was back at the hedge, watching. This spelled trouble, and she had an uneasy feeling that she couldn't shake, which was a shame. She'd been exuberant, celebrating Ethan's success with Karen. Now, she wondered just what the heck the woman was so interested in. She flashed a peace sign which Arlyss frowned at and left for work.

31. HATCHING THE PLAN

"Hello, I am Hans."

"Hello Hans," chorused three voices.

"It has been long time since last I have drank from human." He sat on the metal chair and folded his hands in his lap, crossing one leg over the other. Apparently, he didn't want to elaborate.

How long, Hans? Gladys thought, but didn't say. Had he slipped up recently? A *long time* was pretty subjective.

"Well, that's vague," Ethan mumbled under his breath, echoing Gladys' thoughts right out loud.

"What was that?" Hans asked. He sat up, his narrowed eyes regarded Ethan like sharp daggers.

"Nothing."

Hans glared at him a moment longer, then dropped his gaze.

Ethan took this as an opportunity to do his introduction. He stood.

Hans relaxed.

The air in the VFW was hot and stagnant despite the whirling fans overhead which did little but stir up the dust kitties in the corners and send them cartwheeling. The Veterans didn't want them using up their precious air conditioning, it seemed.

"I'm Ethan."

"Hello Ethan."

"It has been two weeks since I last took blood from a human." He paused. "But remember, it wasn't my fault, so it doesn't count." He sat.

Gladys and Karen each took a turn with nothing to report.

Karen made checkmarks by each name on the legal pad balanced on her knee and then looked up, smiling. "So, what would you all say—"

"I have a plan," Ethan interrupted in a small, uncertain voice. He looked down at his scuffed sneakers and pressed his hands together between his knees. He didn't look up.

"Sorry?" Karen said. She frowned at her yellow pad as if the answer would be there. This must not have been on her mental itinerary.

"I have a plan, I said." His voice was only slightly louder this time.

"Hans, you should see it!" Karen bubbled.

Gladys didn't think Ethan was talking about remodeling, and she was pretty sure Karen didn't think so either. She commended her for her attempt to steer the conversation where she wanted it to go, but Gladys didn't think it would work. She was pretty sure she knew what Ethan was about to propose.

"A plan for what?" Hans asked. "Do you mean for sleeping chamber? Gladys told me about plans." He frowned. "I do not know why—"

"I want to kill Estelle." He announced as if he were saying he'd like to go for a walk. "And then all of us can have our old lives back again."

Thunderstruck silence filled the room. Static electricity made the scant hair on Gladys' head tingle. No one said a word. A page from an old newspaper skittered around the back of the room on a draft that came from nowhere.

"Say that again," Gladys said. She cupped a hand behind her ear. "I don't think I heard that right. Because what I *thought* I heard was something I have expressly instructed you NOT to think about."

"I can't help it." He shrugged. "I wanna find a girlfriend someday. I wanna finish college. I want to have a *life*."

"I want, I want, I want. Young people always wanting," Hans scowled at Ethan.

"Hans," Karen said, using her gentle "diffusing-a-situation" tone, "I don't think Ethan wanting these things is so unusual. Everyone's got hopes and dreams."

"Yeah, but let's be real," Gladys said. "There's no point entertaining the crazy idea that we could take on a head vampire and live. I might not be filled with life satisfaction, but I really don't relish the idea of being torn to shreds. Or worse, she could choose not to kill us and instead subject us to unspeakable torture. Being immortal, that torture could go on for a really long time."

"Or add us to her legion of slaves," Karen said.

What Karen said was true. If they lost a battle with Estelle, that was a definite possibility. She'd do it out of spite. But hadn't Gladys entertained these very thoughts herself, not too long ago? Not taking on Estelle—she'd never really considered that. But she *had* ruminated about the meaning of life and wondered what the point of this was. She wondered if the conversation she'd had the night after their little mushroom party had stuck in his mind.

She looked to her friends for validation. Karen was aghast, but Hans held a finger to his lips in contemplation. That was an unpleasant surprise.

"What, you two have some kind of Rambo complex or something?" Gladys asked. "Or maybe a death wish? A yearning to serve?" Anger flushed from her chest to the top of her head. This was a ridiculous idea, and she couldn't believe Hans was even considering going along with this lunacy. "You think you're gonna tie on a head band and run in there—wherever there is, by the way, we have no idea I'd like to remind you—guns blazing and shoot up the place like a Clint Eastwood movie?"

"You just shipped two completely different movies together there," Ethan said, missing the point in typical Ethan fashion.

"What is this ship—"

Gladys didn't give Hans the time to finish his question. She growled in frustration. "You get it though, right? What could we actually do? I know I'm not suited for fighting. Look at the mess I've been left with here!" She motioned to her lower body. Knees that cracked whenever she moved, swollen ankles that would have been encased in support stockings if it wasn't so damn hot.

"What about you, Karen?" Gladys spat. "You feel like a Terminator right about now, ready to bust out of someone's chest?"

"No more mixed-up eighties movie references, please!" Ethan clutched his head between his hands and squeezed his eyes shut. "If you're gonna use them, do it right!"

Silence engulfed them like a wave. Gladys hadn't even realized it, but her anger had caused her to lift from her chair (legs still bent as if she was sitting) and her eyes to turn crimson.

Karen touched Gladys' arm, and she realized what had been happening. She took a deep breath and came back to earth.

"Look," Ethan said, oblivious to his mentor's vamping out. "I'm working on a plan. It's not finished, but if you want to know how it can be done, then let me put it all together so I can explain. I can't stand the idea of spending the rest of my life like this! And surely all of you aren't exactly living."

Silence spun out in the cavernous space once more. "Not that you all aren't great company; you are." He swallowed. "I'm grateful that you took me in and kept me safe. And I'm grateful for your friendship too. It's just...don't you want something more? Aren't you tired of all this?" His speech completed, he leaned back in his seat and waited for an answer. Each of them considered the question in their own way. Hans was the first to speak up.

"If plan seemed logical, I would entertain ideas." He rubbed his hand over his stubbly chin. "Must admit I would like to see church again. And maybe someday homeland."

Gladys looked at Hans with her mouth ajar. "You can't be serious."

Karen raised her hand tentatively, as if waiting to be called on.

"Yes, Karen?" Gladys clenched teeth and heard her dentures crunch.

Shit. Back to see Dr. Trish. Again.

Karen cleared her throat. "I'd like to hear what Ethan comes up with, at least. I'm not saying a definite yes, but maybe he has a point. It can't do any harm to listen. After all..." Her face went all dreamy and her eyes were unfocused. "It *would* be nice to walk in the sunshine again. Maybe have an ice cream cone at the beach."

"I can't believe I'm hearing this!" Gladys' voice whip cracked, startling them all out of their ideas of possibilities and alternative lives. She turned her glare on each of them. This degree of anger was not in her usual repertoire. "Y'all are serious about the idea of a suicide mission?"

"Well, Glad," Karen said, still pondering, "how long can we keep going like this? It's just living for the sake of living."

"That's not enough?" Gladys shook with fury. Fury at the kid for showing up and planting impossible ideas in their heads, fury at Hans for feeding Ethan's fire, fury at Karen for even considering this terrible idea, but mostly she was still furious at that twat Estelle for putting them all in this situation in the first place.

"Perhaps no," Hans said and folded his hands in his lap. Stoic and stubborn.

Gladys stood, stumbled, and then righted herself. "I'm not entertaining this whacko idea. I'm going to go sit in the car. Ethan, if you want a ride home, I'll wait."

"I can take him home," Karen said and squeezed Gladys' hand.

She yanked it away. "Fine. You all play into this insanity if you want. I'm having no part of this. I'm not some super woman."

She grumbled under her breath, tossing in an occasional swear word as she thumped toward the door. She looked back at them, bent forward toward one another, talking.

Conspiring.

She yanked it open, and went out into the night, still cursing.

Once she was in the car and driving away from the suicide club, she felt her anger intensify, rather than dissipate. Gladys pounded her fist on the steering wheel, as she sped away from the meeting. A few moments passed before she remembered that their whole goal in life was to remain beneath the radar. It would be stupid for her to blow it in a moment of anger.

Ethan was a good kid, she thought. With mostly honorable intentions, but that didn't give him the right to put everyone's life at risk. And those two supposed friends of hers. After all, they'd been through together, how could they even consider going along with this? It was absurd. The worst part was that everything had been just fine until he showed up.

She never should have agreed to take him in. Hell, she could have just let him get caught taking liberties with a patient—sooner or later it would've happened—and let fate play out without intervention. She missed her hum-drum, boring routine. Her safe, unremarkable life and quiet friendships. Evening television programs she didn't have to negotiate with her squatter. And now all that was being put in jeopardy by some dumbass nineteen-year-old kid who didn't even need to shave every day before his run-in with Estelle, and whose voice seemed to crack half the time when he spoke. He still had acne! What could he possibly know about their life after just a few months?

But, look what he did in the basement. He proved he's good at planning. He proved that he was, despite appearances, intelligent. He was motivated and...

"Fuck!" she shouted to no one but herself. She was halfway to believing he might actually be able to concoct a plan that didn't seem completely bonkers. He'd really surprised her with his ingenuity and creativity, but that didn't mean he'd be able to come up with an assassination plot to kill a vampire who'd been lurking around the globe for centuries.

Estelle scared her. That was plain and simple. It was Estelle's eyes that haunted her. The way they'd sapped her will, knowing that when she was entranced, she'd do anything the woman wanted. Maybe even kill her friends if directed to do so. She remembered how euphoric being under her power had been. All she'd wanted the moment she'd tasted her foul blood on her tongue was to please the creature she most hated. What other crimes would she be willing to commit under her spell?

What if she did convert us all into drone slaves in her legion? She'd use Ethan as a sex slave, command Hans to captain the witless soldiers, turn Karen into her willing assistant, and what about herself?

"I'd die," she said out loud as she pulled into the driveway. "She'd have no use for me, and I'd die." She killed the engine and got out of the car. Movement in the corner of her eye caught her attention and snapped her out of her thoughts.

"Mrs. Knight."

"Mrs. Maitland."

"What brings you out so late?" Arlyss asked.

Christ. It just keeps getting worse.

"That support group," Gladys said, hoisting her massive handbag over her shoulder. "I know I've told you about it before."

"Oh yeah. For those people who can't go in the sun. Like you. What's it called?" She tapped herself under the chin in fake contemplation. "Xray or something?"

"XP." Gladys said. She didn't like where this was going. Mrs. Maitland seemed way too interested lately in the comings and goings at her house.

"Oh right. That's it."

"Yeah, that's it." She hoisted her bag onto her shoulder again and turned toward the house.

"How's the young man?" She winked, looking at her over the hedges. Gladys couldn't remember her being so tall. What had she done? Bought a stepstool for the purpose of spying on the neighbors?

"Ethan. My nephew. He's fine."

"Seems like he's been involved in quite the project."

For fuck's sake, woman, will you PLEASE go away and tend to your bunions or something?

"Yeah, he's doing some basement remodeling."

"Ahh. I see."

Gladys turned back again and walked up the sidewalk.

"Oh, one more thing, Mrs. Knight," she called.

Good God, please go away.

Gladys turned toward her neighbor, all smiles. It was hard to keep that smile and civility when all she wanted to do was scream. "Yes?"

"I just wanted to let you know that I'm keeping Mr. Fuzzles inside. So, if you see him out, please let me know. Cats have a way of disappearing around here. You know."

"I don't, but I'll take your word for it." She felt a strange flicker of fear but didn't know why. "I'll let you know if I see him."

"Do that. Good night, Mrs. Knight."

"Good night, Mrs. Maitland."

Gladys shut and locked the door behind her, bracing her not inconsiderable bulk against it as if she expected Arlyss to come bursting in and...and what, exactly? Steal a cup of laundry detergent? She didn't know, but something seemed off. Maybe it was just Ethan and his talk of impotent rebellion that had her riled up.

She dug two ice packs out of the otherwise empty freezer and flopped into her recliner with her feet up. She had a hot date with The Bachelorette. This season's most sought-after bachelor was an orthopedic surgeon with dark good looks, and wouldn't she just *love* to have Dr. Cameron Rickstadt replace her knees! It was dumb entertainment, but she really wanted to know whether he'd get the rose at the end of the show or if the dumb blonde would give it to some other guy who was handsome but lacked brains. If only the network would allow their viewers to vote the losers off like they did in *Survivor*.

32. THAT'S THE WAY THE COOKE CRUMBLES

A tentative tap-tap-tap at the door roused Gladys from her half-sleep. For a fleeting moment, Estelle was back. Ready to punish her for even *thinking* about meddling in her affairs. She had no idea where she was. Then it came to her. The recliner. The Bachelorette. And Ethan.

Ethan.

Frowning, she lowered the footrest and got up. After the two requisite stumble-steps that she had to take every time, she found her equilibrium and hobbled to the front door. She cursed her aching knees, feeling like a toddler who was just learning to walk.

Gladys looked through the peephole only to be treated to the sight of Ethan's giant, eclipsing eyeball. Not that he could see anything. She flipped the dead bolt and pushed the door open, then thumped back to her chair. Ethan entered with the others and had the good grace not to laugh. One point in his favor, she supposed.

"What's this? An intervention?" She asked sourly. "I'm not the one who needs help here. I think y'all ought to take a good look at yourselves in the mirror." She pointed at each of them and rocked gently, pressing the toes of her slippers into the plush carpet with her hands clasped across the twin melons of her bosom.

"But we can't look in the mirror," Ethan said. "That's the problem."

Karen shot him a look that said, "shut up." She was doing the hand wringing thing that Gladys hated to see. It reminded her of a helpless old woman. "Glad..."

The door slammed closed, courtesy of Hans who ducked at the sound of the crack. Always forgetting his own strength.

"*Glaaad,* what?" She said in a high-pitched, mocking tone. She wrinkled her nose and rocked faster, as if she could outdistance the ne'er do wells who'd crowded into her living room.

Karen glanced at Ethan and perched herself on the edge of the couch. "I think we should at least consider what Ethan's saying. There's no harm in listening." She looked at her friend hopefully. "Is there?"

"Of course there is! He's saying, 'hey, why don't we wage a war on the Confederacy, why don't we declare war on the

Republicans, why don't we overthrow the government, why don't we go climb Mount Everest, why don't we organize a half-assed *suicide mission*! I don't feel like committing suicide just yet."

Ethan gave her a look with a little crooked half-smile. "Yeah, but didn't you say that? After—"

"You're gonna hold me to something I said after being on a big drug trip?" But hadn't she thought that herself more than once? She was exasperated and just wanted this whole conversation to be over. Forever.

"But—"

"No buts. No ifs or ands either. Do you seriously picture me being, I don't know, helpful in a covert operation to murder an ancient vampire? Do you see me wielding a crucifix and standing firm before an evil we can't begin to imagine? I don't. Because I can't *hold* a crucifix, and I can barely stand up straight most days! I happen to know that, if there's any need for a quick escape, I'm the one who's going down while y'all take off for the four points of the compass." She paused. "Three points of the compass. You see what I'm getting at here?" She threw up her hands. They fell with a soft fwap on the arms of her chair, shifting one of the little protective doilies which fell off the arm and drifted to the floor. She rocked faster.

"It would not be like that," Hans said, his voice lowering in register as he tried for comfort. It was a hard sell.

"What would it be like?" She squinted at him with one eye shut. "Please tell me what the fortunes have in store for us, oh wizard."

Hans, who had been the only one to remain by the door, now entered and sat on the couch next to Karen, who still seemed ready to make a break for it if this whole thing turned south.

Hans shook his head slowly. "Not wizard. Vampire. I think we could maybe come up with solution," he said slowly. "Ethan...he may have faults but has point. Is possible he could find a way to do this where we do not die."

"Very comforting." Her mouth twisted into a sour grimace. "Possible. Could. Maybe. Not words to inspire confidence.

Karen patted Hans' leg, a gesture that did not escape Gladys' attention..

Well, well, well. What do we have here? Probably nothing but comfort.

"I think we should consider thi—," Karen began, but was interrupted by the sound of a car door slamming outside. She looked at Gladys in alarm. "You expecting company?"

"No," Gladys said as she fought to get out of the chair again. Her internal radar was pinging away like mad.

Hans leaned over the back of the couch and twitched the curtains and black out shade aside enough to see. A blur of motion flew past the house toward the back. "What is this?" He sprung up and was at the back patio door before anyone could blink.

Karen was on high alert, hands balled into fists.

Ethan, however, just looked confused.

"What is it?" Gladys asked as she moved toward the dining room, much faster than her usual tottering pace. She tasted fear.

"I see nothing," Hans said, peering into the darkness of the back yard. "Karen, what is in driveway?"

Karen got up and looked out. "It's an ambulance."

And that's when everything slammed into chaos.

The glass patio door shattered inward, sprinkling the aged yellow linoleum with diamond splinters. Something leapt up onto the dining room table, knocking all of Ethan's hopes and dreams onto the floor in a fluttering cascade of paper and Hans to the floor on his butt. Gladys remained frozen in the doorway, her mouth in a dismayed "O" and her hand rising to her throat.

Crouched on her dining room table was a man who looked slightly familiar. The skin on his face was pulled back tight against his skull. His chin was an elongated exaggeration. The cheek bones protruded, making his eyeballs sink—two hot burning coals in dark black sockets. Two-inch fangs protruded from his upper gums and his hands were twisted into claws. He wore a white coat. A name tag dangled off the pocket.

"Fuck!" Gladys shrieked. "It's Doctor Cooke, and he's totally vamped out!" She grabbed a book from the shelf next to her and hurled it at him. It landed pathetically short of the table and slid underneath. It was *The Seven Habits of Successful people*.

This is why we have no business meddling!

Karen approached fists clenched, and took a deep breath, and released it. As she did, her feet left the floor, and her sharp teeth pushed through her gums, now visible under the bow of her upper lip. Her hair was a floating corona, and the air felt thin and charged with electricity. The faint smell of sulphur danced in the air. Her face changed, becoming monstrous, completely at odds with the mint-green sweater she wore over a white shirt with little pink flowers. Probably a Lane Bryant special.

Ethan could have told the others she looked like a deranged version of Storm from the X-Men crossed with The Green Goblin, but he was incapable of speech. He shrank against the wall, seeming to want to press himself into the drywall and disappear. He watched with huge, round eyes, looking like a rabbit. Looking like…prey.

"Preeeeyyy," the Doctor Cooke shaped abomination snarled, as if it could read Gladys' thoughts. It licked its lips, which had pulled back from its teeth. Its hellish eyes settled on Ethan.

The kid shrieked and ran toward Karen.

Gladys wasn't sure if he'd meant to protect her or cower behind her, but Karen didn't give him a chance to do either. She shoved him backward with a blast of that freaky air and he flew across the dining room into the room they'd just left. He hit the sofa, knocking the wind out of himself.

At least it was a soft landing.

Gladys nearly laughed out loud, catching the crazed terror that hung in the room like smoke from a campfire.

Doctor Cooke locked eyes with Karen, who was now a full five feet off the floor and looking very, *very* un-Karen. She was mere inches from brushing the ceiling with her hair. Her skin had thinned and stretched, and her mouth was frozen in a smile that was more rictus than grin. Cooke crouched lower like a swimmer getting ready to dive, then sprung at her, but his momentum was suddenly thwarted, and he fell to the floor with a thump and an unearthly scream of frustration.

Hans had snapped his hand up and caught the good doctor mid-leap. He managed to get to his feet with his hand still manacled around the doctor's ankle. The doctor screamed with rage. Hans' skin rippled and bubbled as if snakes squirmed beneath the surface.

Gladys felt herself change from the inside out. A terrible heat filled her body like a post-menopausal hot flash on steroids, and all rational thought retreated into a far corner of her mind. Her vision narrowed, and she saw everything before her with precision and clarity. Her knees were the last thing on her mind. Her dentures clicked together as they fell on the floor. Her fangs were on proud display.

Ethan rose slowly from where he had fallen. "Gladys?" He said with a timidity he'd never displayed before.

Of course, he'd never seen her like this before, either.

She turned, nearly grinning.

He recoiled at the sight of his mentor turned monster, and who could have blamed him? Two-hundred and fifty pounds of solid, angry vampire power stood where mild-mannered Mrs. Knight, the kindly nurse he'd met at Golden Peaks, had been moments before. Her skull changed shape, stretching to a nearly comical length, showing every hill and valley through her mostly absent hair. The sockets of her eyes bulged, giving her an insect-like appearance as they protruded and filled with angry flames.

An inhuman growl began in the deep reaches of her chest, sounding like a cross between a huge dog and a prehistoric dinosaur, and finally found its exit through her gaping mouth. She roared and charged after the vampire struggling in Hans' grip. Her knees sounded off like impact drills. The house shook with her mighty thunder.

The squirming doctor lying on the floor uttered a mewling cry as the three elderly vampires swarmed over him. Hans' transformation was complete, and something close to horns sprouted from the sides of his head. His mouth was a wide, bloody slash with a tongue that, between his new teeth, writhed like a snake.

Karen descended upon the intruder with a cry of fury and triumph. Her hands were contractures that ended in claws. She sank them deep into the flesh beneath his doctor's coat, reared back her head, and tore the man's throat out, sending a spray of blood across the room. It dappled her friends like rain as the man's Adam's apple popped in her mouth like an overripe tomato.

Hans and Gladys joined her and soon the man in the once-white coat stopped clawing at them for escape.

Blood flew, hitting the wall, the ceiling, and Ethan's carefully drawn blueprints with a thick scarlet stew of blood and entrails.

Hans thrust his hands into the man's chest and dug until he found the unbeating heart and ripped it from its moorings.

Cooke's jerky movements slowed, trembled, then ceased.

Ethan's new friends backed away from the carnage, panting like animals spent from the hunt, staring with animal-like hunger—then they dug in for a fine meal. Cooke, reduced to mortality when his heart left his body, had become food.

Ethan's face was a mask of horror as he watched Dr. Cooke's desiccated body begin to deflate, now nearly drained of blood. Chip's facial features returned to their previous humanity as he transformed.

Karen beckoned to Ethan eagerly, urging him to come forward and sample the feast, her face covered in blood and globbets of flesh.

He backed away, afraid of all of them, not just the monster who'd come crashing in uninvited. "No," he squeaked. His legs lost their strength, and he slid down the wall streaking the splattered gore of the kill along with him.

The thing on the floor continued to deflate, going from vampire to mortal being to something like a mummy that belonged in an ancient tomb. And still he was losing substance. The fingers curled in on themselves, the eyes fell into deep pits and disappeared, the lips rounded themselves around his gums and after an interminable moment, there was nothing left but a pile of clothes, a pair of loafers, two sharp fangs, and three aging vampires who stood looking at each other with bewilderment. Wearing blood and a flicker of satisfaction.

33. THE CONFESSIONAL

Ethan's face was a greenish pasty color that people got when they were about to throw up. If he *could* have thrown up. He hadn't eaten anything since Mrs. Maitland's cat, which didn't count as regular human food. He sat on the floor with his legs stuck out in front of him and surveyed his friends as if a large-scale re-evaluation was taking place.

"What the fuck was that?" Gladys asked. Her hand pressed against her heaving chest, trying to catch her breath.

"That was Doctor Chip Cooke," Hans, declarer of the obvious, said. "I do not think he will be doctoring again." He nudged the pile of bloody clothes with his foot and grimaced with distaste.

"Well, yeah, I know who it is," Gladys said, rolling her eyes. "But why?"

"I don't know," Karen said, wiping absently at the blood on her face. "But he was really pissed about something."

"That's an understatement. But *why*? Why would he bother coming over here in the first place?" Gladys asked. She reached over and swiped a chunk of Dr. Cooke off Karen's chin and flung it into the pile of clothes. "Had a lil' something on ya there, chum."

"Thanks, Glad."

"He said something," Gladys said. "When he burst in here, he looked at Ethan and said something. What was it?"

"Prey," Karen said and covered her elbows with her hands.

"Prey? Was he mad?"

"Mad, yes. But not crazy. Mad at Ethan. Has the boy done something?"

Hans looked toward Ethan accusingly, and the other two women followed his gaze.

Ethan shifted his eyes away, refusing to look at them. They settled on the blood and gore. He shook his head and finally decided to look at his sweaty, bloody mentor.

"Ethan?" Gladys said with a little uptick, as if she was talking to a puppy who'd piddled on the living room rug. "Do you know something about this?"

He swallowed. His Adam's apple bobbed up and down, and Gladys pictured the good doctor's own larynx as it exploded between Karen's incisors. She willed herself not to look. Blood lust still coursed through her and a remote part of her thought the most rational thing in the world would be to do to Ethan what they had just done to their previous blood dealer.

"Look, you need to tell us," Karen said, wiping her hands on her slacks. "Even if you made a mistake, you need to tell us what it was so we can fix it."

"Or ready ourselves for worse attack," Hans said.

"I was just trying to help," Ethan said in a high-pitched, frantic voice. He begged for clemency with watering eyes of sorrow and shame. "I swear, I was just trying to save you some time."

"What did you do? Fess up!" Gladys said and pounded her fist into her hand. She'd gotten her breathing under control but had made no attempt to wipe the stipples of blood from her face. They were all going to need a serious shower.

"Okay." He tried to get up, but his feet slipped on the linoleum, and he fell back on his ass. His teeth clicked, and he bit his tongue. "Ow!"

"Out with it," Hans said.

Ethan pulled on his tongue as if to examine the damage, then let go and put his palms on the floor. "I went to the hospital, see? We were getting low on blood. You all keep giving me extra, and I knew you were going to have some shifts to cover at work, and since I was off work for the remodeling, I thought I'd, you know, save you a trip and go over there and get it myself."

"Shit!" Gladys slapped her forehead, and fine droplets of blood spattered onto the wall. It would have been comical had it not been for their precarious situation. "I *told* you! Chip doesn't like surprises." She looked at the rumpled laundry and nudged it with her foot. "*Didn't* like surprises. We had a designated day and time for pick up. No deviations."

"Well, I get it now." Ethan threw his hands up in surrender. "But I didn't really think it would be that big of a deal."

"Tell us what happened," mild-mannered Karen said in a soothing "there-there" voice that made Gladys want to slap her.

"I went to the hospital, where we went before. And knocked on the door back by the loading dock. Where we were before, you know?" His eyes pleaded with them for understanding.

Gladys shook her head. "How did you even get there?"

He swallowed. "The bus. I didn't hurt anybody!" He took a deep breath and looked at the mess. A little sob escaped his throat, but Ethan continued. "And some chick answered. I asked for Dr. Chip. She looked at me funny and then went and got him. When he came out, and I told him why I was there, he got really mad at me and started shouting. And then the chick came back after a few minutes, and she had these security guards with her. I thought they were there for me, you know? But when they took a step forward, Chip...um...he, like, turned on them. He was really pissed and shouting and stuff, and I think he might have bit someone. I don't know, I didn't stick around to find out. I ran away."

"Oh. My. God," Karen said. "He *bit* someone?"

"Maybe more than one." He picked at an invisible thread on his blood stippled shirt.

"You basically outed him! Jesus Christ, no wonder! I bet he stole the ambulance and came here for revenge. *That's* why he was after *you* in particular!" Karen stomped to the patio door and looked out to see if there were more blood thirsty killers lurking in the bushes.

"I know, I know. I understand now."

Gladys' face turned to stone. "Is that ambulance still in the driveway?"

Ethan struggled and finally got to his feet. He looked out the front window. "Uh, yeah. It's still there. There's no lights or anything though."

Gladys' mind reeled.

Think fast. Or you're likely to have a bigger problem on your hands.

"Hans, we need to get rid of that ambulance. But we need to make it look right."

"Why do you say me? And what do you mean by looking right?" His bushy eyebrows lifted in a question.

"I mean, we need to get it the heck out of here! And we need to make sure it doesn't look suspicious." Gladys gestured toward the driveway as if she were shooing away an annoying fly.

"How do we do that, exactly?" Karen asked.

Gladys paced in the doorway between the living room and dining room, noting that the couch had a slightly canted look from Ethan's impromptu flight across the house. She stopped. "You," she pointed at Ethan, "and you two." She pointed at Hans and Karen. "Y'all need to shower that blood off you ASAP. Get moving. I'll explain when you're done."

They looked puzzled but got moving without question.

"Two minutes!" She yelled down the hall. "Ethan, what kind of shirts do you have in your closet? Quick!" She snapped her fingers at him.

Half an hour later, Hans, wearing Doctor Cooke's white lab coat (Karen had gotten rid of most of the blood stains with hydrogen peroxide. Even though it was still damp, it would pass) pushed a moaning Ethan toward the back of the ambulance on a gurney.

Karen climbed into the driver's seat wearing Ethan's plain, navy-blue polo—the closest they could come to a paramedic's uniform on short notice. They had pinned Dr. Cooke's badge to the right breast.

Once Ethan was unceremoniously shoved into the back of the running ambulance, Karen screeched out of the driveway with Hans in the passenger seat and took off down the street with the tires leaving twin streaks of smoke behind her.

The lights flashed on as they disappeared around the corner. Moments later, she heard the warble of sirens.

Gladys waited five minutes and then went to the car, clutching her purse under her arm to catch up with them.

"Mrs. Knight?"

Gladys froze.

"Is everything alright?" Arlyss Maitland's voice reflected the concern one neighbor would have for another in a time of crisis, but her face said something different. Like she was in on a joke and Gladys was the butt of it.

"Yes, of course." She tried to smile, but the muscles in her face felt strained. She'd changed her shirt and wiped the obvious blood off her face, but realized she had neglected her pants. Mrs. Maitland pointed to them.

Gladys looked down and then offered Mrs. Maitland a sheepish grin and the quickest explanation she could come up with that sounded reasonable. "It was my nephew. He fell through the patio door while he was changing a light bulb. So, we called 9-1-1." Sweat poured off her forehead through her thin hair.

"We?"

Goddamned nosy woman, why don't you go have a stroke or something?

She didn't really wish her dead, but she did wish she'd get thrown into a rehab facility somewhere for a very long time. And take her stupid cat with her.

"Yes, Ethan and I, I mean." Gladys had had enough. Why did this woman think it was alright to spy on her business?

"Kind of late, isn't it? For changing lightbulbs and such?"

Gladys didn't care for the look on Arlyss's face, but had no time to think about it.

"Yes," she snapped. "I suppose it is. Why are *you* still up?" Her lips thinned to a line like a bloodless incision.

The woman faltered for a moment, which brought Gladys a moment of triumphant joy.

"Oh, I just heard a whole lot of kerfuffle over there, so I thought I'd check in. I do hope the boy will be alright."

Sure, you do.

"I'm sure he'll be fine. He'll need some stitches for sure."

Now get the fuck outta here or I'm going to start screaming at you and I don't know if I'll be able to stop.

She wondered how Arlyss would taste. Her crooked dentures threatened to pop out of her mouth from the force of her erupting fangs, but she held them back.

The neighbor's moony face, filled with false concern, hovered over the black shadow of bushes, and Gladys wished she could punch that look right off it.

"Please let me know if there's anything I can do. Anything at all."

"Right." Gladys gave her a wave and hurried to the car.

You can go to Hell.

She sped toward the hospital where Hans and Karen would dump the ambulance a block away from the loading dock. They'd let Ethan out of the back, get in her car, and go over to Hans' house to regroup and make a plan. Her house was no good now, with the back door shattered. As she drove, she had time to wonder about her neighbor. Why *was* she always butting in? Why *was* she always nosing around? Was it just the cat, or was there something else? She drove faster. If her suspicions were correct, they no longer had the luxury of inaction. Mrs. Maitland was part of this.

34. PALAVER

Gladys brought the car to a screeching halt and three people tumbled out of the ambulance parked on the shadowy street, looking very much like clowns getting out of a clown car.

But we're the clowns.

Gladys watched them approach, her heart thumping wildly with impatience. It was amazing to feel that lub-dub in her chest after a good feeding. She had the car rolling before all the doors had been secured. To hell with seatbelts. Houses zipped by as she sped away from the scene. She would have gotten pulled over, but Hans had enough sense to put his hand on her shoulder—a firm and grounding pressure. She felt rather than heard him tell her to be calm. She took a deep breath and let off the gas pedal a little bit.

She glanced at him with a strained smile. "Thanks."

"Now what?" Ethan asked.

"Now we go to Hans' house and have a little confab," Gladys said.

"A what?" Karen asked.

"She means a palaver," Ethan said.

"What is palaver?" Hans asked. "And what is confab?"

"Palaver," Ethan repeated. "You know, to sit and talk about a problem? Like in *The Gunslinger*?"

Hans looked into the back seat and narrowed his eyes. "Please speak English. Is hard enough to understand without these fancy words."

"Sorry, it's just, in this book I like, it's the Old West, but not really. It's kinda like in the future, but like he's a cowboy and he has these companions...kinda like us, but they come later on in the series through magic doors, and they're on this quest, see? And any time there's a big question, like how to go on or what to do next, the Gunslinger's always like, 'hey, let's palaver' and they all crouch in the dirt and talk." Karen and Hans regarded him with blank faces. "Never mind."

Gladys ignored the chatter, and kept her eyes on the road, particularly to the side roads. It would be disastrous to get pulled over now by a cop who had been waiting for someone to fall into his speed trap. There wasn't a single thing that would explain their situation. She checked the speedometer and let off the gas a little more. As they pulled onto Hans' street Gladys asked, "Is there anything in the garage?"

He looked at her, puzzled. "My car is in garage."

"Well, I figured that," she snapped. "Is it taking up both sides, Hans?"

He still didn't seem to understand.

Gladys huffed in exasperation. "Is there room on the other side of your garage? I don't want my car on the street."

Understanding dawned. "Other side is empty but for boxes. Pull up and I will move boxes for you to pull in car."

She did as he asked and killed the lights while he made space for the Toyota in the empty garage bay. It didn't take long. Gladys pulled in, shut off the car, and ushered everyone in through the service door.

"Shut it!" she hissed. The automatic door was still trundling downward when she slammed the door shut and turned the deadbolt. Gladys breathed in deeply and exhaled all the air in her body. "Thanks, Hans."

As they stood in the garage entrance off the kitchen, it struck her again that she'd never actually been inside Hans' house in all the years they'd known each other. She almost laughed. It was just so...so him. From where she stood, the walls were all white, the carpet grey, and was decorated in a style which could generously be described as minimalist. No art graced the walls, and the only photographs were on a small drop-leaf table in the hall. Everything was low, and small, and angular.

"You are welcome," Hans stammered. The next second, he stood in the front windows.

Gladys hadn't seen so much as a muscle twitch.

"I see no one."

It was spooky how quickly he could move when he wanted to.

"Good," Ethan said. He walked over to Hans' uncomfortable looking sofa and sat down, hanging his head.

"I need a minute," Gladys said. Her hands shook, and she tried to still them. "Where's the bathroom?"

"Down hall. Left side. First door."

As she walked, her knees hurt more than ever. All the action must have really done a number on the joints. It would fade, of course, but only back to the usual dull throbbing. The way they *always* were and always would be. She closed the door softly behind her and leaned against it. The mirror over the dual sinks had been covered with a grey sheet. She splashed her face and then noticed something on the bathroom counter. A hairbrush with brown strands in its bristles. A zippered pouch with pink flowers embroidered on it. She opened it up and confirmed her suspicions with a ghost of a smile.

Good for Hans. And good for Karen.

She decided not to mention anything. If they wanted their business kept secret, she would keep it.

"So, what is all this?" Karen asked when Gladys returned. She leaned against the wall with her arms crossed.

Gladys sat on one of the uncomfortable couches. "I think it's pretty much as you said. Obviously, Cooke got outed by Ethan here," she shot an irritated look in his direction.

He ducked as if she'd thrown something heavy,

"And he went nuts. I don't know what happened to him between the time he met Ethan and the time he showed up at my house, though. How many days would that have been, Ethan?"

"Umm...two. I guess."

"Two days?" Karen counted backward. "That would have been the day after coffee, right?"

Ethan nodded. He looked on the verge of tears.

"Hey," Karen said and crossed over to him. "You were just trying to help, I understand." She pulled his head onto her shoulder and patted him like a favored pet. "But you understand now, you need to run things by us before you go out on your own. We have a way of life that we've relied on for a long time. It's kept us from turning to dust."

He looked up at Karen, and the pitiful expression on his face both softened and irritated Gladys. Yes, the kid needed help and guidance. That was more obvious now than ever before. But he was such a liability! He was very likely to get them all killed. She silently wished he'd never started working at Golden Peaks.

"We have other problem," Hans said. He'd turned on the living room lights, which cast a soft glow. In spite of Gladys' first impression—that his house was sparsely decorated—she realized now that it was just tastefully laid out. Then she realized. Ikea. The Swedish furniture company. The whole place was done up in Ikea. She almost expected a trio of blonde girls bounding up the basement stairs with ribbons in their braids, singing some Swedish folk song. Maybe carrying giant mugs of beer.

"Earth to Gladys!" Karen snapped her fingers in the air with one hand while the other cradled the head of a quietly sobbing Ethan into her shoulder. "Hi! Welcome back. So, what are we going to do?"

"What are we...what?"

Hans paced. "We have big problem, as I said. More than one. First is blood. Without blood supply, what will become of us? We've sworn not to take blood from human. This will be the end of the easy street." He shook his head morosely. "Second, it is seeming perhaps Dr. Chip had more customers than we know? Perhaps there are others alerted? I also have suspicion about drugged blood. What if there is cartel of blood drugs in vampire world that we know nothing of?"

"Hans," Karen said in a voice that was full of gentle authority, "I seriously doubt there's any vampire cartels. In fact, I think we're a pretty rare breed in this little midwestern town."

"Actually," Ethan said, "Iowa City is pretty big. There's like, 80,000 people. And if you add in Coralville, that makes it almost 100,000. That's a lot of people. There could totally be a gang. Maybe more than one. Like West Side Story."

Karen lifted the corner of her mouth in a smile. "Yes, honey. Jets and Sharks and problems like Maria. I'm sure it seems like lots of people to you, but we're just a small town in spite of it being called Iowa *City*. Let me ask you a question: do you know what alopecia is?"

Ethan shook his head, looking completely lost.

"It's a condition where people lose their hair. It becomes very thin and patchy, and I don't mean male pattern baldness. How common do you think alopecia is?"

He shook his head again.

"It's about two percent of the population. Now, do you know anyone with alopecia?"

He shook his head once and then stopped and looked at Gladys who wore a bemused smile while Karen delivered her statistics lesson.

"Yes, that's why my hair looks like this." She tugged on one tight poodle-permed curl. "It hasn't gotten worse thanks to…you know, but there isn't a treatment in the world that can help me with it right now. I've tried the shampoos. It started to get better before my grand transformation. But now," she shook her head. "Ain't nothing growing back on this head again. I'm stuck with it."

"Oh," he said, at a loss of how to respond. "Sorry about that."

"The point is, Ethan," Karen said, "being a vampire is much rarer than having alopecia. So how many vampires do you think there really are? The chances of there being some major vampire gang—especially around here—are less than zero. Sorry if that seems boring."

35. TROUBLE – RIGHT HERE IN IOWA CITY

"I think our first concern should be blood," Karen said. "We have a couple bottles left, right?"

"Yes, but after that, I am not knowing where we will get more," Hans said. He looked more than a little frantic. His eyes darted everywhere, and he clenched and unclenched his fists. "I must not have from people. Is sin. I am damned to God, but will not damn myself to me."

"I think it's safe to say," Karen went on, ignoring Hans' religious dilemma, "that Gladys and Hans and I should be fine for a while after...after tonight." She wiped unconsciously at her lower lip. "We should save the rest for young Ethan here."

She patted the spot next to her on the couch and Ethan sat.

"After that, we will see." Her brows knotted together in fierce concentration. "There is the dentist..."

Gladys laughed. "Absolutely not. Dr. Trish has been through enough, don't you think?"

"Okay, okay. We'll cross that bridge when we come to it," Karen said.

She took Ethan's hand in hers and gave him a little pat of comfort. But Gladys thought maybe she was comforting herself just as much, if not more.

"I have more bad news," Gladys said from her seat on the rigid couch.

"What now?" Hans asked. He seemed tired.

"Mrs. Maitland," Gladys said.

"You mean that old lady next door?" Ethan asked. "What's wrong with her? She seems nice."

Gladys made a sour face. "Yes, the lady next door, and she's not *that* old." She paused. "She's not that nice, either." She shook her head. "Arlyss. Fucking. Maitland."

"What about her?" Karen asked in a quavery voice. She was wringing her hands, a telltale sign of anxiety.

Gladys knew what she was probably thinking about—the time before Dr. Cooke, when they never knew where their next meal would come from. When they had resorted to...she pushed the thought away, took a deep breath, and continued.

"Well, somehow or another, I think she's part of this. I don't know if my house is safe anymore." She thought about that for a moment, then corrected herself. "I'm *sure* my house isn't safe anymore, and not just because the back door is busted to smithereens. Cooke knew how to find us, and I think he had help."

Hans' face cramped with disdain and understanding. "Maitland. She is too much in the business of everybody to worry about just you. She is ziemlich die Tratsch-Königin."

"Huh?" Ethan asked.

"How you say? To be monarch of the gossips?"

Ethan cawed laughter, but it didn't seem to be laughter at Hans, just the keen use of phrase. "You mean, like, a gossip queen?"

"Yes. That is meaning," Hans said.

"No, not everybody, Hans," Gladys said. "Me. And Ethan, I suppose. And now you two."

"Stop round and round talking," Hans said from his place by the doorway with a twirling gesture of his hand. "Say what it is you think."

Gladys took a deep breath. "Mrs. Maitland is—or was—either Dr. Cooke's human servant or she's one of us. I'm sure of it."

Karen gasped and covered her mouth, eyes wide. "You mean…"

"That's exactly what I mean." She ran her hand through her thin hair. She was trying to stay calm for Ethan. For all of them. But the more she thought about tonight's narrow escape and Mrs. Maitland's inquiry, the more her stomach felt like it was on a slow elevator ride to Shittsburgh. Panic filled her like a bad transfusion, but she tamped it down. "I can't think which is more likely." She pounded her fist on the arm of the chair.

"Or, maybe, she's Estelle's familiar," Ethan said.

"Familiar is for witches and warlocks," Hans corrected. "Is animal and shapeshifter. *Human* servant is for those like us."

"What's the difference?"

"As dentist has said, human servant is not a vampire, but human person who looks out for master. Familiar takes animal shape."

"Or mistress," Karen added.

Gladys thought about the makeup bag at Hans' house and suppressed a smile.

"What do the human servants do?"

"They carry orders, protect, serve," Hans replied, "anything that is required."

"Ohh. So, like an executive assistant to one of those big CEO people?"

"What is this CE—"

"Never mind!" Gladys interrupted. "What if Arlyss is actually Estelle's human servant?"

Hans seemed deep in thought. "Also, she could be vampire. Is possible. Woman does spend much time up in the night."

"Or even her bloodfruit," Karen suggested.

"What? What the heck is bloodfruit?" Ethan asked.

"Is human kept for snacking," Hans said. "Some big, big vamps have two. Sometimes three."

"Ha!" Ethan cackled, a little too shrilly. "Betcha they don't sell *those* at Hy-vee."

"Whatever the case, that's…that would be very bad. If she's been spying on us this whole time, who knows what she's found out and reported back. Estelle could know everything about us!"

"How could she?" Ethan said. "If she's a human servant, what else could she be up to?"

"Fetch dry cleaning, type memos. Clean up murder scene," Hans added.

Ethan nodded. "Okay, I get it. So, if she's Estelle's human servant, she can only know what she sees when we come and go. It's not like she has super vampire hearing."

"She might. Some benevolent head vampires gift their human servant with minor powers," Gladys said.

"Or maybe she put in cameras? Listening devices? She could even be a recently turned vampire, out to gain favor," Karen said.

"Or a reward," Gladys added.

"She may have followed for long time," Hans said. "Is important we find out which, slave or sycophant, but how?"

"I could eat her cat," Ethan said. "See if she comes after me in full vamp with her fangs out." He was grinning. "Or chases me down with holy water and a garden stake."

Even in the midst of crisis, Gladys marveled, *the kid can still find something funny.* Maybe his survival skills weren't so bad after all.

"Oh, Ethan, don't," Karen said. She looked sick.

"I'm just kidding. I'm not gonna eat anyone's cat. Again."

"You might," Hans said. "If no other choices."

Everyone was silent, ruminating in his or her own way about how their simple lives had been upturned so quickly.

Gladys flicked her eyes to Ethan. He was the cause of all this. If she hadn't seen him having his little midnight snack with Mrs. Mortenson that night, that *one time,* none of them would be in this predicament. He had moved in, disturbed her peace, rearranged her house, and been a constant source of worry in need of vigilant surveillance. Then he'd started up with his talk about settling the score with Estelle, wanting to get them moving in a direction that could only lead to their deaths.

Had he deliberately provoked Cooke, so they'd be forced into action? She considered. No, she didn't think he was that misguided, and he'd certainly been as surprised as they were to see Dr. Cooke spring through the patio door like a rabid dog. Her heart softened. Despite everything, she'd come to like him. Hell, she'd come to love him like a grandson. But the end result was the same. They were fugitives.

"Ethan," Karen said. "You said before that you had a plan. Was that real? Or was it just wishful thinking?"

"Well, I sort of have a plan. Part of a plan, anyway." Ethan shrugged.

"How much of a plan?" Gladys asked.

"Like, half a plan. Maybe a little less."

"We must make whole plan. No forward motion until all plan. But now are new problems to consider," Hans said.

"There's no time now," Gladys said. "Look."

They looked out the window where Hans had raised the blinds earlier. The sky was changing to the pre-dawn shade of turquoise on the far horizon.

"Where are we going to stay?" Karen said. "I don't want to go home by myself, and we certainly can't camp out at Glad's." She chewed a fingernail, caught herself, and folded her hands in her lap, like a prim schoolgirl.

"Come to basement," Hans said and led them to the door.

"Great. Another creepy adult luring poor Ethan into their basement. I suppose there's a swell little cupboard under the stairs for me? *Harry Potter Two, Electric Boogaloo.*" The kid laughed at his own joke.

They all ignored him. The narrow stairs opened up onto a tasteful man-cave. An ultramodern home entertainment system was built into the farthest wall and a comfy-looking sofa wrapped itself halfway around the room. Again, low lighting and a few Ansel Adams prints made it look chic. He led them past a set of bookshelves filled with leather-bound classics. After sliding one set of shelves aside effortlessly, another door was exposed. He unlocked it with a key from an overloaded ring in his pocket, which Gladys stared at in fascination.

What are all those for? That's got to give him back problems after a while.

The overhead lights flickered on automatically and revealed a rack of storage shelves filled with camping gear, plastic totes full of supplies with printed labels, rolled up tents, and what looked like half of the inventory of the military supply section of their local outdoor outfitter.

Gladys stepped through and surveyed the contents. "My, my, my, you've been busy. Art deco, home movie theater, hidden doorways, magical bookcases. What's next, Narnia?"

Hans frowned.

"What is all this stuff? Are you like one of those crazy preppers? Like that group in that one place who like, had a stand-off with the government?" Ethan asked as he ran a finger along the totes, reading the labels.

"Ruby Ridge," Gladys said dryly. "But this isn't an alt-right anti-establishment compound."

"Is only preparations. Just in case."

"In case of what?" Karen asked with her hands fisted on her hips.

Gladys snickered. *I guess Hans hadn't invited her into his basement bunker before.*

"Emergency. Like this." He pulled four sleeping bags from the shelves and tossed them to the floor. After them went four rolled up sleeping pads. "I say we stay here."

Ethan was still examining the containers. "Why all this food?"

"Begging pardon?"

"I mean, why do you have all this emergency food in here? You can't eat it. We can't eat it. What's the point?"

Hans' face flushed. "When you lived through war, you will understand. War is no joke to laugh at. Many were being hidden in great war." Hans stopped, perhaps trying to find the right words to explain the Holocaust to someone who hadn't even lived through Desert Storm. "Others could need things someday. It is good charity to help neighbors in time of trouble. As we did before. My...wife. And I. Back in Germany. Before Sweden." He clammed up, not wanting to say more, and not sure how to backtrack to where they'd been a moment ago.

"Thank you, Hans," Karen said, seeming to sense his discomfort. "This is truly a lifesaver. I think it'll do just fine, don't you Glad?"

"In the storage room?" Ethan was clearly thinking about his luxury accommodations back at Gladys' house and his fancy new bed.

"Is better than out there." Hans pointed to the open doorway. "And here is locked. Also is security system. Alarm will sound when anyone enters."

"This will do," Gladys said. It looked like she was back to sleeping on the floor in a vampire burrito for the time being. She sighed. Although Ethan's remodeling had looked more like a movie set than actual sleeping quarters, she'd liked the idea of possibly being one of *those* vampires; living in Victorian luxury while a swarm of underlings tended to her unearthly needs.

"So glad it gives satisfaction," Hans said. His voice dripped with sarcasm.

"I suggest we roll up quick. The sun will be up any minute," Karen said.

Hans slid the bookshelf back into place and locked the door.

36. THE MIDNIGHT RIDE OF ETHAN BRADFORD

Gladys was sitting up in her mummy bag when a hand tapped her shoulder. She turned to see Hans handing her a one-ounce shooter of blood. "Thanks, Hans. But I thought we agreed that Ethan should have them." She accepted his offer gratefully anyway and drank. "What about you?"

"I am good for today. We can get...more. Later. If is needed. Perhaps it will not be."

"Huh?" Hans was hard to follow sometimes, but in her bleary state of just-woken-up, it was impossible.

"We talk upstairs. When you are ready." He turned and walked through the open door. The other sleeping bags were empty.

"Everything alright?" Gladys felt alarm bells clanging away inside her head.

"Upstairs," he said, pointing in the direction of the stairway.

Gladys nodded and waited until Hans was gone before she struggled to free herself from the nylon bag in her typical, undignified manner. Something was definitely up here, and from the look on his face, it wasn't good. The man was stoic, but even his emotions were palpable. She didn't know if it was their shared experience, their long friendship, or some mild telepathic connection. In their world, anything was possible.

Karen sat at the kitchen table with Hans beside her. Both looked concerned.

No, they look desperate.

Karen looked up with eyes crazed with worry.

"Is it Ethan? What did they do? Take him in the night?"

Karen shook her head and slid a piece of paper toward her. "Worse."

"What's this?"

"Read," Hans said. "Then questions."

The writing was scrawled across the page unevenly.

Hey guys,

I know I shouldn't be doing this, but I'm gonna find Estelle. And Mrs. Maitland. We can't go on this way and without Dr. Cooke. There's no way for us to feed without violating people

"Oh Christ," Gladys muttered and collapsed into the chair beside Karen. "Any idea where he might have gone?"

"None," Hans said.

"How did he get out?" Gladys asked. Her lips felt numb.

Hans held up the massive key ring. It was empty except for a key with a misshapen peace sign. The one to the car in the garage.

"Aww shit."

Karen, concentrating on her folded hands, shook her head. "I know. It's like we should have put a bell on him or something."

"Where would we even begin? It's not like Estelle's in the phone book. We have nothing to go on." Gladys felt like crying.

Ethan was out there, by himself, maybe doing the things they should have been doing all along. Trying to live instead of simply surviving. It struck her how cowardly they had been all this time. And this kid—this frustrating, charming, clueless, ingenuitive kid—had just shown them all the real meaning of courage. Stupidity, too, most likely. At least he was doing something.

Karen snapped her head up and smiled an unsettling grin. She raised her index finger. Fire lurked just behind her dilated pupils. "I have an idea."

Twenty minutes later, they climbed into Hans' tank-like grey Mercedes. "Perhaps Maitland does not know of my car like yours," he said to Gladys. "Best to be as invisible as possible."

He drove without speaking, but his lips moved like he was having a silent conversation with an unknown entity. He pulled into the parking lot of the DMV and stopped beneath the light closest to the building.

"What are we doing here?" Gladys asked from the back seat.

"I'll just be a few minutes," Karen said, leaning in the rear window to give Gladys' arm a reassuring squeeze. "Don't worry. We'll find him. And *her*. Just wait and see." She smiled unconvincingly and walked toward the back door. She knocked once and the door pushed outward, a white arm visible against the dark metal, and then closed again.

"She's looking for Estelle's address," Gladys said. "That's it, right?"

"Ms. Getty did come for license once," Hans said. "Should have record on file."

"But she could have given a fake address," Gladys said.

"Is possible. Maybe long ago more possible, but not so easy now with all electric records and databases. Perhaps she returned for renewal. Easy to check, I think."

It was worth a shot, Gladys supposed. She just hoped they found Ethan before he found Estelle. They'd need to go together as a group, with whatever weapons they could wield.

The door whacked open against the side of the building and Karen crossed the parking lot in seconds. A human wouldn't have been able to track her movements. "Start the car!"

Hans turned the key. "Where will we go?"

"Out of the lot and a right onto Sycamore. I can't believe this!"

"You got it?" Gladys asked.

"Yep. She was here three years ago getting her damned license renewed!"

"And DMV just gave information?" Hans asked.

"Well, Cindy and I go way back," she said. "I told her I needed a favor and she agreed."

"Just like that?" Hans asked.

She chewed her lip. "Not exactly. Let's say that once upon a time I went to her for help. Two or three weeks after the...the change. I hadn't planned on attacking her at the time, but I was just so hungry. I'm afraid I scared her half to death, but I came to my senses before I did any harm."

"So, you just called her and said, 'hey I need a favor' and she agreed?" Gladys asked.

"Umm, not quite. I demanded a favor in exchange for not eating her. She was happy to help."

"Happy?" Hans raised an eyebrow.

"Oh, turn here," Karen said, looking at the paper in her hands.

Hans flipped on his signal and slammed on the brakes. The tires squealed. "More notice, please," he growled.

"Sorry. Anyway, I gave her the Reader's Digest Condensed Version when she let me in, and I think it made her feel a little bit better. She remembered Estelle."

"You told her everything? And you don't think she'll call the cops?" Gladys asked.

"Turn left on 6th Avenue," Karen told Hans, who mumbled and peered everywhere at once, most likely looking for their missing compatriot, looking for loping vampires, looking for cops.

"And say what?" Hans said. "There is small woman vampire who demands secret government information? They would laugh. Then send men in white coats for ride to asylum."

Karen rolled her eyes. "It's not secret government information, just stats from the DMV database, and besides there's no *asylum* anymore here. Nowadays they just take you to Ward D at University Hospital."

"I don't want to know how you know all that," Gladys said.

"Head downtown, Hans. Then turn on Highway One toward those big houses on the bluff. You know the ones I'm talking about?"

He nodded.

"Stop!" Gladys shouted. "Stop, stop, stop!"

Hans brought the car to a stop and put it in park with his hazard lights blinking.

"Why? We're not there—"

But then Karen saw why.

"Not here. Turn down that street and park on the corner. And shut off your hazards unless you want a cop to stop and see if you need help."

He did as Karen said.

Gladys tried to exit the car too quickly. Her right knee gave out, and she went down onto the pavement. Right before she smacked her head, two powerful hands had her under the armpits. She felt herself lifted and set onto her feet. Her rescuer stood in front of her, disheveled, out of breath, and covered in blood.

Ethan was panting and his eyes looked like a wild animal's. Except most wild animals didn't have crimson eyes of fire. A runner of foamy pink drool glistened from his lower lip in the streetlights.

"Ethan?" Gladys was shocked at his appearance.

"Get in the car!" Karen snarled. "People will see." She opened the door and Gladys shoved Ethan inside, sliding in beside him.

"Get us out of here," Gladys said.

Hans didn't ask questions, just put the car in drive and sped away.

"Where have you been? We've been worried sick!" Karen leaned over the seat and fussed over him, straightening his collar and trying to put his hair back in order, ignoring the bloodstains.

Ethan didn't answer right away. His eyes still had a faraway look.

Gladys put her hand over his and closed her eyes, willing the kid to lower his blood pressure and get a hold of himself. She sent him one word—*CALM*—over and over. She opened her eyes, saw that he was a bit calmer, and restrained an unexpected urge to give him a giant hug. She was relieved to see him but didn't need blood all over herself.

"Where now?" Hans asked. "Continue on to house of horror or *palaver* before suicide mission? Perhaps weapons and plan would increase chance of survival?"

Ethan leaned against Gladys and hummed quietly to himself.

"Your house," Karen said. "Go back so we can talk. We know where to go; all we need is the plan. I say we start by getting there right before sunrise."

"But that won't give us much time," Gladys said with alarm.

She grunted as Ethan's elbow went into her midsection and adjusted him into a more comfortable position.

"It won't matter," Karen said. "Either she's going to die, or we are. The sunrise is irrelevant. We'll watch it happen as mortals or we'll be dead. No more fucking around."

Gladys, surprised at Karen's use of the magic f-bomb, smiled. "Alright then. Alright. Let's do it."

37. OH YEAH, IT'S ALL COMING TOGETHER

"So, what are the things that kill vampires?" Ethan asked. His hair was still wet from the shower, but at least he was no longer sticky with blood.

Gladys had been relieved to learn that the blood had come from various squirrels and nocturnal mammals that had been enjoying a quiet evening in the park until he'd arrived. He'd left with no real idea what he was doing, just hoping to spot the woman who'd caused all this trouble out for a midnight stroll. Which was, of course, ridiculous and as opposite a good plan as you could get.

"Hold up a minute," Gladys said. "Before we go any further, I need you to first acknowledge that your last plan was terrible and promise us you're not going to run off on a fool's errand again."

He stuck out his lower lip in a pout that would have looked at home on a toddler. "Fine. Fine. I promise. It was a stupid idea—I think I might have been delirious from hunger and anxiety. But hey, at least I got dinner, and nobody got hurt, right?" He smiled his goofy, toothy grin.

Gladys could see his fangs in there still, prepared and ready. His blood was up, and he was ready to fight. God bless him, he had courage. She just hoped it would last. And that it would be enough.

"Well," Karen said, thinking it over, "you know the usual: holy water, which we can't touch, by the way, a cross—likewise a terrible choice, a stake through the heart, although that'd kill just about anyone. She could use it against us if we weren't careful. Sunlight, obviously." Karen tapped her chin, searching her mind for more.

"What's special about sunlight?" Ethan asked.

"Are you being funny?" Hans asked. "Because is not funny. And we do not have time to waste telling joke."

"No." Ethan shook his head. "I mean, what's different about sunlight that isn't the same as all the other lights in your house, Hans?" He gestured at the light fixtures and table lamp. "Why aren't we bursting into flames right this minute?"

"It is not same kind of light," Hans said with his woolly eyebrows nearly touching one another, as if Ethan was a dullard.

"Right! It's not! It's UV light!" He clapped as if Hans had solved an ancient riddle. "If we could somehow expose her to it without hitting ourselves, then she'd be gone!"

"And how do you intend to do that?" Karen leaned her elbow on the table with her hand cradling her head.

She looked exhausted. Pale, too. Had she fed?

"I'm not sure. I'm still trying to work out the details, but they're coming." He looked like he was next door to having an aneurysm.

Gladys felt a flicker of something. Was it hope? It had been a long time since she'd felt anything like that. "Easy there, kiddo. Don't blow a gasket. We need you."

Ethan looked at her worshipfully. "We need a light saber or something like that."

"Come on, Ethan!" Karen said and slapped the table in frustration. "We need to be serious! This isn't the movies. We're going to run out of time, and then it won't be until tomorrow night that we get our chance. By then..."

"It might be too late," Hans finished for her.

His face brightened. "No, I mean, we need to *make* a light saber. A UV lightsaber! Hans, do you have some wrapping paper?"

"Why? Are you going to gift wrap it for her?" Gladys asked. Her head was propped on her hand and her expression was one of bemusement. She was having a hard time keeping track of all this. Her thoughts fluttered from fear to excitement to a dull wish for everything to go back to the way it was. But that was never going to happen.

"No, like, you don't get it! We need the tube thingy from a roll of Christmas wrapping paper." He counted on his fingers. "Then we get a full spectrum light of some kind, I don't know. Maybe just a bulb, but it has to be attached to something somehow. Then we find her, we pin her down, and then we point it at her! Fry her face right off! We don't get cooked, but she does, see?" He grinned. "Oh yeah," he said, more to himself than the rest of them. "It's all coming together."

Gladys still wasn't sure this was the best idea in the world, but it did have some merit. The science was sound. But she had no idea how they were supposed to get the jump on such a powerful vamp and then end her. No one else had offered a better idea, so this was their only option.

Ethan had collected everything he needed from the garage and the doomsday prepper supplies in Hans' basement. Wire, a huge six-volt battery, duct tape, a dismantled table lamp. Hans objected, but he lost the argument. Ethan had found everything but a full-spectrum light bulb which Hans (obviously) didn't have lying around. They'd have to make a pit stop at the Walmart on their way to battle. He sat at the kitchen table with his supplies in disarray, looking more like a mad scientist than a college kid.

Hans had been relegated to the position of gopher and Karen sat outside looking dreamily up at the stars on the front stoop.

With nothing else to do, Gladys went out to keep her friend company in what was likely to be their final hours together. She sat down next to her on the step with tremendous effort. Karen patted Gladys' swollen right knee. She'd been hobbling worse than ever since launching herself out the door of Hans' Mercedes. An extra shooter would have helped, but they didn't have any to spare.

"Whatcha doing?" Gladys asked. But she knew. Karen was getting one last look at the stars in case things went badly tonight.

"Oh, nothing. Just thinking. Can you imagine if we come out of this alive? What that's going to mean for us and the rest of our lives?"

"Oh, I've thought about it," Gladys said. "The first thing I'd do is get my knees fixed."

"Well, the first thing I'd do is go out to dinner. I can still taste all those things I love in my mind, you know? It never went away. I know what a nice medium rare ribeye steak from The Outback would taste like. I'd get it with a Bloomin' Onion, a fully loaded baked potato, and one of those huge fudge brownie thingies for dessert."

"The cholesterol in that'd kill you almost as fast as Estelle would," Gladys said.

"Yeah, maybe. But it'd taste better!"

They cackled together, but their laughter cut off when headlights appeared, turning onto Hans' street from the main road.

"Who's that?" Gladys asked.

The headlights turned up Hans' long driveway. The bright halogens swung toward the two women, casting them in garish luminance, and plowed through Hans' mailbox and into the bushes without stopping.

"Christ!" Karen shouted and shot to her feet.

Gladys struggled to get up, failed, plopped down on the step, cursed, and still the headlights were coming.

The lights bounced and jounced as the kamikaze driver tore up the pristine landscaping. They were coming fast.

"Get out of the way!" Gladys shouted and bumped Karen out of the way with her hip.

Karen fell against the brick wall of the garage.

As if to contradict physics and her own bodily limitations, Gladys vaulted onto the hood of the car and punched through the windshield, grabbing the steering wheel and yanking it to the right. The car veered away from the house, missing Karen and the front wall by mere inches. It smashed into Hans' tall evergreens, slowing, but still in motion. Gladys slammed her other fist through the windshield, both arms buried to the elbow in cracked safety glass. She grabbed the unseen driver by the hair and smashed their head forward into the steering wheel repeatedly until she felt no more resistance. The car slowed to a crawl at the edge of the property and Gladys leapt off the hood. She tore the driver's side door from its hinges and yanked the emergency brake, bringing the thing shuddering to a stop.

Karen shouted at the boys to come out as she chased after Gladys.

Hans and Ethan erupted from the house like two pimples and ran after her. They reached the car in seconds, just in time to see Gladys plunge her teeth into the neck of the driver and latch on to the pulsing life beneath the skin. A moment later, she dragged the body from the car and threw it to the ground, an offering to her friends. They spent no time hesitating; the smell of fresh blood was an intoxicating perfume. Even Ethan joined in this time.

The shape of the former Mrs. Arlyss Maitland was falling in upon itself. Unfortunately, it wasn't crumbling into oblivion like a mummified corpse, as Dr. Cooke had. They had their answer. Mrs. Nosey Parker Neighbor was a human servant, not a vampire. To Cooke or Estelle, they didn't know, but they were safe and satiated and at that moment. Nothing else mattered.

38. NOT OVER TILL THE FAT LADY SINGS

"We have to get rid of the body, Hans," Karen said, tugging at his sleeve to get his attention. "We can't leave her out here like this." She chewed at a nail. "And the car. What are we going to do with the car?" She paced in front of the garage.

Hans had shut off the outside lights to get rid of the spotlight effect on their illicit activities, and Gladys had extinguished the car's headlights with two mighty kicks, forgetting the handy switch inside.

Hans' vast property backed up to a strip of woods. The rest of the property was bordered by a line of small bushes in front (plowed into non-existence by Gladys' traitorous neighbor) and tall evergreens on either side. These blocked out most of the view of the neighboring houses. No curious neighbors stood on their porches to see what the commotion was all about. At two in the morning, the decent people of the world were asleep.

"We must do this, yes. But time grows shorter and soon will come sun. There may be others and we must be ready for anything."

"We could, ummm put that," Ethan motioned to the desiccated body without looking at it, "back in the car and push it behind the bushes some more. And maybe we can stick some branches through the holes so it would look kinda more like an accident than umm...a murder."

"Don't say that!" Karen said, looking sick with dismay. She had her arms around herself, her elbows cupped in both hands. "This was clearly self-defense! That woman would have plowed us into the wall." She looked pale except for the dainty little rose blossoms on her cheeks. Fresh blood was good for the complexion. "And time is running out."

"Yeah, but I think the cops would still have a lot of questions, if you know what I mean," Ethan said.

Karen looked to Hans for support, but he was already dragging the corpse back into the car. He tossed what remained of Mrs. Maitland into the front seat like she was a bushel of sweet corn and motioned to Gladys.

Gladys released the emergency-brake, and together they pushed the car back into the bushes between the house and the verge while Hans leaned in and steered with one hand.

"Come on," Gladys said. She dusted off her hands as if that would get rid of the blood. The scrapes from the glass had already healed. "Let's clean up and get going. Doesn't have to be perfect; we'll settle for unnoticed."

Karen hesitated, looked back at the car, and shivered.

Gladys knew what she was thinking. That woman, now dead in the front seat of her car, had deserved her fate, but Karen still hated the idea that a moment ago a living person was driving toward them and was now nothing more than an empty meat sack. Worse was the fact that her life-giving blood was now drained. Maybe this would be the last time. It was that thought that got Gladys going.

Ethan was back at the table, constructing his makeshift death ray. His hands flew like a surgeon's.

"How much longer?" Gladys asked.

Ethan's look of concentration made him seem older. "Almost done," he said.

"Can you finish in the car?" Karen asked. "We really need to get a move on."

"Give me just…one…minute…" He stuck his tongue out the side of his mouth as he connected more wires together. Then he assessed his work. "Yeah, we can go. I can finish these last two things on the way." He scooped his tools back into Hans' handyman bag unceremoniously.

Hans groaned.

"Never mind, Hans! He can tidy up later. Let's go!" Gladys prodded Hans toward the garage, and Karen carried Ethan's tools as they clambered in.

"Don't forget to stop down at the *Wawl-Mart*," Ethan said with a southern drawl. He was eerily calm, the death ray project swallowing all his attention and focus.

They headed toward the expensive bluff-side properties that overlooked the Iowa River. Gladys sat beside Ethan in the back of the Mercedes like a surgical nurse while Karen navigated and Hans sped them on toward a possible future or demise. Only fate would decide.

Hans turned into the twenty-four-hour Walmart off First Avenue.

"I'll be right back," Ethan said and trotted toward the front entrance.

Five minutes later, he returned, and Hans started the engine.

"Did you get it?" Karen asked, seeing that he had nothing in his hands.

He shook his head. "No. Hey, Gladys, can I borrow some money?"

"I can't believe this," she said and opened her giant handbag. She handed him a ten, but he didn't go back.

"You need more than that? For a light bulb?"

"Maybe, but I want to get a Snickers, too. For, you know. After. For our victory dance. I've been jonesing for one for weeks. And I thought it would be a good victory dance. Anyone else want one?"

"Victory dance?" Gladys asked.

"Yeah, like in that movie Independence Day? Where Will Smith and that geeky smart dude, Jake Goldenbloomers or whatever his name is go up in the alien ship and Will Smith's all 'It's not over till the fat lady—"

"Get going!" Gladys growled. She thrust a twenty at him through the window and shooed him away.

"I'll take a Reese's," Hans called out the window to his retreating figure.

"Really, Hans. You shouldn't encourage this," Gladys frowned.

"Is good to be hopeful in situation like this. Picture victory in mind. Power of positive thinking." He tapped his temple with a finger.

Ethan came hurrying back and chucked a Caramello at Karen. He got in and handed a Milky Way to Gladys.

Twenty minutes later they were driving slowly down Blackberry Lane with the headlights off, a ridiculous name for the residence of an ancient vampire. They parked a block away, just past the address Karen had gotten from her former colleague. Ethan had just finished strapping his contraption together when Hans unhooked his seatbelt.

"So, what's the plan, exactly?" Gladys asked, fearing the answer would be less than concrete.

"Well," Ethan said, concentrating. He examined his weapon. "I wish there was some way to know if she was home or not. Like, if you had to guess, what would you say? Home or not home?"

"She has the ability to day-walk," Karen said. "She wouldn't necessarily be worried about sunrise." She groaned. "It's impossible to tell."

"I vote home," Hans said. "Is no need for her to roam streets looking for victims. That is purpose for underlings."

"I think she was the one who sent Mrs. Maitland," Karen said. "I mean, think about it. The woman saw us last night. She had to have known that Chip was there to take us out and then failed. No doubt she reported back to Estelle that we were meddling, and she sent her to finish us off tonight. I vote home as well."

Ethan nodded. "Probably thought we wouldn't put up a fight. I mean, in all these years you never did before, right?"

"Right," Karen said.

"Which also means that she's probably waiting for Mrs. Maitland to come back and report," Ethan said.

"That ends now," Gladys said. "We all agree. She's most likely at home. I think the best bet is to rush in together, overwhelm her, and then Ethan hits her with his light stick."

"Light *saber*," Ethan said.

Ethan's saber was a sad-looking, odd conglomeration of an astounding amount of duct tape, cardboard tubing (which had become slightly bent in the middle), and a bunch of crazy crisscrossed wires leading to a big battery that stuck out of the voluminous pocket of Ethan's cargo shorts. It looked more like a bomb to Gladys, but maybe that was for the better. Let Estelle think they were coming with bombs. She'd think she was safe.

"We go in back door," Hans said. He pointed to the wooden fence pickets on the rear floorboard, leftover from Arlyss Maitland's failed assassination attempt. "We take stakes as if that was plan, yes? She will think we are there to drive them into heart. Then, when cornered, Ethan turns on ray of death. Agreed?"

They nodded.

"I called it a light saber, but death ray sounds even cooler. Just let me do one little thing here." Ethan frowned at the compromised portion of his weapon and ripped off more duct tape.

"Come on, come on!" Gladys moaned.

"Hang on," Ethan said. "I just gotta fix this or it won't work right."

"I'm so scared," Karen said. Her hands shook. "And not just to face her, but what if we win? What will become of us?" She shook her head. "Can we even live like normal people?"

"It'll be fine, Karen. We'll figure it out. If we live, it will be the best revenge ever." Gladys reached over and squeezed her shoulder. "And if it doesn't work, well hell. I'd rather die with my friends around me than alone." She kissed Karen on the cheek and got out of the car, being careful to close the door as softly as she could.

They ran in two-by-two military formation around to the back side of the lawn, with Hans and Karen in the lead. A wild tumble of vines, trees, and fallen logs tangled in the underbrush crept around the house. No landscapers tended this untamed vegetation.

Adrenaline coursed through all of them and heightened their connection with each other. Their vampire senses were honed to a lethal sharpness, and thanks to their recent feed (courtesy of Mrs. Maitland) they maneuvered easily enough and lined up behind the huge oaks and maples that separated Estelle's fancy mammoth of a home from the jungle. Even Gladys was able to keep up. She smiled viciously.

Hans turned to his unlikely fellow soldiers. He pointed to himself and held up one finger, then pointed to Gladys and Karen and held up two. He nodded at Ethan. The plan was understood. Now it was time.

39. A CLASH OF TITANS

Hans lifted his hand, fingers splayed out, waiting to give his unlikely Seal Team Four the signal to invade.

Gladys felt as if every tendon and ligament had been cranked tight and would soon snap if they didn't get moving. The muscles in her legs were thrumming, ready to spring into action.

At last, he closed his fist, and they all darted with superhuman speed toward a massive oak door at the back of the house, having no idea what they would find on the other side when they entered.

Gladys no longer cared what they found. This was right, by God. She wondered why they had waited for so long to make their move.

Her knees crackled like an autumn bonfire as they ran across the patch of open lawn which had not yet been swallowed by nature.

Karen hardly touched the ground. Her hair flew wildly, for once not holding its careful beauty. Her face had shifted from mild-mannered human to an unearthly killer's grin. Her red eyes flashed at Gladys in an expression that almost looked like...what? Fun? Amusement?

Ethan crashed into Gladys' back as she slowed her advance. She nearly went down, but he grabbed her collar with a strength she would not have suspected and kept her on her feet even as they moved toward the door.

"Warp speed!" he shouted.

The heavy wooden door splintered as Hans ran straight at it with a weird sort of flying front kick. He tumbled through, did a forward roll, and came up on the balls of his feet like an elderly, German Simone Biles sans sequins, ready to fight.

Gladys and Karen burst through the debris right behind him, shielding Ethan and his secret weapon from sight. A hissing sound coming from their right caught their attention. Hans whirled in that direction with Gladys and Karen backing him up, stakes held like spears.

In a darkened corner of the room, Estelle sat in the corner of a voluminous red velvet couch wearing some weird Elvira lingerie get-up. A young man sat beside her. She held his wrist to her mouth, and Gladys could guess what they'd been up to. This must be Estelle's human bloodfruit.

Poor kid. How'd you get caught up in all this?

Estelle slowly opened her eyes, clearly not alarmed or even surprised by the sudden appearance of three aging vampires. She must have had a psychic inkling and, considering who was in the cavalry, hadn't bothered to confront them.

Ethan remained mostly hidden and unnoticed.

A grin spread across Estelle's face, and she knocked the young man who'd been donating blood to her aside. She pointed at them. "I wondered when you'd show up here." She cackled, then crossed her legs and stroked the young man's head like a cat's, while keeping her eye on the quartet of hapless invaders.

He rubbed against her hand, which intensified the impression of feline affection.

"To what do I owe this pleasant visit? You really should have called first. I'm rather occupied at the moment if you couldn't tell." She stared at them and lifted his other hand to her mouth, biting in and feeding leisurely. Clearly, she felt no threat from them at all.

Hans stood almost hypnotized, his stake-spear held loosely in one hand as he watched. He wasn't just watching. He was captivated.

Gladys realized that in a moment, Estelle would have him completely under her control. "Hans!" She whispered and pinched the tender skin beneath his upper arm. "Now! We have to do it now!"

That broke the spell. "Schnell! Schnell!" Hans shouted in a deep voice. Saliva flew from his lips.

Karen and Gladys shrieked in harmony and ran forward.

Estelle leapt to the ceiling in an instant—one moment she was relaxing on the couch, the next she had long claws dug into the plasterwork overhead. Her pinched, angular face transformed from small, petite woman to monster. She growled deep in her chest, a raspy sound that made Gladys think of a giant, full of awful phlegm, tearing wildly at tent fabric. Her head twisted around in a way normal humans couldn't move, and she erupted in horrible laughter, and then in deadpan monotone she said, "You shouldn't have interrupted my dinner."

Karen howled. Two disparate gales of wind battered one another overhead. Her feet left the floor as she hovered, suspended by invisible threads. That crackling, maddening static electricity filled the room and seemed to sizzle the edges of Gladys' vision. Her ears popped as Karen launched herself at Estelle. She sank killer's talons into the throat of their nemesis, their maker. Mother of the damned.

They spun in the air, spitting curses, shrieking wild unintelligible cries, gouging, and trying to get at each other's throats. Blood sprayed the walls like a wayward garden hose. The wind continued to grow—a collision of their lust for blood and victory—rose to a deafening roar.

Papers and books flew in a tornado. The house shook. Cracks cris-crossed through the walls like lightning. The whirling cacophony increased in volume until a sound like a locomotive filled Gladys' head. She strained to track their movements in the chaos, but they moved so quickly.

Estelle's bloodfruit-boy cowered in the corner—he obviously wasn't there as a soldier, just another tasty treat in a fruit bowl—and Gladys fought the urge to go to him and give comfort, to tell him this would all be over soon.

Estelle hit the floor with a resounding thud.

Karen landed on top of her, gaining the upper hand temporarily. She ripped and tore at Estelle, but was unable to do real, lasting damage.

The horrible woman healed almost as quickly as Karen was able to wound her. Estelle's teeth came perilously close to Karen's throat, but the pink clad, former Queen of the DMV fought hard. Estelle's claws tore at Karen's midsection. Seeking her heart. Karen was losing.

"Move!" Gladys shouted, breaking their spell of paralysis.

She and Hans ran forward, grappling with Estelle's arms and legs, yanking her hair back, trying to keep her fangs away from Karen, but they weren't strong enough. Their adrenaline was fading.

"Ethan!" Gladys cried above the shrieking wind. "Now! Do it now!"

From behind them, an earsplitting scream split the air. Ethan whirled to find a gathering group of vampires emerging from the darkened hallway past the massive kitchen.

Estelle grinned. "I have friends too, you know. My precious legion. They are the ones who sought me out," she snarled, still laughing.

It sounded like rats on shattered glass.

"You should have sought me out too, instead of hiding like vermin." She bared her teeth and reared back to strike Karen's exposed flesh. She freed one arm and continued her excavation of Karen's chest, searching for the thing that would stop her in an instant.

Karen struggled to pull away, but Estelle held her close.

Ethan shouted for help.

The monsters in the hallway moved forward, hissing in sibilant syllables that were not even words.

Gladys looked at Hans and sent him a thought with all her might, not knowing if he would hear. *Are you ready?*

He nodded.

She leapt to her feet like a boxer and jumped over the scatter of plaster, bodies, and splintered boards. She ran to protect Ethan, not wanting him to unleash his secret weapon until the last, perfect moment. She roared like a prehistoric monster, her mouth opening three times its normal size. Her poor battered dentures fell to the floor. Three dozen teeth skittered across the floor in every direction like ice cubes from a shattered drinking glass.

The first vamp in line—a young man turned when he wasn't much older than Ethan—ran at the four interlopers, skittered on the pebbly teeth, and went down.

Gladys rammed her fence picket through his chest, and the pitiful look of surprise and pain almost made her feel bad for doing it. Almost.

The next moved forward, but with far less conviction. They were just pawns. Pesky mosquitos with no ambition or courage, and faltering loyalty.

She shouted at Ethan over her shoulder. "Go! Do the thing!" She rose up taller than she could have done in normal circumstances, yanked the fence picket out of the first vampire's chest, and squared off in front of the rest of them. Dim shapes continued to fill the hallway.

We'll never defeat them all if it comes to that. There must be a hundred.

And still, they continued to throng.

Gladys could never have imagined that there were so many, right here in the city where she'd lived for so long. How had they not *felt* them? Had Dr. Trish? They knew there were others turned like they were that had returned to Estelle, but Gladys had no idea there were so many.

She shielded *them! Up here on this parapet of suburbia, Estelle had hidden them away.*

The vamps spread out into the kitchen and waited to swarm at Estelle's command.

Gladys nearly laughed as she realized that there was a strong resemblance to *West Side Story* after all. Ethan had been right about that when he'd mentioned it after the attack of the Chocolate Chip Cooke. She felt him behind her, his will flagging from fear. She shoved him backhanded. "Go!"

He froze a moment longer, but Karen's scream of pain got him moving.

She could *feel* her friends now—somehow sharing their thoughts in this moment of need more than the little twinkles and intuitions they'd had before when they were losing ground. In her mind, she knew they all felt it. This was no time to lose their mettle. She screamed like a deranged martial artist before a kick and threw the stake like a javelin.

It skewered the first two vamps together like a kabob. The others faltered again.

Gladys had bought them time. She rose up above the melee and flung herself into the pile, joining her friends who were locked together in mortal combat with one of the most dangerous creatures on earth.

Gladys descended upon them.

Estelle's hand was now deep in Karen's chest, reaching for her heart. In a moment she would grasp it, squeeze, and tear it out. The other was stuck in the back of Hans' neck, pulling him toward her gaping shark's mouth, filled with not just two, but dozens of fangs that tilted every which way.

Gladys wailed a banshee's cry and pried the horrible thing's hands out of their flesh before it could end their lives.

Estelle howled in frustration and almost succeeded in jerking herself out of Gladys' grip.

"Grab it, Hans!" she shouted.

Hans took control of Estelle's right arm as she secured the left.

"Karen!"

Karen clutched at her damaged chest, breath rasping and little red bubbles forming in her mouth as she tried to speak. She locked eyes with her best friend and Gladys could read the fear and pain inside them. Somehow, she smiled.

"Off!" Gladys shouted again and shoved her friend off Estelle and out of the bloody fray to allow passage for Ethan's death-ray.

"Now!" Hans cried.

Ethan stepped forward, smiling with a calm serenity that made him beautiful. He crossed the wires at the end of the tube and a light burst forth —straight into Estelle's face. "Take that, you murdering cunt!" He cackled with triumph as his own feet left the ground and he rose on the wave of his power and fury. He descended on his victim, crashing between Gladys and Hans. He straddled the writhing thing that was their maker, knocking them aside. He planted his feet, teeth bared in triumph, with the makeshift light saber still trained on Estelle's horrible face as it began to run like wax.

Estelle tried to wriggle away as the flesh melted off her face, but Gladys stomped down again on her arm and Hans pinned the other back to the floor.

An inhuman shriek, shrill and high, rose above the din, threatening to split Gladys' eardrums and rupture her skull.

Glasses in the kitchen shattered. The windows cracked, and the foundation canted one way and then the other.

Gladys doubled down on her efforts to hold the beastly thing to the floor while Ethan continued to burn away Estelle's face. Her hair caught fire and the stench of burning filled Gladys' nostrils, making her eyes sting and blurring her vision with tears.

After a time, Gladys could not have said how long, the shrieking sound began to falter, diminishing into a wail, a whimper, and then a shuddering sigh. Estelle's movements slowed and the body beneath them erupted into flames.

They backed away, watching in silent horror as the thing that had tormented and changed them into the bloodthirsty undead slowly burned first to black coal, then dusty ash. It was over.

40. THE VICTORS AND THE VANQUISHED

Ethan flipped the switch on his death ray, and the light went out. He ripped the wires away from the battery and broke the light bulb for good measure.

Hans stood up on shaking legs and helped Gladys get to her feet.

"Karen!" Ethan shouted. He tossed his weapon away and ran to her.

She hunched over, still trying to catch her breath. Raspy inhalations rattled in her chest.

"Are you okay?"

She smiled. "Yes, I'm okay. She looked down at the front of her sweater and realized that only a few tattered shreds of fabric remained to cover her modesty. Her chest had knitted itself back together, thankfully, before Estelle succumbed to the deathly light of the artificial sun.

"Here." Ethan pulled off his T-shirt and handed it over.

She took it gladly and slipped it over her head. It reached nearly to her knees.

"Thank you, Ethan." A single tear fell from her eye, and she reached for her friends. They stood, holding hands in a circle around the dusty ash pile in stunned silence.

"You alright, Glad?" Karen asked in a wavery voice.

Gladys nodded and took a shuffling step toward her friend. She enveloped Karen in a crushing hug, laughing and crying. "Yes! I'm okay, I'm okay!" She held Karen at arm's length and looked her up and down. Leftover cuts remained on her neck and some on her arm. They weren't serious, but they weren't healing. "You're not healing!" She cried and held Karen's arm up. "Look! You're not healing!"

Karen burst into tears. "I can't believe it! I can't believe this is real. Is it real?"

Gladys nodded and embraced her again.

"And look! Look at you!" Karen said.

Gladys wiped a hand across her face and her palm came away sticky with blood. She'd come through the ordeal fairly unscathed but had a few scratches as well. And they weren't healing either. She looked for Hans in the dimly lit living room, now a wreck with furniture strewn hell to breakfast and broken drywall scattered across the dark wood floor. The kitchen looked diamond studded with shards of glass everywhere.

"Hans! Are you alright?"

He stood next to Ethan. They shared twin expressions of dumbfounded surprise, as if they, in their deepest hearts, hadn't thought they would make it through to see another day. Hans grabbed Ethan's hand and held it up in the air as if the kid had just gone ten rounds with Mike Tyson. The look was a bit spoiled by the fact that Hans stood only five-foot-eight and Ethan was over six feet tall when he wasn't slouching.

A slow smile spread across Ethan's face as the enormity of what they'd done pressed down on him.

Hans smiled back, and it made him look ten years younger. Maybe more.

"It's over!" Ethan shouted. "Is it over?" Doubt clouded his face as if he hadn't anticipated the victory could have been that easy.

"Yes, honey," Karen said and opened her arms. "It's over."

He fell into them, laughing and crying. Karen held him tight. They broke apart, and Ethan wiped his eyes and nose with the back of his hand.

"Like, I didn't think...I mean, I *hoped,* but I really wasn't sure this would work." He dragged the toe of his sneaker through the ash pile. A lopsided smiley face materialized in the center. A burn scar surrounded the space Estelle's body once occupied and now it resembled a chalk line around a murder victim. "What do we do now?"

Movement caught the corner of Gladys' eye. The kitchen was dark, but she could see the outline of the people standing there. Estelle's former minions, now free to go and live their lives. How many of them had been vampires until moments ago? How long had they lived that way before they were liberated? And how the hell could they have been stupid enough to forget about them? She nudged Karen and gestured at the gathering mass of confused bodies.

"Oh!" she said in quiet surprise.

"I think it best that we go now," Hans said, motioning to the shattered door.

The silence in the house was eerie now that they knew how many people had been inside with them, watching the spectacle, too frightened to intervene.

"Vampire mafia." He chuckled and shooed them toward the door.

Gladys had never felt so alive as she did when she exited the house of horrors and breathed in the free air of the wonderful summer night. "I guess we'll just go back the way we came." She reached for Karen's hand. Then a tickle of intuition pinged in her head like sonar, but it seemed far away and faint. More like a wind chime than a fire alarm. It was also a moment too late.

From behind them, a sound like a wounded dog cut through the still air, and Gladys and Karen turned just in time to see Ethan's eyes suddenly fly open as he screamed in agony and fell forward.

Karen shrieked, and Gladys caught Ethan as he stumbled into her. She struggled to hold him up and then they both went down together with Ethan on top, knocking the air out of her in a painful whoosh.

The attacker ran out into the tree line.

Gladys felt her knee shrieking with a pain so intense it would have filled her head had she not been so terrified for the boy. For Ethan.

"Oh my God!" Gladys squeaked. "No! No, no, no..." She moaned it like a mantra and scrambled out from beneath his lanky body onto her knees and cried out as they popped like firecrackers in a new flash of pain. "Hans, help me!"

"Where did he go?" Karen cried, looking everywhere at once for their assailant.

Hans shook his head, frozen, fists clenched at his sides, watching the scene before him. His mouth opened and closed, and Gladys had an absurd, momentary flash of Hans as a German goldfish with a funny little mustache.

"Gladys?" Karen kneeled beside Ethan, who was face-down in the grass, struggling to catch his breath. A high wheezing sound came from his mouth. Gladys turned his head to the side so he could breathe.

"This is bad. Oh God, this is really, really, bad." Karen looked in all directions again, but they seemed to be alone. No sign of Ethan's attacker.

A three-foot-long cedar fence plank jutted from between the kid's shoulder blades. Blood spilled down his skinny, naked side over his ribs like a stream over submerged rock. Ethan managed to scream in pain and tried to reach for whatever had stuck him in the back. Gladys grabbed his hands and looked up at Hans, pleading.

A yell rang out from across the lawn; the same kid who'd been feeding Estelle when they burst in through the back door stood with his feet braced wide apart, crying. He held a second broken fence picket and rushed Hans, holding it like a jousting lance. He yelled incoherently as he rushed forward.

"No!" Karen shouted. She yanked the stake out of Ethan's back and Estelle's murderous walking food source. No longer a vampire, yet her reflexes were still lightning quick.

It pierced his belly. He clutched at the protruding picket and looked at Karen incredulously, clearly saying without words that it wasn't supposed to happen like this. That he and Estelle had been fated to be together forever.

Gladys knew Estelle never would have agreed or held to such an arrangement, but the look on his face was that of utter surprise. His small starfish hands grappled at it, but it was fruitless. His knees crumpled, and he fell to the ground. Blood pooled around him and for the first time in decades, Hans, Gladys, and Karen had no desire whatsoever to lap it up.

"Help me," Ethan gasped. The blood was flowing faster now that the object that had been shoved through his back had been removed.

"Gladys!" Karen said, with tears streaming down her face. "What do we do?"

Gladys had seen a lot of wounds during her career as a nurse. She didn't think there was much that could be done to save him, but maybe...

41. THE SUN ALSO RISES

"Should we call 9-1-1?" Karen asked.

Gladys crouched on the ground, trying to stop the blood coursing from Ethan's back.

Karen whapped Gladys on the shoulder as she tried to stop the blood.

"Yes. Wait, no," Gladys said. "How would we do that? None of us has a cell phone." She shot a look of desperate irritation at Karen and then turned her attention back to her wounded patient. She ripped off a strip of her shirt and pressed it down hard on the wound, knowing it would be pointless. The blood appeared almost black in the moonlight as it seeped out of the wound.

"Hurts," Ethan croaked, his voice barely audible.

Karen looked toward the busted back door. Faces like white balloons stared back at them. It was impossible to know how many. These people were an unknown element. Those left behind could be friend or foe, and there was no way to know for sure which.

"I think we'd better go," Karen said quietly. She grabbed Hans' shoulder and turned him toward the gathering crowd.

Hans snapped into action. He scooped Ethan up in his muscular arms and stumbled toward the car, knocking Gladys aside. His vampire strength had fled and now he huffed and chuffed like *The Little Engine That Probably Couldn't*.

Karen hurried ahead, opened the door, and got in the driver's seat.

Gladys grunted as she struggled to keep up with them, wincing with each step she took. Her knees were now filled with tiny piranhas that bit at her every time she took a step. She climbed into the back with Hans and Ethan, gravel spitting up from the tires before she'd pulled the door closed.

Ethan groaned, but he sounded so far away.

Hans turned Ethan over so Gladys could tend to the wound on his back. They bounced and rocked in the back seat as Karen sped toward University Hospital.

Gladys pressed hard against the flow. It was slowing now; that was a good sign. "I think the bleeding is going to stop!" She shouted. The triumph in her voice was loud in the small space.

And then Hans touched her hands with a gentleness she would not have thought possible. "Stop now," he said. Sorrow dripped from his eyes and ran in rivulets down his face.

The boy was still looking up at him, past him, toward the fading stars. Ethan was gone.

"What? No, I need to keep the pressure on—"

Hans took both of Gladys' hands in his and gazed sadly at Ethan's still body. Then she knew. Her frantic eyes locked with Karen's in the rear-view mirror.

Karen opened her mouth in a little "o" of dismay and yanked the car over to the side of the road and shoved it into park. "Is he...?"

Gladys felt for his pulse, then nodded. She stroked his hair and pulled him gracelessly up onto her bosom, rocking him like an infant.

Ethan's hand fell away and dangled by his side.

Huge tears plopped onto his head as she cradled him against her. She thought about how she'd first found him that night at Golden Peaks; how lost he'd been and how badly he'd needed a mentor. How badly he needed a friend. Hell, he'd needed a mother. And as reluctant as she'd been to take on that role, she had grown to love him as one of her own. "Ethan...Ethan...Ethan..." She shook her head and chanted his name over and over, a spell that could bring him back from the dead.

"Best stop now," Hans repeated and wiped at Gladys' tears.

His grief mirrored her own and great tearing sobs tore loose from her throat. Her job had been to protect him, guide him, and teach him. And she had let him down. Why couldn't it have been *her*? Why did this awkward, clueless kid, who had started out life so confidently, have to be lying here in her arms?

Karen looked out the windshield at nothing, saying nothing. A dull, dazed expression clouded her face. She put the car in drive and went to Hans' house without thinking.

When she pulled into the driveway and her brain began functioning again, she asked, "What are we going to do with him?" Karen parked and got out. She wrung her hands, looking from the dead body of Mrs. Maitland in one car, to Ethan in the other. Her eyes were dry. The grief would overwhelm her later, but for now, she was mechanically following some sort of internal protocol, planning their next steps with methodical care.

Hans, who must have been working this out as they drove, shook his head. "We cannot go to hospital. Also, there is no help for him. We have choice to return him to Hell house and allow authorities to find him and others or we put in car with Mrs. Maitland."

"And do what, Hans?" Gladys cried. "Push it into the reservoir? Burn it? He's a *kid*! And I let him *die*! I refuse to pollute his memory by trying to dispose of him somewhere like a piece of garbage!"

"There may be another way," Karen said quietly, chewing on a thumbnail. "Two, actually. One is to stage an accident with Mrs. Maitland and Ethan in the car. It might be hard to pull off considering her...condition. The other is to drive them both to the hospital in her car," she pointed to the nose of Mrs. Maitland's would-be death machine, barely visible behind the bushes with foliage still caught in it, "and leave the car in the ER parking. We'd get away, and he'd be taken care of properly." She made a face. "So would Mrs. Maitland, which is more than she deserves, but at least Ethan's family would be notified, and he'd have a proper burial."

"What would we say? There is no way to explain this," Hans said sorrowfully.

"We wouldn't." Gladys understood perfectly. She sat with a whump on the porch step, gazing out over the trees. "That would be for them to determine. We couldn't go in and explain."

It was a sad truth. There was nothing they could say that would make the situation make sense. It would be up to the police and the medical examiner to figure it out.

At least it wouldn't be Dr. Cooke.

He'd been the ME at Mercy Hospital, but it still brought her savage glee knowing that creature would never touch another human being, dead or alive. It sucked. She didn't want to leave Ethan that way, but that was the best they could do now.

The sky was a brilliant pink as the sun began its climb out of the eastern horizon line.

"If we're going to do it, we need to go now," Gladys said. "It's getting light." She sighed as the sadness washed over her. Ethan. The kid deserved a medal, not abandonment. He deserved recognition for his heroism, but the events of this night could never be exposed. Karen was right. At least he'd be tended to.

"Look, friends. It is sun. We are alive." Hans allowed tears to fall from his eyes in a rare display of raw, naked emotion.

Karen slipped her arm around his waist and laid her head on his shoulder. Gladys struggled up from the stairs and joined them, snuggling Karen close to her with her arm around her waist.

"I am happy to be with friends."

They spent several moments enjoying the nearly forgotten sight of the sun casting its brilliant glow—something they'd been missing for decades, but time was still of the essence. They couldn't leave the car out in broad daylight.

They quickly laid Ethan in the back seat of Mrs. Maitland's car.

"He looks peaceful," Karen said, and kissed his forehead tenderly. Then she slid into the front seat and started the engine.

Hans got in his own car and started the engine.

"Remember," Gladys said. "Be sure to park at the end of the little circle drive, where the security camera can't pick you up. And pull something over your head."

Karen fished around in the glove compartment and tossed out napkins, parking tickets, and old receipts, which landed on the late Mrs. Maitland's lap. Finally, she found one of those old lady plastic rain hats that tie under the chin. "Will this do?"

Gladys nodded, then got in the passenger seat of Hans' Mercedes and they took off. She rode quietly with her hands folded neatly in her lap as Hans drove. It smelled of blood—a scent which now brought her nausea instead of hunger.

Karen pulled into the emergency drive up, making sure to follow Gladys' directions, put the car in park, still idling, and ran like hell down the street to where Hans and Gladys were waiting.

"Thank you, young man," Hans spoke solemnly. "Thank you for giving us the sun, thank you for giving me my God back, and thank you for...being young." All three of their faces were wet with tears as they pulled away from the ER parking lot.

Later, when the three remaining XP support group members were gathered around Hans' dining room table savoring hot, fresh lattes from The Java House, they decided it was best to make an anonymous phone call on Ethan's behalf.

They drove to one of the few remaining pay phones in town, just outside the same Walmart where Ethan had gotten his death lamp, and Gladys did the honors. Then she went in, bought three candy bars, went back to the car and passed them around solemnly.

"What is this?" Hans asked as he examined it like a found relic at an archeological dig.

"Our victory dance," Gladys said. "Now eat up."

It took the authorities months to figure out how the two bodies had gotten there. Mrs. Maitland was easy to identify—it was her car, after all—but identifying and explaining Ethan in the back seat created an epic mystery that was never fully solved.

42. VICTORY DANCE

"Hey, Glad! How ya feelin'?" A chipper voice chirped from the doorway of Gladys' hospital room. Karen was there with Hans by her side, holding the biggest arrangement of flowers she'd ever seen.

"Hey," Gladys said.

"That good?" Hans strode from the door to Gladys' bed. He kissed her cheek, then stood back, hands clasped in front of himself like a groomsman.

"We wanted to cheer you up!" Karen said.

Gladys could barely see her lunatic smile over the big bunch of hydrangeas.

Gladys rolled her eyes. "I'm cheered. Thanks for coming."

"How do they feel? The knees, how feeling now from surgery?"

"Ugh," she said with a grimace. "They hurt like seven hells, but the torture experts tell me they'll feel like brand new before I know it. I don't even remember what brand new feels like, so I'll have to take their word for it."

"Well, it's all up from here, right?" Karen chirped.

"Except for the physical therapy," Gladys grumbled. "Hurts worse than the surgery."

"Aww, it'll get better. Promise! Now, where do you want these?" The twinkle in her eye couldn't hide her underlying sadness. The sadness they'd all felt since Ethan's passing. The funeral had been nice, all of them standing anonymously in the back, trying hard, as always, to go unnoticed.

In the intervening months, they'd spent their time together healing, trying to regain life as breathing, living human beings again. Playing countless games of Scrabble (not Hans' favorite, being German and all), Trivial Pursuit (Karen remained the reigning champ) and Risk (Hans' favorite), and seldom going out while they patiently awaited the day of Gladys' surgery. Rejoining the daytime society they'd so long ago been forced to abandon was not as simple as it seemed.

"Okay," Gladys said. "If you want me to be optimistic, I'm optimistic. Happy?"

"Of course I am," Karen said. She took Hans' hand and intertwined their fingers together. They'd be married in the fall, and Gladys was happy for them both. It was funny that as vampires, they'd never been more than friends.

But they had been. After all, hadn't that been Karen's makeup bag on Hans' bathroom counter?

At the very least, they had kept their feelings a secret until their curse had been lifted. After that, they'd decided that their love would endure and decided to make it official. If they hadn't fallen in love, Hans might have moved back to Germany or Sweden and resumed the strings of his old life there. But, as he'd explained one late night over too many beers, everyone and everything he'd known before was gone or had changed so much it would never feel like home again.

"Gross. Get a room, guys," Gladys said. She muted the TV, where Bob Barker's replacement was enthusiastically explaining to the showcase showdown contestants that their bid had to be below the actual retail price without going over.

"Sorry. I just cannot help myself. She is like lovely flower."

"Oh, spare me," Gladys said with a fake grimace, but she was happy for her friends and their new-found love. It was a rare thing indeed, and one that she had written off long ago. As for her, she was liking her new life alone just fine and didn't want to complicate things by inviting another person into the mix.

They stayed for an hour and by that time, Gladys was so high on Vicodin that she drifted in and out, barely able to track the topics of conversation that never included Ethan. The pain was still too close.

Three days later, they came to collect her from the hospital and return her home, where Hans had built a ramp to the front door. Gladys strangled the handles of her walker as she made her way up in that side-to-side, rocking gait of hers. The physical therapist had told her to start walking without that motorboat movement, but old habits were hard to break. She'd been stomping around the city that way longer than the baby therapist had been alive.

"What do you think?" Karen asked as she helped her friend into the house.

Gladys didn't speak. Couldn't speak. The house had been upgraded and modernized. There were signature Hans touches—modern, angular furniture, sleek lamps, simple, tasteful rugs—and some of Karen's influence as well. Huge Georgia O'Keefe paintings graced the walls of the living room and pastel accent colors offset the light and dark grey furniture.

"What?" She cleared her throat. "What have you done to my house?"

"You needed a fresh start, Glad. No good sitting around and sulking in this old eighties museum. Time to move on and move on up." Karen gave her a tentative smile. "Do you like it? Because if you don't—"

"Like it? I love it!" Gladys said. She reached out to hug her and nearly went ass-over-teapot over the top of her walker.

Hans reached out a strong hand to keep her on her feet. She was still surprised by that strength. Some of it seemed to have stuck around since his vampire reversal. Lucky him.

"Did you..." She swallowed a lump that had risen to her throat. "The basement. Did—"

"Is same. We did not touch work of young man," Hans said.

Gladys felt a flood of relief. She could not imagine those pieces of Ethan and their former life being chopped up and thrown in a dumpster.

Karen cleared her throat. "Now, the home health therapist will be coming twice a week. And you *have* to do your exercises. Hans, tell her she has to do her exercises."

"You must exercise," Hans said before excusing himself to collect the rest of Gladys' rehab equipment from the car.

Karen watched him go, mouth twisted in exasperation. Then she looked back at her friend and smiled.

Gladys smiled back, and then winced in pain. "Right now, I'm gonna exercise my right to sit in the only piece of furniture I have left. The only one you didn't send to Good Will." She thumped over to her beloved recliner and sat down gingerly, grimacing at the discomfort of her spandy new knees learning to do their job.

"Okay," Karen said. "I'll let you off the hook. For today. But I'm going to be here every day, so don't think you're gonna get out of it. The sooner you get moving, the sooner you'll be back on your feet and as good as new."

They left after supper and Gladys thought to herself that she was a lucky woman to count those two as friends. She'd never get over the loss of Ethan, but without his courage and ultimate sacrifice, they wouldn't have this new, second chance at life. She'd always be grateful to him for that. She pulled the scrap book out of the little hidden pocket on the side of the recliner and turned the pages as Price is Right gave way to Wheel of Fortune. Pat Sajak on the TV encouraged his little entourage to spin the wheel while an aged Vanna touched the panels that illuminated the letters.

43. MESSAGES FROM THE GREAT BEYOND

Gladys opened the cover. The first ten pages were filled with candid Polaroids, all taken by Ethan: Karen sitting on Gladys' back steps looking with childlike wonder up at the stars, Hans looking ever-so German, scowling at the camera, Karen and Hans standing together, her looking up at him with an expression of obvious love, even though they hadn't proclaimed their feelings.

It was so obvious.

Gladys snorted out loud with laughter. The next page was a photo of Gladys' large rear end as she bent over in front of the mini fridge and handed a bottle of blood to an unseen someone outside the frame. She frowned at that one and a tear threatened to escape. Ethan had thought it was so funny. She wiped it away.

The next two pages of the book were of Ethan and his remodeling project. Stacks of lumber and upholstery material neatly divided into piles in the basement, the frames of the new structures as Ethan looked at the camera with a ridiculous grin. This one he must have set up and used a timer for. Several photos of stages of construction, and then the final two of his completed masterpieces. These pictured Ethan standing before his work, looking like a hunter who'd just bagged a lion while on an illicit safari trip.

Then there were the pages of the three of them gallivanting through Gladys' back yard, clearly leftover relics from the free love era of the 1960s. She was glad he'd ignored their express instructions not to take pictures. Hans cradling his lightning bug jar, Gladys with her flower crown. She remembered what she had told Ethan afterward. A pang of regret wrenched her stomach. She'd told him that she'd thought about ending things, that the life they were living wasn't *really* a life, just an existence. He'd taken that as confirmation that he needed to help them free themselves from the undercover life they'd been living.

Ethan. God bless your ridiculous little self. I miss you.

She brought her fingers to her lips and touched them to the final image in the book. All four of them inside the VFW hall, posing while Ethan held bunny ears up behind Karen's head.

The remaining pages Gladys had filled herself with various newspaper clippings she'd found since the showdown at Estelle's house of horrors.

RELIGIOUS CULT EXPOSED IN UPSCALE IOWA CITY NEIGHBORHOOD

The Iowa City Press-Herald—July 18th

No one knows how the quiet house at 4202 Blackberry Lane became a home to a dangerous religious cult, but after neighbors called police to report a disturbance, they arrived to find three dozen young men and women wandering in the backyard and inside the home. In the upper level of the house, they found another fifty or so individuals who appeared dazed. Police discovered blood in the back yard and a burned area inside, confirming that the cult had been performing blood rituals. Human sacrifice is believed to have been a part of their so-called religious activities. A number of artifacts were removed from the home. Those found there have been detained for questioning.

Authorities linked the cult to the mysterious dumping of two bodies on the University of Iowa Hospital property. Earlier hospital staff had been alerted by a security guard of a car idling in the emergency parking area, seemingly empty. Upon investigation, two bodies were discovered abandoned in the back seat. One had been reportedly impaled by an object, the other mutilated. Rumors that the mutilated individual had been drained of blood have not been confirmed...

She turned the page and a huge headline blared out at her.

ARRESTS MADE IN MYSTERIOUS KILLING, POLICE QUESTION SUSPECTS

The Coralville Current—July 20th

A recent raid on a religious cult engaging in human sacrifice has confirmed police suspicion that nineteen-year-old Ethan Bradford had been murdered on the premises in some sort of ritual. Police confirmed that the other body found with Mr. Bradford's in an abandoned vehicle was Mrs. Arlyss Maitland, 72. Police have not been able to ascertain if Mrs. Maitland was a cult member, nor the relationship between the two deceased.

Most of those detained have remained silent during questioning. Those who have spoken with police told strikingly similar, bizarre stories—that a woman who had turned them into vampires had been holding them there for an undetermined amount of time. Their claim that three unknown individuals in the company of Mr. Bradford had broken into the home and dispatched the missing cult leader has not been confirmed, and in fact, no evidence of such a woman has been found to support their claims. Of the thirty-eight people arrested, twenty-six remain in police custody, pending formal charges…

The articles got smaller as she went. The public being so fickle that they'd lost interest as the time went by.

THIRTEEN PEOPLE CHARGED WITH MURDER IN CREEPY CULT KILLINGS

The North Liberty Times—August 30th

Of the thirty-eight originally arrested, police have managed to charge just thirteen individuals with the gruesome murders of nineteen-year-old Ethan Bradford and seventy-two-year-old Arlyss Maitland. What of the other cult members? The identity of the mysterious leader, a self-styled "vampire" members still call The Mistress, remains a mystery. Police have declined to answer reporters' repeated requests for more information, but public speculation points to a lack of sufficient evidence to hold all the cult members responsible for the loss of life of two known Iowa Citians and countless others. How many did the cult sacrifice? One can only speculate.

JURY DELIVERS JUSTICE

The University Press—September 29th

In a whirlwind trial lasting only seven days, a jury delivered a guilty verdict for all thirteen individuals charged in the so-called Cult Killings from last July. Lesser charges have been filed against nine other members of the cult, but their whereabouts are still unknown. Warrants have been issued for their arrests, though it is believed that a number of them may have fled the country to avoid prosecution.

The families of Ethan Bradford and Arlyss Maitland now have closure and can grieve the loss of their loved ones, knowing that the guilty parties will be serving life sentences without parole.

Police still have not completely ruled out the presence of a cult leader, described as a woman who dressed all in white, nor have they been able to determine the identity of three individuals who may have been responsible for breaking up the cult and making the initial report to police.

Gladys smiled but felt tears sting her eyes. She wished there was more they could do to honor Ethan's memory and his sacrifice, but this was something they were just going to have to hold for themselves.

Maybe she'd add more to the pages as time went on. She ran a hand over her eyes and returned the album to the recliner pocket. Pat Sajak was yammering about a trip to the Bahamas. *That sounds nice.* She clasped her hands across her chest and fell asleep with a soft little smile on her face.

The following week, Hans picked her up and drove her to the VFW hall. A sign greeted them as he held onto her so she could make it up the steps with her walker.

XP SUPPORT GROUP MEETING TONITE

She rolled her eyes but smiled. There were four folding chairs, and Karen sat perched on the edge of one, pen and legal pad on her lap. The twin-set, it seemed, was something she wasn't ready to let go of.

Gladys felt a surge of love and loneliness when she looked at the empty chair set out where Ethan should have been fidgeting and going off on tangents about movies and books.

"Welcome to the XP Support Group," Karen said. "Who'd like to start?"

Gladys pulled herself up on her walker, which was becoming easier to do now that the initial pain of her knee replacements was fading. "Hello, I'm Gladys," she said as she stood in front of her army green metal chair.

"Hello Gladys," the others recited.

"And I'm no longer a vampire.

Acknowledgments

This book would never have happened without being jump-started by my sister, Colleen, who not only got this project going, but who also helped me form my sense of humor. When I first thought about writing about Gladys and her friends, I had planned to post the story as a serial. Unfortunately, that was about as far as I got. Even the title was all wrong.

One day, as I was recuperating from surgery and feeling bitterly sorry for myself, my front door opened, and someone plopped down beside me. It was my sister who had driven nearly a thousand miles to cheer me up. Instead of greeting her with a gigantic smile, I said, "What the f-ck are you doing here?" I was surprised and flummoxed, but definitely wasn't mad. She laughed. As I said, we have twin senses of humor. As we sat on the couch giggling like idiots, I told her all about my idea and she gave me great advice. Not to mention a much better title. Thus, Gladys was born.

My Shut Up and Write group, the Online Creative Collective, The Horror-ible Writers Critique Group, Writing Heights Writers Association and the Horror Writers Association have been instrumental in helping me hone my craft, telling me when the writing is terrible, and giving me ideas on how to fix it. You all are pretty awesome.

My husband is ultimately responsible for every word I've written since 1993. Without his encouragement and insistence that I was wasting my talents, I might never have had the confidence to begin my writing journey.

Additional thanks go to my mom and step-dad who have cheered me on all along, my best friend Kim who lives too far away, the kind folks at Stodgy Brewing and Wolverine Farm Publick House, my tolerant children, and my furry writing buddy Blue. Also, thanks to all the people that have inspired me—Aunt Fern, Hans Klauffman, Cindy Hudson, Melissa Mullane, Auntie Janice, and my hideous neighbor. You know who you are.

Finally, thanks to Penny at Kiki's Castle Independent Press, LLC for your patience, your fantastic ideas, and your ability to gently pump the brakes when I start to wander. Without your guidance and perseverance, not to mention your ability to talk me down off the ledge when needed, this never would have happened.

Thanks, y'all. This Blood's For You.

About the Author

Heather Hein is a Rocky Mountain Wordsmith who lives in Colorado with a menagerie of people, pets, and plants. Though her heart belongs in the west, she spent her high school years living in Iowa City where she (really!) worked at Hy-Vee Food Store before moving on to bigger and better things. She attended the Iowa Writers Workshop, edited her junior college paper, and taught professional writing as she completed her bachelor's degree.

Heather is deeply committed to her local writing community and helps organize writing support and accountability groups, teaches classes, and coaches new writers to help get them started. She is a member of Writing Heights Writers Association, Rocky Mountain Fiction Writers, Pike's Peak Writers, and the Horror Writers Association.

Her first official short story, Aisle 16, was accepted for publication in 2018, and that's where the whole thing really got started. Since then, her work has been published in print anthologies, on Amazon's Kindle Vella, and other online platforms. She won third place in the 2021 Colorado Short Story Contest and her work has been nominated for a Pushcart Prize.